Praise for Lilith Saintcrow

"Incredibly timely, well written and important....A testament to Saintcrow's skill." —*Los Angeles Times* on *Afterwar*

"Vivid prose highlights the immediacy of battle, and the war-fractured landscape and the emotional and physical toll of fighting are realistically drawn....An unsettling vision." —*Publishers Weekly* on *Afterwar*

"So refreshing and original....With non-stop action, you won't be able to put down *Cormorant Run*!" —*RT Book Reviews*

Praise for Gallow and Ragged

"Saintcrow deftly mixes high-minded fantasy magic with rough, real-world rust using prose that veers between the beautiful and the bloodcurdling." —Chuck Wendig, *New York Times* bestselling author

"Painfully honest, beautifully strange, and absolutely worth your time. Lilith Saintcrow is at the top of her game. Don't miss this." —Seanan McGuire, *New York Times* bestselling author

"Saintcrow's urban fantasy series launch is expertly crafted with heartbreak and mistrust, far darker and lovelier than the title suggests.... Saintcrow's artful, poignant descriptions remain with the reader long after the tale's end, as does the persistent sense of dark, unsettling unease." —*Publishers Weekly* (starred review)

Praise for Dante Valentine

As Lilith Saintcrow

As S. C. Emmett

THE
FALL
OF
WATERSTONE

BLACK LAND'S BANE:
BOOK TWO

LILITH SAINTCROW

orbitbooks.net

Copyright © 2024 by Lilith Saintcrow
Excerpt from *Doom of the Elder* copyright © 2024 by Lilith Saintcrow
Excerpt from *Song of the Huntress* copyright © 2024 by Lucy Hounsom

Cover design by Lisa Marie Pompilio
Cover illustration by Mike Heath | Magnus Creative
Cover copyright © 2024 by Hachette Book Group, Inc.
Map by Tim Paul

Orbit
Hachette Book Group
1290 Avenue of the Americas
New York, NY 10104
orbitbooks.net

First Edition: June 2024

Orbit is an imprint of Hachette Book Group.
The Orbit name and logo are registered trademarks of
Little, Brown Book Group Limited.

The publisher is not responsible for websites (or their content)
that are not owned by the publisher.

The Hachette Speakers Bureau provides a wide range of authors for speaking events. To find out more, go to hachettespeakersbureau.com or email HachetteSpeakers@hbgusa.com.

Orbit books may be purchased in bulk for business, educational, or promotional use. For information, please contact your local bookseller or the Hachette Book Group Special Markets Department at special.markets@hbgusa.com.

Library of Congress Cataloging-in-Publication Data
Names: Saintcrow, Lilith, author.
Title: The fall of Waterstone / Lilith Saintcrow.
Description: First Edition. | New York, NY : Orbit, 2024. |
Series: Black Land's Bane ; book 2
Identifiers: LCCN 2023046869 | ISBN 9780316440530 (trade paperback) |
ISBN 9780316440639 (ebook)
Subjects: LCGFT: Fantasy fiction. | Novels.
Classification: LCC PS3619.A3984 F35 2024 | DDC 892.—dc23/eng/20231010
LC record available at https://lccn.loc.gov/2023046869

ISBNs: 9780316440530 (trade paperback), 9780316440639 (ebook)

Printed in the United States of America

LSC-C

Printing 1, 2024

For those who travel far.

Marukhennor

Icehaunt

The Wild

Nithraen

Eastronmost

Redhill

South Gap

...ns of Dis Aethas

Southronmost

To The Riverlands

Map by Tim Paul

And through the drifts the snowy clifts
Did send a dismal sheen:
Nor shapes of men nor beasts we ken—
The ice was all between.

—Samuel Taylor Coleridge

Several problems have tormented the translator of this tale; many a term in the Old Tongue or the southron dialects holds nuance not easily explained in other languages. The reader's patience is humbly solicited. Any error is unintentional, any inaccuracy likewise.

May the Blessed smile upon both reader and scholar alike, knowing there is neither insult nor injury meant.

PART ONE

WATERSTONE

Caged Creatures

Thus did the folk of the High-helm pass swift and silent, over tree-crowned hill and through murmuring valley, until they reached the place shown unto their king. The first stones of Laeliquaende were laid with joy, and as the white towers rose Taeron's people sang. Even so close to the Enemy's land the music flowed unceasing, until the day doom arrived in the form least suspected...

—Gaemirwen of Dorael, *Concerning the Lost Kingdoms*

A t least they did not throw us in a pit," ruddy-haired Arneior snarled, tapping a disdainful fingertip against the bars. The slim metal pillars were light, even decorative—for the Elder make no thing without attention to the most pleasingly efficient shape for its function—and their powdery surfaces were utterly impervious. Even had we some implement to cut through, where on earth would we go? "Though that would be easier to escape."

No freeborn creature likes to be caged, and a shieldmaid less than most.

I sat upon the cell's shelf-bed, which now bore a thin cushion of wondrous softness and blankets of surprising warmth. The guards were not impolite, though regarding us with a great deal of curiosity. They were Elder, had presumably seen mortals enough in their time...and yet.

There was nothing else to do, so I combed my hair with surpassing slowness. As well as bedlinen and small necessaries, the politely inquisitive guards had also brought my mother's second-largest trunk, hauled this far north by what *seidhr* I could not tell—and it did not seem they had searched its interior, at least.

The appearance of our luggage bespoke some graciousness upon the part of our hosts, and further intimated the men of Naras might not be finding their own confinement overly difficult. Our prison was amply sized, contained a water-room, and once the sun left the sky a soft glow remained in shell-shaped patterns painted upon the wall, dying gently as we readied ourselves for sleep.

I tried to discern the *seidhr* in such a wonder by laying a fingertip against luminescent stone, but it granted no illumination other than the physical. In fact, the meat inside my skull, usually so painfully active, was hard-pressed to find a solution to any quandary. Even twisting my hair into braids starred with red coral beads—all of Dun Rithell's supply until traders brought more upriver in summer—did not help.

To make matters worse, I still occasionally shivered with the cold of our passage across the Glass, not to mention the memory of a snow-hag and a great lich, attempting the healing of Eol of Naras, the final terrible effort to reach this hidden city where Aeredh said some great Elder weapon lay waiting for my use. The shocks lingered in my flesh, echoes not fading as an ordinary nightmare but acquiring new and terrible resonance whenever I shut my eyes.

My shieldmaid's attention was wholly taken with peering down the stone hall, testing the bars at intervals, listening intently for any sign of our guards, and performing what practice she could within the barred room's confines. Her spear was too long for the space, but those women taken by the Black-Wingéd Ones may fight with anything to hand—even sand, and grass—so she performed the stretches and quick movements of unarmed battle assiduously every rising and dusk, and when the sun reached its apex as well.

I was content to sit and brood, to consume what liquid victuals the Elder brought us, and to attempt some manner of contemplation, so far as I could through the clamor vying with strange humming distraction inside my head.

"Solveig?" Arn half-turned, regarding me narrowly. Her hazel eyes were hot as banked coals, and normally I would have said something to ameliorate her temper.

There seemed little which could accomplish such a mighty feat at the moment, though. "I am trying to think," I repeated, for perhaps the fifth time that day. My throat was dry, though a graceful silver ewer and two gemmed chalices rested upon a small table carved, like the rest of this room, from pure rock. It was akin to the dverger-crafted halls of Redhill, except the stonework of the Elder seems more grown than shaped.

Inside the jug was a version of what Aeredh and his Elder friends called winterwine, that memory-flavored drink filling as meat and bread, though not nearly quite so satisfying to the teeth.

"Oh, aye." My shieldmaid did not mock me, though 'twas a near thing. "What good is that, though? We must do something."

"I find there is little to be *done* at the moment, small one." The name carried no little affection—I barely reach her shoulder, despite my father's brawn and my mother's tall slenderness. Even Astrid held more height, and she the youngest of Eril and Gwendelint's children.

The image returned once more—our riverbank home under the shadow of Tarnarya reduced to a shattered, smoking skeleton, strewn with baked, shrunken corpses. If I sought sleep, sooner or later I dreamed of it; if I closed my eyes and attempted to still my thoughts in the way of a *volva* the vision thrust itself upon my inner eye. I could not tell if it were a true sending, a foretelling, or merely my own fears given deadly strength by passage so close to the terrible shadowed peaks of the Black Land.

The Marukhennor is hung about with gloom that eats hope, pouring despair into all living things. We had passed near indeed to those sawtooth masses of frost-choked stone, and even our leader had seemed prey to bleak imaginings in their shadow.

At the winter solstice, being concerned wholly with my own problems, I had been certain the Enemy was merely a tale of past danger to frighten children with. Our journey had not consumed more than a few moonturns, and yet I felt as old as some of the Elder are said to be. They do not die as the Secondborn do, those favored first children of the Allmother, though they hold that we mortals are her favorites, given the greatest gifts of any beings.

I cannot tell the truth of such an assertion, even now.

That morning, awakened from a fitful broken doze—I did not toss or turn, since Arneior slept upon the edge of the shelf-bed, closer to the door as befit a shieldmaid with a charge to protect—and not only clean but warm as I never thought to be again after the last terrible part of our trek, I had no energy for such philosophical matters.

The red coral did not help, though it is said to keep its wearer from being led into a bog. My favorite scentwood-and-horn comb, miraculously unbroken, lay in my lap; heartsblood-red wool, the second-finest dress I had, probably appeared drab to our Elder captors. It took far more concentration than usual to twist my hair properly, and I often gazed at my hands or comb as if I had forgotten how to use them.

"Nevertheless." Arneior was not willing to admit any defeat, or even uncertainty. Battle or protection were her duties, negotiating with and winning over our new captors should have been mine.

There was no purchase upon that cliff, for all the spike-helmed Elder guards were courteous enough—when they spoke at all. Aeredh had promised to return when he could, but would he be allowed after parley with the Elder king whose lands we had reached? One did not build a hidden city in order to look kindly upon visitors; perhaps our guide and leader had been placed in a cell of his own after attempting diplomacy.

Four days since our arrival, all told, Arneior chafing more and more at inactivity when she was not performing the forms of weaponless combat or examining the contours of our quarters for any weakness, and I? I sat slothful, staring at the fall of light in the stone hallway, rousing myself barely enough to take some nourishment or wander to the water-room when the need arose.

Perhaps I could have tried harder to befriend the guards. Blond Floringaeld appeared daily as the sun reached his highest point, passing naught but greetings through the bars along with our daily repast. No information did that captain grant a lowly pair of Secondborn women.

I had not even enough wit to attempt a riddle or some other manner of enticement, letting my shieldmaid meet him with stiff politesse instead.

"Do not rattle the bars." I was hoarse as if I had been screaming, and my head ached. "Please."

Arn spread her slim capable hands. "I doubt I could shift them. Even the Wingéd Ones are silent; this is a curst place, and us dragged here by *Northerners*." The last word was not obscene, but her tone almost managed to make it so. "False are they, claiming weregild where instead your brother did them a service, and now look. These Elder will probably keep us here until we die. 'Tis no more than an eyeblink to them."

I almost winced at hearing my own fear given voice, and examined my comb afresh. My braids were done; now I had to fill the rest of the day with something before I could lie down once more and seek elusive sleep.

Some volva *you are*, the soft terrible voice of self-loathing whispered. A wisewoman may send her subtle selves free of any confinement; all it takes is will and concentration. Yet I lacked both at the moment, and I could not tell if my weakness stemmed from the strain of our travels or another, less wholesome direction.

"We are as nightjars to them, dashed upon rocks." The words startled me. They were not mine but Tarit of Redhill's, and now I wondered if I should have insisted on going to Dorael, where yet another Elder king reigned.

Perhaps we would have ended in a barred cell there, too. Even Lady Hajithe's son had been loath to accompany us southward. The deep, inarguable certainty that I would never return to Dun Rithell taunted me, along with the vision of my home blasted by some unspeakable attack. The *orukhar* of the Enemy were fierce indeed. My father and his fellow warriors might hold those back for a time, yet the liches, not to mention other foul things…

Those were an altogether different matter. And here I lingered, trammeled in an Elder hutch like a rabbit in an osier cage, waiting for the sharp knife or the sacrificial fire.

"Sol." Arneior's shadow blotted out the light from the hall. She rested her fingertips upon my chin, tipping my face up like a dish. "You are not well."

"Well enough." If I admitted any weakness, what would my shieldmaid have to lean upon? She trusted me to know what *seidhr* to perform, my weirding ways more than adequate at home.

Ever since we left that haven, I had failed miserably in every way that counted.

She might have said more, but a soft sound interrupted us with far more efficacy than shout or clamor. When you are locked in a silent prison, every footfall is as a festival drum.

My shieldmaid whirled, darting for the end of the bed, and had her spear to hand in a trice. Every time the guards arrived she was armed, and it would have been comforting if I could have readied some manner of *seidhr* as well.

I could not. It was midday. And we had visitors.

A Change, at Least

Great choking fumes rose from torn earth where the eldest
son of the Allmother ended his flight, and shrouded his
new home in shadow. His servants fear the great eye of day
no less than their dread lord and perhaps it is their misery
which provides fuel for the brooding dark; the Black Land
is vast, but in the end no more than a prison cell.
    —Faeron One-hand, *The Nature of the Black Land*

Floringaeld was not merely a captain, but the head of Waterstone's royal guard. With a spiked helm tucked under his arm,
his fine green cloak draped over bright silvergold armor, and his long
golden hair, he would have been accounted more than handsome
enough in Dun Rithell even though he bore no beard. It was strange
that the Northerners and Elder did not grow such a crop upon their
cheeks and chin; one would have thought that the cold would induce
them to the measure in self-defense.

He halted at the other side of the bars, and he was not alone. Of
course, even while exchanging pleasantries through our cage-door he
was usually accompanied by at least two other Elder—as if my shieldmaid and I were mighty enough hostages to need such caution—but
this time, his companions were familiar figures.

Aeredh son of Aerith no longer wore the black garb Secondborn
lords in the North preferred. Instead, the Crownless of Nithraen

appeared in clothing of Elder make and style, with the particular grace of Laeliquaende. Soft is their fabric, and wondrous light even when woven for warmth; trews and a long velvet tunic more closely resembling a robe, both near a young birch's bark in hue, suited him rather well.

His blondness was paler than Floringaeld's, though the pointed tips of their ears were of like kind and rose through their hair. Aeredh's eyes were a richer blue, and seeing them together one would be hard pressed to say which man was younger, though the son of Aerith was slighter in build. A silver fillet rested upon his brow, and he smiled upon seeing us.

Behind him, slightly taller and dressed in unrelieved black, Eol of Naras glanced at the bars of our cage. His mouth was a straight line, his dark eyes cool and distant, and the glitter riding his shoulder was the colorless gem in a swordhilt. Since we were not journeying in the wilds, he had not wrapped it with leather to deny pursuers its gleam.

They had taken all our group's weapons save Arn's spear. It seemed rather important that Eol wore his blade openly, but the scalding passing through me was not for that reason. He was walking about, whole and well. Naturally the Elder here would have healed the wound in his shoulder; I had only managed to draw out a shard of the great lich's blade. A poor *volva* I proved to be, unable to fully stanch the bleeding, and even the burning vitality of one who had a second form had not been able to close the flesh properly.

I had glimpsed the wolf in him more than once. It peered through his coal-dark eyes for a moment again, but I closed my own lids, stricken with relief that my incompetence had not killed him.

When I did so the image of my home, blackened and burnt, rose before me once more in pitiless detail. I could not dispel nor had I spoken of it to my shieldmaid, though she was the one to record a *volva*'s oracular utterances from dream or vision before they fled waking memory. I had been hoping it would retreat as any normal nightmare, since I could not discern if it were truth or mere fearful imagining.

"Well." Arneior addressed an invisible point above Aeredh's golden head. "I thought we had been forgotten."

"We would rather forget ourselves first, my lady shieldmaid." The Elder's smile was instant, and warm; at Dun Rithell we had mistaken him for a mere youth. Of course his kind have means of appearing near-mortal when they walk among us, and did so more often than one might suppose even as we southrons forgot the menace beyond the Marukhennor.

Perhaps the Northerners' appeal to the Althing might have met with some manner of firm reply instead of silence had they been openly accompanied by such a fabled creature; perhaps my brother Bjorn might not have struck an Elder's companion with one large fist, knocking the other young man down to meet his end upon a loose, skull-cracking rock.

Wondering upon what might have been can drive even the most sensible person mad.

Would we have believed what was before us, had Aeredh shown his ears to the Althing? Safe on familiar banks, protected both by our river-mother and Tarnarya's white-hooded bulk, we had known the age of wonders long past, the Elder all departed, and the Black Land merely a tale to frighten unruly children with.

I wished Arn and I were still there, cradled in that blessed ignorance. Even if it meant we might be unaware of impending disaster as the Enemy stirred.

"The king of this place is an old friend," Aeredh continued, and though he spoke to my shieldmaid his gaze rested upon me. The *seidhr* in it was a heaviness, but did not meet with my own. I merely sat upon the shelf-bed, my comb loosely clasped in both hands, and sought to appear interested instead of almost too exhausted to stand. "He wishes to meet one whom the *valkyrja* have blessed, and my lady *alkuine*. The entire valley is most curious about you both."

Arneior half-turned, glancing over her shoulder. Her *seidhr*-cleaned ring-and-scale was bright as Floringaeld's armor, and her spearblade glistered almost angrily. She clearly expected me to do my duty in this situation, since there was nothing for her to fight—or kill.

I had to say something, yes, but what? My throat ached dryly, no matter how many Elder draughts I drained from gem-crusted goblets. "No doubt you have not seen your friend for some time, Lord

Aeredh." Each word was a husk of itself, as if I were shaking free of a winter illness. "Your reunion must have been joyous."

"Blame me." Eol of Naras's gaze had a weight to it as well, though he possessed no weirding save a second skin and that is not properly *seidhr* but another wonder entirely. He took a single step closer to the bars, and his expression was strange, almost as if he were the one trapped in a cage instead of breathing free air. "I lay near death for some while, and could not be called upon to give counsel."

Was I supposed to believe a Secondborn would sway an Elder king's mind? All I had seen of Aeredh's people so far was much pride, and no little disdain for those of us who suffer mortal death and disease.

Although that was not quite fair, for they were mighty allies. Daerith the harpist had fended off the great lich upon the Glass; the others of our band had fought with skill and bravery against *orukhar* and worse while shepherding not just Arn and me but the wolves of Naras through the killing freeze.

Yet we would not have left Dun Rithell at all save for a lie. I could not tell how to properly weigh each individual event since setting forth from home—one more sign I was not a true *volva* at all, despite the inked bands circling my wrists and the runes between them speaking of each test I had passed.

"Step back some little, my lady shieldmaid." Floringaeld pronounced the word for Arn's kind cautiously, handling the southron dialect with care. He had grown far more facile with its use over the past few days, though only exchanging commonplaces. Still, Elder love all manner of language, from their own and past ours into the speech of birds, the long slow sighcreak of trees. 'Tis said they woke and conversed with many things long before the very first sunrise, while the sky was a great river of Vardhra's star-lamps and the Enemy merely laying his plans in a forgotten corner.

The captain also produced a ring of keys, jangling musically as he moved. Arn retreated a few paces, but her knuckles were white upon her spear.

"I believe they mean to free us, small one, and to show us in their Hidden City much as prize livestock during a riverfair." I lay aside my comb and rose, though my knees were none too steady. "It will be a change, at least."

I meant it as a jest, however bleak. Aeredh's smile fell away, and Eol looked pained. But the stiffness in Arn's shoulders eased, and when I reached her side to lay my fingertips carefully upon her left arm a warm humming sense of breathing life filled me, pushing back the persistent chill.

I was still *volva* enough for that, at least.

The bars slid aside, grooves at floor and ceiling letting them move with only a faint metallic ringing, sweet as the keys' jangling chorus. "You are guests of Taeron Goldspear the High-helm, king of Lae-liquaende," Floringaeld intoned. "The son of Aerith has pledged to your good behavior, and you may tread where you will save for private houses. Our safety here depends on secrecy; should you attempt to leave this valley no mercy shall be shown."

How often does he give this speech? I could not tell, and to ask would be insulting. Yet I was sorely tempted.

Instead, I kept my hand upon Arneior's arm. "Considering there is nothing but leagues of lich- and *orukhar*-infested wilderness in every direction, my lord Floringaeld, we might think it wise to tarry even without such warning. We thank you for your care during our captivity."

A somewhat stiff half-bow was all I received for my restraint. Arneior exited our cell with her head high and her spear ready; I followed slowly, my joints creaking as Idra sometimes complained hers did near the end of her life.

Of course the air held no appreciable difference outside the cage, yet I breathed a little easier.

Only a little.

Waterstone

The cunning word, the bright eye, the quick hand, all these are seidhr. *But the word means much more, for it encompasses the weirding wonders performed by the Wise, the natural laws which seem miraculous to those unknowing, the powers of the gods themselves, and the secret spark in every living thing. There is still more contained within—loneliness lives there, and the will to surpass one's own mortal self...*

—The Saga of Icevein

Our other traveling companions had been freed as well, and there were two white Northern horses to bear Arn and me across the green fields and pastures. Though I was glad enough at the prospect—it was some distance to the shining city—I also could not suppress a flinch when the Elder-bred mount given to my use turned her head.

Her mild gaze reminded me of Farsight, the mare most likely lost in the wrack and ruin of Nithraen. If she had escaped the city's collapse and eluded the *orukhar*—not to mention the great wyrm making its home in the now-darkened caves—she would still have to contend with winter's bony, ravenous grasp, no longer held back from the hills over the Elder city.

Arn hardly noticed my hesitation, and fairly tossed me into the saddle. Perhaps she was simply delighted to be breathing free air again; she vaulted atop her own horse with enviable ease.

A bright nooning lay over the great green cup-valley holding Laeliquaende, called Waterstone in our southron tongue. Once it had been a mountain-girt lake, so deep the tallest spires might have only pricked its surface from underneath, but those days were long past. Now broad stone-paved roads, proud cousins to the ones running near the Eastronmost Steading of Lady Hajithe or from the great gate of Nithraen to Dorael, spread in lazy patterns from the shining city to outlying steadings and halls, running alongside several leftover brooks and streamlets. Copses clothed in dark evergreen or vivid autumnal leaf dotted the plain, and though the depths of new winter—the most grievous time of year, after the solstice heralding sunlight's lengthening but before any melt is possible—held the land outside in its iron-iced palm, the Elder somehow kept such murderous weather at bay. While the trees might change color they did not shed their robes; a thin veining of green remained at the heart of each leaf, as in the center of every yellowed grassblade at Nithraen.

Only Arneior and I were granted mounts. The wolves of Naras made a cortege about us, the Elder who had accompanied Aeredh from the riven city both before and behind as well as a small contingent of the Hidden City's green-and-gold-armored guards. All in all it was a grand sight, but I felt no wonder.

I was too busy clinging to a saddle of design far different than the southron kind or even the equipage of the Northerners visiting Dun Rithell. The cavalry of Taeron Goldspear was legendary, and their tack reflected all the art of the Elder. The seat was surprisingly comfortable, the mare's gait so easy I hardly had to touch the reins—which were in scarred Efain's hands anyway—but my head throbbed abominably and the steady motion threatened to make me ill.

Were I to retch the only thing produced would be Elder winterwine, and though that drink does not burn with bile during an upward journey it also does not taste half so good as upon its downward path. Besides, the Elder do not suffer such physical upsets, and my pride, though much smaller, would not permit it either.

Not if I could help it.

Each hoof-fall chimed upon pale stone, and to the others it must have seemed musical indeed. Arneior suffered Soren to take her own reins and glanced often in my direction as we rode, each time wearing a disbelieving smile. It was not quite the bemused grin she displayed after our ride upon antlered winter-deer, but I understood her joy.

After all, we had survived the ruin of an entire Elder city, endured the Wild, the Mistwood, and the Glass, not to mention the killing cold of the Marukhennor. *Orukhar* and liches and the many-legged weavers of the dark woods were left far behind; now we rode white horses under an achingly blue winter sky. There were Elder about, and most sang as they wandered or attended to vineyard and field. Some danced too, apparently from a manner of overwhelming joy, like my sister Astrid upon certain summer days.

Efain gave me many a curious glance; he hardly needed to guide my mount. He had his sword again, as did the other Northerners. Their black-clad forms were blots against white stone and rolling green; I made no effort to inquire after his health.

I was too busy keeping my stomach from wringing itself dry.

As we drew nearer Laeliquaende's walls, the music intensified. No doubt my companions found it sweet, but discord lurked under the notes. I tried to discern whether it was simply the pain in my head, spilling down my neck and radiating outward from my stiffened spine, tainting the melody so. Yet each time I gained some equanimity the vision of my charred, broken home rose and every tradeweight of pleasure, no matter how small, vanished.

I shudder to remember that ride. Though it stood wide, the great southronmost gate of Waterstone—the color of horn and bound with mellow brassy metal—appeared to me merely a larger cell-door, and the streets beyond resounded with that jarring, discordant noise. Houses with steeply pitched or rounded but always brightly tiled roofs did not crowd each other too closely, gardens peeped through filigreed gates of powdery metal or stood open to the admiration of passersby, fountains played in every courtyard or square. Each building seemed not to have been built but grown, trimmed and shaped as it rose from the earth itself, and they were all different shades of paleness—nacre to riverfoam, summer cloud to the fleece of a spring lamb, horn to parchment, and all the different hues of bleached linen or wool.

Even the towers, rising to piercing spires or bulb-tipped, graciously melded with their surrounding buildings instead of looming over them. Elder crowded in many a doorway, their gazes lambent and their high-pointed ears poking through hair of every shade, a few even ruddy as my shieldmaid. They all bear a certain similarity, the Children of the Star, and to see it repeated in a crowd is to suddenly doubt one's own mortal lineaments.

The Northerners smiled as they walked, even Efain's mien far less forbidding than usual. Daerith the harpist was at the head of our group with Aeredh, conferring as they walked; each Elder was in the flowing, comfortable costume of the Hidden City.

It should have been glorious. In an Elder settlement, a traveler's weariness falls away. There were even children about, though few compared to the number of adults and looking a little less...well, *alien* than their parents and teachers. Indeed, the very young among them may oft be mistaken for bright, laughing mortal younglings, like my own beloved Astrid when she was but four or five summers high.

The Elder are born knowing much, 'tis said, but also arrive from the womb amused at the world's follies.

Occasionally pairs of littles darted toward our group to hand over flowers; Eol was granted a nosegay instead of a single bloom and thanked the black-haired child who handed it to him with a grave, smiling bow.

None approached me, though—or Arn. My shieldmaid viewed all with an interested air, and her spearblade shone bright as the armor of the guards. She seemed to be having a fine time, her hair alight in sunshine, and hers was the only face that did not seem sickly or vaguely malignant, hiding some secret purpose.

And I? Every hoof-fall was a torment, the endless singing scraped my already frayed nerves, and salt damp collected along my lower back, under my arms, in my palms. The red coral beads in my braids were chips of ice, as if fragments of winter still clung to me.

"My lady Solveig?" Efain had finally decided to address me. He dropped back slightly, the reins clasped in one half-gloved hand, and the mare did not find this at all amiss, plodding placidly along. "It has been some few days. Are you well?"

How could I be? Yet I essayed a smile, though it felt more like a rictus on a frozen corpse. "Well enough. Was your captivity endurable, my lord Northerner?"

"Well, Gelad would not stop pacing, and Soren fiddling with bits of leatherwork, and Karas fretting when there was fresh news of our captain, or no news at all." Efain's scars—one bisecting his eyebrow, the other along his jaw—were pale compared to a warrior's weathering upon the rest of his face. "Even the Elder held with us seemed a trifle out of countenance. The folk are passing cautious here."

"So it seems." I could find nothing else to say.

After a short, excruciating pause, he cleared his throat. "I must offer you our thanks," he said, quietly. " 'Tis a wondrous deed, drawing forth a heartseeker. Eol owes you his life."

Then he may take it, and use it elsewhere. I wish to go home. It was a child's response, and childish anger fair threatened to choke me. The wolves of Naras had sharp ears; I wondered that they did not hear the jangling in the music. There were pipes nearby, and other instruments I might have enjoyed but for their sawing at every inch of skin.

"I am an ally to the house of Naras." Even to myself I sounded stiff, though not nearly as brusque as Eril my father when beset by flowery words he suspected a snare within. "Such was my duty, and I sought merely to perform it. No thanks are necessary."

" *'Tis courteous to give, even when unnecessary.*" Efain used the Old Tongue, that ancestor of the southron dialects. We had journeyed long before they had any intimation I understood their language, being tutored since childhood by both Idra and my mother; perhaps he thought me a liar or worse for refraining.

Arn and I were alone among these men, and every small advantage to be carefully hoarded. Now we were one less.

So I made no answer. My hands tightened, inked marks upon

my wrists filling with sharp sweet almost-pain. The road was rising, and we approached the heart of Waterstone upon a wave of limping, agonized melody.

Efain did not speak again. I shut my eyes, and prayed the ride would end soon.

A Brazen Voice

Of the Elder kings who left the West that day, Taeron Goldspear was not counted least. His folk followed Faevril for love of their kin, and to right a great wrong. O, bright the horses of the High-helm's people riding to war, and the gleams upon their lances; O, sweet the sound of their battle-song, like the voice of the sea itself! Yet so many passed into darkness; aye, only a remnant remain.
—Ancilaen Gaeldflor, *The Fallen Helm*

Arneior set me upon my feet with more care than usual, study-ing my expression. Her freckles glowed, and a healthy flush mounted in her cheeks. The stripe of blue woad upon the left side of her face nearly leapt into thin air, so vivid was it in the noontide. "What a place, Sol. Such gardens. But they live so close—'tis a warren."

Better than Nithraen. The cave-city had been beautiful indeed, but I preferred open sky to so much rock overhead, no matter the weather's fury. "At least we are not underground." A dry cough clawed at the last word; I denied it.

At the center of Waterstone a great shining palace the color of fresh cream basked in wintry sunshine. Perhaps my anxiety was sim-ply the jarring difference between that light and the temperature, for when the great lamp of day looks pale in a drained sky it should be cold. Yet I did not need my great green mantle, its hood and back lined with fur from a shieldmaid-hunted wolf, nor did I need my sturdy felted overboots.

It was utterly, simply *wrong*. At least the hideous discordance was somewhat muted here.

The palace was of much grander form than Nithraen's, and its great silver-chased doors stood open at the head of marble stairs veined with gold. I held fast to Arneior's arm as we climbed, securely contained in a knot of black-clad Northerners, velvet-wrapped Elder, and the armored guards.

Did they fear us—two lone women, levered from their home and brought here all but unwilling? Eol and Aeredh exchanged meaningful glances as another group of armored Elder appeared, taking charge of visitors with precise movements. Floringaeld did not leave, however—the captain simply slowed, and when he drew level he examined us with much interest, as if he had not seen me and my shieldmaid enough the past few days.

I did not return his gaze, being wholly occupied with placing one foot before the other. Halls folded away upon either side, pillared or lined with bright tapestries and murals I might have been interested in had my head not throbbed so awfully. Arneior glanced down at me several times, especially when we passed gardens and courtyards open to the sky, each with its own plashing, jangling fountain.

"Sol?" Her mouth barely moved; it was the whisper we used in our closet at home, away from prying ears. "You're pale."

"So many people." I had thought the folk of Nithraen beautiful with their shining eyes and bright hair, but every Elder I now saw looked furtive or outright haughty, viewing us with secret disdain and more than a hint of malice. "I can barely breathe."

"Do you require rest?" Floringaeld stepped nearer; I almost blundered into Arn's side, flinching from his presence. "Our king gave orders that you be brought, yet at your own pace."

"I am well enough." My throat was almost too parched to grant passage to the words; I pushed my shoulders back and set my chin. "This is only the second Elder city I have seen, my lord. Our settlement is small by comparison." *Though fine indeed, for it is full of honest folk.*

I kept that thought trapped behind gritted teeth, and wished my stomach would cease its rolling.

"*Our journey was long, and few our companions.*" Blue-eyed Gelad moved forward, almost as if to step between the Elder and me. The Old Tongue, familiar though of archaic Northern accent, pierced my head like an awl forced through heavy leather. "*No doubt this is a great change.*"

I could have been grateful for his intercession, but there were yet more stairs to climb. I almost wished to be on horseback again; my knees were soft as Albeig's sops for ill children or the toothless elderly.

At last another set of glittering doors fit for giants swung open, quiet as a whisper, and we were ushered into a vast space full of trees.

Spreading branches met overhead, bearing broad yellow leaves veined with green. I recognized the foliage—the Northerners' dense sweetish waybread had been wrapped in them, and the forest above Nithraen populated by these smooth greyish trunks as well. In this hall the trees were far more ancient; if Arn and I clasped hands their boles would be too large for us to encircle. They grew from a mirror-like stone floor which imperceptibly turned to soft grass-clad earth where their roots delved, and small pale-blue flowers peeked over their gnarled feet.

I had seen those blossoms before as well—after leaving Redhill and traveling far upon the backs of winter-deep, we had reached a stone-ringed clearing full of them. I strained to remember their name in the Old Tongue, and could not.

That was another wrongness; a *volva*'s memory does not misplace such small details. My unease turned sharp as a good blade. So did the nausea. Something dire approached, yet I could neither halt nor evade it. A whisper of *seidhr* trickled into my bones, easing some of the discomfort—but not nearly enough.

"Sol?" Arn, whispering again. I had no attention to spare for her concern.

The center of the space held a slight, natural rise, and upon it stood a simple bench of white stone. Such was the throne of Laeliquaende, and Taeron Goldspear chose no further decoration for his seat. The music here was muted, which was a distinct relief.

Or it might have been, were I not sweating and trembling like a frightened horse.

He was tall and dark-haired, the king of this place, with piercing sky-blue eyes very much like my mother's. He sat with one leg drawn up, resting an elbow upon it as casually as my brother Bjorn when taking his ease upon a fallen log between practice-ring bouts, and rested his chin upon his hand as he regarded our group. A silver fillet like Aeredh's clasped his brow, and nearby a bright-haired Elder girl—Naciel his daughter, the treasure of Laeliquaende—with skirts of pale new green like soft early fir-tips set aside a graceful harp. She rested in a nest of pillows, all covered with muted jewel-color velvet. Next to her was a Northerner in the garb of the Elder inhabitants though black as Eol's cloth, dark of hair and proud of nose, his gaze bearing the same weight as Tarit of Redhill's.

Not quite *seidhr*, but very close.

At the king's left hand stood an Elder man appearing of Aeredh's age, though that is little indication among their folk. He was another black blot, as if he wished to dress as the wolves of Naras—armor of matte finish, engraved with flowing, near-invisible lines. His eyes showed little difference between pupil and iris, and he wore an air of pronounced vigilance; Maedroth was he, called *the Watchful* after a star well-beloved by the Elder, and he was Taeron's nephew.

Their names I learned later. At that moment, I saw only their physical forms as if through a sheet of clear rippling water, distorted as the so-called music. I swayed, pulling upon Arneior's arm, and the whisper of *seidhr* became a thunder.

No, please. I cannot.

But fighting this flood was a doomed battle; Idra my teacher would have tweaked one of my braids with ruthless precision. *Ride the power, child. Don't fight it.*

But I was so tired, and everything hurt.

"My friend." Aeredh's voice should have been comforting—after all, he had carried me upon the last leg of our journey, as if I were a youngling sleepy after a great feast—but it near tore at my cringing nerves. "I bring you Solveig daughter of Gwendelint, *alkuine* of Dun Rithell, and her shieldmaid Arneior, taken by the Black-Wingéd Ones."

It was a great honor to be announced thus, presented to an Elder king by the equally royal Crownless. I might even have enjoyed it, had my stomach not suddenly plunged and a red-hot wire of pain run through me from scalp to heels.

The black-eyed Elder at the king's side cocked his dark head, and a shadow lay over him. *No,* I pleaded silently. *I don't want to see. Stop.* My wrists flamed too, as if every bit of ink forced under the skin pinprick-by-pinprick was suddenly full of molten lead.

It was no use. In the great thronehall of Nithraen I had spoken in couplets helpfully provided by a passing spirit, but this was different. Perhaps something about an Elder throne was inimical to me, or provoked *seidhr* in those who carry the weirding? I could not guess, I knew only the pain.

"Welcome are your friends in my demesnes, son of Aerith." Taeron's tone was pleasant, and he used the southron tongue instead of the Old—another signal mark of honor, especially for mortal guests. "So, this is another *alkuine*? Great indeed is the—"

Agony roared through me, not merely a wire but a heavy sword-blade. The *seidhr* drew me from Arneior's side, my hand sliding nerveless from her arm, and I took three staggering steps as if mead-drunk upon a festival day.

My head tipped back, my mouth opened. Even submitting to the prophecy-speech granted no relief, for I was ill indeed and had hidden it much as a dog or caged bird will, unwilling to show any vulnerability.

A great brazen voice rose from my lungs, scorched my swell-aching throat, rattled my teeth, and tore past my lips. I was vaguely surprised no crimson sprayed forth with it, for it *felt* as if I bled, a great gout of force rammed through a channel far too narrow.

"Taeron," it boomed, and the entire hall rattled, darkening. A salt-smelling wind loomed over the trees; their ancient pillars groaned, branch and twig thrash-dancing. A great soughing as of a summer storm in the forest swept the name high, tossing it back into the hall's cup like dice into a leather container before the gambling begins. **"Taeron, my child, I told thee once, and sent one fated to tell thee twice. Now arriveth my final warning."**

The Old Tongue it spoke in, that terrible tone, and the sky over Waterstone turned the color of a fresh bruise. Salt and fish the wind smelled of as it whistled through the white city; I sought to collapse, but the *seidhr* would not let me. My spine arched, my head thrown back, and Arneior sprang for me, attempting to reach her charge.

She was pushed away, not ungently but clumsily, as if the invisible force inhabiting me for that brief moment did not wish her ill yet would brook no interference. Again the voice was drawn forth, this time from my heels as they touched the earth.

"Love not the work of thy hands too much," it intoned. **"Be not so proud of thy House that thou scruple'st to join it to another. Thou know'st my voice, and know'st the truth in thy inmost heart."**

The king had risen, and for a moment I glimpsed a cold blue brilliance about him—for the Elder have *seidhr* too, though not of our mortal kind, and their subtle selves burn bright-hot. My eyes squeezed shut, tears slicking my cheeks, and for the last time, the voice wrung me like a rag in our housekeeper Albeig's capable, callused fingers.

"Hope has been offered thee, Taeron. The hour is late; let it not grow later."

The thing speaking through me—certainly some divinity instead of a mere passing spirit, though at the moment I could not even wonder which—perhaps also tried to be gentle as it lifted up and away like a white bird upon chill salt-freighted breeze. I had only seen the sea with my inner eye, subtle selves freed from my physical body by drugging fumes from Idra's brass brazier, but its smell was everywhere in that city. For that brief tearing instant I was free of all pain, gliding over the deep cold spear-harbors of the westron shore so far from Dun Rithell.

"Sol! *Solveig!*" Arn was calling, but I could not answer. Does a pipe feel exhausted when the breath forced through it ceases? I had been used as an instrument, and collapsed at last. A vast soft darkness enfolded me, welcome because it was painless, and the last thing I heard was Aeredh's voice, the Old Tongue ragged and breathless.

"We passed too close by the Marukhennor; she is in the despair. Fool that I was to not see it."

For a brief interval I knew nothing, not even to be grateful at the cessation of discomfort. Such was my greeting to Taeron, and little did I guess he knew that voice, having heard it before Tyr's burning first rose and a few times thereafter as well.

But I? I landed upon stone floor with bruising force, saved only from skullsplit by Arneior reaching me at last, her spear clattering free as she thrust her hand between my cheek and cool, hard, mirror-glossy stone to cushion the blow.

Even upon the Scales

'Tis oft not the simple which heals, but the strength of the hand that gives it.

—Proverb of the riverdwellers

Slowly, gently, I drifted. Occasionally a cold blue light bloomed, pushing away the devouring dark, and I heard the Old Tongue as if muffled through layers of cloth. Soft and steady it sang, almost familiar. For I had heard some of the saga before.

The song told of an Elder princess whose glance was like a knife, and of the Secondborn who loved her—at first from afar, then with his affection returned. The tune was lovely, lilting and slow, yet with the sadness which lies within a great many Elder stories.

Anything granted life—short or long—must have some experience of suffering. Even gods; do not the old tales tell us so?

Eventually the blue radiance gave way to a hazy, colorless glow. I found myself possessed of breath again, and for some while simply enjoyed the ability to draw air without pain. From there, though, I discovered my physical body, and expected it to ache more. *Seidhr* flowed in concentric rings, rippling through me as if I were eleven again, feverstruck while Idra tended to me.

A bleak wind had blown from the north that winter. I almost flinched, expecting the vision of my shattered, fire-blackened home to strike snake-quick, but the blow did not arrive.

What did, however, was further consciousness of existing. I had fingers and toes, ribs and a head, my hair was unbound, and I became aware the softness was something like a bed, and the weight upon me very much like blankets. The new illumination was daylight pressing through my half-open eyelids.

The song faded into humming. I lingered upon the threshold of waking, reluctant to discover what new ill-luck returning to myself would bring. Yet I could not tarry forever—there was Arneior, after all, and she relied upon me.

As if the thought summoned her, my shieldmaid spoke. "I think she wakes. Sol?"

Oh, please, let me stay dead. I hate this. It was no use; there is no rest when duty—or *seidhr*—calls. The gates of my eyes opened fully, day flooded in, and I found myself flat upon my back, staring at a stone ceiling carved to look like interlocking, vine-covered branches. A fresh cool breeze touched my cheek, and I tasted the dregs of some Elder draught at the back of my throat.

"Arneior?" The word slurred, caught halfway, and firmed like bread in the oven, developing its proper shape. My arm lifted, and I reached out.

Warm fingers threaded through mine. The invisible haze of another living, breathing being swamped my *seidhr*-senses, heartbeat and lungwork thump-sighing under the formless faraway mutter of another creature's thoughts. The jolt was salutary, like Idra's walloping upon my back when my breath refused to seat itself properly.

The first few times a *volva* sends her subtle selves forth, their return can shock the body's processes into halting. A teacher's blows, while uncomfortable, serve to bring an unruly beast to compliance, or merely to its own natural behavior.

"*There* you are." Relief made her tone sharp as one of Frestis's flint knives. Arneior sat at my bedside, her spear leaning easily to hand, and her hornbraids glowed ruddy in light like that of a new-winter afternoon. "By the Wingéd, I've half a mind to thrash you like your father does Bjorn. What were you thinking?"

Despite the situation, I was absurdly comforted. If she was using breath to scold me, any danger was well past. "I think 'twas a passing divinity, small one. What did I say?"

"Not that, you stubborn little fishhook; I'll repeat the god-talk word-for-word later." Her glare intensified, if that were possible. "But Aeredh says you were struck by some weirding, and hid the wound. Why?"

"Easy, shieldmaid." Aeredh's face appeared over her shoulder. The Crownless looked weary, as an Elder hardly ever does unless some great feat is performed or grief has occurred. The fatigue sat uneasily upon his unlined face, for when they are tired it is mostly shown in the eyes and somehow, in the lack of expression instead of how the flesh pleats with mortal age. "The mists of the Marukhennor hold dangers more than physical, and our lady *alkuine* is not the first to be sickened by the despair. It is a shapechanging foe, and hides itself even from its sufferers."

I longed to shut my eyes again, retreating into lassitude. The veil of distortion was lifted, and the music rustling through fluted pillars along one wall—a door or large window, I could not tell—was no longer a cruel mockery of the Allmother's gift. The shadow lay in my memory, and did I think upon it, I could see how it had grown, silent as chancre breeding in bones or inner organs, turning the faces of my companions into malignant masks and the Elder city into a twisted mockery.

Mighty that *seidhr* was, and I had not even known its working in and upon me.

The room was pretty enough, its walls carved with vines and a wardrobe of dark wood opposite the bed. A stone table and two filigreed chairs of that light powdery metal also stood ready for use, and I heard liquid rilling from a fountain or water-room, for it was Laeliquaende after all and no corner of that land lacked the sound. I was not chilled, though the uneasiness of winter light married to a merely cool breeze remained, a taunting reminder of this place's essential alienness.

Arn and I were mortal, and even if honored guests I did not think us truly welcome here.

All this passed through my skull in a flash. It was a relief to *think* again, without looming, nameless horror grasping at every breath. "It was *seidhr*." Had I not been lying down I might have staggered with relief, for that meant the awful vision of Dun Rithell might not be true. "A great and lying weirding."

"Indeed." Aeredh regarded me gravely, shadows lingering in his blue eyes. "I must beg your forgiveness, my lady Solveig, for I did not notice it. I thought you merely quiet, as is your way."

Arneior's mouth twitched; she knew I was not truly so. Watchful, certainly, as those born to weirding often are, but no one who has ever seen a *volva* enforce peace between arguing smallhall-lords or brawling warriors would name me *quiet*.

"No use in asking what will not be answered." *I sound like Idra.* It was one of my teacher's sayings, though usually accompanying a tweak of my braids or a dismissive snort. "So, I listen instead."

"Indeed. I did not even guess you knew the Old Tongue." Aeredh studied me, much as a *volva* will a recalcitrant patient who must be bullied into greater health. "*You have a great deal of cunning, my lady* alkuine."

The term he used meant *a hunter's wisdom* instead of *treachery*, and I decided it was a compliment. "*As do you, son of Aerith.*" Listening to the Northerners throughout our journey meant my accent was tolerably pure, though not like Floringaeld's or even Daerith the harpist's. "I was weregild, taken from my home and among strangers. You did not show your ear-tips at Dun Rithell; I did not show my command of your language. We might be said to be even upon the scales."

"Hardly." The weariness upon him did not alter. In fact, it intensified somewhat, and he straightened almost self-consciously as if my gaze was unwelcome. "We brought you from your home with a lie, and you have suffered much upon the journey. Make no mistake, daughter of Gwendelint, I am in your debt, as is the House of Naras."

Little good it does any of us, I suspect. "Well, you have achieved your purpose. We are in the Hidden City you spoke of. And since I am not returned to a cell, I may understand the king of this place is not infuriated by a Secondborn's *seidhr*-speech?"

Aeredh did not quite give a start, but he did allow himself a slight, bitter grimace. Arneior leaned back in her chair, wearing the slightest of smiles. She enjoyed hearing me negotiate; sometimes visitors to Dun Rithell made the mistake of thinking my lack of age meant a lack of sense, despite the slow accumulation of inked bands upon my wrists.

"If Taeron wishes to vent a measure of wrath, he may do so upon me." He had been a smiling youth at Dun Rithell and calmly, patiently amused through most of our journey, but now the Crownless was grave indeed. "None can deny the hand of the Blessed in bringing you hence, and it is beneath him to treat a gift of theirs with disdain. Yet I am not comforted, my lady. We have arrived at some small safety. What lies ahead will not be so easily surmounted."

"This Elder thing you wish me to wield, you mean. I already told you I cannot." Caelgor's toy had almost killed me, and I did not like the thought of what Aeredh intended me to attempt next. Though no pain remained, a great exhaustion still gripped me. Returning to health is often an uphill trek, like climbing our mother-mountain Tarnarya to search for certain plants useful in *seidhr*-workings.

Aeredh's hands flickered, a graceful motion, and silver glittered in his palms.

The *taivvanpallo* seemed innocuous enough—a simple orb, the lines etched upon its surface moving lazily. I knew what that fluid writing said, and what lay locked in its flower-opening segments. The Elder toy had almost boiled me to death from the inside, but that was not what truly frightened me, for I had survived its touch and could count myself lucky. A danger surmounted is one which may be almost forgotten, else even a seasoned warrior might be reduced to a quivering rabbit-heap when battle approaches, simply waiting for the sacrifice knife.

No, the fear came in a different form. Because as much as I knew the thing was dangerous, I still longed to open it again and feel the heart-pounding satisfaction of accomplishing something an Elder could not do.

Only one among Aeredh's kind had been born elementalist, what they called *alkuine*—able to touch all branches of *seidhr*'s great tree instead of merely one, able to bring open flame from the air itself instead of a mere spark amid piled tinder. Faevril was his name, mighty his gifts and wondrous his works. He was long dead, and some of his cherished art could not be used save by another capable of that weirding.

I could not even be glad of signal proof that I was of his kind. The greater part of me held it an honor I could have done without, the quite justifiable pride of one wearing inked bands notwithstanding.

"The Blessed brought us to your home, my lady." Aeredh set the small silvery orb upon a tiny table at the bedside, carefully avoiding intrusion upon Arneior's invisible borders. "I cannot think they would offer hope merely to snatch it away. I promised you answers when we reached this place, and will be glad to give them as you please. For now you should rest, and when you are ready, summon me. No matter the hour, I will appear."

He turned sharply, and left through a door of light, deeply carved wood I had scarcely noticed.

Arneior considered the *taivvanpallo*, her bright head cocked and one of her leather-wrapped braids falling over her shoulder. Her ring-and-scale armor was polished to even greater brightness than *seidhr* could grant; she must have been at it with mortal methods and vengeful thoroughness while waiting for me to wake.

"Three days." Her profile, familiar as my own, was set and stony. "He sat and sang, while others came and went with Elder draughts and other things. I prayed, but the Wingéd Ones were silent. You almost died."

"I am sorry." It was an effort to lift my right hand from soft sky-blue cloth once more. The blankets were light but warm indeed, though I did not sweat. I did not wonder who had stripped my heartsblood wool dress, leaving me in a sleeveless linen shift bearing Astrid's careful embroidery at neck and hem, for my shieldmaid would have allowed none other that duty. "I did not guess it was weirding, Arn. Idra would be so disappointed."

She clasped my hand, but her expression did not change. Her freckles stood out through paleness, the only mark of discomfort she would allow. "I wish you would have told me, instead of hiding it."

"I cannot tell what I do not know."

"What good is weirding, then?" A quick shake of her head, like a granary cat suffering an unwelcome shower of cold rain. "You must not do that again, Sol. We are far from home; you are all I have."

It was unlike her, and a strange slipping sensation filled my chest. "You speak as if you are not all I have as well."

She squeezed my fingers, bruising-hard, and let go to rise, striding to the pillared window. Later that day I learned it was a balcony far larger than the one attached to our quarters in Nithraen, for such was the healing I could rise and take a few steps back and forth, my legs unsteady as a newborn colt's.

We were not troubled with other visitors, and my shieldmaid was largely silent. I did not like that, for her temper is unlike mine— quick to rise, and just as quick to recede.

And I had never before thought she might be afraid of anything at all.

Mortal Envy, Sharper Teeth

Alaessia returned to her brother's city with her tall, somber son, and the High-helm welcomed both. Yet hard upon their heels her silent husband tracked; perhaps 'twas even a form of love which drove him, granting skill enough to find the hidden door. For Gethsael the Quiet held a wild strain, and in it cherishing was wound with possession, tight as strangling vines...

—Fragment, *The Annals of the Long Vigil*, attributed to Varaecil the Daggerwise

The palace of Taeron was a world all its own, like Fryja's land of plenty or Odynn's halls where warriors and shieldmaids, found worthy after their last mortal battle, feast with the *valkyra*. I thought then it might bear some resemblance to the fabled land of the West, that bright myth-drenched place the Elder were then barred from.

Quiet halls with pillared sides looking onto gardens with bright spangled fountains, small round rooms holding cushioned benches or deep soft chairs for easy conversation with a companion, one's own thoughts, or even a painting upon the wall. There were rooms full of curiosities in well-designed wooden or metallic cabinets, strange treasures or interesting bones, stones, and other items. Even the stables were a joy—airy, well-kept, more fit for a riverlord's domicile than beast-shelter. There were meeting halls and feast rooms, strange follies like the chamber with its walls sheathed entirely in some curious nacreous substance carved from the teeth of great slow creatures with columnar legs—or so Naciel explained once, showing me finely wrought illustrations upon a yellowing page—and on, and on.

I could sing for a long, long while without exhausting the wonders shown to a daughter of Dun Rithell in that place.

Nothing could outdo what was revealed the first day Arn and I left our quarters, though. Floringaeld and Aeredh both insisted to my shieldmaid that we were free to wander where we chose, save into private homes—not that we would have ever done such a thing, being raised well by my mother Gwendelint. But I suppose the Elder suspect all Secondborn lacking in even such basic courtesy, or perhaps the inhabitants of the Hidden City believed us akin to granary cats, who walk where they will.

In any case, upon a bright crisp morn we sallied forth, and at the end of the hall were greeted with a wide stone staircase spiraling in easy steps to a round space with benches running along either side, pillows scattered about its floor, and a great harp—easily taller than me, though not quite so tall as Arn—upon a small stone pedestal seemingly crafted solely for its rest. And, looking out one of the broad window-casements onto a garden of blue foliage and pale flowers even in this season, was an Elder woman.

She owned a head and a half on Arneior, though much slighter than my shieldmaid, and she wore soft blue cloth of Elder weaving—a dress like a sauna-robe but heavier, and with a longer skirt brushing the floor in her wake. Her wide dark eyes were full of amusement, like my sister's, and her hair was deep gold as Astrid's as well. Laughter lurked about her pretty mouth, and her nose was proud as Eol's. A necklace of silver filaments held a white gem just a little below her collarbones, and delicate silver drops hung from her ears.

"Hail, daughter of the river," she intoned in the southron tongue, bending one knee in a melting courtesy. Her accent was exceedingly archaic, though every word was softly distinct. "And hail to thee, maiden-of-steel."

I could not tell how to respond. I recognized her, of course—she had been in the thronehall, a bright bird in a soft nest with a Second-born man beside her.

"Is that the correct greeting?" She absolved me of any requirement to find an appropriate response by continuing, with barely a pause, as she straightened. "Tjorin could not tell, for he doth ken not much of the south, and Eol's men of chatter are not overfond. Aeredh said I must avoid fright or insult, and you knoweth our tongue—but 'tis better to greet a guest in their own, my father speaks. Are quarters-of-yours sufficient? Do you thirst? How may we make you welcome?"

Indeed it was slightly difficult to understand her, for she spoke a very old variety of southron, salted with the Old Tongue in the bargain. Arneior cocked her head, her spear dipping slightly as she leaned upon it, and I am certain I looked just as baffled.

I also attempted to copy the Elder's courtesy, though I suspect I did not do so with any real grace since my legs were still a trifle unsteady. *"Hail and well-met, Child of the Star. May the Sun shine upon our meeting."* I made every syllable as precise as possible, accented as the Northerners did. Then, in our own language, I continued with likewise care. "I am Solveig of Dun Rithell, and this is Arneior my shieldmaid, taken by the Black-Wingéd Ones. Your welcome warms us; we would be good guests."

"Sol-ve-ig." She nodded thoughtfully. "Ar-ne-ior. You must correct, if badly I speak. Naciel am I, Silverfoot they call me, daughter of Taeron Goldspear."

"Naciel Silverfoot," I translated for Arn. "Daughter of the king, and she wishes to learn our dialect."

"Better than me learning weirding-speech." Arn tapped her spear's blunt end thoughtfully against stone floor, punctuating the sentence. "And she is a woman; no doubt she has some sense."

I could not help smiling. Those taken by the Wingéd Ones have little use for men, save as sparring fodder. "I think it likely." I addressed the princess again, hoping she was indeed as friendly as she appeared. *"We are honored, king's-daughter; if you will teach me the Old Tongue, I shall teach you ours."*

"Indeed I think you need little instruction." Naciel's brow wrinkled

for a moment. "Your...shieldmaid, is it? *Does she speak the Elder tongue?*"

"Arneior prefers our own language, my lady." Perhaps I should have chosen a different mode of address—but I was *volva*, and though now doubting myself completely worthy of the name I still wore bands upon both my wrists. One with the *seidhr* may speak regardless of rank, though never without politeness.

Such a distinction is beyond many in the world, yet exists nonetheless. Besides, I was a daughter of Dun Rithell. Had I a habit of rudeness my teacher would have tweaked my braids thoroughly, and my mother's quiet disappointment was ever punishment enough to induce any necessary change in her children's behavior.

"Well enough." The princess's manner was all warm welcome, and I could find no hint of ill intent in its depths. She moved from the casement as if dancing, her dress fluttering in several layers. "A wonder would I show ye, guests-of-honor. Tjorin says..." She halted, clearly searching for the right words. "He says 'tis summat interests-would one-who-is-wise." The last term was the antecedent of *seidhr*, the older form of describing one who may see beyond the visible, speak with the intangible, and discern the secret patterns of the world.

"We are in your hands then, Princess Naciel." I halted in near-confusion as she regarded me, a deeper smile blooming upon her lovely face.

I had seen others become tongue-tied when Astrid regarded them thus, and it was a strange experience to feel wonder instead of fond pride in a like situation. It occurred to me then how some mortals could hate the Elder, as some seem to despise *volva* or others born to the weirding—like the blackrobe priests farther south, with their blasphemous god and their virulent execration of quite natural cunning.

The Children of the Star are simply too beautiful sometimes, and mortal envy has teeth sharper than an *orukhar*'s sawtooth grin or lich's cold blade.

The moment passed. My shieldmaid and I followed our hostess, exchanging a single look. Arn's was puzzled; mine, however, might have held a touch of something darker.

After many a passage and a few short, easy flights of stone stairs, a pair of highly carved doors opened upon whisper-quiet hinges. Arneior glanced through, nodding before I moved to follow the princess.

A vast round room swallowed us, full of such light I almost thought it roofless though the air was still. But there was a great dome with slender-seeming stone ribs, and between them panes of crystal so clear only refractions at their edges told what they consisted of. The tall, narrow windows were crystal as well, instead of scraped horn, and lingered between shelves of stone and polished wood. Like so much else in Elder settlements, the rock and tree-stuff seemed grown or shaped while almost liquid, instead of mortal-carved.

Yet the architecture, while wonderful enough, was not the true treasure of that place. I longed to know how the walls were constructed, how the dome and window were made, but what took my breath away...I can feel the awe and deep reverence even now.

Shelves filled that place, ranks of them radiating from a central space with tables and chairs. Some of the tall structures held ladders for reaching their tops, and others were enclosed by thin folding doors of a fragrant wood which repelled both chewing insect and perhaps time itself.

For every shelf and cabinet held scrolls of birch bark, or of some thin material very like parchment, or flat-bound books with heavy barklike faces and backs. Not a single shelf, nor a small chest holding an entire settlement's store of knowledge transmitted through runes either carved or linked-and-falling—no, whole *cases* of them, entire *stacks*.

"What is..." Arneior took in our surroundings, somewhat mystified before she recognized the treasure. "Scrolls? Ai, I will never pry you from here." She shook her head; for one who can track all manner of creatures across mountainslope or through fen, she rather oddly regards the deciphering of written footsteps as a slightly sinister act.

Some hold that very common weirding in wonder, even if they

may puzzle out a word or line. The wise of Dun Rithell taught the *seidhr* of reading to all who wished, though many who could practice it disliked writing other than single runes to be blood-fed when the need arose. And of course, being riverfolk, we all knew how to figure sums, debits, tolls, and credit with trade-partners.

But this...so much learning, such a wealth of scrolls all in one place? I forgot my legs' unsteady protestations as well as the terrors of the journey, and any lingering unease was lost in sheer wonder. "Are they..." I could not find words for a moment, staring at the closest set of shelves. "Are they in southron falling-runes, or..."

"Some are in Secondborn writing, others in Elder script." A deeper shadow in the valley between two towering shelves was a mortal man in Northern black, but the cut of his cloth as well as its weaving was Elder. He held a thick bark-bound volume, and I recognized him from the throneroom—he had been next to the princess. "Ah, forgive me. I am Tjorin son of Hrasimir, of House Berengar. May the Blessed upon-our-meeting smile."

His southron was not nearly so archaic as the princess's, but exceeding formal indeed. I laid my right hand over my heart as I had seen some of the Northerners do, and nodded. "Solveig daughter of Eril, *volva* of Dun Rithell. This is my shieldmaid Arneior, taken by the Black-Wingéd Ones."

"Yes." He glanced at Naciel; though her smile never altered, the warmth in their meeting gazes was very nearly uncomfortable to witness. "The gift of the Blessed, who speaks with their voice. And her protector, a mighty *trul*-killer."

"I did not kill it," Arn immediately objected, for a shieldmaid must not claim valor unearned. "Should I meet another, though—"

"Gods, no." I could not help but shudder. My skirts swayed, a soft sound unlike the silken whisper of the princess's dress. "I would not like to see another of *those*."

There were dangers at home, of course. Warlords both petty and strong, illnesses rising from the river in hard winters or wet springtime, wolves, bandits, ill-luck, bad weather—to be alive is to worry over such things. Yet ever since setting out with Aeredh and the wolves of Naras, my shieldmaid and I had seen far worse.

Liches, mostly of the lesser type—as if it mattered, for even a mere contagion-bred wight is deadly enough. The many-legged weavers of the Mistwood. Pale *orukhar*, and the twisted, invisibly burning *trul*. A snow-hag and a *nathlàs*, one of the Enemy's seven great captains.

Even worse than knowing the Black Land, that fabled horror of long ago, was alive and sending forth its servants once more was the thought that somehow those terrors would, sooner or later, descend upon Dun Rithell. And what of the thickly clustered settlements to the south, or the greater lands past the Barrowhills?

"Then wise indeed are you, my lady." Tjorin set the volume upon its shelf with a great deal of care. The swordhilt set with a gem very like Eol's, save with a reddish cast instead of water-clear, glittered over his shoulder. "I must practice your tongue; forgive me if I speak not aright."

"Then we may teach each other, as the princess and I have agreed." I could barely look at him or at the bright-haired Elder woman, my attention straying repeatedly to the cases and spines. Though I had been taken as weregild and suffered in the snows of the Wild, all that could be counted little enough if I could plumb these depths. The thought that I might even have run hence willingly if I knew this place existed could not be voiced, but I do not deny it crept through my head. "Elder script, you say? Is it like our runes? I would wish to study, if time permits—"

"Those of Naras call you *Lady Question*, and I see the name well-chosen." Tjorin's smile, like Naciel's, held no hint of arrogance or ill-will. "You will find many an answer within these stacks, and I shall help all I am able."

"Wonderful," Arn muttered. "Where am I to practice, if you are here for long hours? There is no room."

"We shall move a table or two," I offered sweetly. "As long as we replace them when you are finished. Or you may go elsewhere to find warriors to duel. It is no worse than when I am in the stillroom at home, small one."

Naciel laughed, a sweet silver trill. "Fortunate this is, indeed. Tjorin may stay with the books as he loves to do, while your maiden-of-steel and I find more active amusements." And though she salted the words with the Old Tongue her accent was improving, even in such a short while.

Arneior did not demur, though a shieldmaid and her charge are rarely apart save when the former judges there to be no danger in separation. Once she satisfied herself that nothing untoward lurked in the environs, she would find summat else to do, but I could not think upon that. I was too busy marveling.

The princess and Northerner guided me through a fraction of the library that morn while their hands occasionally strayed toward each other's, fingers tangling and separating shyly. They traded lingering looks as well, perhaps when they thought Arn and I would not notice.

That was how I met Naciel Silverfoot and her husband-to-be, and the memory still makes me smile. Yet all was not well, for though he was an honored guest, Tjorin's affection for the king's daughter was not welcomed by Waterstone's ruler.

Capable or Not

No mortal came to Waterstone without escort save one,
And when he arrived all marveled—all save the Watchful,
The son of Alaessia, brimful of deadly temper
For upon the newcomer his fair cousin's gaze fell
And longing was there plainly writ...
                    —The Second Saga of Hrasimir's Son

Even Elder healing takes a heavy toll upon the body. I would have given much to stay in that wondrous crystal-roofed chamber, but after assurances that I could wander thence at will I retreated, with Arn, toward the rooms given to our use. I did not think our withdrawal unwelcome; no doubt Tjorin and the princess treasured every moment spent alone, much as courting couples in Dun Rithell.

During our return journey Arneior repeated the words which had forced their way through me in Taeron Goldspear's throneroom, imitating even the cadence since sometimes the key to a riddle lies not in what is said, but *how*.

"I indeed marvel that the Elder king did not order me returned to the cells." I did not have to lean upon her arm, but a quiver ran through my leg-bones as if I were about to take the ague. "Am I to be spoken through every time I meet such rulers? I would rather not have the honor, then."

"You did not prophesy for the princess today." Arn's brow

wrinkled as she shortened her strides to match mine, glancing absently down a hallway opening to our left. She had not been this watchful at Dun Rithell, but the Wild will make even the tamest creature cautious, as the proverb goes, and we had been traveling long indeed.

"Why bother, when I can see how she and the Northerner look at each other?" There were no bars holding us in a confined space, nor anyone to overhear; 'twas luxurious to be walking where we willed, unwatched by Elder or grim Northern men. Had I not been in need of rest, I might have suggested we test the limits of this new freedom.

As it was, I was glad to see an archway carved with trumpet-shaped flowers, which Naciel said was the symbol of the women's quarters. I wondered if Elder men had to risk pinches, pokes, or thumps with a spindle if they intruded, unless they were under a kinswoman's skirts.

"Sol." Arn halted, tapping her spear-butt upon the stone floor—not a sharp crack of irritation or to mark an utterance of portent, but a simple sound of emphasis. "We must discuss something."

"Here?" I longed to sit down, or lean against something solid.

"I can sense no nearby ear." Her expression was not quite grave, though her mouth was a thin line. "You?"

"None." I did not say I doubted I was *volva* enough to tell. We were far from home in a hidden Elder city, surrounded by creatures of sagas and lore—allies instead of weregild since I had negotiated us free of the latter, yet still far more helpless than I liked. And the corrosive whisper of doubt in my own abilities, despite the inked bands and runes upon my wrists and forearms, was not wholly of a bleak *seidhr*'s making.

Idra would have made a sharp spitting sound and set me some task or another, not merely to keep me distracted from dire thoughts but also to grant me proof of at least some competence. Confidence is largely built upon victory, no matter how small, and attempting any *seidhr* with less than complete will is an invitation to disaster.

I was elementalist, true—able to touch all branches of weirding's great tree, able to call open flame from the very air. I had never questioned whether there were others, since Idra only said she had not trained any and therefore must rely on lore and rede for my teaching. But if there had been only one among the Elder in all this time...

When I thought of it at home, I had always assumed there *had* to be others of my weirding-kind, perhaps farther south in the more thickly settled regions. After all, my teacher never showed any uncertainty, merely due consideration of how my talents might possibly differ from that of a wise one bound to a single branch.

"We may simply have exchanged a small cage for a larger one." My shieldmaid glanced over my shoulder, alert as any hunted beast and trusting me to watch for any creeping thing behind her. "Remember Redhill? Tarit's father was said to have passed time in this place, and was allowed to go forth for some reason. They seemed to consider such departure a signal mark of honor, and Efain remarked that we might not gain like distinction. We may not be allowed to leave."

"Why would Aeredh bring us hence, then? If he expects me to use some Elder weapon..." It was, I must admit, somewhat of a relief to have something other than my own failures to reflect upon. "I told him the *taivvanpallo* almost killed me."

"Yes, at that council you spoke well indeed. Yet you did not truly express to *me* how badly the thing hurt you." Her gaze sharpened; it is no comfortable thing to face a shieldmaid's disappointment. "And you did not tell me of that foul weirding upon you, either."

"I did not know I was suffering it." A paltry excuse, to be sure. "Arn..." *What if I am not a true* volva? *What if Idra was wrong? What if...*

Arneior's task was to protect us from physical danger, no matter how dire. All else was my responsibility, whether I felt myself capable or not.

"What else have you not said?" Her knuckles were white, I realized, and her freckles glared because she had turned pale again. The stripe of blue woad upon the left side of her face, carefully applied that morning, gleamed bright. "I know you are weirdling, Solveig, but I am your shieldmaid. I cannot protect you if I do not know such things."

What else would you have me say? "The Elder cannot mean to keep us here for long, especially if they wish us to wield something against...against their foe." I could not bring myself to say *the Black Land*, or even *the Enemy*.

Not at that moment, with the trembling still in my limbs. A being who could hang such vast darkness upon mountain-peaks, an enemy so old and ancient, once the Allmother's brightest and most powerful child...perhaps the Elder could fight that manner of creature, but Solveig of Dun Rithell was merely a riverside wisewoman. It was ridiculous to think my mother's daughter, Eril's uncanny get, Astrid and Bjorn's serious, sharp-tongued sister, could match such a foe.

At home I was proud, and powerful. Here, I was...otherwise.

Arneior's eyebrows rose. "Aeredh's city is gone, he may as well tarry here. Our lives are shorter than a hound's to them; they will not care if we spend them trammeled. Do you not long to go home?" She leaned toward me, light upon her toes as if watching a particularly interesting sparring match. "I know you wished for adventure, and knowledge. And yet, if those pale things go conquering southward..."

It was uncomfortably like hearing my own thoughts spoken aloud. "My father has the battle-madness. In any case, Dun Rithell is small. If *orukhar* and liches wend south they may well miss us entirely."

"Have you dreamed of home? Of your mother, at least?" Of course, when she was proved to be taken by the Black Wingéd Ones Arneior's own kin had been severed from her, and once the ceremony tying us together was completed my mother was the closest thing to her own she would ever know.

Gwendelint of Dun Rithell had always prized Arn as much as a child of her own body. I had never wondered before if my small one missed her own upriver steading, a place I had never visited.

"I did dream, and they were safe enough." The consciousness of not being completely truthful was acute—I had dreamt of them before the shattering vision of our home lying in smoking ruins, yes, and the terrible contaminating *seidhr* upon me was almost certainly full of lies.

But any creature possessing speech may mislead with not-quite-falsehood, with omission, and with the truth itself as well. I could have been granted a vision of what would happen in the future, not an event already past.

Indeed, 'twas more than possible.

"Perhaps you should try again." Her generous mouth turned down at the corners. "I...have been unable to dream of home, despite asking the Black-Wingéd for aid."

Did it cost her to make such a confession? I could not tell. "They have no reason to be displeased with you, Arneior. You have done more than well, and performed mighty feats. I heard the Northerners call your spear *Trul*-killer, even if you have not named it yet."

"Ah, well." She shrugged, but her tense watchfulness did not abate. "We must explore this place, and be ready. This king Taeron does not please me, though I like his daughter well enough. And if this was indeed Aeredh's goal, he must have some further plan as well."

When you are ready, summon me. No matter the hour, I will appear. So Aeredh had said, and soon enough I would put it to the test. My legs were unsteady at that moment, though, and perhaps I swayed a little more than was absolutely necessary. Arneior's hand shot out, closing about my upper arm.

"I need rest." It irked me to admit it yet again, but what else could I do? "I cannot question him effectively at the moment, but when I can I will make certain he grants some indication of how long they mean to keep us here. And do not forget 'twas my choice to come hither, since we are allied to Naras. Eol does not seem the type to take his ease in an Elder cage for long."

"Oh, aye. But had you chosen that Dorael-place, what is to say they would not have dragged us here anyway?" She made certain I was steady, then gently tugged me for the doorway. "They are better than those *things*, Sol. But they may do us ill nevertheless."

She was right, of course. Inside the chambers given to our use there was no sense of a listening ear either—but my shieldmaid had grown cautious indeed. We gave each other many a significant glance, and her brow was troubled.

So, I suspect, was mine.

Too Often Fearless

Most hold Dorael was the fairest, for there the Cloak-Weaver of the Blessed lingered and the forest was that of Lithielle's birth. But artful Nithraen, Galath of the willows and blue fields, Tol-Naralin the dreaming, proud Faeron-Alith, shining Laeliquaende, Gaeliquenden of the fragrant gardens, the delicacy of Isdrassil-named-Icemarn, and so many more—who can say which was most beautiful? Only that they are lost...

—*Song of the Scattering*

The contrast between thin bluish winter daylight and the lack of snow and ice made the whole glittering city into a dream, even the gardens. Trees which would have long shed their robes in the Wild—or upon the slopes of Tarnarya—still bore them, albeit in bright autumn finery. Many were the same kind we had seen in Nithraen and Taeron's throneroom, but others made their home there too, from silverbark birch to wise gnarled tahami, larch to the ever-dancing shiverleaf and more.

I rarely saw Elder about the work of tending their gardens, and when I did it seemed more a contemplative activity than one with any real urgency. Even Idra had to blast a weed or two with a muttered curse in the small plot just outside her thatched cottage, but in Waterstone the line between copse and field, garden and pasture, blurred easily. Things simply seemed to know where to grow, and how. Perhaps it was the constant singing *seidhr* drenching the air.

Though at any given moment I would have much rather been in what Naciel called *the smaller library*, Arn was restless. The discomfort between us was new, and deeply unwelcome. So, the day after being shown a treasure-trove of knowledge, I forewent the pleasure of pillage. Instead, I settled upon a stone bench amid a bank of rustling bluegreen grasses with white feather-heads, listening to a stone fountain half-buried among waving tufts, and watched my shield-maid use a wide flagstone space for her daily spear-swinging.

Closing my eyes, listening to the faint afternoon breeze, I sought some measure of peace. I did not need my great green mantle, though the wind was cool. The heartsblood wool of my second-best dress sufficed, and I had taken much care with my braids that morn, every scrap of red coral placed at appropriate junctures. My grandmother's silver bee-end torc rested lightly against my collarbones—women armor ourselves just as warriors do, though in skirts and bright accoutrement—and I laid my hands in my lap, palm-up.

Summon me, Aeredh had said. *I will answer.*

Well enough. Yet the soft, lying voice of the Marukhennor's gloom still lingered in my head. I had not dreamt; my sleep was as thick and dark as rivermud, and my bones still remembered the killing cold outside Laeliquaende's mountain-girdle.

What vast weirding kept winter itself at bay? Would I ever unravel it? What need did the Elder have of any mortal when they could perform such a wonder?

Enough, Solveig. You have chewed that question until it is dry. Find a better one.

Arn's faint huffs of effort when a spear-strike would meet the flesh of an enemy, the scuff of her boots—sounds so familiar they were almost unheard, like the sough of my own breath. I shut them away.

The soft breeze teasing plumed grass, whispering through branches bearing painted leaves, brushing against stone buildings before it escaped the city to play in the fields beyond; I also shut that away, and it left without trouble, a polite guest aware of welcome overstayed.

It was harder to ignore the fountain's soothing, everchanging chimes. And yet more difficult was the music of Elder voices, a great tapestry of song rippling as the breeze shifted, rising and falling like the breath of some vast clean-limbed animal.

Yet it faded, and I was left with my own heartbeat. Idra's training was thorough, and some might say harsh. Discipline, even tempered by love, can be uncomfortable. She ever had little patience with my lack of confidence.

First you were too prideful by half, now you behave as a shamed thrall. Who among them wears the bands you do, Gwendelint's daughter? You earned them, else I would not have forced the ink under your skin myself.

Was it her voice, or merely what I wish she could tell me? Idra was gone, and though the dead might speak during times of great need and a *volva* knows how to provoke such an event, it is never wise to disturb an ancestor's rest.

I did not think it likely my teacher had gone to the halls of Odynn's feasting, nor to the sybaritic pleasures of Fryja's innermost halls. Perhaps she would find one of Hel's mist-shrouded lands more restful, for it was on days the clouds came to earth and the river breathed moisture upward that Idra seemed most content, though the damp oft made her bones ache until her last student could ameliorate the discomfort with a wire of vital warmth run into the marrow.

Brooding upon that was a distraction, and hardest of all to put aside.

My heartbeat slowed. My hands tingled, palms warm as if full of summer sunshine. I thought of Aeredh.

At first he had appeared a youth in Northern black, blue-eyed and smiling as if he knew a delightful secret jest. Singing softly upon the mist-shrouded Elder roads, lifting his cup to Lady Hajithe of the Eastronmost, patient and of good cheer no matter what the weather brought—I had been somewhat proud of myself for noticing he was Elder, though it had been Arn whose vision pierced deeper, uncovering the secret of Naras.

In Nithraen Aeredh was the Crownless, regal though his father's circlet lay discarded upon an Elder throne. And in battle he was deadly, a sliver of his true age showing sharp as splintered metal.

But it was after crossing the Glass I began to think I knew him, for we walked almost as one, his arm over my shoulders, and he carried me the final stretch to this harbor which might yet be a trap. And while some of the Elder were prideful and surprisingly petty considering their great age and many gifts, he had proved himself otherwise—even if I were inclined to dislike the lie told to bring me to this wondrous place. He led his Secondborn friends with neither brutality nor cunning, but calm certainty.

My fingers tensed. The sending leapt from my hands like a bird, a small brown sparrow brought from its thornbrake-hiding by a whisper of *seidhr*.

It is not right to kill something so small and trustful when you have lured it to your grasp, though sometimes hunger might win over every consideration of fairness. Still, there is a far greater weirding in returning such a creature to its business, unharmed and untroubled, suffering no lingering shock.

It was far easier than I expected, as if the Elder *seidhr* pervading the air strengthened my own. I exhaled softly, letting the wind and the fountain fill my ears again. Arn was still at her practice, so I drifted in that state a *volva* knows as well as waking—not of the daylight but not of slumber either, caught between and rocking like a coracle upon waves of slow soft lung-fill and empty.

My fingers twitched. I returned to full wakefulness with an internal jolt, for laid across my open hands was something that had not been there before, and the Crownless settled upon the bench to my right.

"Then did she speak, though many leagues between them lay." It was the Old Tongue, a quotation from some saga or other work, judging by the accents upon penultimate syllables and the pleasing arrangement of rhyme. He wore dark blue, and the Elder fashion suited him; the tips of his ears were clearly visible, for his hair was pushed back. Upon one high ear-point a filigree of silver winked—such is the fashion of some Elder, the whorls in metal replicating certain glyphs of their writing.

Southron falling-runes can only approximate the sounds of their ancient language.

Relief burned through me, so hot and sudden I almost swayed. I was still *volva* enough for a sending. "What is that from?"

"An old song. My father used to hum it sometimes." Aeredh watched Arneior's practice; by now, he knew better than to think my shieldmaid unaware of his presence. "The first time our people went West some could not finish the journey. There were those who tarried, and those who were…lost."

The weight in my hands was a knife. A short, curved healer's blade, it was plain but beautiful, like many things of Elder make. The handle was fine-grained, very dense wood, carved like fishscales and worked with thread-fine silver delineating each one; the sheath bore no gem but instead a single decorative glyph, repeating with slight variations as it marched to the tip. It fit my palm perfectly, as if it had been made to, and its weight felt…good.

I already had a very serviceable healer's knife for herb-gathering and stillroom work in my embroidered *seidhr*-bag, a blade Bjorn had made under Corag's watchful eye and presented to his weirdling sister upon my twelfth birthday. This one, I suspected, would be more than sharp enough to dig an arrowhead out of resistant flesh, or lance an infection.

"It sounds a sorrowful tale." I lifted my hands, examining the play of light upon the hilt. "But beautifully made, as is this."

"*A small gift.*" He slipped into the Old Tongue, but with care upon each syllable, as if he doubted my understanding. "*It is of the kind you may carry, is it not?*" Did he sound anxious? It could hardly be credited, but then again, he seemed most polite.

Even for an Elder.

"Oh, yes. A *volva*, like any with *seidhr*, must not touch proper weapons. It is bad for us, and bad for them." I felt the fool, explaining such small things to one of his undoubted age and power. "This does not trouble your kind at all; I have seen you fight with both."

"Efain says your shieldmaid is so sharp any other weapon is unnecessary. Eol said it was more likely you simply disdained to carry one, as you oft disdain to speak." Now Aeredh sounded amused. He stretched out his legs; his boots were of Elder make too, patterned as leaves wrapped in several layers. "At first I thought you remained quiet out of fear. Then I thought you angered, for you had noticed we were not all Secondborn, and many hold those like the wolves of Naras in some caution."

"Better to listen than to speak." I used the Old Tongue carefully as well, as if it might turn against my throat. To mispronounce a word at this stage would be utterly embarrassing. "Especially if a weregild finds herself suddenly among Elder and those with a second skin."

"It was a surprise to hear you use my language, I must admit." He sobered. "I swore to answer any question you might have once we reached this place. You have been far more gracious than we deserve."

"You sound like Eol." I watched Arneior spin, her spearblade a solid bar of silver as it clove air. "Is he well? His shoulder."

"Well enough. Such wounds heal slowly, and rarely completely." Aeredh paused. "Do you know what you saved him from?"

I saved no one. It was all I could do to light the snow-hag on fire, and I could not have drawn the splinter without your aid. "Heart-seeker," I murmured. Even the name sounded ugly, and I had to quell a shudder. "That thing, the *nathlàs*. Was it one of the Seven?"

"Yes, though unmounted. Which rather worries me." He shook his head slightly, a feline flicker. "The shard you pulled forth would have continued working inward. When it reached his heart he would become the thing's servant, his will wholly subsumed by the darkness. He would become the Enemy's thrall."

"Ah." It was a sickening thought. "Gelad would stay with him, then, to..."

"To grant his lord peace before he was turned, and seek his own end in battle afterward." Had Aeredh paled ever so slightly? It was difficult to tell, he was so serene. "It is a terrible thing to bear a heart-seeker. Of all deaths, it may be the only one the heir of Naras fears."

"So there is something he is afraid of."

Perhaps my honest surprise sounded like sarcasm, for Aeredh's laugh was pained. "If anything, I would say Secondborn are too often fearless. It is a marvel."

Not I, my lord Elder. My own cowardice was a deep shame, and not one I wished to speak of. "The sagas say we are to meet death well, after all."

"It is the Allmother's great gift. I often wonder…" Another small shake of his head. "Eol owes you more than his life. He is also my friend; thus, I am in your debt thrice-over."

Thrice? I cannot tell even once, Crownless. "I could not have drawn the cursèd thing free without your aid, and Arn was near to killing you for granting that help. I am merely glad you do not take offense upon that count."

"Offense?" Once more Aeredh sounded pained; his hands lay easily in his lap, palm-up as if he liked the feel of sunlight and sought to hold it like water. "We owe you so much I would bear even your enmity as a blessing. I am here to explain, my lady Solveig, yet I know not where to begin."

"Some Elder weapon rests here, and you brought me hither to attempt its use." That much I knew. "If I learn nothing of import and prove I cannot wield this thing, will you send us home to Dun Rithell?"

Arn whirled lightly and halted, spear held perfectly level, her eyes half-lidded and the stripe of blue woad upon her face glowing as her ruddy hair flamed. A soft feather-brushing filled the air—a sign that the Black-Wingéd Ones had not abandoned her, and no doubt she welcomed the feeling.

"This is no simple matter." Aeredh's smile did not falter, merely turned somewhat pained as he rose. "Will you walk with me, my lady? There is summat I would show you; it will help you understand."

There was nothing else to do, so I rose. At least my legs were much steadier, for a full night's rest had worked well upon me. Arn fell into step upon my other side, smiling and at ease, as Aeredh set off.

I was not quite completely recovered for all the steadiness of my limbs, but that did not matter.

Amusing Insults

The Greycloak's wrath was great. He would not alter his decree, but neither would the Secondborn's heart turn. So it was Bjornwulf set out from Dorael to gain a shining bride-price, and he took the road to Nithraen, seeking counsel. For Aerith of the Shining Caves was ever a friend to mortals, though oft repaid with bitterness.

—Daerith the Elder

The gleaming towers of Waterstone rose high indeed, most tipped with needle-spikes but some swelling into bulbs as if they sought to worship Fryja's most tender gift to men. But we did not tread upon the paved streets that late afternoon, instead following a chain of gardens through Taeron's palace. No carved-rock dome soared overhead as in Nithraen, but I was still uncomfortably aware of many buildings crowding relatively close, brimming with living, thinking beings. Aeredh's city had been an assault to the senses, but Laeliquaende was truly massive, and weighed upon the breath.

There were quiet spaces within its bustle. Music—Elder voices, fountains playing, instruments I did not recognize adding to the flow—turned soft, a murmur in the distance, and though no bright-armored guards were visible, I knew we were watched.

Arneior studied our surroundings with much interest, occasionally taking my elbow as I craned to look at some detail of the buildings. I longed to know how they constructed such towers, what *seidhr* or cunning held them steady, how the Elder melded earth with stone or fashioned the sheets of window-crystal. A cool breeze flirted with my skirts, teased at Arn's leather-wrapped braids, and swirled about Aeredh like a small tame animal wishing to play. And as we walked the Elder spoke, softly at first, then warming to his theme.

Of Faevril he told us, that blessed son of an Elder king, the only *alkuine* among his people. Mighty in craft and battle ere the Sun first rose, his works were still spoken of with wonder. The *taivvanpallo* was only a toy, a small amusement; I looked at my feet as Aeredh spoke of Faevril's other, more serious artifices.

He had told us something of this once before, but I did not begrudge the repetition.

I did not need felted overboots for this journey either. Soft embroidered slippers of Elder make were more than adequate, for the garden paths were smooth even as their borders turned rustic-ragged, disarray looking at once planned and utterly natural. We descended an easy slope, a smaller cup within the valley holding the city, and in its center a hill, clothed with green sward and starred with five-petaled blue flowers. At its crown, a small tower the color of summer cloud rose.

I say *small*, but only by comparison to its fellows; its shadow could have swallowed Dun Rithell's largest hall with little difficulty. A glittering cylinder, light playing upon its sheerness like the sheen of a snail's trail, rose skyward and no path ran to its base. Nor was there any hint of winter yellow upon the greenery, and we had seen those flowers before. Of old the Elder named them *ildora*, but more recently they were called *sudelma-lithielle*, Lithielle's Kiss.

As we circled the tower-crowned hill, ambling at an invalid's pace, Aeredh spoke of the works Faevril held most dear. It was then I first learned of the Elder Jewels.

His tone was hushed and reverent. A clutch of artificial stones, translucent and yet holding silvergold light within their depths, so beautiful even the Blessed of the far West were enchanted by their sheen. By the will of the Allmother's mightiest children the Jewels were hallowed, for the light they captured was last seen during a long and blessed peace in the Elder's once-home across the sea.

The gems had been stolen by the Enemy upon a day of fear and lamentation; deep grief followed the loss. Much else also ensued—an oath that led to murder, Elder shedding the blood of their own kin, banishment from that lost shining island, and a great darkening only broken when Tyr the Ever-Burning slipped free of his own skin to kindle the Sun's great bonfire-heart, for he took pity upon newly awakened Secondborn suffering under the Enemy's thick shadow.

Of all the gods Tyr is the one said to love mortals most, and he proves it by immolation.

The Enemy had thieved many other treasures as well, committed a spate of horrific murders as he fled, and now kept his hoard in the Black Land's great iron fortress, gloating over it much as his great wyrms do over precious metals and other shining things.

Faevril's greatest works could not be turned to the Enemy's use, no—but he could and would rob the world of their solace, denying all who might find comfort in the echo of lost beauty.

"Like any petty warlord," I murmured. Arn's soft exhale, not quite a huff, said she agreed. Perhaps we were both surprised to find the great Enemy of both Elder and gods behaving so, but then again, many of the beautiful immortals we had met so far had proved themselves startlingly like touchy, self-important Secondborn in certain respects.

"Greed makes its own weather, we say." Aeredh glanced up, checking the sky, a motion familiar from our journey hence. He walked with his hands loose, or sometimes clasped behind his back. "And no doubt you have noticed some peculiarities in the construction of this tower, my lady."

Indeed I had. "No windows. And no door yet."

"Yes. This building can claim neither, and only Taeron knows the secret of its opening. It holds something the Enemy much desires to attain once more. Can you guess? One of Faevril's great Jewels."

He told us then—without song or saga-rhythm though the tale well deserves both—of an Elder princess, the Secondborn man who loved her, and how their affection had resulted in a deed so stunning it was celebrated in song even by the people of this hidden place.

For Lithielle and Bjornwulf had stolen a single radiant Jewel from the lord of the Black Land, and escaped his wrath afterward.

"Where is she?" Arn was immediately interested in a woman who could perform such a feat. "An Elder, surely she still..."

"She died a mortal death." Aeredh paled, though his eyes had darkened. The filigree upon his ear winked cheerfully. "Such was her love, and such was the grace granted her."

"Grace?" Arneior tapped her spear's blunt end upon the turf, halfway between thoughtfulness and disbelief. "And for a man. Disappointing."

"A shieldmaid never marries." I murmured the old proverb. "These jewels, my lord Aeredh. What do they do?"

"Do?" He seemed puzzled; we were approaching the place where we had begun our circuit of the hill. The tower was indeed feature-less, blank as an egg. "They are beautiful, and sacred. 'Tis said their light is painful for any evil thing to bear."

"And yet the Enemy—" I was about to ask if he were powerful enough to overcome such injury, but a clear, cold voice rang against the tower's sides, the Old Tongue accented strangely.

"*So.*" The dialect of Waterstone had diverged in isolation, though 'twas still understandable enough. "*You bring a Secondborn witch to attempt a theft? Your father would weep, Crownless. Or perhaps you think his part in the great quest gives you some claim?*"

It was the black-eyed Elder I had seen at the king's side. He wore the light, beautifully forged armor of Laeliquaende, yet not polished to smooth brightness as upon the guards. Instead, his metal was dark as volcanic glass yet unshining, and his beauty was sharp as the healer's knife I had just been gifted. Bladed cheeks, dark eyes, a fine nose—if he had a beard, the young women of Dun Rithell would have counted him handsome indeed.

He was also armed, one gauntleted hand resting upon a sword-hilt. His blade was of the Northern style, straight and heavy, though its metal was blackened as well; they called him *the Watchful* for that steady gaze and fierce silence.

"Maedroth." Aeredh bowed but slightly, and did not lay hand to his own hilt. I suspected it was not for lack of desire, though. "The son of Taeron's sister, my lady. He has a sharp humor; 'tis said to be like his father's."

"My father is dead." Maedroth's gaze flicked across Arn, settled upon me, and I felt again the weight of an Elder's regard. In Nithraen a son of Faevril had looked upon me thus, but Curiaen's attempt to discern my inner self—common enough, among those with *seidhr*— had not the well-honed edge of this man's.

"So is mine." Even in his home city Aeredh had not sounded thus. Not quite offended, but thinly polite, a shield of ice over swift-running water waiting for an unwary step. *"We are akin in that, and equal enough. Your uncle would chide you for impoliteness; must I?"*

Arn's grip did not tighten upon the spear, and her expression held nothing but mannerly interest. She did not shift so much as a muscle, but her attention settled upon the newcomer.

He was, after all, an armed stranger. And a man.

The darkness I had seen upon him in the thronehall was nowhere in evidence now; he was merely an Elder, though that is like saying a wolf is *merely* a wolf. Either way, 'tis a creature deserving of respect and careful handling.

There was a great deal of arrogance in the Watchful's *seidhr*, and I thought him touchy as Ulfrica when a new freeborn girl arrived for service in my father's hall. The initial glimpse of a visitor is often of much deeper import than any later events, and I suppose that day outside the tower could be said our first real meeting.

I have often wondered what he saw upon that short new-winter afternoon, as the sun nearly touched the horizon. The days were lengthening, yes—but spring was still some distance away.

I did not have to sting him with my own weirding, for he altered, swift as the frozen carapace upon a river's back cracking in the melt. The storm upon his features vanished, a smile bloomed, and the dark of his eyes turned to velvet instead of sharpshatter shards.

"Forgive me, Secondborn ladies." The same bladed accent scraped his words in our language free of the Old Tongue's moorings, but he was much better at it than even Tjorin. Like Caelgor the Fair, he sounded as if he had been taught the southron language by mountainfolk. "I am of an abrupt temper, and accustomed to the…oh, the combat-of-jesting. You call it flyting, do you not?" He bowed in the Elder way, but with a swift grace like a hawk's stooping, straightening afterward with the greatest possible efficiency. "It is a saying in this city that the Watchful never utters a killing insult, only amusing ones."

"There is little need for either." Aeredh took a single step, his shoulder breaking the thin line of humming force between me and the new arrival. He loomed somewhat in the manner of a brother with an injured sibling to protect; I was reminded of big, blundering Bjorn, and my eyes prickled for a moment. "Your uncle knows my intent."

"Does he? That is a great comfort." Maedroth also took a single step—to the side, which placed Aeredh yet more squarely between us. I could not decide if he wished to mock the Crownless, to laughingly imply he feared a pair of women—or if he had another purpose, some turn in the arcane dance of Elder etiquette. "Well, we are the *Hidden* City, I suppose there is no better place for a few dangerous articles to be kept. I look forward to friendship with these Second-born, brief though it may be."

"I would not want you to suffer any inconvenience," Aeredh returned, stiffly. This was a side to him I had not seen, even with Curiaen and Caelgor in Nithraen. His shoulders almost seemed to spread, like a bullock's when preparing to pull a heavy plow.

"Oh, it is none, I assure you." Maedroth's smile never altered, and winter sunlight fell into the curiously matte surface of his armor. "I am quite fascinated. An *alkuine*, here? I would invite the lady to visit my workshops; it would please me much to have one of Faevril's kind view my work."

I was relieved of any responsibility to respond by Aeredh's swift reply. "I do not know if my lady Solveig will have time, king's-nephew. Naciel likes her a great deal, and will keep her close."

"Oh, yes, my sweet cousin loves her pets. But as they age...well, what seems short to us is not to others, my friend. Cherish your days. And, my lady Solveig?" The Watchful's accent turned my name into three disparate syllables, all of them graceless as the Old Tongue would never be. "My invitation stands. You—and your fascinating blue-painted companion—are welcome at the House of the Maker at any moment."

I could have made answer politely enough, but Aeredh again denied me the chance. *"Keep thy distance, watchful one."* The Old Tongue was inexpressibly pure in his mouth, an accent far older than any he had used before edging each word steel-sharp. *"You may attempt tormenting the son of Hrasimir as you please, but this Secondborn is beyond your reach."*

My jaw felt suspiciously loose. Arneior watched intently, and though she did not know the Elder tongue she had no difficulty understanding the tone.

"Ah, I see you have grown fond." Maedroth's fingertips tapped his swordhilt in quick succession, a gentle, thoughtful smile pulling up the corners of his lips. "I am merely being hospitable; even brief as the lives of Secondborn are, your *alkuine* may seek other amusement when her captivity palls. And then I shall welcome her."

With that, Maedroth the nephew of Taeron turned and glided away across the green, his armor soundless as his step and his shadow long as the light of day lowered. His hair glowed with blue highlights like Eol's in thin golden sunshine, and later I learned the same sheen was imparted to blades of his making. It was said he learned that particular craft from his own silent, keen-eyed father, and guarded it well.

In the pained silence, a realization struck me. My stomach rolled, a wringing motion like a great silver-sided fish brought from the river's cold embrace, drowning on dry land. As Maedroth left, the tension receded from Aeredh's back, but he did not turn. Instead, his chin dropped. The Crownless studied the grass at his feet as if he had never seen such vegetation before.

"So I am not to use this thing at all." Therein lay the answer to the riddle, and I spoke not in verse but with the slight embarrassment of one who had been bested during a dinnertime game of rhyming. "You merely wished an *alkuine* kept away from the Enemy, lest he hear of my existence and seek to collect a prize."

So simple, and yet I had not seen it before.

Taeron's Tower

No gift will she take, no notice of one
Who haunts her steps. A lament
Turned inward gnaws at the bones
Of any man. Yet can I deny it?
The pain is better than living without…
                                        —*The Traitor's Song*

The tower glowed with its own light, even as that day drew toward to swift dusk-shadow. In the silence, a faint unheard hum came from smooth, seamless white stone. Had I not been told what rested there I still would have guessed at some mighty *seidhr* locked within its embrace, if only by the way the inked bands upon my wrists ached.

Or perhaps all of me hurt, and I was only now noticing. There are some forms of weirding, drawing upon vital inner resources at the root of being, which may cause a mortal or animal to surpass physical limits until the very foundation of their bodies tears itself apart. It is akin to the battle-rage my father Eril had; a berserker will slay his opponents until there is nothing left but piled, broken bodies and only then die of wounds that would have immediately killed one not gifted with its dubious honor.

"Ah." Arneior tapped her spear-end against the turf again, a heavy, disappointed strike. "So we are indeed merely exchanging a smaller cage for a larger one."

"All this world is a cage, my lady shieldmaid." Bitterness filled the words; the Crownless still did not turn. "The Enemy will not look for you in this corner. You are safe, it is enough."

I was safe at home. But was I, if *orukhar* and liches spilled south and east? My father and the rest of Dun Rithell's warriors could deal handily enough with warlords and bandits; when Astrid married her husband would do the same, aided by Bjorn's strength and thoughtless speed unless my brother wed into a hall far away from home.

Did they know of the approaching danger? Was that what the elders refused to speak of after the Althing? I had been wholly occupied with holding the solstice fire steady all that night. Yet what manner of *volva* was I, not even dreaming of looming disaster?

"Had I chosen to go to Dorael instead…" I could not finish the question. My left hand blindly sought the healer's knife, now hanging at my belt. I freed it, sheath and all, with a hard yank.

"I did not think you would," Aeredh said, softly. "You had declared yourself Eol's ally, and he trusts my judgment. Besides, my lady Question, you were curious. Elder and Secondborn alike share that trait, at least."

"Sol?" Why did Arneior sound worried? It was not like her.

My hands were knots, my knuckles bloodless. The twist-lunging of my stomach would not abate.

"There has never been another *alkuine*, among your kind or mine," the Crownless continued, soft but pitiless. "The Blessed led us to you for some reason, and I cannot be other than glad. There must be a meaning to it; there *has* to be. I have done what I must."

"By bringing me here to rot until I die, and Arn as well." My tongue was numb; so were my lips. The humming in the white tower filled my ears—suspecting a thing is not the same as enduring it, and I had after all thought better of Aerith's son than *this*. Why had the Elder bothered healing me at all? "Tarit's father was allowed to leave Taeron's lands, and you were once before as well. So you may eventually take the wolves of Naras and search for other *alkuine*, if any may be found. What has happened once may happen again."

"Unlikely." Aeredh stiffened as if struck—or as if he suspected Arn might unleash her spear upon him again. "You are the first since the Sun rose."

"The first you have heard of," I corrected. Yet I was uneasy, for now another secret fear of mine had escaped my head and was given voice in clear air. Idra trained me as best she could, and said elementalists were merely rare. How had she known enough to say it with such certainty?

Or had she simply been guessing, following her own *seidhr*? The world rocked underneath me, a boat upon choppy rapids.

I dropped the knife; I had not the strength to fling it. The beautiful curve of Elder metalwork and sheath landed near Aeredh's heels, but he did not move.

"*I do not think my soul could stand another,*" he murmured in the Old Tongue. "You are angry, and though there is more to tell the day grows late. Shall I accompany you to your quarters, my lady?"

During our journey I had wondered if my father's battle-rage lurked within my own bones, despite the fact that women are not often prone to such things. At that moment I thought it possible, for the tower's hum had become a rattling buzz, as of a heavy cart dragged by runaway bullocks shaking itself to pieces upon a stony path.

"No need," I heard myself say. Strangely, I sounded very much like my mother in that moment, and the likeness was at once a comfort and a deadly, indecent hurt. "Arneior and I had best learn to find our way without Elder aid."

He did not move, but strangely, the son of Aerith almost seemed to stagger. "I am...sorry, Solveig."

We are as nightjars to them, Tarit of Redhill said, *and we dash ourselves against their rocks.* He was right, of course. I had mouthed a pretty sentiment in return, but at that moment all I could do was writhe inwardly at my own blindness. "It does not matter," I answered, heavily, and turned my head, staring at Arneior's knees.

I did not wish to watch him walk away.

"I have a spear," Arn repeated, stubbornly, and smacked the bedroom's floor with said weapon's blunt end for emphasis. The sound was heavy, jarring every rediscovered ache. "I should like to see these men set themselves against the Black-Wingéd Ones."

"I doubt Odynn's maidens will come riding to our rescue at the moment. They must have far greater concerns." I leaned against a pillar at the very large balcony-window, for my knees were not steady at all. I also wished she would stop expressing her displeasure with such sharp, staccato taps. My head spun, and each time her spear hit a bolt passed from one temple to the other. I was hard-pressed not to flinch.

Arn swung about, and the high color in her cheeks was akin to a wolf's growl, or an adder's warning hiss. She stared at me for a long moment, and for the first time in my life I wished, with sudden, startling vengeance, that I had no *seidhr*.

Better to succeed as a simple riverlord's daughter than to fail so miserably at being a *volva*. At least if I had been born without weirding I could have married well and been blissfully unaware of all this madness. I had been outplayed at every turn, and by *men*. No doubt Arn was too kind to share her ire at being shackled to a piece of bad bait, but I could very well suspect her true feelings.

If not now, then later. We had years ahead of us in this Elder trap; eventually she would take my stupidity to task. And then...

Then I would be truly, irrevocably alone.

I held her gaze while the breeze through the window stroked my hair. Crisp and cool, it was soft despite the freeze lurking outside this Elder realm. If by some miracle my shieldmaid's spear overpowered the guards of the Ice Door and Hidden Passage, we still had frostchoked, lich-infested wilderness to traverse.

And—I could not deny it—I was pained to have misjudged Aeredh so thoroughly. I had not thought him capable of...of coldly trammeling a mortal until her death, especially with all his talk of owing debt.

"I know that look," Arn said, softly, and thankfully did not pound the floor again. "You are discouraged, and need to ramble. Idra would send you out to gather rare herbs or ask the river some question."

Idra is not here. Wherever she rests, she is no doubt disappointed in her last student as well. "I should have seen. I should have known." My hands throbbed with the need to do something, but there was nothing to occupy their yearning. Even the sewing packed carefully in my mother's second-largest trunk held no attraction for me at the moment. "I am...sorry, Arn."

"For what? Their treachery? *Elder.*" She all but spat the word. "Sheepshit, I say."

"Which one?" I could not help but laugh, though the forlorn little sound died halfway through. "The Crownless, or the other?"

"Both. All of them." Her free hand made a swift, flicking motion, consigning the Allmother's most graceful, immortal creatures to the midden-heap. "And their lapdogs, too. The House of Naras should be ashamed, lending itself to this."

"Do not forget Eol lost his brother, even if a mere stone had the deciding toss of the game." *And even if they suspected him of treachery.* I rubbed at my arms as if chilled, and was glad of the stone windowframe's support. A slumbrous dusk enfolded the garden below our quarters, and though I could easily hate the entire city at the moment there was no denying the sound of the fountains was wondrous soothing. "He may not have fully known his Elder friend's purpose."

"I should have known you would take his part." Her nose wrinkled with disdain, but at least she was no longer in the first hot flush of anger and would do nothing...inadvisable.

I did not shrug, though I longed to. "We are allies now." In other words, she could give me some time to work upon the heir of Naras, as upon a stubborn neighbor at home. Even if Aeredh claimed greater friendship with a Northern lord, I could appeal to Eol's conscience. He seemed to have one, at least—and I knew some of his men did, as well. "I negotiated that much, and now wish I would have wrung more from them."

"The lord of Redhill warned us." It was unlike Arneior to sound so approving of a man, but the son of Hajithe had been of a temper we both understood. For my part I liked him a great deal, especially in retrospect. "Perhaps we should have gone to this Dorael."

"'Tis another Elder kingdom, safe behind some mighty *seidhr*-wall. Which means they could hold us there just as well as here." My sigh was heavy as my mother's when a quandary with no happy solution presented itself, like a spat between powerful nearby clans with long-held grudges. "It will be spring soon."

Arn strode across the room, took a post on the other side of the pillar-gap, and peered into swiftly falling darkness. After a few moments, she turned her spear, the blunt end grinding against stone—a quiet, meditative sound. "Spring," she said. "And us not home to see it."

So she understood. Attempting escape now would be folly—even if we managed to slip past the Elder guards in one direction, the winter waste could well defeat us. It was much better to wait, learn the dimensions of our captivity, and see what allies of our own could be found.

"There is a summer afterward, and harvest season as well. I was promised for a year-and-day in any case." *Please, Arn.* I was not quite pleading with her, though I longed to. *I will rack what little brains I possess, and might redeem myself by finding us a way out of this trap.*

There was also the library. Who knew what tools lay hidden in its depths?

"You're angry." Did she sound surprised? Now Arn stared at me, hazel eyes unwonted wide. "I can feel it. You *never* get angry."

While the last was not quite correct—I was frequently irritated with the world, much as Idra used to be—the first was indisputable. A hot, prickling ball had settled in my chest, and it grew as I inhaled.

"I do not have your temper, small one. But I do have one." I forced the sensation away, for *seidhr* is doubly dangerous when fueled by rage. "Nevertheless, there is nothing to be done at the moment. We are in an Elder palace; we might as well enjoy its comforts—like that bed. It is a marvel, I must admit."

"I do not need rest." Still, Arn's own fury abated somewhat. The promise of future action salved her temper wonderfully. "You are but newly healed, though. Come along."

I let her fuss over me—clumsily, it must be said, for that is not a shieldmaid's preferred duty. Yet we both drew comfort from the ritual. She pulled the covers high, tucking me in much as Albeig or my mother, and even touched my forehead with callused fingertips before straightening swiftly, spear braced in her left hand. "There. I will practice, and think. You must dream."

"I have been trying." I could not suppress a sigh. "Arneior…"

"No. You rest." She glowered, as if threats could induce someone to slumber. "Lying point-eared swine, and their false gifts. Better thrown at their feet, indeed. You did well."

At least I could be certain she meant it; a shieldmaid will not offer false praise. I could make no reply, so I simply closed my eyes. Tears prickled hotly behind my lids, but I denied them. Better to rage than to weep, and slumber is more useful than either.

I would need all my wits—and patience—in the coming days.

Full of Danger

When one who is wise speaks, 'tis well be mindful,
And when they are silent, beware!
— Southron proverb

Many things I learned in Waterstone over the following moonturns, and only a few of them rested among scrolls and bark-bound volumes—for the crystal-domed library, overwhelming as it was, paled beside the larger one I never had the chance to visit more than passingly.

Oh, of course I absorbed the Elder script, with its flowing curves so different than our falling-runes. Tjorin was a good teacher, though he did not drive a lesson home with braid-tweak or clouts upon an unheeding ear. Instead, he praised my small successes, smiled at any errors, and was so even-tempered I nearly feared some explosion later, like a volcanic peak suddenly deciding to vent its wrath after centuries of quiescence.

Dun Rithell's mother-mountain had never done so even in the days our settlement bore an Elder name, but we heard stories from travelers. And any fool knows great heat lurks within the earth, breaking free of its sheath like insect-guts when the shell is punctured. In days lost to history we learned the use of saunas from traveling near pools heated by such deep fires; even the Enemy harnesses those forces for his own ends.

With the son of Hrasimir I learned some portion of Elder and Northern lore as well, for he was of a lordly house said to be passing scholarly and had been among the library's volumes since his arrival besides—a tale in itself, but not one he ever spoke willingly upon. I learned more upon that count from Naciel, who would appear, merry as Astrid on market-day, to draw Arn and me forth for summat more active.

For the daughter of Goldspear was ever barefoot, and danced with every step. More than that, she loved to run, and it was from her I learned the Elder *seidhr* of fleetfoot, speeding light and near-trackless over almost any surface. To her it was natural, near-effortless, and she could race from dawn to sunset, her hair a golden banner and her joy visible as a playful river-otter's.

Being mortal, of course, I could only run so far in that fashion. Arn had more success, for it is very akin to a shieldmaid's tracking-gait used for hunting or pursuit, and though I lagged behind them both I was still more fleet and enduring than Tjorin, who much preferred sparring with the wolves of Naras or hours of study among fragile bark scrolls.

We did not run in the city. Instead, we passed through one gate or another, guards in bright armor studying the princess's Secondborn pets with much reserve, and once past the city's shadow the entire valley was ours to roam.

Most Elder lived inside the walls, but others preferred privacy and there were smaller outlying settlements, groups and solitary dwellings. Houses of white stone seemed grown from the earth itself; there were fine vineyards and other crops, though most lay fallow during the season of long nights and it was eerie to see threads of green veining each winter-yellowed leaf or grassblade.

Streams coursed through the soft green bowl, and one great river—perhaps the eldest child of that which had carved the valley—roughly bisected it. Naciel showed me fantastical shapes embedded in ancient sediment hardened to rock, effigies of creatures long since extinct; she took us along waters the Elder named *Egeril* for their white foam, and *Naricie* for their speed.

Cascading from tall peaks untainted by the Enemy's grasp—for these mountains were not part of the Marukhennor, though hard by those terrible, shadow-hung crags—the great river of Laeliquaende's valley took several hard turns, veered through some stony hills on the periphery of more-arable land, and ran crashing over greater rapids before smoothing and widening as it passed near the city and away, vanishing under a massive shelf of stone in the extreme southwest of Taeron's domain. The whirlpool there was called the Leap for a pair of lovers who had cast themselves from its height, but those of Waterstone never sang the story of its naming.

At least, not where Secondborn could hear.

Their Naricie-Egeril was nowhere near as mighty as our own river-mother. Still, every child of my folk knows even a puddle might be dangerous, and the rapids were surpassing perilous in more than one place; the vast crashing, sucking drain of the Leap, hard against the wall of mountain stone, one of the more frightening things I have ever seen. Its horror was wholly impersonal instead of evil; anyone who has stood in some high place and thought of falling can understand.

At first I thought the sensation of being watched during those rambles was the Elder king's guards, making certain we would not attempt some kind of flight. Then I glimpsed flashes of black, like ink splashed upon an oiled plate, and sometimes a familiar winking gleam of swordhilt-gem; then I understood it was the wolves of Naras—they did not follow us every time, but often enough while we ran with the Goldspear's daughter.

It galled me, for I did not otherwise glimpse our former captors. And why did they bother? So long as winter endured we were surely trapped, as if in another barred cell.

And *still* I did not dream, falling into that cloud-soft mattress on its stone stead, asleep almost before Arn settled beside me with a sigh. Dark was my rest, but not with terror or pain. It seemed I no sooner closed my eyes than the dawn rose in gentle stages, heralding another day full of lessons.

The Elder say time is a river too, and I say in their vicinity it flows oddly—a threeday might feel like twelve, a year as a sevenday, a moonturn like a single afternoon. Even now I remember only flashes of Laeliquaende during that period. The weariness and fear of our journey faded, bit by bit, held at bay by the wonder of the library and Naciel's merry laughter.

***

"'Tis fragile," Tjorin said, his hands moving with swift efficiency to weight the corners of a large sheet of strange Elder material somewhere between pounded bark and parchment. Small, heavy ingots carved into stylized animal-shapes held the map in place without damaging it. "I have a thought to recopy this, with Naciel's additions."

His grasp of southron language, like his lady's, had improved beyond measure. I could only hope mine of the Old Tongue was likewise. "How do they do this?" My fingertip hovered over the representation of Waterstone in the middle of the valley, then moved to the Egeril and traced its course northward. "The lines are so fine."

"Brushes, I should think." A smile lingered on his mouth, and in his tone as well. Though rarely truly merry, he was astonishingly easy-tempered. "Though I would not be surprised if they had quills from some rare bird."

"Ah." I bent closer, peering at the words in Elder script. "The Ice Door is not marked."

"No." Around us, the crystal-roofed dome was saturated in drowsing hush. He indicated a spot in the mountain-girdle, east-southeast. "'Tis around here, I should think."

"Yes, she never takes us in that direction." I straightened, pressing my fists into my lower back as my mother did after a long time spent at her sewing, and realized I sounded bitter when he glanced at me, a line appearing between dark eyebrows.

But he said nothing. Tjorin's silence was not like my father's, or Bjorn's, or any other man's I ever met. It was more akin to Idra's, or the quiet regard of some wild creature. He had traveled long in the empty places, hunted by the Enemy's dire servants, before arriving in Waterstone; even the wolves of Naras did not possess his particular stillness.

Once he even remarked upon seeing the Great Sea itself, but could not be induced to say more.

I bent again, studying the map closely. I could match several symbols to their counterparts outside the city walls, yet my gaze kept returning to the largest river's curves, then jumping guiltily to the space where our own entry to the valley had to have occurred. Then, a curious set of glyphs over the northwestron mountains drew my attention. "What is there?"

"*Raven's roost*, it says. 'Tis very old writing, I had to ask the same question." Tjorin's fingertip hovered a breath from the map, circling the glyph and what I could now tell was brushwork denoting the shape of certain crags upon a mountainside. "They say the birds of the Blessed linger there, and may be asked for counsel if any are brave enough to climb. Sometimes they visit Taeron, bringing him news of the outside."

Ravens were Odynn's birds, and powerful. If Arneior and I went in that direction, would we be gainsaid? "You speak of the Blessed. Do you mean the Aesyr or the Vanyr? Or both, or all the other spirits?"

"The Elder see no difference. I am told that in the West they walk as men and women; here, they take other shapes or none at all." He glanced at me, restrained curiosity bright in dark eyes. "Do you know which one spoke through you in Taeron's throneroom? I have a guess."

"Do you?" I did not like to brood upon it; as the proverb goes, 'tis as well the memory of pain flees quickly, for otherwise no woman who has borne once would consent to further childbirth. Still, even a faint remembrance will make one cautious, if sharp enough. "I cannot tell; it is Arn's duty to remember what I say when the fit is upon me. Or when I wake from certain dreams. My teacher often had a steading child for year-and-a-day to perform the same duty, though she did not prophesy much."

"Fascinating. Eol says you did much the same in Nithraen, and . . ." Tjorin halted, straightening, and looked somewhat chastened. "Forgive me. It cannot be pleasant to think upon."

His courtesy was old-fashioned, and almost made me smile. "In Nithraen it was merely some poetry from a passing spirit. Here, 'twas otherwise." I could not suppress a shiver. "Still, that is part of being a *volva*. It would be much worse were I not trained for the event; *seidhr* eats the unwary whole."

"So may battle-weariness, or the Enemy's curse." The jewel in Tjorin's swordhilt flashed a ruddy gleam as he shifted into relaxation. "Or even a hungry bear in spring."

"The world is full of danger," I agreed. Every conversation with him granted me further knowledge, though rarely in the direction I had been hoping. "What forms does it take here?"

"None for you, lady *alkuine*. I would wager you are safer in Lae-liquaende than anywhere else in the world, for all it lies hard by the Black Land." He paused, a tentative smile fading. "You do not look comforted, nor do you disagree."

"A wager?" It is ill done to cheat-whisper bone-dice, but if one is held prisoner perhaps it could be permissible? Still, my conscience twinged. It is the greater gods who watch over games of chance, and mayhap I had angered them in some fashion already.

Though I could not tell what I had possibly done to earn this misfortune. Wishing for adventure is no crime, and it is natural for a *volva*—or any other with the weirding—to be somewhat ambitious. We are born to look beyond the seen, to delve past the expected.

It is what *seidhr* means, at least in part. And one cannot do such things without the urge to *know*.

"They say southron folk love such things." Tjorin moved one of the mapweights, metal carved into a fanciful, leaping fish-shape. "Is it true that a man may wager thralldom upon a toss of the dice, and go into servitude without a murmur if it falls ill?"

The library was full of soft mutters itself, waiting for my answer. I told him and Naciel much of southron ways in those days, and they returned the favor with Northern knowledge. There is a joy in such exchange. It is never ill to learn of one's neighbors, no matter how far afield they may be.

"Very true, though not often done anymore." These were modern times—though I was now in the North, faced with ancient dangers. It beggared belief that such things still existed, walking in the same daylight that held our sheep-folds, looms, and riverboats. "More often, 'tis alter-marriages decided in such fashion. Women may play a game with the man they want, and if he loses, she has him for a year-and-day no matter his other ties. Like weregild."

"Weregild." He nodded, and in thoughtful repose Tjorin looked almost Elder. Perhaps it was that stillness, or the almost-serenity resting upon his features. "A cruel custom, but better than the alternative—I do not mean to pry," he added hurriedly, "and it must be distressing for you to think upon."

A laugh rose in my throat; I clasped my hands amid my skirts. "You have taught me much, it ill becomes a *volva* to take umbrage at honest questions about my people in return."

"Once our people were one."

"Do the Elder say so?" I meant no sarcasm; I might have even asked Aeredh, had our conversations ever turned in that direction. The Crownless had taught me some of his own folk's *seidhr*, especially to do with the care of horses during long voyages, and had done so with good grace.

I had not seen him for many days now. Perhaps he feared my temper, or perhaps even an Elder could feel some little shame.

"My father did, and I believe him." Tjorin returned his gaze to the map, but I doubted he was seeing its markings. He did not often mention his kin. "The Elder do not know everything, my lady Question. Just a little more, by virtue of living longer."

"I shall keep that in mind." Again I could not help but laugh. It was easy to see why the princess prized him so, and I found it difficult to brood while in his company. "The light tells me 'tis past noon; I should go to the garden and find Arn. She says the dust in this room makes her nose itch."

"I know my lady agrees." As usual, when he mentioned Naciel his mien softened considerably, and he seemed almost as young as Bjorn. "Shall I walk with you?"

"This place is safe, is it not?" I found I did truly not wish company, even the most pleasant, at that particular moment. "And *I* would wager you do not wish to leave that map, son of Hrasimir."

"Indeed you are correct. I begin to think you wise indeed, my lady." He bowed, and I took my leave.

Or, more precisely, my laughter had faded and I was almost to the door before I thought to ask again, for the conversation had flowed so easily I had almost forgotten. "Tjorin? Which of the Blessed do you think spoke through me?"

"*The Lord of the Seas,*" he said quietly, in the Old Tongue. The phrase was ancient, and strangely sonorous. "Njord himself, Ulimo the Elder name him, the one who knows all deeps. For he spoke to Taeron at least once before, and not long ago as the Elder count it."

Now there was a piece of news. "You were present?"

"I was." The son of Hrasimir had paled a few shades, but his gaze was clear enough. He stood near the table, the gem in his swordhilt glittering rubescent, and with the dome's light upon every surface he once more looked like an Elder—though far less alien, indeed. "The memory is disturbing."

"Then I ask your pardon for raising it, my lord." I made him one of Naciel's pretty courtesies, like a drooping flower though I had not even a fraction of her grace, and left to find Arn.

Halfway there, I was waylaid.

Three in Succession

*Rarely do the gods send only one warning; often none at
all is granted. Perhaps it amuses them to watch the results.*
                              —Idra the Farsighted of Dun Rithell

By then I knew at least three routes to the garden my shieldmaid
liked to practice in while I visited the library's wonders; I used
neither the shortest nor the longest but the most pleasing, for it passed
along a gallery open all along one side, its pillars wound with rustling
vines from a greenery-clad wall below. The leaves were glossy and
tapered to points often dewed with crystalline drops; the Elder named
the plant *weeping-bright* for its glitter upon sunny spring mornings.

There was not much to dislike about Waterstone, and almost my
every waking breath was drawn in Arn's company. Still, that nooning I felt the urge for a few snatched moments of solitude, so I walked
slowly, my head down and hands clasped in pale-blue skirts. Naciel
had made me a present of several Elder-style dresses, finer than even
my green festival gown last worn at the winter solstice—the night I
lit the bonfire upon the great stone at Dun Rithell and held it steady
until dawn, unconscious of approaching danger.

The first night I saw Aeredh, and Eol as well.

My head was full of strange thoughts, and I did not like that I
could not dream. I paused halfway down the gallery, turning away
from the open air to study a statue of white stone set in a niche.

The carving at its base said it was of a woman named Alaessia, and the face was serene, beautiful as the Elder always are yet with sadness lurking around a mouth full-lipped as Arn's. The material was slightly altered where her dress was carved, not discolored but simply a few shades darker, eggshell instead of snow.

Something in the statue's lines called to me, so I waited to see if it would speak—not physically, though I would not have put that past the art of Taeron's folk. Instead, the tongueless voice of *seidhr* whispered, but no omen could I discern.

I had not the time.

"Ah, a happy chance." A soft, courteous male voice broke my reverie; he shifted to the southron tongue. "Solveig, is it?"

I turned sharply, and found Maedroth the Watchful. Fortunately I remembered his name, though Naciel never mentioned him unprompted. The king's nephew wore unrelieved black velvet instead of mail; still, his garb was very much like a Northern mortal's, for all he seemed to disdain Tjorin's and my kind.

I had not heard his approach. His accent no longer chopped my name into unpleasant portions, and at the moment there was no hint of scorn in his tone.

Still, a prickle spilled down my back. "My lord Maedroth."

"No need to be so formal, Secondborn. You make my gentle cousin happy, and for that I am disposed to be your friend." He smiled kindly enough, I suppose, but the gleam in his dark eyes was sharp indeed. I had heard Aeredh speak and sing of the princess whose glance was like a knife, a lovely saga-saying—had not the heir of Naras used the same phrase in Nithraen?

Proverb or not, Maedroth had such a look. At least he did not try to pry into my heart with *seidhr*, but there is a way of observing the merely visible which treads close to such a feat, requiring only attention and intelligence in equal measure.

The statue glowed, catching light from the gallery's open side, but he was in the shadow of a column, his boots just at the dividing line between sun and shade. "This is of my mother," he continued, indicating Alaessia's likeness. "She wandered far from home, into my father's lands."

"Ah." I searched for an appropriate politeness; a guest must always be mannerly, as the saying goes, and all I knew of Taeron's sister was that she no longer lived. "Naciel tells me she loved to sing, and eased her brother's mind many a time with music."

"She sang to me oft indeed. My sire was of a quiet temper by comparison, preferring to let his works communicate instead." Maedroth paused; often, the Elder do so in conversation. Since all of time is theirs, they do not often hurry in speech. "I am glad to see you, my lady Solveig. I was not…kind to you near Taeron's Tower, for which I crave your pardon. I thought you in league with the Crownless, instead of his victim."

Victim was a strange word, carrying overtones of physical attack in the particular form he chose. "It is difficult to be in league with one who will not share his plans," I said, carefully.

"Just so, just so." He nodded and turned his chin slightly, gazing up at the likeness of his mother.

I could close my eyes and call up my own dam's face, but I could not imagine seeing it replicated in stone any more than I could compass losing that inner vision—or hearing of her passing. Certainly anyone knows tragedy may befall a loved one, and yet…who does not think one's parents eternal?

If I were trapped in this strange and lovely city for long enough, would I remember Gwendelint of Dun Rithell's features clearly? Or my father's, or Bjorn's, or Astrid's? If I could not even dream of them, I might forget small details. Then larger ones, for memory even when trained can be unreliable.

The thought unsettled me to a surprising degree; my heart hurt, a swift glancing pain. Aeredh and Naciel both said Maedroth's father was dead as well, and though Eril the Battle-Mad held his weirdling daughter in caution—especially as I had grown to adulthood—I still could not imagine a world in which he was not the lord of Dun Rithell, striding about with his big boots, loud laugh, and fell axe, protecting us all.

I wondered if this parentless Elder had come here to commune with a statue, which made me an intruder upon something deeply private. "I shall leave you to your thoughts, my lord." I moved as if to perform another courtesy, but the Watchful gestured with sharp grace.

"Please, do not flee my presence." His tone held a hint of almost-sadness. "Many do, for I am not easy to like as Naciel is. I was wrong, and will admit it. Will you not stay a moment, and let me invite you to my workshop again?"

He was polite enough, and he was undoubtedly correct—the silent sense of sneering pride lingering behind much of his speech was not easy to like at all. Some Elder prefer to wear their arrogance like a shield slung upon a warrior's back; I had even traveled with a few from Nithraen. Daerith the harpist, for one, and Yedras the spearman who called me *Secondborn witch*.

"*The House of the Maker.*" In the Old Tongue, it had a pleasing ring. "Such is your home, is it not?"

"*You know our language, and speak it well enough.*" Maedroth's smile broke free as the wind ruffled weeping-bright; the vine-leaves glittered as they moved. "I will not lie, I am a crafter and there are some items I would have an *alkuine* look upon. Faevril was mighty among those of us inclined to that pursuit, and you are of his kind."

It was a high, heady compliment, and the lure of seeing an Elder create something, anything, was not to be discarded lightly. Yet I hesitated. The same sure inner sense which led me through negotiations between scornful, axe-ready warriors, each with a grudge and his honor to uphold, gave a muted, warning twinge. "You do me great honor, likening me to one of your own. Especially one so renowned."

"*And cursed in the same breath.*" He spread his hands; a heavy silver ring glittered upon his left second finger, bright yet undecorated. Its very restraint drew the eye more than ornamentation would, and perhaps that was why he dressed as he did amid the rest of Waterstone's easy luxury. "But you are Secondborn, of the Allmother's favored ones. Some say that with your kind she corrected the errors in our making."

I should have taken the shorter route to the garden. I was glad my hands were clasped before me, for a nervous movement seemed inadvisable. "I have not yet met an Elder who thinks so, my lord Watchful."

"There are some even in Laeliquaende; I could introduce you

to them." He studied me for a long moment, the little difference between pupil and iris perhaps responsible for the eerie quality of his gaze. "But you are reluctant, I see."

"It would be another great honor to view your work." I could not deny I was tempted indeed. "Yet I am not sure where I am given leave to tread, my lord. This place is not my home, and I am barely even a guest."

Maedroth's smile made light of that difficulty. "Anyone in the city will direct you to my hall. It is well known that my doors are open, even to those who have slighted me. It was not always so, I admit, but—"

"*A fine invitation.*" For the second time that morning, a man's voice interrupted; this time in the Old Tongue, with a thread of growl under the consonants. "*Tell me, watchful one, would I be greeted kindly in your hall?*"

Maedroth half-turned. Eol of Naras strode through the gallery's repeating patterns of sun and darkness, his swordhilt's colorless jewel glittering balefully over his shoulder. A restless twitching flicker under his skin was the wolf sharing his form; the sigil upon his blackened armor, its mouth open in a silent howl, looked sidelong at me. Next to an Elder's elegance his Northern garb was stark and somewhat graceless, though functional enough, and his blueblack hair was as unkempt as ever I had seen it.

"*Ah, it is the son of Tharos. I thought you with your companions today, roaming the fields.*" Maedroth's politeness was not quite icy, but certainly much less warm than that aimed in my direction. "This one knows where the Hall of the Maker is, my lady Solveig. Should he accompany you, he will also find my hospitality blameless."

With that, the Watchful turned and left. He passed close enough to Eol that their shoulders almost touched, but neither man changed course by even a fraction. No flicker of expression crossed the heir of Naras's face, either, and he halted a mannerly distance from me, his back to the retreating Elder.

Perhaps this passageway saw too much use for me to find it pleasing in the future. But then, it had been deserted every other time I traversed it, with or without Arneior.

Who would be looking for me soon, no doubt. "I am bound for

the garden below." Why did I feel as if I had been caught doing something...untoward? I was no longer this lord's weregild, bound by those stringent, unforgiving rules.

Yet I had rarely been alone with any man not my kin; now I had been near three in succession this morning, though Tjorin did not give me the slightly unsteady feeling the other two did. Besides, even though a *volva* may do as she pleases I was also a lord's daughter, and expected to act accordingly.

"Then I will accompany you." Eol did not move further, simply regarded me. Half of him was dipped in golden afternoon winterlight; the edge of a column's shadow fell diagonally across his face. The wolf in him had retreated but the vitality of one who possessed a second skin burned throughout, a different blaze than an Elder's blue flame. "Unless you do not wish it."

"We are allies, are we not?" My fingers ached. I realized my fingers were twisted together, snarled as scrap-yarn a granary kitten steals to play with. "And you seem in good health."

"*Better than I would have been.* But forgive me, I..." A slight shake of his dark head as he shifted to southron; the blue highlights ran in his dark hair and for the first time, the captain of Naras wore a rueful expression showing how he must have looked as a youngling. "'Tis difficult to remember you speak our language."

I did not wince—at least, not outwardly. "I was weregild among strange men, my lord Eol. Surely you do not begrudge my silence."

"Of course not." His right hand flicked, brushing away the question with all the imperiousness of a lord. "But I would ask, did you learn it before leaving your home, or by listening to us speak? Both are difficult endeavors."

"It is the language of *seidhr.* My teacher spoke it, and taught it unto me." I longed to be free of this conversation, and heartily wished I had chosen a different route for returning to my shieldmaid. "My mother's people are traditional, so she speaks it too—though she might have sought to avoid insult by mispronouncing, for she does not use it oft."

"I see." He nodded slightly, as if I had told him something of great import. "So you simply...kept quiet?"

Did he think a woman incapable of such a feat? Men may make sagas, certainly, but speech itself is woman's *seidhr*, for who else teaches children how to use it? Still, no weapon needs constant use. "Underestimation is sometimes the only defense a woman has."

For some reason, the heir of Naras smiled rather broadly, in a manner I had never witnessed before. It was a strange expression, half-pained, and yet his eyes lit with something close to warmth. "Blessed grant I never underestimate you." The tension had left him; perhaps he simply did not esteem the Watchful overmuch.

"Ah, I see. You did think me defenseless." *Yet I have Arneior, and my bands.* Abruptly, some confidence returned. I had been all but ineffectual upon the journey here, I could not have drawn the *nathlàs* splinter free of his flesh without Aeredh's help, and I was trapped in this Elder city, yes.

Yet I had held my own in conversation with Maedroth, I thought, and though Eol was strange and grim he was also Secondborn. Mortal, for all he shared his skin with a wolf. Those with such a gift are held to be strong, quick, and well-nigh unkillable, but he was of my kind and not so deeply foreign as the Children of the Star.

"My lady Solveig, so long as I draw breath you are never so." Fine lines fanning from the corners of his dark eyes deepened, the smile receding and its aftereffects not quite reaching his mouth, tight even in repose. "But I sense you wish to be free of my company. Shall I withdraw?"

"*My ally leaving the field, so soon?*" I aimed for Naciel's light, laughing tone, and do not think I did too badly.

At least, Eol's smile broadened once more. But I do not know what reply he would have made, for there were voices at the far end of the corridor.

Arneior and Naciel had found us.

Useful, Not Trust

*What goes North seldom returns. If mischance does not take
the traveler, wanderlust might; 'tis best to stay close to your
hall and your fields, among those who share your speech.*
—Harald the Skald

T he princess does not speak ill of him." Only an act of will kept
Arn from fidgeting, though she ever enjoys my fingers in her
hair well enough. "In fact, she seeks not to speak of him at all. Curious, for such close kin."

"Aeredh does not like him, Eol does not like him, Naciel does not
like him." I massaged her scalp, coppery strands sliding between my
fingers. "And I think he does not truly like me. But the fact remains
he might be useful."

"Hm." She did not quite stiffen, but she did turn still as a cat seeing prey. When she spoke again, it was the half-whisper we used in
our closet at home. "So you are indeed thinking of escape."

A soft cool breeze tiptoed from the balcony into our shared room;
my hair was unbound as well, free of the pressure of braids or the
weight of red coral. My trunk stood open near the wardrobe, which
now held even more Elder garb the princess deemed suitable for her
new friends. A trio of light, wondrously carved wooden stands held
both sets of Arn's armor, best and second-best, from Dun Rithell;
the third held an entirely new set of scale-and-ring, Elder make and

bright silvergold with green padding, both like and unlike that of Laeliquaende's guards. There were tunics and trousers for her as well as a few dresses, though my shieldmaid ever disdains to cover herself solely in peaceful cloth.

Those the Wingéd take must be ever-ready, though they are given lee to sleep without iron if they desire to. Both of us were prepared for rest, my linen shift of Elder make embroidered with seven-petaled flowers in slightly contrasting cloth, her sleeveless tunic and trews severely plain but still beautifully stitched.

I had not wielded a needle in what seemed like forever, save to repair some small damage to our travel-clothes. Even the pieces Astrid had packed to keep a weregild occupied in the North lay neglected under other items. I missed the peace of pulling thread through cloth, and the satisfaction of making something solid from flat panes—a marvelous *seidhr* that is indeed, and one who claims otherwise will recognize the error as soon as they are naked to the weather.

"The days grow longer," I said, softly. "It will not always be winter. An Elder our captors dislike may well have his own reasons for wishing us gone, and once we are outside this valley..." I went to work with my scentwood comb, separating her hair for fresh hornbraids. Her back rested firmly against my knees; her hair was a bright shawl against sleek-muscled shoulders. "What then, Arneior? League upon league of *orukhar*-infested wilderness, liches sniffing our tracks and quite probably the wolves of Naras hunting us as well?"

For so long as Aeredh had use for us, I was certain Eol would do as his Elder friend thought best.

"If this king lets them leave." Arn's wrists were propped upon her knees, her capable, callused hands dangling. "He could just as easily trammel them here after we slip free of the net. But I would not trust this Watchful, my weirdling. He sets my teeth on edge."

"I said nothing of trust. I said *useful*." I began the first braid, taking much care though sleep would disarrange my work in short order. "What would the Wingéd think of us leaving allies in such a fashion?"

It worried me. I had sought to behave in exemplary fashion ever since leaving my father's hall, and could not help to think perhaps that course was in error despite my mother and Idra both regarding proper behavior as a bare minimum in any situation, no matter how outlandish.

"I have prayed." Arneior tipped her head back slightly, not needing a nudge to know which angle would best help my efforts. "There is no answer."

"And I do not dream." I quelled the shiver rippling down my back. "Yet I think we are watched quite closely, and not by spirits. There was no reason for Eol to be there, otherwise."

"Are you so certain?" A laugh bubbled under Arn's words. "Perhaps he meant to thank you for saving his life."

I almost tweaked the braid developing under my fingers. "If not for his Elder friend, I would have failed. It was…" My hands paused, but I returned them grimly to their task, staring at ruddy, silken strands. The cold of our journey hence returned at odd moments, stealing my breath and running a tremor through my bones. During the sun's hours I was too busy to think upon it, but once night fell the memory of ice had no fence to stay behind. "You were with Idra almost as much as I was. She never said I was the only one of my kind, only that I was capable of becoming *volva*."

"You wear the bands," my shieldmaid loyally pointed out. "I like not this cringing, Sol. Idra would—"

"Idra is not here." I could not even be certain my teacher was watching, from whichever of Hel's lands she had journeyed to once the burden of her flesh was eased.

"'Tis for the best. She would have hated this adventure. Can you imagine her taking Aeredh to task?" Arneior's laugh now burst forth, her entire body quivering slightly, and I could not help but smile.

"One such as you should behave better." My impression of Idra's needling tone held too much amusement to be true-to-life, but I did not think it a bad effort, and Arn's merriment increased. It had been a long while since I heard her chuckle so heartily.

I continued braiding, and thinking upon the Watchful. We spoke no more, but then again, my shieldmaid and I did not need to.

That night I finally dreamt, but not of Dun Rithell.

Instead, my sleeping self gazed upon orange stars burning in blue depths. Bells rang and Elder singing filled soft night air, but terror clutched my throat with bony claws and the smell of smoke and sickly roasting filled my nose when I awoke, shaking, a howl trapped in my throat. My shieldmaid listened to my stammering recitation, but we could not tell the vision's meaning.

I wish we had.

PART TWO

THE RIVER RACE

Current, Skill, and *Seidhr*

Take care, my friend. No winemaker knows which pressing shall be his last.
    —Elder proverb, attributed to Vardhra Star-Kindler

I did not quite collapse, though my sides heaved and my lungs burned. I did bend double, palms upon my knees, and sought to draw as much breath as possible. The turf was springy under my thin slippers, and the scent of water rising from the river was almost that of Dun Rithell.

Yet not quite.

Arn skidded to a halt, her boots leaving little impression upon thick grass. Neither of us ran barefoot as Naciel, who clearly did not wish to halt just yet, but that particular Elder *seidhr* of swift motion works even when one wears heavy hooves.

My shieldmaid's spearblade shone, not angrily but with great cheerful sun-darts. It was a fine day, barely a feathery cloudbrush in an aching-blue sky; were we outside the valley we might well be frozen solid. But here, I cherished the breeze patting my flushed cheeks.

Joy boiled in my middle, shook my already trembling ribs, and for the first time since before my teacher's death I laughed without restraint.

After Idra's passing the weight of responsibility had settled upon me, along with a thousand other cares. Not only that, but I had daily worried over lighting the solstice fire, the specter of possible failure stalking closer each day, fraying my nerves. Journeying north was not a merry occasion, and though Waterstone was beautiful I did not feel at ease in valley or palace. Even in the library I found only mild amusement at Tjorin's sallies or certain passages, the fact of being caged robbing near every word of its savor—but running as we did with Naciel, fleet as summer-sleek deer, provided a few precious moments of relief.

My merriment ribboned along the water; we were far from the city, having left the gates at dawn. I straightened, though muscles in my side gripped hard, the claws of mortal weariness digging in. Tipping my head back, I stared at white brushclouds across the blue vault, and the thought of freeing all my subtle selves at once to lunge upward was so enticing I did not think I would mind the abandonment of my physical form.

"Wingéd be praised." Arn's voice recalled me to the duty of staying earthbound. "*There* is my weirdling; 'tis good to hear you, Sol."

"Almost like being home," I murmured, and glanced about.

A winter-yellowed bank sloped to the chuckling Egeril, silver foam combing over worn boulders before widening to smooth fast-flowing torrent. On the other side dark evergreens came almost to the water's edge, their roots buried in mud that did not smell like that at home, heavy branches bearing no ice but no hint of soft new growth either.

I did not know if spring would come late to this place, or indeed at all. Was it simply, eternally autumn where the Elder rested?

As always, even after something so pleasant as running lightfoot in Naciel's wake the consciousness of our predicament arrived, hemming me in. My breath returned swiftly even as the princess ran in a wide arc, cutting away from the river's course, returning to her companions at leisure.

I wondered that other Elder women did not accompany her, but she did not seem to feel the lack.

"Except there you would be keeping Bjorn from mischief, hearing tedious legal cases all day, and attending to every chilblain and mead-sour head in range." Arn's grin held no anxiety, yet she glanced over her shoulder, the habit of alertness too deep to break. "Not to mention locked in the stillroom muttering about cures, and singing the same sagas every night for warriors too lazy to make their own."

I could not argue. How many times had I wished for some measure of solitude or leisure, or even a few moments of simple quiet? In Laeliquaende was all the peace I could ever long for, and yet I was dissatisfied.

"And you would be knocking the same warriors into the training-yard's dirt, instead of sparring with Elder and two-skins." I still smiled; I was helpless not to, joy filling me like clear sweet mead. "Efain seems to delight in bruises."

"As well he should, each one is an honor." The garden she practiced in had lately become the haunt of a few Northerners and even one or two Elder, eager to find if a shieldmaid was a worthy foe. She had rarely been so exercised, and gloried in it. "I have not seen Aeredh, though. I would not mind sending him sprawling."

So, she no longer judged the mention of him unwise. I shrugged, stretching; we seemed to have outpaced any guards this morn, and perhaps that was Naciel's aim. She was running toward us now, her hair a bright banner and her dark-blue dress fluttering.

If Tjorin saw her at that moment, he might well swoon like a lovesick calf.

"There is no need for him to visit. He has what he wants." Even the thought of the Crownless could not dampen my mood.

"Ai, you sound like an old married woman." She examined her spear, critically, and the brightness of its long, leaf-shaped blade was matched by her smile. Her woad-stripe fair glowed.

The sun rose slightly earlier, fell just a few moments later each day. It was impossible not to be cheered by that fact alone. The Naricie before us—and other streams within the valley's bowl—would rise as melt occurred high on white slopes, so at least I would have that marker of time passing, as well.

It could not be much longer, could it?

The princess seemed to shrink as the ground dipped beneath her, then rose like a wood-spirit as she continued up the hillslope. She halted between one step and the next, skirts swirling and her hair turning into shawl instead of banner, looking intently past us.

I turned, and saw what had caught her interest—a high-prowed boat of silvery wood, moving swift upon the river's shining length.

Ah. So that is why she brought us out today. And that answered another question, they *did* have such craft—I could not think the Elder unaware of shipbuilding, but I had seen none yet upon the many waterways. Slim and high-necked, the rowboat danced like a leaf over the rocks, but the black-clad figure in it handled his paddle awkwardly as an Elder never would. The craft was far too large for a single rower, even one of more-than-mortal strength.

Arn turned to look as well, shading her eyes with her free hand. "Huh." Her coppery eyebrows drew together. "It's Tjorin."

"So it is." I watched as he struggled to right the boat's passage, and all my merriment turned to unease at once, as a single drop of wyrm-venom will taint an entire cask of ale. "Arn, he does not seem—"

Naciel saw it too. The boat lifted over a final submerged rock as if it meant to fly; the princess gasped, the sound carried on a breeze that was, after all, softer than it had been a few days before.

It is not quite polite to laugh at one who takes a ducking in such fashion, but no riverdweller can help it. For the second time that day I chuckled, but the sound curdled in my throat as Tjorin plunged into a smooth, fast-flowing section after the rocks and before another set of rapids.

"Sheepshit," Arn muttered, but I was already running, fingers tearing at my dress-laces.

For the boat landed with a tremendous splash near the figure in black, and it was clear from the way Tjorin's arms windmilled furiously that he could not swim.

⬯⬯⬯⬯⬯

Cloth ripped, I left my slippers in juicy mud between runners of slowly greening grass while shedding layers of Elder gown with indecorous haste. I had to, for extra material will drag a swimmer down if it can and Arn was in armor. She could not help.

All I retained was the thinnest linen shift. The ground fell away and my body stretched into a flat skimming dive; 'tis faster than attempting to run into a river's embrace.

Cold closed over me like a blow. I expected the shock, my breath leaving in a rush to clear both nose and mouth before swirling back in as I gasped above the water's surface. The current was much stronger than its deceptive smoothness showed, but I expected that as well, aiming myself accordingly. Tjorin was being carried past, and if I meant to catch him before he was dashed upon the rapids I had to work *with* the flowing.

For all that, our mother-river at Dun Rithell was far mightier than this Elder torrent, and I was well used to her casual, terrifying strength. Albeit a trifle colder, Egeril of the white foam cradled me almost gently, and I was aware of the Elder boat spinning away, ready to fling itself upon the rocks.

The fool is lucky it did not fall upon him. There was no more time for fear or thought, for the rapids were approaching swiftly and Tjorin still thrashing. The greatest danger was that he would strike me or cling, his body attempting survival by drowning us both before we were tossed amid boulders and then the Elder need never worry about a mortal *alkuine*'s existence or presence again.

Yet there was Arn at the riverside, giving a high piercing cry I recognized; it was the traditional *Come, the river means to take one of us*, meant to bring anyone from a nearby steading at a run to offer aid.

I arrowed for the black-clad man with the help of current, skill, and *seidhr*. This was, after all, a battle I knew how to win.

The son of Hrasimir slipped below the surface just as I reached him, and the cold gnawed deep. A few moments in a snow-fed stream can rob the vital warmth from even a strong man, leaving him mazed and witless while the river-spirits pull at his feet. They are lonely, those daughters of Ráen and her giant consort, for all they live in great tribes; they do not ever hesitate to take what companions they may.

Woe betide you if there is not something valuable in your pocket to gift them upon arrival, too, for then you shall be as a thrall in their grottos instead of a captured spouse.

But I had a firm grasp upon Tjorin's collar, and though he was taller and much heavier the river was helpmeet as well as danger, for it eased the burden. The *seidhr* of fish-lunge bloomed under my skin and I aimed us for shore, barely aware of a bright flash—Arn, leaping nimble as a young goat across boulders both dry-headed and only slightly submerged, her spear and mail sending up vicious stings of sunshine.

Firs crowded the opposite shore, their feet breaking the rush of headlong passage; my charge struck a dipping root and gasped, his mouth filling with river as I hauled him grimly along. There was a scallop of muddy, reed-heavy ground, and I just managed to aim us at it.

Another great, wringing burst of *seidhr*, my marks flaming with bright pain at each wrist—seven on the left, five on the right, and a few of the runes dancing between them are for just such an occasion. They must have spun several times that day. I spat earth-flavored liquid, coughed, and my free hand managed to grab at another knotted root protruding amid the reeds; Tjorin almost slipped from my grasp, for the river still clawed at more than half of him and the fool was wearing his boots.

Arn had reached us, wading and splashing; her spear sank deep among other roots, capable of bracing a much heavier pair than me and the son of Hrasimir. Her free hand, sure and strong and flaming-warm, grabbed my left wrist. I was a rope between her and Tjorin's weight, and heard a voice rising in furious chant, *seidhr* dropping from my lips like chill rain.

One more effort, choking as the river made her displeasure at being robbed full known, and we had the lackwit safely free of her grasp. I could have halted, retch-heaving while braced on hands and knees, but the work was not finished, for our friend had taken more than a cupful of Egeril and mud both.

"On his side!" I barked, and Arn was already obeying, dropping to her knees. Tjorin was limp, no longer struggling; the breeze coated my clinging shift with ice as I struggled half-upright, rack-coughing again to clear my throat.

My left hand rose skyward, pointing; I screamed a word in the Old Tongue and my right palm struck forth, walloping him upon the back. It was not merely a physical blow, for my marks flamed once more and vital force exploded from me, wringing him much as wet laundry in capable, work-roughened hands.

A gout of foaming liquid spluttered between his teeth, jetted from his nose. I struck him again, my voice a curlew-cry. Arn cursed, willing him to breathe, and finally he drew in a long tortured gasp, then curled up much like the armored bugs which hide under rotting wood do when threatened.

But he was breathing—splutterchoking, as was I, yet air was reaching his lungs and the two blows had hopefully expelled every particle of mud and other matter from those abused organs.

Sometimes one may drown even upon land, if the air-sacs are not freed.

He would naturally require other care—no doubt the Elder could supply it, having no need for Dun Rithell's mortal cures. But he was safe enough for the moment, and I collapsed in near-freezing mud, wearing only tattered linen turned transparent and clinging, my braided hair streaming, my eyes full of hot tears.

"*Idiot!*" Arn bellowed; if she was taking him to task, the battle was over. "You *sheep*shitting *fish*gutting fool! Are you trying to die?"

His eyes half-closed, his black cloth sodden, Tjorin lay in the mud alongside me without a word. Naciel arrived a few moments later, her skirts wet to the knee.

Such a Prize

*Even her ladies and childhood friends withdrew, for the
Silverfoot had little enough time to spend with her mortal
husband. None wished to rob her of a single moment; in
the end, they well knew, they would share the burden of
her grief…*

—Gaemirwen of Dorael

"Here. Let me." The princess bent, pushed my numb fingers
aside, and swiftly tied the lacings. My shift was a sodden
mess, but stripping bare, even amid the trees, and shrugging into dry
cloth left upon the bank held no charm. Besides, I had *seidhr* for this;
I inhaled smoothly, focusing upon the body's inner heat. The last
time I had done so we were in the Wild, and this was little hardship
compared to the killing freeze.

If we ran back to the city, the extra effort would dry me in short
order.

Naciel had also produced a small glass flask much like Eol's, and
Arn held it to Tjorin's lips. "Slowly," she said, though her mien was
still fierce and her woad-stripe bright. "It would not do to drown
upon land."

"I did n-not think—" His teeth chattered, but he swallowed obe-
diently enough. "M-my thanks, Lady Minnow."

She made a short, irritated sound in reply, though I thought the name rather pleased her; Efain called her that, for her spear's swiftness. At least that particular wolf of Naras took being knocked to the ground in nine out of ten bouts with good humor, but that was no matter.

A man who would take that ill should not spar with a shieldmaid.

"Hand me the flask." Naciel fretted much as Albeig did, albeit in the Old Tongue. It was strange to see such a beautiful, ageless creature so worried. *"I have no mantle, but perhaps one of my layers—"*

"I am well enough," I husked, the taste of mud still clotted in my throat. "Simply glad we were about to see him go under; it is not wise to treat a river so. Have you no sense, son of Hrasimir?"

"The boat is probably in splinters now," Arn added, "and you could have been likewise. By the Wingéd, you are a fool."

"Oh, I am." Propped against gnarled roots, his black garb sodden as my shift, Tjorin still smiled wanly. Whatever draught his princess carried had worked its wonder, and he no longer shivered. Water gemmed his forehead, dark hair clinging to skin. "But determined. It is the only way."

"It is not," Naciel retorted, hotly, and snatched the flask from my shieldmaid's hand. *"I do not need my father's permission, I am of age."*

"Is this some Elder custom?" I accepted the small glassy container, and did not bother to sniff to discern its contents. A single mouthful told me, however—the heat of *sitheviel*, bright and full of tangled herb-tastes, hit my throat, continued down to my middle, and spread in rings of soft welcome fire. "Ah. It tastes the same."

I do not know why I sounded so wondering, even as memory assailed me—it was exactly as the drink given by Eol on the first day of our journey, or by an Elder hand during the last terrible struggle.

"Get up." Arn prodded him. "You must move to keep your limbs from freezing. Silly man."

"And your boat was too large for one man to handle," I added, my fingertips finding the cap upon its thin silvery chain. I stoppered the small flask with a decided twist. "You need at least four, and a singer would not be amiss either."

Naciel took back the *sitheviel*, and her strong slim fingers grasped my wrist as we rose together. "You are correct." Her southron was full of sharp consonants, the Old Tongue rubbing through. "But he will not listen; I dread what he will do next. How many times, Tjorin?"

"As many as it takes." He gained his feet, barely needing Arn's help yet staggering some little.

My shieldmaid steadied him, stepping away as soon as he had his balance to glare downstream, no doubt searching for the boat. "Huh. It still floats, but will go past the city at some speed."

"Someone in the fields will see, and bring it to shore." Now Naciel rounded upon her beloved, and was somber indeed. "Will you not cease? Even for me?"

I would have left them to wrangle, for Idra held such quarrels too tangled for *seidhr* to sort. Like attempting weatherworking—unless true famine threatens—love is best left to itself. Many a saga warns of the so-called wise who ignored that rule, and the resultant havoc.

But the princess turned away, almost angrily, and slipped her arm through mine as if she were Astrid excited at the prospect of a festival fair—though my sister was not nearly so tall. "Come. We may stop at any house, and gain dry cloth."

"I am well enough—" I began, but she did not listen, and drew me along.

We had to re-cross the river on the line of boulders Arn had used, and though I am not Elder-graceful I have been performing such feats almost since I could walk. With Naciel ahead and my shield-maid behind there was little danger, though my outer skirts were draggled almost to the thigh afterward, and as we walked Tjorin told Arneior of his design while the princess kept a barbed silence.

Every spring, the Elder of this valley held a race—light boats, four rowers and one more to keep the rhythm with silent gestures, guiding them through rapids. They competed largely for the joy of it, testing themselves against the swiftness and rapids of melt-swollen Naricie.

But that was not all. The captain of the first boat to reach a glade just south of the city, where the river broadened enough to become mirrorlike-still and its current lessened somewhat, could ask a boon of Taeron Goldspear, the High-helm himself.

At this point Naciel shook her bright head, her stride lengthening. I resisted, gently, and her arm slipped free. Ahead of us the princess walked, and every line of her body expressed how she longed to run.

So that is why he studies that particular map so closely. I halted, letting my shieldmaid and Tjorin draw abreast. "You mean to ask for marriage."

"She says 'tis not necessary, that we already belong to each other. But..." Even wet clear through and daubed with rivermud, the son of Hrasimir carried himself proudly. For a man who had almost drowned a short while ago he looked hale enough, though I longed to reach my *seidhr*-bag and find something to keep lungrot or pneumonia away.

Not that it mattered; the Elder would treat any mortal ailment with alacrity and *sitheviel* had probably put him far past any harm. But it was a *volva*'s thought, and I had drawn him from the river's grasp.

A little victory, and yet it braced me wonderful well.

"But you wish to prove it." Arneior nodded, and her gaze settled upon me as we walked. "Yes."

Do you think... her eyes asked, and mine replied, *I do not see why not.*

We were trapped in this place, certainly, yet it never hurts to gain an ally wherever one may be found. 'Twas a deep and sudden comfort to find a quandary I could *do* something about; all during our journey I had been mere useless baggage, but here I could be of some service to one who treated us kindly. Not only that, but an Elder princess well-disposed toward me and my shieldmaid for making certain her stubborn paramour did not drown himself might be grateful indeed.

There were advantages to be gained, as well as some exercise and a testing of our skills. More than one stream lingered in the valley of Laeliquaende. Waters will seek an exit, and if we had access to a boat...

"Well." I rubbed my hands together briskly, as if still chilled despite an Elder draught burning amid my ribs. "You will need a boat, either that one or another. Arn knows how to call the strokes; I do not weigh enough to be a burden and matched against Elder a *volva*'s song can be said fair play. All we need are three more rowers."

"How to call..." Tjorin did not halt, but he studied me with great interest, then glanced at Arn as if he expected her to speak against the notion. " 'Tis a dangerous feat, my lady Solveig. The rapids are terrible at more than one point, and even a few Elder have lost their lives attempting merely to finish the course. Else Taeron would not offer such a prize."

"I compass little of Elder history, and less of their draughts," I said. My heart had lightened to an astonishing degree. "But river racing? That is something my small one and I know a great deal about, my lord."

"I already owe you for saving my life." Tjorin looked a little dazed. "Yet—"

"Then 'tis decided, we shall help you." My face felt strange, for I was smiling again—and broadly, too, the expression mirrored by Arn's. My shieldmaid's eyes fair sparkled, and she tapped her spear-butt upon the ground as she strode along, a solid sound denoting agreement. "And if we are with you Naciel does not need to worry you will be lost to the river-daughters."

"But—"

" 'Tis not wise to refuse a *volva*'s gift," Arneior said, and though her tone was mocking the edge beneath it was not. "Better to thank my weirdling, and turn your wits to acquiring another boat. We shall need a place to train." She glanced at the sky, checking the weather. "Where shall we find more backs to bend, though?"

As soon as she asked the answer became evident to me, like a good, contest-winning riddle delivered by a beneficent passing god. "Leave that to me." And, unable to contain myself, I all but skipped a few steps, as I had not since I was a child. "Fear not, son of Hrasimir. You are as good as wed, and I shall ask a toast at the feast in payment."

And mayhap I could ask summat more.

I had thought to put my plan into action that very afternoon, but as soon as we reached the city gates—late, for we did not run but walked, despite Naciel protesting that mounts could be found—an Elder in glittering mail informed me, in painstakingly correct southron, that my presence was required elsewhere.

Taeron Goldspear had remembered my existence, or judged I had been left to my own devices long enough. The king of Laeliquaende wished to see his captive *alkuine*, and her blue-painted companion as well.

Stay Where Unwanted

*Colder than lichburn is the suspicion cast among friends.
Is this the Enemy's true victory? For he has oft been content to let our division do the work, while he takes his ease
behind Agramar's iron walls.*
                    —Collected Sayings of Aenarian Greycloak

S oft violet dusk enfolded Waterstone; the Elder could keep winter at bay but for all their might and craft, they still must wait
as mortals do for the days to lengthen. A hasty scrubbing-away of
rivermud still tingled in my skin as Arn and I, shepherded by a smiling blond Elder youth with bright sky-colored eyes, approached the
throneroom once more.

It was just the same—a vast polished stone floor holding our
shimmering reflections but turning by imperceptible degrees to
earth under tree-roots, the huge, living grey bark-pillars stretching
in every direction, the rustle of leaves overhead. Yet it did not seem
so dangerous or malformed as it had the first time I walked here, and
instead of the music from Elder throat or instrument, birdsong filled
the gloaming.

Small blue lights bobbed among the branches, reflected in the
floor almost like Fryja's veils in the northern sky, save these illu-
minations were shaped into rounds instead of shimmering cascades.
A brighter light bloomed about the gentle rise holding Taeron's

bench-throne, but the ruler of this place was not seated to receive his humble visitors.

Instead, he stood at the hill's foot, hands clasped behind his back, his dark hair shining as it fell past his shoulders. The silver upon his brow glowed as if bathed in sunshine, and when he turned at our approach, his blue eyes were bright holes in the twilight.

A murmur in the Old Tongue and our guide glided away, soundless amid the gleams reflected in polished stone. Arn's spear did not tap the floor, and her step was soft as well. She looked about with interest, but had not chosen to wear the gifted Elder armor. Instead, it was her second-best hauberk and breeches, fit for travel; in silent accord, I wore none of Naciel's gifts but my green festival dress.

It was of the finest Dun Rithell could offer, along with the silver bee-torc of my father's mother resting against my collarbones. Well might a haughty Elder king consider us uncivilized, yet appearing in borrowed finery would be worse.

We Secondborn, even of small river-steadings, have our own pride. Mine was that of my mother Gwendelint, for though I have seen many a powerful woman since, none have ever seemed more regal. Perhaps every daughter views her mother thus...yet I do not know, for some of the sagas speak of what may happen when that bond curdles.

Silence stitched with liquid, lilting notes brushed against us. The birds had to be hiding in the trees; who would not sing, in such a place?

I half expected another terrible, deep-wringing voice to bubble up through me, and was grateful the only *seidhr* seemed to be in the heavy glance of the Elder king. Arn could no doubt see well enough in this gloom, and a *volva*'s eyes are sharp—but the Children of the Star roamed over hill and valley before the Sun rose, and midnight is hardly less bright than noon to them.

Taeron wore a long tunic-robe of indigo velvet in the fashion of Laeliquaende, and boots of highly tooled leather, likewise dyed and vanishing into the dimness. He bore no weapon and why would he need to, faced with two mortal women? He took two steps, three, approaching almost as if wishing to see us more clearly—yet slowly, as if he felt some caution at being so near unto presumably wild creatures.

No guards lingered to hear any converse save the pair at the thronehall's great doors. We were alone with a being who had lived both our lifespans several times over, yet he seemed younger than my father, albeit passing grave in that moment, studying me from slipper-sole to coral-studded braids.

"*Mere children,*" he said, finally, in the Old Tongue. His accent was ancient and inexpressibly pure, though softened by the lilting flow of his people's dialect. "*Yet marked, I see.*"

I made no reply, though Arn tensed beside me and the feather-brushing of the Wingéd Ones' attention ran in a soft stream under bird-music. For some short while the High-helm watched us, and I felt the strength moving in his gaze. Like and unlike my mother's own scrutiny it was, and he might have succeeded with gentleness where Curiaen the Subtle of now-vanished Nithraen had tried overwhelming force.

Weirding may be used to pierce the secrets of another's heart, and perhaps the Elder king thought I would be easy to read as the scrolls in his libraries. The bands upon my wrists ached, only a little at first, then intensifying as if the needle were moving, ink forced below bleeding skin afresh.

That pain must be borne in silence. After a short while it turns into another sensation, indescribable but well known to one who may call upon even a single branch of *seidhr*'s great tree. In Nithraen I had used a sharp single clawing stroke to sting an arrogant Elder's nose; amid these shadowed trees the needle-sensation was a shield— frail and flimsy, naturally, since Taeron's kind may fight with weirding and physical weapon both, without loss of vigor or the twisting a mortal suffers from the attempt.

And yet, I bore the buckler as a warrior might use a half-broken wooden round in final defense, willing to trust even that imperfect shelter in order to gain a few more moments of breathing.

For while one yet breathes, any battle's favor may yet be turned.

I did not stagger, nor did I sway. A slight quiver went through my skirts, and that only. He did not bring the immensity of his will to bear, though I sensed it like thunder behind Tarnarya in late summer, before the autumn storms race over our mother-mountain's shoulder to sweep southward.

To turn those storms aside is impossible. But bending under them, protecting the fields from lashing, encouraging the lightning to strike away from greathall and steading—that is well within a *volva*'s skill, and Idra had taught me as much.

When he spoke again, it was in southron. Perhaps he had been listening to his daughter, or perhaps the ravens who brought news from outside allowed him to practice our tongue.

"Do you have more messages for me, *alkuine*? Or did the Crown-less teach you to deliver the one you uttered before?"

Sharp was his tone, and his eyes paled. He was not quite the picture of a not-so-petty warlord well aware of his own power and smarting at former defeats…yet it was very close, and the similarity gave me courage enough in answering.

"I say what I must when the gods require, Taeron Goldspear." More crowded my tongue, but any man who will accuse a *volva* of lying does not deserve the honor of extended reply.

Another silence, not so long as the first, nor so uncomfortable. A certain relief loosened my shoulders, and my breath came more easily. I had expected the ruler of so much beauty, an ageless Elder of immeasurable wisdom, to be…well, less petulant.

They are given much, the firstborn of the Allmother's mortal cre-ation, yet many of those I had met so far spoke with unbecoming arrogance. Aeredh might have lied to bring us to this place, but at least he had the grace to seem somewhat ashamed of the fact.

Not only I was far in the North, witnessing legends and saga-creatures, but also in a position to compare multiple Elder tempera-ments. It fair boggled the mind; had he been mortal, the urge to take this haughty warrior to task might have provoked me to sharp words indeed.

Had I not pulled Tjorin from the river that afternoon I might have been fearful instead, and covered it with anger. But *seidhr* responded to me; I had the greatest possible proof of being *volva* still. Small that might be counted by this proud Elder, and yet it meant I could not be impolite. Nor could I act in any craven fashion.

I might have been captive, but I was neither defeated nor thrall.

"The Secondborn used to come as friends." Taeron turned slightly, aiming the words just slightly past me. Even in this shadow the resemblance to his sister's son was striking, and I almost heard the echo of the Watchful in his tone. "Now one comes to steal my daughter, and another arrives for Lithielle's Jewel."

Arneior inhaled sharply.

I lifted my right arm, as if to bar her from striding forward to strike one who would accuse a *volva* of thievery as well as falseness. "I have no desire for your Elder bauble, my lord. I was carried here with a lie, and would return to my home if you would but let me." *Though Aeredh would argue against it, and I cannot see you making cause with me against one of your own kind.*

His reply was instant. "Were you allowed to leave, you would spread news of my people's refuge to our Enemy."

"A Secondborn left before, and did not do so." I could thank our sojourn in Redhill for granting me such knowledge, and was more than willing to use it. "He did not even tell his son Tarit, who called you a fair king and a just one. I am saddened to find the report so untrue."

If he would insult me so thoroughly, I did not think my own reply entirely undeserved.

"Now you malign me." Taeron's tone shifted to bitter amusement. "I could have you and your spear-child there thrown from the Leap."

Spear-child? I was confused for a moment, a shock as if I had been slapped. Arneior *did* start forward then—and with a muttered oath as well, for that is nothing to call a shieldmaid.

"Peace." I caught at her left arm, my fingers hard against metal scales sewn onto tough leather. "He does not mean *that*, Arn, 'tis a lack of understanding."

"A king should not speak so." Her arm was iron under mail, leather, and padded tunic-sleeve, but she did not shake away my fragile tether. "The Wingéd Ones witness this." And, to provide emphasis, her spear's blunt end struck the floor. The sound cracked against birdsong; all liquid leafrustle and wingmurmur stilled.

"He does not use our language well." My hand ached, and so

did my bands. I would rather believe an Elder did not know how to speak our tongue than dignify such an affront by acting as if 'twas truly meant. "Do not, Arneior. It would dishonor your weapon."

The High-helm observed this in the sudden hush, his eyes a paired, scorching gleam and the rest of him blurring into shadow. Had he called us here merely to offer insult in darkness?

It took some pressure upon her arm, but my shieldmaid finally, resentfully subsided. The soft feather-brushing around her had turned edged, almost metallic in its ringing, and had I needed it the sound—striking just behind my ear instead of arriving through its aperture in the usual way—would have warned me to consider my own speech carefully as well.

The Black-Wingéd select worthy fallen upon the battlefield, 'tis true. They also have a darker duty. It is they who pursue malefactors—oathbreakers, blasphemers, kinslayers, violators of innocence or hospitality, those who are utterly beyond the application of mortal vengeance. They drag those who have misused sacred things to the very depths, a country even Hel does not visit though she rules it as she does every afterworld save the few belonging to her fellow gods.

That is why their attention rests ever and anon upon the shield-maids they take, not only to fill them with holy purpose but also to watch how those selected use their many gifts.

A few moments' worth of restraining my shieldmaid's anger also gave me time to think. If an Elder king wished to act thus without others witnessing the event—it was not even a proper flyting, for he did not speak in verse—he must have some deeper purpose.

I decided a neutral tone would be best. "The proper word is *shield-maid*, my lord." I said it slowly, enunciating each syllable as if teaching Naciel the finer points of southron pronunciation. "Have you aught else to ask your captives? We would not stay where we are unwanted."

The silence trembled. Even the trees dared not whisper.

"I begin to think you almost half of what Aeredh claims." Now Taeron Goldspear did me the honor of direct address, instead of aiming his words just past my skirts. "Tell me, *alkuine*, if I gave you safe passage from my lands, would you take the son of Hrasimir with you and never return?"

Is that his goal? "I doubt Tjorin would leave, my lord." I sensed the true shape of his intent looming behind the words, but could not quite see its dimensions. It could not be so simple, could it?

But fathers are alike the world over. I could only imagine my own sire's reaction, did Astrid seem enamored of one Eril the Battle-Mad considered deeply unworthy; naturally, if I were home I might even agree, and do my best to dissuade such a match.

"If you were to persuade him?" The Elder's tone turned soft, cajoling. I could hardly believe it the same voice so insultingly mis-naming my shieldmaid. "Surely it is within your capabilities."

The metal-scratching noise mounted, soft and irresistible. I had never felt this during a negotiation before, for all I had been at my mother's knee while she dispensed judgments and heard legal cases before I could speak.

"You wish us to buy our freedom by ridding you of a daughter's suitor." My voice spiraled high into disbelief, and I must have looked like Astrid after a child-simple riddle had been overexplained.

An *Elder king*, a fabled creature of power and wisdom, the author of all Laeliquaende's beauty—impersonating a jealous father in a comic saga? The killing ice, the terror of liches and snow-hag, the destruction of an Elder city, the Mistwood with its pale, horrifying, long-legged weavers—and this king sounded like Erlik the Sheeplord at home, anxiously offering yearling ewes or a fraction of the flock's shearing to a *volva* in order to turn aside a distasteful marriage pros-pect or bring about a better one.

A giggle rose in my throat, and I could not contain it. For the sec-ond time that day I laughed without restraint; I nearly bent double as after running with Naciel, my breath stolen and my heart thunder-ing. Perhaps Lokji was passing by, for in his shadow much of import seems ridiculous and trivial matters assume large significance. He ever reads the secret desires of men and often grants them—but always with a twist.

Perhaps he had discerned my buried longing for adventure while going about busy days in Dun Rithell, and gifted me a terrifying realization of the desire.

I laughed until I wheezed, and Arneior's silence beside me became far less cold. Invisible birds in rustling branches began to sing again, and the darkness did not seem nearly so deep. In fact, the gently bobbing blue lights brightened, at first imperceptibly but with gathering strength, and hot tears filled my eyes. One trickled down my cheek, a tiny flame-trail.

The fit passed in a series of gasping chuckles; I could barely draw enough air for words. "You..." I coughed, waved one hand helplessly like Albeig our housekeeper when overwhelmed by a barrage of useless tasks. "My lord..." Another spate passed through me, though of much diminished strength, and I was conscious of perhaps affronting this Elder king beyond any hope of repair.

And yet I could not care. "My lord," I began again, wiping at my cheek, "you may cast me from the Leap if you think you have warriors enough to lose accomplishing the task, or you may return my shieldmaid and I to your barred cells. But I will not betray Tjorin son of Hrasimir in any wise, for he has been far more a friend to me than you. And when your daughter weds him I shall raise a toast at the feasting."

And now I *had* to help a mortal win a boon and wed his Elder princess, for this king's behavior provided me with more than just cause. I did not think he would see things in quite that light, but my mother raised me to know what the gods consider proper, and that is good enough.

Taeron Goldspear stood, a statue like many decorating his palace's halls, and observed my merriment finishing its course. His expression did not change, but his eyes were no more than ordinary piercing blue once more and the silver at his brow did not flame. The throneroom's gloom lightened considerably as he nodded, a short, thoughtful movement, and let the echoes of my words die before speaking again.

"Well enough," said he. "Forgive my behavior, my lady *alkuine*; and you, shieldmaid of the Blessèd. I wished to discern your true natures, and such a thing is not done with empty politeness."

"A test?" Arn was audibly underimpressed, but she did not strike her spear again. "You could have simply asked."

"We live in the shadow of the Black Land, young one." The

sense of breathless menace had drained completely. Now the king of Waterstone was merely an Elder man in indigo cloth, his hands loose at his sides and his true age hidden behind their ever-seeming youth. For all that, a few fine lines were graven upon his face, almost shocking when one was so used to the amusement of his subjects—or even Aeredh's light humor. "Nothing from beyond our walls is as it seems; all must be thoroughly examined. The son of Aerith vouches for you both, my Naciel has found you fit companions, and even my sister-son praises a Secondborn *alkuine*'s thoughtfulness. But 'tis with me the heavy burden of ensuring safety lies. I trust you will see the necessity, and grant me the chance to make amends."

I had to half-turn; my gaze met Arn's. Her eyebrows were drawn together, a thundercloud upon her brow, and her woad-stripe was dark in the halflight. For all that, her grip upon the spear was not white-knuckle with rage, and her mouth, while tight, was not entirely grimacing.

"If 'tis amends he seeks to make, I do not object," she said, finally. "But I still say a king should choose his words with more care."

"I shall seek to learn your language better then, shieldmaid." He pronounced the title slowly, even mimicking the riverdwellers' accent upon each syllable. "Will you do me the honor of a short walk, and share my evening table for the rest of your sojourn in Laeliquaende?"

The invitation was highly prized even among Elder, for it is not everyone who may attend a king's daily banquets. I gave a somewhat neutral assent, still uncertain, but Taeron smiled as broadly as his daughter, and with such evident goodwill I could hardly believe him the same man.

※※※※※

That night we passed through evening gardens accompanied by bird-song, and the ruler of Waterstone exerted himself to be charming indeed. Of history he spoke, and of Elder ways, and sometimes of the properties of certain herbs or flowers as they nodded under a slackening breeze. With Arneior he discussed spear-play, and com-plimented the tales of her skill reaching him through her Elder sparring-partners. She did not quite thaw, for it is no small slander to call even a thrall what he had, let alone a shieldmaid.

For my part, I did not speak upon anything of import, nor did I inquire at the possible end of our captivity. If the Elder king hid a subtler test in his sudden politesse, I would not fail it. I did not mention the son of Hrasimir again.

Nor did he.

Guards in armor observed a polite distance, and other Elder strolled along the paths as well, sometimes singing, other times silent. The sky was dark, for clouds covered the stars, and when Taeron finally bid us good night my eyelids were heavy.

I did not know quite what to think, but at least he did not insult us again. And afterward the sense of being watched whenever we set foot outside our quarters was much diminished.

Which suited me well, for I had other matters needing attending.

Every Effort to His Cause

Wed they were and the prize was theirs, yet both were spent and their friends struck down. The mortal was grievous wounded, and even Melair's daughter was at the end of her strength. With no companion save each other, Bjornwulf and Lithielle found the Ice Door; there her despairing song found an echo, and in the realm of the High-helm were the lovers granted refuge.
　　　　　—Anonymous, from the Paehallen Manuscript

The next morn rose silver-dripping and hushed, for clouds had come to earth. Mist filled the valley's green bowl, though not nearly so thick and clinging as that of the Elder Roads, and for the first time I did not shudder thinking upon that part of our journey from Dun Rithell.

Arn told me I had awakened in the darkness again, gasping with terror and speaking of orange stars. I did not remember the dream, and though we were both disturbed there was no key to its meaning.

Tiny droplet-jewels decorated both leaf- and roof-edges, the fountains' singing was hushed, and the Elder voices in the fog might have raised fine hairs all over both of us had we not become accustomed as mortal creatures could to Waterstone's constant music.

Still, it took some courage to ask an Elder guard at the palace gate where the wolves of Naras could be found. The dark-eyed youth—he could have been as old as Aeredh, or Taeron himself—answered very politely indeed in the Old Tongue, yet looked somewhat surprised when I thanked him at the end of a long recitation of turnings and landmarks, setting off with Arn at my shoulder.

Any *volva* only needs a single listening to capture a saga in her ears; a shieldmaid hardly needs more. We passed into the vapor creeping between pale houses, gardens both green and varicolored softly blurred. Even with the fog I had little difficulty following the thread of directions, and finally Arn and I heard flurries of clash-chiming metal, low conversation, and laughter.

It sounded so much like the sparring-yard at Dun Rithell—warriors exchanging rough blows of sympathy, celebration, or practice—that I halted before peering around a corner as if I were a child again, fascinated by giants playing at the deadly business of combat.

A square building of stone the color of oatcakes stood proudly, low and rough but somehow welcoming as well, for though its proportions were elegant and its roof damp-darkened slate, it did not seem as remote or impersonal as many an Elder dwelling. Its windows had shutters of cheerfully painted wood, its doorways were full of oak bound with iron; two torches burned on either side of the largest, mortal orange instead of blue-tipped *aelflame*.

The Northerners were in their black garb, each familiar from our journey. There was stocky, heavy-browed Soren, his sword glinting as ruddy-haired Elak parried with a high shivering slitherclash. But they were both smiling, the former abstractly and the latter beaming with genuine goodwill. Their fight seemed more a dance, blades springing apart as soon as they touched.

Blue-eyed Gelad spun a dagger over his knuckles, giving the hilt a finger-tap as it flashed past, not looking at his handiwork while he spoke to Karas, whose hair was caught as usual in a leather club. Karas also had a knife out, its blade bearing the sweet curve of Elder work, but he was engaged upon whittling a length of dark wood. When he smiled at his fellow Northerner's words the flash of teeth was very like the wolf who shared his skin, much whiter than many of Laeliquaende's textures.

Efain was a little apart, as always; he had a stave nearly his own height, a dark-oiled length whirling through complicated forms. It did not look like spear-play, but there are ways to strike even with a length of firewood, and clearly he knew more than a few.

There also lingered the Elder who had accompanied us from Nithraen. Daerith the harpist perched upon the end of a stone trough, deep in conversation with Aeredh and Eol.

The captain of Naras listened as the Crownless made some point, his hands spread and eyebrows rising; Eol shook his dark head and seemed to disagree, a mutter of conversation too far away to pick out more than tone and rhythm. The other Elder were scattered about, watching the practice like Kaecil or engaged upon their own pursuits like Kirilit Two-Sword, who was examining arrows one by one before sliding them into quivers standing ready near his workbench.

Arn leaned close, looking over my shoulder. Her warmth was a comfort, for the mist was chill. The light Elder cloth of Naciel's gifts was wondrous comfortable, but my fingers were almost numb. I could not tell if it was the weather or what I was about to attempt.

My shieldmaid did not sigh, nor did she speak. But she did bump me with her elbow, either a rough reminder that she was with me or an invitation to get on with affairs.

For now, all at once, we had much to achieve. I set my chin, pushed my shoulders back, and stepped forth to do battle.

Kirilit saw us first, and nodded a greeting. Next was Gelad, who smiled immediately, a fan of wrinkles spreading from the corners of his eyes to match the lines bracketing his mouth. Karas's hands paused, a curl of wood falling away from his work; Aeredh caught sight of me and halted between one word and the next. Eol turned, following the line of his friend's gaze. Daerith's expression, after a quick glance in my direction, turned set and somber as if I were a bad smell.

I did not nervously touch my torc, nor push my sleeves back to show my bands. At another steading or greathall I would not have approached warriors at their work without displaying those, even with Arn at my side; it did not seem necessary in an Elder city.

Eol did not look away, though his brow creased as I approached.

The music of swordplay did not diminish, nor did the slight whistle of Efain's stave as it clove air, married to the slight rough sounds of his footwork.

All else fell silent, though, and 'twas as uncomfortable as delivering a legal summons to an angry warlord.

"Eol of Naras." I did not perform one of Naciel's courtesies, for we were both Secondborn. "I would speak with you."

"Ah." Eol glanced at Aeredh, who swiftly averted his gaze. Small beads of moisture were caught in the heir of Naras's hair, and the Elder's as well. "Yes. Certainly."

I waited, but he said nothing else. "Privately, as an ally." *Come now, son of Tharos. Surely you will not force me to make my errand public.* Of course, if he did I could use the event to my advantage... but it would not be fitting.

Not with the Elder listening. Who knew what they thought of Naciel's intended husband? I had no reason to think even Aeredh would look upon the matter kindly, for all he seemed to like the company of certain mortals well enough.

"Yes." Eol straightened, and motioned with one hand toward a deserted corner of the stone-paved courtyard. A great black-barked tree stood there, gnarled roots digging between blocks of dressed rock in a fashion half-planned, half-natural, as many things grow when the Elder are nearby. "Of course."

"Ai, Lady Minnow!" Gelad hailed my shieldmaid, but softly. "Care for a round?"

"I have no time to dance this morning, son of Aerenil." Still, she paid him the honor of a nod. "But when I am at leisure I will send you into the dirt again."

"What of Efain?" Karas's grin was nearly ear to ear. "He will not spar with us now, says we are too slow."

"Soon enough." Arn's cheeks pinkened, even the left one under her woad. She paused a few paces from the tree and rested her spear's blunt end upon stone, turning away from the conversation I was about to attempt.

Which left me in the shade of spreading, mist-drenched branches with the heir of Naras. The leaves did not rustle, hanging still and gilded, and I took a deep breath. "I have not seen you for some days." I sounded anxious even to myself. "You are well?"

"*How can I not be?*" The Old Tongue, accented sharply; he gave a slight shake of his dark head, as if tossing away an unpleasant thought. "Has Maedroth approached you again, my lady? If so—"

"The Watchful does not trouble me." I wondered at the immediate question, and the sharp glint in his dark gaze. "Though I will see him at table in the evenings from now on, I am told. Naciel does not let him near us, but that is not what I came to speak of."

"My apologies." Eol's hands hung loose at his sides, though even in this presumed safety he bore his sword. The hilt, its clear jewel unwrapped, did not glitter vengefully today. Perhaps it slept, lulled by the mist. "Speak, then, my lady Question. What would you have of me?"

Very well. Let us see how well I toss my dice. "I would ask the use of your three strongest men."

"The…use of them?" So often while speaking to me, the heir of Naras looked slightly puzzled. Perhaps my southron was too accented, or my Old Tongue not precise enough.

"We are allies, are we not?" I had to restrain the urge to add more; a warrior must not spend his strength too soon in a match, and neither must a negotiator.

"My three strongest?" Eol's jaw firmed, and he stiffened slightly. "Escape from here is neither possible nor advisable, and in any case winter still—"

" 'Tis not for that, my lord." Did he think me stupid enough to risk an open attack on the Hidden Passage? It almost stung. "Oh—do they know how to swim, your wolves? I should have asked that first."

"Swim?" It was the first time I saw Eol of Naras look most entirely baffled, and a sliver of the boy he must have been peered through the expression. "By the Blessed, my lady, what exactly is it you intend? I may ask your purpose, may I not?"

"I suppose so." It was far too early to tell if I had the battle's advantage, and my heart beat thinly all through me. " 'Tis for Tjorin's sake; we need rowers, for the boat."

"Rowers." He repeated the word as if he did not know what it meant in southron; I wondered if I should use the Old Tongue.

"Yes." Bjorn would have understood in an instant, Astrid even more quickly. I glanced aside and caught sight of Aeredh watching this conference with a curious expression, blue eyes bright and his mouth drawn down at either corner. "Tjorin means to win the spring race upon Egeril. Arn will call the rhythm, and I will help as well. But we need rowers, and I would not ask any Elder, for both Taeron and Maedroth are against the marriage."

"By the..." Eol trailed off, and he studied me as if I had begun speaking in a language neither southron, Elder, nor of the fabled lands south-over-sea. "You mean to..."

"Are you unwilling?" I pressed. "There is none other I may ask, Eol of Naras, but should you refuse it will not alter my course."

"I believe that much, my lady." The Northern captain paused, examining my expression. A plain dagger hung at his belt, familiar from our journey. "So, Tjorin has earned your aid."

"Naciel has treated me well, and so has he." No more explanation was needed, yet I sensed granting a further detail could perhaps aid my case. "They are my friends."

Eol absorbed the news with no change of expression. His armor, equally familiar, had been mended at the shoulder where the *nathlàs*'s blade-point had pierced; the repair-work did not look Elder. "And were I to grant this, would I be your friend as well?"

I could not answer for a moment. I was his sworn ally, yet little more than a prize for his Elder companion; why did he feel the need to utter such a question?

"Never mind," he continued, hastily. "I should not ask such things. If this is your desire, my lady Solveig, I will see it done."

I had to pause again, for I had expected far more argument. All my carefully arranged points, my appeals to logic and right behavior, proved unnecessary yet still crowded in my throat, wishing to be used. "You will?" I quelled the urge to take a step backward, my skirt whispering as I shifted from one foot to the other.

"You have little reason to trust my word, I know." A faint stain of bitterness lay upon the words. His right hand tensed slightly, as if he wished to touch the dagger's hilt. "But I have sworn full truth in our dealings henceforth, and to that I hold. I am merely surprised, for the race is in a nineday."

Only nine? Well, we had been here for some while already. I wondered why Taeron had not called us to his presence sooner, but the Elder see no delay in mere mortal moonturns. "Time moves strangely amid the Elder indeed," I murmured.

"I have found it so, yes." Eol glanced aside again, a quick-shifting movement like the wolf sharing his skin. There was no ripple of its attention passing through him, though, and the sigil upon his shoulder did not howl, merely seeming thoughtful though its jaws stretched wide. "We have heard summat of the race. Efain is our best archer and Gelad knows how to swim, I think; in Dorael he spent much time with the fisherfolk. Aeredh will want to—"

"He is Elder," I objected, immediately. I did not see what need we had for an archer, but that was a small matter. "And the king's friend, is he not? I do not think it wise for him to know our purpose."

"We can hardly hide it from him, if we mean to practice. He will not take it ill, my lady. Trust me." A shadow passed over Eol's face. "If you can."

"Very well." The thought that I would not willingly trust the Crownless again was not fit to be uttered, so I dammed it in my chest. Now, like a good ally, I had to add what I could to the agreement, in thanks and as a hedge for further negotiation. Or simply because I wished to behave with exceeding correctness, as befit Gwendelint's eldest daughter. "Eol." My hand twitched, fell back to my side; had I been about to touch his arm? "I have not forgotten."

He did not notice the movement, thankfully. "Forgotten?"

"Others have mentioned a curse upon Naras." I had practiced this speech in my head more than once, and I was lucky or blessed, for it unreeled smoothly. "I thought at first you wished me as weregild in order to deal with it, for a *volva* is often called upon to break maledictions. Even if you denied me aid in this I would seek to offer all the remedy I may for your trouble. It is only right."

"You thought...ah. I see." A flush touched his shaven cheeks, perhaps a reaction to the chill damp. He studied my shoulder as if it were a statue's offered for study, and the stone in his throat bobbed as he swallowed, hard. "Do not trouble yourself upon that matter, my lady. The curse is of the Enemy's making, and only death will free me of it."

Did he think me so incompetent? "For every bad *seidhr* there is a remedy; it is the nature of the thing." I could not say his estimation was incorrect; I had been of singularly little use during our entire voyage to this strange place. And yet, it stung. "I am merely a riverside wisewoman, but I might be able to offer some relief. Do not discount me so easily."

"*The Blessed know I do not.*" The Old Tongue slipped between his teeth, almost as if drawn by force. "Forgive me. I mean to say, you are no doubt meant for more than *that*. Put it from your mind, and tell Tjorin he has his rowers. Naras will give every effort to his cause, for our ally's sake."

"I thank you upon his account and my own, then." Perhaps it was the joy of success after such a long string of failures. My heart leapt, and I bounced upon my toes like Astrid preparing to go a-marketing. I was also, I could tell, grinning like a fool—but that was of no consequence. "But do not think I shall forget your troubles, my lord Eol. I would be a poor ally if I did."

"No need." The flush mounted, and he looked pained again. Perhaps he disliked being maneuvered into something Aeredh would not approve of. "But none of us have used oars before, my lady."

"Tomorrow at dawn, Naciel will meet your chosen ones at the northwestron gate and bring you to a place where we may practice. As long as your men listen to Arn's commands, they will do well enough—and we are riverfolk, Eol. We will not let them come to harm." My heart beat high and hard within me, for the thought of being upon the water again was unexpectedly comforting. Arn and I hurried away, for Tjorin was in the library poring over maps and accounts of previous races, learning what he could of the river's tricks.

Finally, *finally*, there was summat I knew how to do, and I could perhaps redeem a few of my failures.

Through the Oar-Paces

*Elder and mortal are at variance in so many things, yet
upon at least one point all agree—to save a life is to acquire
a debt. Even does it lead to treachery and tragedy, 'tis still
an act beloved of the Blessed and of the Allmother herself.*
　　　　　—Uldwulf of Dun Svesboj, *The Rede of the Wise*

Time, which had been so strange-slow and quick at once, now
began to trip over itself with hurrying, like a greathall's servants before festival feast. There was so much to do—I spent most of
the following mornings running along the Egeril's banks with Naciel,
learning what I could of its mood and rapids along the course. There
was only one place which caused me real concern, a sharp bend midway through. But that was why, as Eol said, we needed an archer.

Which was not my concern. I would have more than enough to
occupy me once we were upon the water. It was a joy to have something other than fretting about our captivity to consume my thoughts.

Arneior did not spar with the wolves of Naras. Instead, she put
Tjorin, Eol, Efain, and Gelad through the oar-paces from before
dawn to well past nooning, calling out commands and giving the
rhythm from her perch at the stern of the boat Naciel had produced.
Tai-yo, tai-yo, right, right, left, left, up, tai-yo, tai-yo, up, up, down!
They set to learning with a will, and obeyed her as well as one could
expect dryfoot warriors who have never wielded a paddle.

Every afternoon, once the practice upon the water was done, Arn made them do the same upon land, seated upon handy rocks in a meadow and mimicking the motions to drive them deeper into muscle and bone. I lay in the boat, drawn high on a scallop of sandy shore, while she taught them all she could in so short a while.

Silvery wood high-prowed and slim, seemingly not hewn but sculpted, the oarlocks wonders of simple Elder design...oh, it was a beautiful craft, and as I gazed into the pearl-grey sky I sang softly, enumerating its fine qualities and seeking to make friends.

I knew the fog and lowering skies meant spring was coming at last. Not only that, but the Naricie was rising, running bright with silver foam over her many rapids. The nights were softer, with a slight edge of warmer dampness, and the songs in Laeliquaende's streets now held a note of anticipation. The trees were not yet awake, but even one without *seidhr* could feel the shift within trunk and branch, sap not quite rising but no longer frozen.

Arn and I were expected to appear at Taeron's evening banquets, which often lasted late enough for the stars to glimmer through rents in high cloud. Perhaps he meant to weary us before the race, though he never mentioned its advent. In fact, he did not truly speak to us at all, and nor did the Elder nobility who shared his board. Maedroth— a black blot among the indigo, silver, pale green, and other shades of Elder cloth—watched me closely when he was not gazing upon Naciel, and often when I lifted a goblet of winterwine I felt his gaze upon my swallowing throat.

Ten days after pulling the son of Hrasimir from the river's embrace, we woke well before dawn to a great susurration of excitement filling all the valley, from outlying steading or smallhouse to the heart of the palace itself.

The race was upon us.

No Other Outcome

*The Secondborn love games, and learned no few from us.
'Tis said even the Allmother gambles, and do not those who
stayed in the West play upon the bright beaches, or in the
houses we left behind? If we somehow return, will we find
the boards and cups, the carven figures and the taivvanpallo where we left them, ready to continue? And our kin
will weep with joy to see us once more, once more.*
                              —*Unfinished Saga*, attributed
                                    to the Crownless

A bloody stain in the grey, mist-drenched east turned lazily to gold. The mist burned away, streaks of blue sky widening like dye tipped into a slow-flowing stream. From the white towers and singing fountains of Waterstone the Elder came, along the paved roads or over gentle hills striped with vineyards, dancing through the copses, the young ones dressed in bright festival garb and the elders in more muted jewel-tones, all smiling, most singing. Pennants fluttered on the wind, guards stood in their light, glittering armor, and palpable excitement filled the entire green bowl.

Some few stayed in the city, treasuring its peace; many wended their way to a wide velvet-nap green south and west where the race would end and the winning captain be crowned with a wreath as he reached the crest of a slight rolling hill within view of the pale walls. Pavilions in many colors crowded there, the largest viridian and bearing a great flag with Taeron Goldspear's device.

My heart beat high and hard; a single draught of winterwine for breakfast had slid down my throat much as mead of my mother's brewing with its aftertaste of sweet fire. Naciel stood aside upon the rocky beach where the racers' boats were drawn up; any Elder with friends enough to wield an oar could attempt this course, and even those who failed were accounted brave and blessed by their fellows.

Tjorin bent his dark head slightly; the princess's murmurs were for his ears alone. We received many a curious look from the assembly, though the Elder were at least polite enough not to point. Arneior waited, for once wearing only her quilted padding, no ring-and-scale; she turned her spear meditatively, its blunt end grinding in wet pebble-strewn sand.

The air of anticipation was familiar—any gathering upon a festival day feels much the same—but there were no fires, nor sacrifices in osier cage or well-dug pit. Nor did any soon-to-be contestants approach a *volva* to ask for blessing or advice.

Of course, I would be upon the water with them soon. The similarities to a Dun Rithell river-race were outweighed by the differences; both crowded me, an odd sensation indeed.

I looked over the throng, deliberately avoiding a direct gaze which could be mistaken for ill-wishing our rivals. Maedroth the Watchful was nowhere in evidence; perhaps he was with his uncle? His absence was strange, for at last night's banquet he had commented upon the river race, asking which captain Naciel favored for victory.

She had not replied, turning to me and inquiring of certain southron customs instead. Her cousin did not seem to take this as an insult, merely smiled as if she had replied with a jest.

I rose on my bare toes, bouncing lightly. My grey travel-dress was a familiar friend, its skirt cut higher than gifted Elder robes. Once I was in the boat the shortened hem and lack of shoes would be an asset; bare skin grips better than any footwear. Gelad, Efain, and Eol stood silent and stolid, though Gelad did not like being without his boots; his expression as the river lapped at his toes was that of a long-suffering elder brother drawn into a younglings' game.

I could not help but smile. "We shall not capsize, if that is what you fear. Arn and I are river-children; we know what we are about."

Efain shrugged. Eol was rather pale, but it could have been the dawnlight strengthening in steady increments before the sun's head lifted above knifelike eastron peaks.

Gelad answered my grin with one of his own, though he quickly sobered. " 'Tis not the water I fear. Even attempting this is a mighty thing, according to the Elder."

They are ageless, true. But this river is only a shadow of ours at home. I would not say it, for boasting in such a manner is unseemly. "I am told those who have two skins have strength above that of mortals." Before we climbed into the boat 'twas my task to bolster confidence, like a proper *volva*. "We will not make a bad showing, I promise you that. Simply listen to my small one, and all will be well."

I could have continued in that vein, but Aeredh drew close as if to grant the mortals some further wisdom. I half-turned away, politely, settling my attention upon Arn. She watched the river filling with reflected light, its nighttime face receding and the foam upon the rapids to the north beginning to spark.

Quick initially, but only enough to warm us. Then Arn will take us through the first rocks, and we shall see how well the wolves have learned their mistress's call. Another smooth portion, then I must sing us through what they name the Teeth, and after that the river bends and 'twill be up to Efain... Then the truly tricksome part, and we must use every means of speed and seidhr we have. My eyes half-closed; running along the bank with Naciel was not even remotely like what we would face upon the water, but I could guess, could I not?

We would win this thing. We had to. No other outcome was acceptable, was possible. My bands tingled, every drop of ink under the skin alive with anticipation.

"My lady Solveig?" Quietly, as if the Crownless expected me to pretend sudden deafness.

Oh, for the love of Lokji, leave me be. But one must be gracious before this manner of undertaking, so I faced him once more, my cheeks feeling strange since I now wore my smile as a mask. "My lord Aeredh."

"We have watched over your craft since Taeron's daughter selected it." Still soft, the Old Tongue refusing to tiptoe far from his mouth. Clearly he did not wish to be overheard. *"Daeron has given his bow to the endeavor as well; the line is strong and light."*

Did he crave forgiveness, or congratulation? I could not tell, and it was difficult to meet his gaze. What was his purpose? There was nothing left to say, and yet it felt as if we were upon the Glass again, his arm over my shoulders and his thoughts moving alongside mine, twin silverscale fish in a frozen stream. *"My thanks for your care, and for the harpist's."* I took care to make every syllable clear and soft, polished with a simulacrum of Naciel's laughing accent; it irked me, and I slipped back into my own tongue. "You need not worry, my lord. I will not let the river take your friends."

"Will you take care with yourself, as well?" Aeredh studied my face as earnestly as Astrid or Bjorn ever had. His eyes were very like my mother's, only lighter and without the thin lines of gold in her irises. Gwendelint of Dun Rithell had a summersky look; his was... otherwise.

"Does it matter? I am here until..." I swallowed the rest of the sentence; it was ill-tempered, and ill luck before a river-run to boot.

A sigh went through the assembled Elder. The breeze freshened, tugging at every pennant fastened upon slim wands by those cheering on their friends—the devices of Elder houses carefully worked in thread, paint, and gilding, bright glyphs or representations of valorous feats, ancient names and ancestral victories. Some I knew from conversation with Naciel or reading in the domed library, like the tusked bear of Aerindael or the crossed arrows of Naevril the Arrowmaster's line.

No family among the Elder is so mean as to lack one mighty progenitor, and the tents at the end of the race bore larger flags blazoned with their names and deeds.

The east was a furnace. Very soon the sun's rim would appear between two peaks they named *Yvaerillith*, a word denoting graceful shoulders rising from a draped shawl. The race would begin at that moment, this being the only day—the first of spring, as that folk counted it—the fiery heart would rise so precisely balanced.

The princess clasped her lover's hands, then let him go and stepped away. Tjorin turned to us; Arn approached Naciel and handed over her spear, gazing deep into the princess's eyes. She spoke quietly, an ancient prayer to the Wingéd used only when one of their taken mortals lays a geas.

A shieldmaid will not trust any mere passing stranger with the duty of spearwatch. Taeron's daughter accepted the weapon's weight with a queenly nod; I had explained the duty to her with much care.

Efain muttered something under his breath—prayer or obscenity, I could not tell. Gelad winced slightly as he set off for the boat, his captain at his shoulder. Eol's jaw was set hard as stone, and his step was that of a man eager to begin a duty.

My marks twinged. It was the deep breath before a plunge; the wind fingered red coral beads among my braids, plucked at my skirt, and damp sandy earth thrilled below my bare soles.

"*I go,*" I said in the Old Tongue, a single imperative word slipping between my lips on a breath of winterwine. For a moment, Aeredh the Crownless met my gaze directly, both of us surprised; I felt that sensation again, his thoughts and mine running parallel like wagon-ruts, never meeting save by some trick of sight in the far distance.

"*Then you carry my—*" His lips moved, but I did not hear the rest of it.

For the sun's first limb lifted free, red as fresh blood. Horns cried out, silver-throated and imperious as the Elder who winded them, and I was already running over sand and splashes of cold river before hopping into the boat. Arn gestured as the craft was pushed free of clinging earth, each man swinging aboard—Efain ponderously, Eol with swift graceless efficiency, Tjorin's face white and his dark eyes blazing, Gelad as lithe as one of our own steading's sons.

Boats turned into the current, oars bit, spray rose. The wait was over; Tjorin—and the wolves of Naras—were in our hands.

Arn began to chant.

Swiftwing, Leaflight

Riverfolk! None drive a harder bargain; no others laugh quite so loudly even in defeat. Quick of hand and eye are those who gain their living from trade and raiding, changeful are their tempers, stubborn as rocks under smooth flow. Take care when dealing with a riverlord or his lady, my friend. For the only thing more treacherous than lesser waters is the Sea itself, and the folk born of any shoreline are slippery to match.

—Erdjil the Lame, to his lord Athlat
Forkbeard of the East Barrowhills

The first part was merely a matter of keeping pace. Elder boats skimmed over the water, all carrying five save for ours. We were Secondborn, naturally accounted of less speed and strength, and my weight before the prow was an additional impediment—yet Tjorin and the wolves bent their backs with good grace and attention, making Arn's first task to hold them below a too-early effort.

I had not realized there would be so many competitors. Bobbing upon Naricie's broad rippling back, pulling from shore and swinging into depth, a flock of wooden birds crowded close. None of the Elder called aloud as Arn did; they preferred hand-signals, for they knew the waters so well silent cooperation was their ideal. Yet they jostled, and this was the first test of skill and daring—many were thrown from the race in the very first flush of speed, capsized or losing rowers to cold water as boats collided.

"*Tai-yo! Tai-yo!*" my shieldmaid called, a lonely cry echoing from shore to shore. Though others sought to bar our way and oars clashed with dull wooden thudding, we swung and darted through the press, nimble as the minnow the Northerners called my small one.

Arneior's cheeks flushed and fine spray hung about her, glittering silver as sunshine mounted and high grey clouds shrank. Her woad glowed, a much brighter stripe than the sky itself; for one used to the river-mother at Tarnarya's feet, her sudden currents and melting floes in spring, this was not quite child's play.

But it was close.

The rowers faced her, but unlike Elder they had no time to gaze upon a shieldmaid balanced loose-kneed in the stern, her hair afire with dawn. It was her voice our Secondborn friends heeded instead, *right, left, ship, now down, tai-yo, tai-yo, two, two, three!* It is a matter of trust between rowers and their caller, and those who can guide such efforts are counted hardly less than bards or songmasters.

The first rapids loomed, and crouched in the stern I felt the water change under the boat's skin, humming upward through my bare soles. I was not looking either, my eyes half-shut and my palms against wet wood. My sole concern at that moment was to be as small and light as possible, trusting in both strong backs and Arn's lungs to carry us through.

I was not idle while I waited, though. The marks upon my forearms twinged as the boat surged and dropped; I had to hope I had been friendly enough, that our leafshaped steed would not shake us away and go spinning downstream, free as her cousin who had thrown Tjorin and almost landed upon his skull as well.

It is no small thing to attempt weirding in a rocking, roving, splashing, heaving boat upon a river combing over half-drowned or grasping boulders. My skin became hers, her prow rising beautiful as a silver goose's and her shuddering infecting my own bones, the joy of skimming upon waves hitting the back of my throat like strong mead. Splintercracks and unwilling cries lapped at the white foamsound of the river's laughter, for the cold water did not like being used lightly, rewarding any inattention—even momentary—with a sudden clutching, a craft smashed to flinders and Elder shorewardens hopping nimbly onto the rocks with long carven crooks to rescue their kinsmen.

Yet Arn's voice rose, a storm of imprecations harrying the wolves and Tjorin. They responded as a horse will to a well-trusted rider; we whirled, stern and prow exchanging places twice with dizzying velocity before *thump*, we landed in a cascade of froth and the banks drew away on either side.

Now was the time for greater speed, since we were past the first rapids. Arn chanted, hazel eyes wide and hornbraids darkened with flying mist. The rowers' backs swelled and shrank as they obeyed, oars dipping and pushing, and we hummed over a riverback gone sleek and tame as a sleeping hound's.

But under the surface the current gathered itself, and a roaring arose. I had heard it from shore, of course, approaching with every light-skimming step as I ran behind Naciel Silverfoot, but it was another thing entirely to feel the river flex under the keel, lazily inviting us along.

Come and dance, Egeril Naricie said, *for I carry all to the whirlpool and beyond, to the sea where the gulls cry over waves much larger than these. Let me show you, hold you, strip you of flesh and polish your bones like the pebbles I have turned silken; time and branch, stone and sorrow, the river takes all.*

I felt the boat tense as well, lifting as the rowers worked in unison, no longer four men or three wolves and a mortal lord but a quad-chambered beast with a single will. Arneior cried my name—*Solveig! Solveig, now!*

I was already rising, knees fluid and my hips moving with the lunging of water over rock. The men obeyed Arn's cry to *ship, ship the oars now, draw them in, lads!*

The Teeth were upon us.

※※※※※

No shorewardens waited upon Egeril's banks here. Evergreens drew close upon one side, dark-frowning, and the river had gnawed at the rock opposite, cutting deep and sheer. Some parts had crumbled, spring's first melt adding force to the water's clawing, but a forest of stone spears thrust skyward all across, begging fingers ready to rip the bottom from our fragile craft. Such rocks could dash even an Elder's body to paste, and here the daughters of Ráen would have fine sport. The current could hold a strong man underwater for long enough to kill even the most lung-sturdy, and Naciel had told me softly of those lost attempting this stretch of rapids.

They were few, for the Elder are hardy and cautious, their boats light and strong. And yet... no wonder she argued against Tjorin's purpose; no wonder she had been so pale that morn.

A single touch of an oar as we careened past and even a two-skin could be yanked from the boat; one miscalculation and my captivity in this beautiful alien place, along with Arn's, would be over for good. Yet I rose while the boat shot into the roaring, my arms lifted, grey sleeves falling back and the bracelets on my wrists and forearms— holy seven and powerful five, the runes between them dance-shifting under skin—flamed hot enough to turn the river's cold to steam. My lungs filled, my head thrown back, and the song burst from me like a sleekwing riverbird.

All who have *seidhr* may perform some basic tricks and wonders, for every branch of the weirding springs from a central pillar. Yet as a child grows into one of the Wise a particular bough-road calls to them, and they learn the secrets of water, of air, of stone, of black earth. Some learn the forge's heart, others the living mysteries of wood; many are the riddle- and runemasters. Some may enforce their will upon their bound element; others are beloved of theirs and even stone or fire will rise at the bidding of cherished friends.

But I was elementalist. All branches are available to me, though most not to any great depth. I could not bend Naricie the White-haired to my will; even one who had a lifetime to sing and much strength to spend would have lost that battle.

Yet I could *persuade*, and when dealing with so mighty a beast, sometimes that is all one needs.

The Old Tongue scoured my throat, lifting high and keening silvery, bouncing from sheer rock to the trees hard upon the other side. My feet melded to the leaping, spinning boat; we whirled merrily, a hairsbreadth from one set of rocks, lunging past another, shooting between sharp shivering stonefingers. Arn crouched now, the men clutching their oars and Efain's feet braced on either side of a bow tucked below his rowing-seat, Gelad keeping a coil of light Elder rope from being flung elsewhere. I could have laughed, for they were wholly in my power at that moment, and the weirding filled me like silt-dark wine.

I sang to Egeril the swift, the cold, to Naricie the foaming; *mother* I named her like the vast streaming depths at the foot of Tarnarya, *sacred one* and *white-clad*, and each looming rock buried under her skin or breaking free to catch us was my brother, as big and blundering as Bjorn.

But that was not the end of my weirding. The song mounted, my throat scraped by its passage and my lungs heaving.

To our boat I sang as well, hoping the few short days of attempting some kind of communication had reached into its curves and overlapping tight-clamped boards. She seemed more hammered or grown than carven, and her skin bore no pitch for waterproofing. She was a light dry leaf upon a fast-flowing torrent, and if we even brushed one of the rocks she would break asunder.

But I called to her, and she responded. Her wooden hide became mine, the river beneath us a cold parental hand—large and protective, though sometimes terrifying as all omnipotent power—and I cried aloud the craft's name too.

What is named is known, and may be fought. Or befriended.

Swiftwing I called her, *Araenail elussieae* for the fowl passing overhead each spring and autumn in V-shaped flocks. *Nacamasiae* I named her for the white-winged birds I had only seen when my subtle selves were freed by drugging fumes from Idra's brass brazier, flying to the west where the spear-harbors meet the sea. *Leaflight*, I chanted, *Wave-skimmer, Wood-dancer, Daughter of forest and stream*. Each kenning was a thread between us, and in the cradle of overlapping strands we were borne fleet and light as the foam itself, whipped into flying gobbets by a heedless rushing roar under the infinitely thin wooden shell bearing her burden along.

And she responded. So did the river, and for a long endless breath I was the cord between them, the link by which a mother is bound to the one in her womb. The boat could have broken to wooden shards at any moment; the river could have decided to consume the tiny motes upon her foam-itching back.

Yet they did not. Lulled by a *volva*'s voice they cradled us, albeit with shattering jolts, drenching spray, and several hairsbreadth-scrapes, the rocks not quite certain we were friend instead of prey.

Arneior laughed, the sound lost in crashing spume; I am sure one or more of the rowers cursed as they clung grimly to their oars and hoped not to be thrown overboard.

But I? I *danced*, voice and body both weaving *seidhr*, and for a long dilating moment I was the river itself, from high springs so cold even an Elder would not survive their freshets to the whirlpool before it submerged, passing under masses of black stone. My heart slammed against its moorings like a terrified horse in a burning stable, and I glimpsed the eventual meeting of Naricie Egeril and great Jarstvik the Elder call *Ancarimael* for its brownish breadth, water pulled ever onward until it meets the great salt depths and loses itself in forgetting every other name.

Again there was a sense of dropping; our craft sailed airborne for a few moments, light as the bird I had called her. The shock of landing grated all through me, but there was no time for wonder or thought, for Arneior's voice rang out again and I folded down, realizing I was cold and wet clear through. I had to twist, settling my back against the prow's comforting solidity, and blink away the spray.

Tjorin's and Eol's oars shot out, dug into the river's skin again. But Efain rose, swaying with the river's rocking, and we shot along silken rippling at a speed even the glimpse of silvergold on the now-rolling bank could not rival—Naciel, running as she rarely did, at the edge of even her Elder swiftness. She bore a shieldmaid's spear as she raced and its bladeglitter rivaled that of her hair, a floating banner upon morning breeze, both receding—for she had turned away, cutting across the base of a triangle.

Next the Egeril bent sharply, and I could not sing us past that deadly curve. There was only one way to meet it, a feat of skill any remaining Elder would be proud to say they had accomplished, and it was Efain who must somehow perform it now.

Whip-Tip, Whisper

*Then did a voice lift high and bright, sweet singing such as
the Goldspear's folk had never before heard.
Then did they hear the wonder, not merely of a mortal's
gift. For there was an answer that day.
Many swore they saw it, too; many swore they witnessed
The Riversinger dancing, and their waters replied
One voice was two, and the second was of the Blessed...*
     —Ancilaen Gaeldflor, *The Alkuine's Tale*

"*Tai-yo! Tai-yo!*" Arn chanted. Eol and Tjorin had to do the
work of twice their number, and they bent to it grimly.

Efain did not ride the rocking with grace as my shieldmaid did.
He swayed, ever seeming at the edge of being cast from the boat's
shelter headfirst, his skin twitching like a wolf's hide each time he
avoided the fall. In his hands was a curved length, a bow of design
even few Elder had seen. I hoped the string was not too wet for service, my heart hammering in my throat; Gelad shook sodden hair
from his face with a quick irritated motion and handed his battle-
brother the arrow.

The bend was approaching, and swiftly. I could not look. I gazed
at the scarred man in his sopping black clothes, teetering as our craft
heeled, Arn exhorting Tjorin to dig his oar deep, *deep as Hel's country, now, now.*

Efain half-turned, and the boat rocked again. He nocked, and Gelad was wholly occupied with keeping his own balance as well as making sure the coil of line was not wrapped around an oar, a leg, an arm. Of Elder make was that rope, plaited finely, looking far too thin for what it was to bear.

I was praying, unheard in the rush of water, the sound of slapping oars, Arn's chanting, the *huff*s of effort from our rowers. Efain was pale, though the scars upon his jaw, forehead, and cheek flushed, and his dark eyes shone with predatory glee.

In that moment I saw his wolf with clarity, instead of the merciful shaggy inkspot blur of shifting. It waited, teeth bared, for prey to appear, and his stance dropped slightly. He still swayed, but it was the lolloping of a four-limbed beast over rough ground, each foot placed near-thoughtless yet effectively, no motion wasted and no grace sought.

My heart nearly throttled me. *I can feel the river shifting*, I wanted to scream, *do it now, by the gods!*

But he waited, the bow dangling loosely. It was a complicated affair, for it had small turning pieces and clattered as it loosed, but the harpist of Nithraen was proud of it, and swore it the finest of its kind. Darker wood was inlaid along its curves, and it hummed with the force of a named weapon.

The arrow was strange too, its head ungainly with barbs in odd places and its fletching from no bird I had ever encountered or heard tell of. But I had to trust it would serve; so did my Arn, who was wholly occupied with her own work.

I shook not with cold, but with the urge to *act*. Holding back that flood was harder than weirding, worse than singing a long saga, more difficult than enduring the few confusing, clamoring battles I had seen upon our journey.

At the last moment, when the need for action chewed my bones like ague, Efain smiled. He raised the bow, the nocked arrow taking its place with an unheard *click*, and Gelad watched, hands busy with the line. He would have to loosen his grasp the instant the bow spoke, or risk losing a finger.

Possibly more.

Efain drew in one smooth motion, his chest swelling as he inhaled. He sighted, but his eyes were half-closed, and I do not believe he saw his target. Rather, he *felt* for it in some unphysical way, with the near-*seidhr* instinct of those who may whisper a shaft into flying as they will instead of as it prefers. His scars had drained of their flush, his cheeks ran with riverwater, and as soon as his fingertips reached his ear the bow spoke, a single hard sound with a whistle at its end.

I was aware then of other high sharp cries; those of Laeliquaende called these particular arrows *kwislael*, akin to the word for a sound the flag-tipped blades of *orukhar* made before they buried in flesh yet with a softness at the end.

The Elder rope smoked between Gelad's palms, uncoiling swifter than a thought; he grimaced, but held to his task. Efain dropped the bow with seeming inattention, ending with its clatter into the bottom of the boat; I had to tap it into place with one foot without disturbing Arn's rhythm or anything else in the chaos. The boat heaved as if it wished to throw us all into the depths, and my shieldmaid's hawk-cry of warning fell from a sky now clear and blue, innocent of any cloud.

The mist was gone. Pitiless golden light drenched us, and Efain's hands flashed out. The arrow vanished into a stand of old, massive trees and moss-shrouded boulders just before the tip of the triangle, hopefully burying itself deep in a surface strong enough to bear our weight.

Efain planted one foot against the boat's side; Gelad wrapped the line about his own forearm and lunged, nearly upsetting us again. Arn screamed an imprecation, Eol's oar slapped instead of digging...

...and the line snapped taut, a shock communicating through Efain to the rest of us. Our poor boat bucked like a horse pushed past patience into terror, Gelad threw his arms—one tangled with the line—around his battle-brother, and Efain leaned back, a wolf's snarl distorting his entire face.

"*Up! Up!*" Arn called, and the two oars wielded by Eol and Tjorin rose free of the water's skin. The rope added a thin singing noise of stress answered by its kin; we were not the only ones who had achieved this feat. Around the sharp bend we shot at the end of a spiderstrand thinness, like a cradled stone before it leaves a shepherd-boy's sling, and we had to hope we would not tangle with another line nor find ourselves in the way of any other archer's aim.

Skimming swiftly, my stomach jolting to my throat and crowding my wildly throbbing heart, a coughing growl from Efain's lungs vying with Gelad's scream of an obscenity in the Old Tongue I would blush to repeat if I could remember its exact dimensions, we were as the tip of a whip as it cracks through air. Arn dropped into a crouch again, whiteknuckle grasping at gunwales to keep from being flung, and a pair of oars rolled in a few fingerwidths of shipped riverwater, Daerith's bow close to being crushed under Gelad's bare toe-spread feet.

The most perilous moment, all annals of previous races agreed, was the releasing of the line so those in the boat could continue, having turned the water's corner. But again, Efain's eyes half-closed, and he was not listening to the sounds of effort, the cries of dismay as others missed their shot, a splintering crack from a craft which had found a rock hidden in smooth swift deepflow. His attention still focused wholly inward, and much sooner than I thought possible his hands loosened. He tumbled into Gelad's lap, the other man somehow freeing himself with a convulsive motion as well, and the Elder rope's now-freed end flew, curling, striking with snakelike swiftness diagonally across Eol's back.

The captain of Naras stiffened before his shoulders hunched, but he did not let go of his oar. Nor did he cry aloud, though blood flew scarlet as the line vanished, its falling length now a danger for those behind us.

"*To oar!*" Arn cried. Quick and smooth she rose, shaking out her hands and gesturing, motions familiar from other races upon our home waters—a shieldmaid is lucky to have as a caller, though it was oft judged unfair for one bearing *seidhr* to compete. "*To oar, my brothers, to oar! Tai-yo! Tai-yo!*"

They caught her rhythm again, and now I had to turn once more to the prow. But I stared for a moment at Eol's back, black cloth flapping free, blood now invisibly soaking into river-sodden fabric. I could not tell how deep the wound was, but he did not falter, bending to riverwork as fiercely as any son of Dun Rithell.

"*Sol!*" my shieldmaid shrieked, and the boat shook like a dog gaining a far shore, bringing drowned fowl to its master.

After the bend were more rapids, and the greatest test of all. Savage exhaustion filled my bones, and my vision shrank to the waters before me. A great liquid comb fell over a shelf of stone, the river wearing away but not quite managing to flatten this stubborn prominence, and beyond it an expanse of white foam rose again, hungry and beautiful.

Now every separate mortal in the boat had to trust the others, and do their own task besides.

My legs pushed me upright. My hands snapped free like birds uncaged, wet woolen sleeves falling free, and the song rose from my chest again.

This time the music did not soar. A droning undercurrent furled behind me, slapping-cold against my cheeks, striking the backs of the rowers. Strength I sang into them, weirding fusing to their bones. Any with the *seidhr* may spur warriors in battle with voice married to will; what came unbidden from my throat was an old, old chant Idra had taught me in the depths of a terrible winter. That particular half-song is said to be one of the first of its kind, ancient and strong, a recitation from the time before we knew the Elder or the Black Land's master existed. Of monsters it howled, and those who left the shelter of caves to put an end to their depredations.

In those days we did not know how the weirding twisted when physical weapons were wielded with it, so the tales are largely tragic and a hero usually dead with their opponent amid shattered trees and stinking mud. But they gave their lives willingly, those considered and named mighty among our primeval ancestors, so the rest of the clan could survive.

Of Grivik I sang, and the very first Bjornwulf who hunted a foul many-limbed thing in the high fells under cold stars. Of Sigurl the manwoman who first spoke to wolves and made them hounds, leader of a pack bringing down a twisted mockery of a stag upon the smoking side of a shuddering, ash-choked mountain. Of Astranna, no shieldmaid but mighty enough that the Wingéd carried her bodily from her place-of-dying, of Gesilda the Firewitch from whom many a warlord claims descent if there is even a tinge of red to his beard. And to give him his due, of Odynn I sang, hanging upon the tree of *seidhr* to gain wisdom, and of the stars wheeling overhead as his sacrifice endured and his dripping godblood nourished the roots.

Later we mortals met the Elder and learned different songs; later we tamed both kine and granary cat. Later we built greathalls; later we plowed and spun. But though the Children of the Star might disdain our short history and call the South forgetful—no, we do not forget this.

How can we? The knowledge lies in our very bones and blood and skin, and needs only a whisper of *seidhr* to burst forth.

Arn's voice throbbed counterpoint and the rowers called upon their last reserves in a glare of sunshine, white riverhair flung high as Naricie sought both to kill us and to bear us safely along. Between those two longings we spun, just barely avoiding the rocks, and so great was the effort I might have sung until my throat shredded itself, my heart torn free, my bones broken like dry branches, and all of me but a single wavering note upon the wind.

We burst from the last veil of riverbreath, rainbows like Fryja's veils shimmering in every direction, and onto another great glassy section just as the sun reached his apogee. A bright clear noon enfolded us, and we were not alone. Two other boats crewed by Elder appeared, and upon the far shore a loud cry went up, though we did not hear it.

Or rather, *I* did not hear it, too far lost in my weirding. But Arneior's rhythm changed, and the boat—named *Swiftwing*, named *Leafwhisper*, named *Solveig* in the depths of my song for I was her and she was me—hummed across the river like a fish-hawk whose wings almost brush the surface but not quite, not quite. So quick was their motion the oars nearly blurred, appearing to bend as they scooped and lifted. Spray curled upon either side, lifting high, and though more Elder craft freed themselves from the last rapids, even the two who chased us could not catch.

Like a well-rested hart before tired hounds we raced, and barely slowed as we aimed for the green shore where bright pennants fluttered and a crowd stood, some cheering, others singing, a medley of horns and pipes and harps lifting to the blue vault.

Arn's chanting changed; my voice fell, a falcon plummeting earthward. The keel grated upon sand with tiny agate pebbles buried in its wet flatness, and my legs almost failed as I hopped from the wooden shell, something in me crying out as my soles left her skin. I pulled, and there was splashing behind me as the wolves of Naras staggered knee-deep. We hauled our faithful craft from the water she longed for, beaching her upon unforgiving ground, and Naciel burst from a crowd of Elder, the joy upon her so bright I could not bear to look. She carried a wreath of glossy dark-green leaves, and as Tjorin swayed with the exhaustion of a mighty feat accomplished, his princess crowned him.

Above the beach, on a slight shelf of rock with a balustrade of silvery wrought-metal seeming to grow from it like a hedge, Taeron Goldspear witnessed this. Draped in green like new leaves the king smiled, though the expression was pained.

My stomach quaked. I longed to retch. I reeled; Arn drew alongside, her arms closing around me like rope over a mooring-pole. We made a single pillar upon the shore, our feet sinking in sand, her face in my wet hair, my knees full of the water we had just been upon. The remaining wolves of Naras clustered their companions; there was much backslapping and shouting. Aeredh brandished a flask, holding it to Eol's mouth as the captain, white-faced, stared over his Elder friend's shoulder, drinking unwilling.

I rested my cheek upon Arn's muscled upper arm, and could not tell if I smiled or wept. A pang passed between *volva* and the heir of Naras, some silent chord resonating unheard amid the tumult. Other craft were reaching the beach, each fresh arrival greeted with joyous tumult.

But we were first. The son of Hrasimir, nominal captain of our crew, was counted the winner of that spring's river race.

Nor Men

Even Aerith's songmaster lent his aid, the great bow Kaesgrithil given to a mortal. Well-named was the weapon indeed, the same bow which hunted the Enemy's creatures upon the banks of Nith-an-Gaelas, its string speaking in Laeliquaende before the fall, and later wounding Saeril the Accursed himself.
—Raelin of Nassan-Daele, *Saga of the Ringmaker*

The Elder held that spring's arrival was formally accomplished once the race was finished; the valley was full of celebration. All of Laeliquaende sang, danced, drank. The day's orb began to descend. An afternoon of merrymaking filled the white city, spread into the fields, ran gaily through hall and settlement, lapped at the edges of vineyards, and threaded through stands of trees whose leaves held thicker strands of green than they had last night.

The wolves of Naras were hailed from every quarter, given great honor, crowned not with the dark-green *laekeri* but plaited bright-green grapevine. Soren laughed much, a note of disbelief threading through his voice as Gelad spoke of Efain's shot, and before the sun fell a handsbreadth from the summit there were already songs of Daerith lending his bow and the use it was put to. The harpist himself beamed, toasting the scarred Secondborn with a plain silver goblet—filled by every passing jug—each time a new chorus rose.

Many restoratives were poured down Tjorin's throat as well, while he was clad in dry cloth of green and silver like a lord of Lael-iquaende. After that he roamed, his hand caught in Naciel's; he was cheered and she radiated both pride and relief. They finally settled in Taeron's great pavilion, and the princess took up her harp to sing of the morning's work as well.

A tent was given to the use of Naras, and before going inside Eol stripped his sodden tunic and linen undershirt, dislodging his grape-vine circlet. The weal across his back, already mostly healed, glared amid a mass of similar but long-healed marks, yet I was granted only a single glimpse before he was hustled inside. Aeredh lingered in the doorway, casting a bright blue glance over his shoulder.

Arn and I, shivering in wet wool and padding, were given circlets of new-green grapevine as well, but ours were woven with small blue *ildora*. We were also shown by smiling Elder girls to a smaller round fabric house; Naciel had arranged everything that might possibly be of comfort except a sauna. I might have fallen asleep in a steam-room, though, and almost slid below the surface of a round cask, copper-bound and large enough for two women, full of bathing-water far, far warmer than the river's embrace.

Sounds of celebration splashed against heavily felted walls. My head still rang with the last effort of *seidhr*; I longed to collapse. Thin curls of steam rose from the bathwater; Arn levered herself out of the tub with something like a groan. Her spear rested against a highly carved wooden holder, its blade glittering in a sun-shaft from the vent-flaps overhead; she dressed swiftly, though she paused often and finally settled upon a wooden stool to deal with her boots.

I should have hurried to help with her armor, but the silken heat of water was delicious and I was still not yet quite myself. Part of me lingered with the boat, beached and useless, perhaps as weary as I felt. I drifted, my head resting against the cask's rim.

"Here." My shieldmaid thrust a goblet at me; a small table, near the rack where an Elder dress of green and gold waited, held two graceful flagons as well as cups for our use. She was hoarse, each word scraped thin as a hide window-cover. "Drink, and do not hes-itate. You are pale."

"Such a feat." I sounded mead-mazed, slurring. "Arn, you were magnificent."

"The Wingéd are pleased." She pushed the goblet's rim in my face again. "Come now. It won't do to drown in a bath after *that*."

I had to laugh. It was a thin, tired sound, but her own chuckle answered and I found I could lift my hand, clasp the cup, and drink.

That was my first taste of springwine. The winter vintage tastes of memories; this variety flowed clear and bright down my parched throat. It was flavored as nothing, or perhaps only of water, but it was strong as the finest clear ferment ever made from honey. A rushing filled me, spreading from my empty stomach in overlapping rings. My fingers stretched, my toes pointed, and even my hair tingled as if it wished to grow at visible pace.

I had not even loosened my braids. Red coral satin-warm, though my hair was still heavy with riverspray; I touched a braid-rope knocked awry over my left ear and drained the cup's dregs. There was no bitterness or silt, and as the drink settled within me I felt new-wakened. Aches from being rattled about a boat and the fire in my throat from battle-singing retreated before a wave of seeming health.

All the same a thin thread of unease knotted about my heart, and my subtle selves were not refreshed. I settled back in the bath and began to work at my wet hair. Arn drained two goblets, and there was familiar fire in her dark gaze as she donned Naciel's gifted armor. She examined her spear from blunt end to sharp tip, muttering softly while almost-heard feather-brushing cloaked her, and at last reapplied her woad.

She might need more of the dye soon. I thought that plant grew everywhere, but had not seen it in the valley yet. Maybe the change of seasons would bring it, for 'tis hardy as a shieldmaid itself.

My own equipage did not take long. I combed my hair with another of Naciel's gifts, an implement carven from a large chunk of greenish amber. I wished I could dry thoroughly before braiding; the silence between us deepened.

Finally, Arn sighed, setting aside her dye-bowl. "It is a festival. They will be celebrating into the night, I daresay."

We knew where many of the boats were kept now, in sheds along the riverbank. And yet... "We cannot pass through the whirlpool. There is no other river likely to give us egress, the streams are many yet few of them touch the walls." The maps of the valley Tjorin and I studied agreed on that, at least. "If we knew the guards at the Hidden Passage were likely to be sotted...and yet I do not think so, for the Elder do not seem to suffer such things."

She frowned—not angrily, merely thoughtful. "The mountains cannot be entirely impassable."

"But finding a way over them while being pursued, possibly by both Elder and our wolf allies, whom we will have forsworn by fleeing? I like it not, Arn." I worked at damp hair with fingers and combtines both, wincing. "And I cannot dream. Not of Dun Rithell, not even of our journey here. Just those fishgutting orange stars."

"I saw them too." She regarded me somberly. "In a deep blue sky, like summer twilight but unlike as well. What does it mean?"

"I wish I knew." Well should she ask me, for deciphering visions are part of a *volva*'s duty. But I could not tell, and I could not lie either. "Perhaps a god is punishing me."

"Why, though? You did everything you should." She eyed the jugs upon the small table; there was a burst of merry noise from outside, Elder voices high and sweet singing in the Old Tongue. The words were so archaic as to be nonsense, but *they* no doubt understood the meaning.

"Perhaps it is as Aeredh says, and there is some purpose to this." I did not like to say as much; I sounded weary as my flesh did not feel. "I cannot see it, though."

Arneior was silent for a long moment, staring at the jugs. "We are not gods," she said, finally. "Nor are we Elder, nor men. Whatever their purpose, at least *we* have done as we should."

"True." I was abruptly cheered; I could always trust my small one to cut the heart from any dilemma. "And at least...well, if I were alone in this, I would perhaps go mad. It is a fine thing to have a shieldmaid."

"Ah." She nodded, and a pink tinge crept to her freckled cheeks. "There is that. Sol, sometimes I am glad to have traveled. Home is home, but..."

Had she felt my secret, silent craving for adventure as well? She had never mentioned boredom or longing in Dun Rithell. "I am too."

She turned her head as if startled, gold threads in her hazel irises glowing. She might have said summat else, but there was a soft commotion near the door-flap of our temporary domicile, a courteous mispronouncing of my name accented in the Old Tongue. 'Twas an Elder guard in full armor, bearing a summons disguised as a request.

Taeron wished to see his captives again, and we barely had time to take up our victory-crowns before answering the call.

Victory and Weariness

Yet the son of Hrasimir heeded the counsel which had spoken to him from the sea, and did not beg for what he already possessed. Nor did he seek aught for himself, instead rendering aid to one who had not asked it. His wife's father was silent for a long while, the sounds of merrymaking roaring as stormy surf all 'round. And the Crownless turned pale, for alone of his companions he guessed what grief lay ahead...

—Daerith the Younger, *Of the Unfinished Council*

I have ever disliked crowds, finding even riverside fairs difficult to endure for long. Among the celebrating Elder were a sprinkling of children, but none clamoring for a *volva's* minor *seidhr*-tricks; women, but none seeking brewing-blessings or a word upon their sons' marriage prospects; warriors, but none looking for a legal judgment or approval of a saga-rhyme; girls, but none approaching bright-eyed to ask for a spindle-blessing; youths, but none seeking a prophecy for future greatness or aid in negotiating a good match.

Most Elder paused in their merriment to lift goblet or rhyton in our direction. Others cried aloud at our approach. I was hailed as *alkuine*, Arn as *maiden-of-steel* since the Old Tongue does not have a word for shieldmaid. *Here comes the Riversinger*, they sang, *and Minnow-so-sharp*—for my *seidhr* upon the water had been witnessed, and the wolves of Naras named Arneior *Lady Minnow*, remarking upon the quickness of her spear.

The titles might have delighted both of us in a different setting, for to earn such names even at your own hall—let alone elsewhere—is no small honor. Arn accepted the cheers with a shieldmaid's polite indifference, inclining her coppery head at intervals. It was my duty to smile graciously, occasionally lifting my hands to display my marks, and my face felt ever more like a mask.

The springwine burned in my limbs, but inwardly I felt only weariness, and longed for quiet.

Taeron Goldspear's pavilion was vast, fabric the color of evergreens embroidered with pale verticals impersonating a grove of slim young silverbark birch, and I could not examine the ropes holding it aloft or wonder at the secrets of its construction and raising. Elder guards saluted as we passed, and even Floringaeld the golden-haired seemed glad to see us, shepherding Arn and me through heavy-draped flaps serving as the main door.

Once inside the crowd-noise was muffled and sweetness lingered upon the air from smokeless braziers scattered at intervals. The carpets were woven to resemble grass, and laid cunningly so as not to damage earth or plants underneath. Cloth dividers stitched with lifelike forest scenes rippled slightly as the breeze made the entire structure move—not enough to seem dangerous, merely imparting the semblance of life to a stitchery doe raising her shy head, a cloth bird flapping its wings, sewn branches swaying.

I cannot say I was unimpressed. Nor can I say I felt the wonder I once would have at the sight, either.

The king was not alone. On a vast carpet-lawn strewn with tiny blue fabric *sudelma-lithielle*, pillows like boulders gave shelter. Naciel looked up from her harp and smiled, her happiness so intense a faint blue shimmer rippled about her just as her beautiful hair. Tjorin, looking almost like an Elder save for his ears as rounded as mine or Arn's, rose and came to greet us, still wearing the *laekeri* victory-wreath.

Eol stood a little apart, in a fresh set of Northern black cloth;

Aeredh had a hand upon his shoulder and was speaking earnestly in low tones. Daerith the harpist raised a silver chalice in our direction, for it seemed we had temporarily earned his approbation.

Floringaeld did not precisely crowd behind us, but he did let down another fall of cloth, further shielding our small gathering from outside noise. He saluted his king; I could not study Taeron's mood, for Tjorin had reached us.

"*Gifts of the Blessed*, Aeredh calls you twain." The son of Hrasimir indicated his own dark head with a swift motion. "By all rights the crown belongs to you instead. I doubted you before the race, though only in my silence. I was wrong and freely admit as much. My House is in your debt, now and hereafter."

" 'Tis no large matter." This was, I told myself, no worse than the morning after a solstice feast when the thorniest legal cases are brought and a *volva* must lend her weight to or against certain judgments even if exhausted from merrymaking or other duties. "Arn is one of our finest callers; I did not compete often at home, but any child of Dun Rithell is at home upon the water. The wolves of Naras must be given their due, for they wielded the oars well, and Efain's shot was a marvel to witness." I inclined my chin in Eol's direction, attempting to include Daerith in the motion. "Not to mention the songmaster of Nithraen, who lent his bow."

"*A modest child.*" Daerith took a draught of whatever filled his cup, but the phrase in the Old Tongue held grudging approval with no tint of scorn. "It was used well," he continued in southron, "and has earned its name afresh."

I was full of springwine, but I longed for some of Albeig's roast fowl or daybread with river sand in the crumb. Even a rind of hard cheese, bitter greens, or the marrowbones of a feast would have been welcome. Something honest and mortal to chew, and a place to rest without music or voices. Returning to the boat and climbing into its shelter sounded *wonderful*; I simply could not tell how to free myself of this current obligation in order to do so.

"Come." Naciel laid her harp aside and rose, fluidly. The gleaming about her would not abate no matter how much I blinked; I was seeing too much after the morning's vast effort. "Sit beside me, victory

does not preclude weariness. Arneior, my strong friend, your spear
was touched by no other; that I may swear."

Arn acknowledged the princess's care with the salute shieldmaids
perform to a woman they respect, and followed me to Naciel's side.
The men drew closer, giving pride of place to Taeron, and I realized
this was to be a council instead of interrogation or banquet.

Very well. I settled upon one of the boulder-pillows, grateful it
was not oversoft. Arn disdained that comfort, but she did brace her
spear upon the carpets and stand at my shoulder. Floringaeld and Eol
chose to stand as well, the Captain of the Guard with hand to hilt
and the heir of Naras with a set jaw, his palms still pinkish-raw from
the bite of oars.

Those with two skins heal swiftly, but even their great strength
may be taxed by such a feat. And I wondered about the other marks,
covered by his tunic.

❧

Many are the songs of our Althing, like the tales of the Council of
Redhill; contrary to most assertions we did not each craft a verse of
poetry extolling Laeliquaende or the might of white-maned Naricie
while the valley celebrated spring's return. Instead, the Elder and
Northerners spoke largely in southron, perhaps out of new-gained
deference to their captives, and Taeron began not by invoking the
gods nor by threatening to have Tjorin cast from the Leap for his
daring as some would have it.

Instead, the king fixed Aeredh with a steady look. "Say what you
will, old friend. I am not so shameless as to be angered when proven
wrong."

"I have never thought you thus." The Crownless, perched upon
a large dark-grey cushion bearing a resemblance both to well-felted
wool and hard stone at once, tilted his dark head with a rueful smile.

His ear-tips poked through silken hair, sharp and distinct; I was
surprised such things no longer seemed strange. There is no oddity
so great that constant sight of it will not induce a manner of nor-
malcy; all who travel outside their own steadings know as much.

"Then you do me great honor." The High-helm turned his address to me next. "Lady *alkuine*, you seem to have recovered from your journey hence, and now I would hear how you came to my valley. I have heard Aeredh's tale, and that of Naras. Yet it is my preference to weigh what every creature would say, not merely those whose words may please. Before you begin, though, allow me to apologize once more for testing your temper upon our second meeting. Many are the snares of the Enemy, yet it is not fitting to do his work by offering insult to guests."

So Taeron's restraint had been merely to allow us recovery? And we were *guests* now. Yet I did not think it likely we could take our leave at will, nor did it seem wise to say, *My brother murdered Eol's, and thus I was taken.* I had maneuvered us into allyship instead of the paying of a life-debt, freed of galling over-obedience and answerable to Naras only as a fellow warlord might be.

But I well remembered the hints of treachery before they knew I understood the Old Tongue as well as my own. What guest will comfortably speak of such things? Not to mention the morning's work, helping to win a boon from a man who did not wish his daughter married to one of my kind.

What, indeed, could I reasonably say?

These considerations and more flashed through my head as I arranged my skirts, as if admiring the weave of Elder cloth. Arn's silence at my shoulder was a comforting steady glow, like coals deep in a winter night, and had this been a contest of physical strength she might have taken a moment to brace herself as well.

"How came we to your valley?" I said it slowly, as if surprised by the question. "My lord king, we walked."

My statement was greeted with a long pause. Eol's mouth twitched; Aeredh gazed at me as if I had said summat faintly obscene. Naciel's finely sculpted eyebrows rose, and Tjorin glanced at Arn as if she could translate the words.

"You...walked." Taeron did not sound baffled, merely pleasantly interested. Wise was the king of Waterstone, for I suspect he sensed my dilemma when I paused before speaking, and waited to see how I would surmount it.

"Sometimes we rode," I amended. I raised my chin, and the *seidhr* still resonating inside me leapt across the space between us.

He, like Curiaen son of Faevril, had attempted to use that force to discover my intentions. Now I offered what I would not let either of them take, inviting him to peer inside my heart.

Not far, mind you; there are things in anyone, Elder or Second-born, which should remain private. Yet there is a flavor discerned from such contact between two creatures, each with weirding of their own, and if there is evil intent it smokes with bitterness.

Naciel's father was much like winterwine, though distilled to clear burning strength instead of the filling almost-solidity of that draught. A giving tension stretched between us like skilled fingers spinning wool into thread, or a mother's hand guiding her daughter's first work with a small shuttle.

I was aware of a half-swallowed laugh. "*We should name her Lady Answer instead*," Eol muttered, and Aeredh made a stifled sound as well.

But Taeron merely settled further upon his seat. His hands lay upon his thighs, palms upward, and again the fillet at his ageless brow caught more than its fair share of light. I did not quite see his subtle selves, yet for a moment we were only a breath apart, sounding like adjacent strings upon his daughter's harp.

A burst of music lifted outside, Tjorin's name clearly audible in a long string of accented Elder words, paired with Naciel's at the end of the phrase. The king of Laeliquaende nodded in answer, though I had not spoken; I felt the motion in my own flesh.

"I am not what you think," I said, quietly, as if he were Idra upon a long afternoon spent in her small, snugly thatched cottage, *seidhr* passing between teacher and student. Some things cannot be taught, they must be *felt*, sure as Efain's grasping for a target or Arn's inward sense of propriety and right action.

"No," the king agreed. "But you are, in some measure, what I have feared. Do not be alarmed—" His right hand twitched, as if to forestall Daerith's interjection, which died upon a sharp inhale. " 'Tis a mere fact. A pattern is at work here, as Aeredh of Nithraen says."

"Would that I did not see it." The Crownless was no longer

smiling. "I would give all that remains unto me for the certainty of being wrong." A shadow of the Old Tongue rode behind the words; what he wished to say could be more perfectly expressed in its syllables, and pressed against the bars of another language. "Never have I heard of a second *alkuine*, Elder or Secondborn. And to find this one as we did beggars belief."

Perhaps you did not ride far enough south. I throttled my immediate objection, yet Taeron must have sensed it.

"Nor have the ravens upon the peaks or the waters which whisper through my lands heard tell of another." He looked to Floringaeld. "What of our borders, my captain?"

Our erstwhile jailor cleared his throat. "The woods outside the Ice Door are cold, and darkness gathers. You would not think it spring, for there is little melt; there is movement, but of what we cannot discern, for it stays just beyond the limit of our sensing. The animals are frightened, and the trees do not speak. It could merely be the end of a hard winter's quiet... yet my heart misgives me, my lord. The Guard is likewise uneasy, to a man."

"And you, heir of Naras?" Taeron addressed Eol, whose gaze did not move.

Indeed, he watched the tips of my slippers as if some mystery was to be solved in the stitchery. "Nothing but a trace of mud in a few streams," Eol said, heavily. "Where the waters enter the valley, and it could simply be the loosening of winter's belt. But it smells of something ill—though only a whiff. A whisper."

Naciel studied her hands, lying in her lap. I thought Taeron might ask her summat, but the king merely regarded his daughter for a few moments, then addressed the gathering as a whole.

"So far our fastness remains undiscovered; the Enemy, like many an evil creature, is so busy with subterfuge he does not compass what is in plain sight. Faeron-Alith keeps its ancient watch, as does Galath. Dorael is yet too mighty to fall, though that grace may be of short duration." The High-helm paused, a shadow dimming his bright gaze, and the tent's interior turned still. "Aenarian Greycloak is dying."

Shock printed itself upon every face save mine and, I suspect,

Arneior's—we did not know enough to be surprised, and I was busy absorbing the implications of the watch kept upon the valley's borders. No wonder Taeron could deal with Arn and me at leisure; why hurry, when one is ageless and there is no chance of prey's escape?

I had heard of the Greycloak, true, a high king among the Elder; even in the south his name was spoken, though 'twas held he had passed from our lands to the West long ago like all his kind, and collections of sayings or sagas featuring him were ancient indeed. Some even thought him a garbled legend like all things to do with the Black Land or the Children of the Star, a distant truth embroidered over and over until the original pattern is lost.

"You know this of a certainty?" Daerith stiffened, and his shoulders curved inward as if he had been struck. "But...the Cloak-Weaver..."

I had not just studied maps of the valley, of course, but also what I could of the North itself. I had seen the breadth of what they called *Dorael*, embellished with stylized trees—for it was a vast forest, wrapped in a maze of bewilderment even the Enemy's servants could not pass through. We had brushed its edges before turning north into the Mistwood's numbing shrouds upon our journey here, emerging onto the Glass.

"Melair's love is great, and her grief at losing their daughter just as sharp." Taeron's tone was studiously neutral. "Her husband has been bleeding of the wound since 'twas made. The ravens spoke to me in the high places, my friends; it will not be long. And then what of Dorael?"

Naciel's hand had crept to Tjorin's. Their fingers interlaced.

"Melair cannot mean to leave their people unprotected, even if Aenarian embarks for the Shadowed Halls." Daerith shook his head, almost angrily; he had, I thought, some kin in that land. "Surely... surely she..."

"Even grief may kill," Aeredh murmured, his gaze resting near my knees—clearly not seeing green-and-silver cloth, but merely his own thoughts.

"The secrecy of Laeliquaende does not merely protect our own folk." Floringaeld, too, spoke as if the Old Tongue wished to pierce the screen of its descendant; he did not look at us, but I sensed it took effort to refrain. "To send forth what was gained with such great cost is a fool's errand, and if none other will say it I must."

I could also grasp the implications of *that*. The Elder weapon in its doorless tower might be carried elsewhere and I along with it, to keep from being used by the Enemy.

Arn and I had won a victory upon the water, yet it was utterly empty. Nothing had changed; we were still to be dragged hither and yon at the pleasure of these men.

Eol of Naras cleared his throat; after the Elder voices, his was much harsher. "Perhaps we should ask Lady Solveig's counsel, since she is the gift of the Blessed."

Oh, so now he thought to ask my opinion? Better late than not at all, as the wife of Narjik the Tardy said to their ill-tempered lord. I had little chance to answer, though, for Naciel spoke once more, aiming the words at clear air instead of any particular person.

"And where is my cousin the Watchful? No royal move is made without his counsel, after all."

The Council of Laeliquaende

She did not loathe her cousin at first, not until the shape of his desire was laid clear; the Elder do not marry so close, and her heart did not turn in his direction. The son of Gethsael struggled with his longing, and most agreed he did so with much grace. Yet under the seeming, his very being twisted into madness.

—Elaedie the Swift, of Aerindael

C an you not guess?" Floringaeld did not quite hiss, but he sounded scandalized as Albeig when some steading-gossip was brought from a neighbor's sparring-yard or sewing-room. "No doubt he roams the hills alone, listening to the sounds of festival."

"I would have thought him eager to render duty and counsel to his uncle," she returned, sharply. "Despite whatever base desires linger in his heart."

Arn shifted, an uneasy movement. My cheeks were hot, and I studied my hands in my lap. I could not close my ears, but I could pretend to.

Sometimes that is wisest. Besides, I had to think. Did they truly mean to send me from this place to a shadow-locked forest? Why? And if they did…the mountains were a deterrent to wandering; a mighty Elder *seidhr* capable of barring the Allmother's eldest son from entering was as well. The journey to reach another place might afford me some chance of freedom, yet I thought it unlikely.

At least Dorael was a comparatively larger cell than this valley. Still, the thought that I might spend my entire life being shuttled from one Elder prison to the next was chilling.

"I have oft found profit and solace in Maedroth's counsel, and he is my sister's child." Taeron's tone turned forbidding, and the tent's walls rippled with the breeze. "He has borne his shame with courage, and his habit of telling truth earns him few friends. I do not wonder he wished to avoid witnessing the morning's work."

"Is it truth he tells, my father?" Naciel was a tense blur of silver and green at the very periphery of my vision. "Or is his honesty merely the leavening of ash-bread?"

"*You have gained what you sought, my beloved child.*" Strange, how an Elder speaking the Old Tongue should sound so...well, at that moment the High-helm seemed very like Eril the Battle-Mad chiding Astrid, with far more gentleness than he ever used upon our brother. "*Be gracious in victory, so you may be strong in defeat.*"

A pained silence descended, not quite the same as the quiet when a passing spirit slips invisible through a mortal crowd. This was an entirely familial pause, and the music outside the tent only underscored its dimensions.

"Yes," Naciel finally said, and a soft sound of cloth was her shifting. Slight bitterness, well-reined, edged her tone. "We must turn our attention to weightier matters, as always, like where to stow a precious item so others do not even glance upon it. Yet I would advise you to beware of using small things so. Even a master grower asks a blade of grass what it wills."

I could not help it; I raised my chin. The daughter of Taeron tilted her bright head, and her smile was just as ageless and pained as her sire's as she regarded him. They resembled each other very much indeed in that moment.

None—save Arn, perhaps—would see the stamp of Eril the Battle-Mad or my mother Gwendelint upon me. I knew I would never see Dun Rithell again, but the realization kept returning, a hungry bear at an inadequately fenced midden-heap. And each time, my heart gave a hard wringing pang.

"And yet, to hand over Lithielle's Jewel..." Floringaeld stiffened as Taeron turned in his direction. "That is what we are discussing, my lord. Is it not?"

I stirred, sensing a change in the discussion as surely as a shift in riverflow. "I do not want your Elder gem." My tone was soft enough, but seemed unmusical as Eol's after Elder voices. "Faevril's *taivvan-pallo* nearly killed me in Nithraen, and Caelgor called it a mere toy. This other thing may stay in that tower for all eternity, I care not a whit."

"You have not seen it, child." Taeron now leaned forward, propping his elbow upon his raised knee, and rested his chin upon his hand. It was a familiar pose; he often sat thus upon his throne. "The Enemy himself was helpless against such beauty, for he halted in his escape to steal them first and other treasures only as an afterthought. And none knows what even a single Jewel might do in the hands of another *alkuine*."

Now was my time to speak, as a wise but seemingly reticent warrior will turn after luring his opponent into ill-judged pursuit. "Perhaps it might be dangerous wielded by an Elder, but I am merely Secondborn, am I not? You count us lesser in everything—sheep to be won upon a dice-toss, not even thralls." I did not mean to sound so rancorous, but the truth had its head like a runaway horse, and if it pained them to hear such facts it also stung my tongue to utter them. Indeed, I spoke much as Tarit of Redhill then, and welcomed the likeness. "What threat am I, Taeron Goldspear? If your terrible Enemy found this place, would you cut my throat to keep me from his clutches? Or do you mean to simply trammel me like a rabbit in a wicker hutch until I die of old age? It may be a mere eyeblink to an Elder, but it is all the life I have, and what will I say to the gods when they ask me how it was spent?"

Arn lifted her spear, and its blunt end struck the carpeted floor. It did not have the crisp sound it would upon stone, but was still clearly audible even through the muffled music.

All of Laeliquaende celebrated that afternoon; my own feelings were otherwise, and mattered less than naught.

Eol rocked back on his heels. Aeredh's gaze fastened upon me, and I could not tell if he looked chastened or merely shocked at my temerity. All the silence and forbearance I had used upon our journey to this place curdled within me, every word I had dammed behind the screen of a weregild's obedience and the prudent quiet of a woman among armed men not her kin now jostled for release.

A *volva* must speak carefully, yes. So must a weregild, and an ally. But by the gods, I had held my tongue long enough.

"Tjorin did not even ask for our help," I continued. "We offered it freely, for he and Naciel have been kind. Wise you may think yourself, Elder king, and ageless your counselors. But as I see, your daughter and her husband far outrace you in both wisdom and honor. Keep this jewel of yours in its doorless casket; even had I known of its existence in Dun Rithell I would not have stirred a single step to seek it out."

"You say that now, but should you look upon—" Floringaeld began.

"Why was I summoned to this meeting, merely to hear my doom?" Perhaps the river was still within me and the morning *seidhr* filling my veins, for my tone demanded silence. I fixed the Elder captain with a glare that would have done Ulfrica at home proud. "Or did the High-helm think to punish me for rewarding kindness with aid? You have not heard of another *alkuine*, but the world is wide; have you looked in every possible corner? Has the son of Aerith? He and his friends rode south to ask for allies against the Enemy, yet this is how your friends are treated?"

"Yes." Eol, pale and rigid, took a single step forward. A ripple passed through him, the wolf inside his skin turning restlessly. "Each time some alliance seemed likely it was withdrawn, and the creatures of the Enemy dogged our heels until Lady Solveig's brother felled mine with a single blow, for Arvil made rude comment upon her younger sister. And afterward my brother's pyre smoked foully, refusing to burn clean; when we left that place we were not followed so closely." He spread his hands, the rawness upon them all but healed. "I deserve your anger and am in your debt besides, my lady. If you are trammeled here so am I, for I will not leave you to suffer such fate alone."

He had not said it so baldly before, and now I was not the one who had told the tale of my leaving Dun Rithell. Still, I had not meant to provoke him, and disliked the event.

"Ah," Taeron said. "*So that is why the heir of Naras stays.*"

"*You cannot keep wolves who do not wish it,*" Aeredh answered. "*Yet I still hold this a design of the Blessed, Taeron, and do not regret bringing her here.*"

"*It is as well you do not regret it, son of Aerith.*" The words leapt from me, the Old Tongue sharp as one of their well-wrought blades. "*For it cannot be undone, and you are not the one who pays the price.*"

"By the Blessed." Daerith eyed me, and perhaps it was his aim to calm the conversation, for he spoke in southron. "I have never heard you speak so, *alkuine*, and would have thought you of gentler temper. *Valkataela* we should name you, for you hide your fire well."

As far as I could tell, the name meant the light from that which precedes thunder—poetic, but hardly hidden. Aeredh all but flinched; so did Floringaeld. Taeron's mouth turned down at both corners, but Naciel smiled as if well pleased.

"I invited you because your counsel is sought, Lady Solveig." Taeron's expression forestalled any interruption. "I would not keep any creature unwilling, did not the safety of my entire people rest upon it. And I would not send you forth from sanctuary either, for I think the Enemy knows another *alkuine* has been found."

A cold shiver rippled down my back. Arn tensed, and glanced down at me. Thick silence enfolded cloth, pillows, Elder, and Secondborn; pipe and harp, voice and drum faded in that tense hush.

"The Accursed One does not move against Dorael or Faeron-Alith yet, even with Nithraen gone." Tjorin spoke softly and nodded, as if confirming a private guess. "You were not tempted forth after the fall of your kinsman's city, as you came once before to the field. He does not know where the High-helm is, and that disturbs him."

Taeron clearly agreed, and if he was sour at his daughter's suitor seeing his meaning so clearly it did not show. "The Enemy's spies comb the lands around Dorael's edges; if I know of Aenarian's failing, so does he. The likeliest answer is that he is watchful, and furthermore keeping Faeron's land for last, hoping we act in haste."

"Or..." Naciel shook her bright head, as every eye turned to her. Rippling gold slipped over her shoulders, strands pooling in her lap. "We should go to Dorael, my father. Swift and silent, as we came here."

"Leave Laeliquaende?" Floringaeld's objection was swift. "Even with every secrecy, we would be discovered as we marched. Our children, our families, all our treasures—"

"Swift," she persisted, "and silent. What use is everything we have wrought if all our people perish? And if Aenarian dies of grief we may yet hold Dorael with or without the Cloak-Weaver's aid, and keep the Enemy penned."

"*Alkuine.*" The High-helm's gaze turned to me again. "You spoke with the voice of the Blessed before. What say you now?"

"I cannot force the gods to utterance, only accept what is given." And in truth I felt rather faint. I had seen the names upon maps— Dorael, Faeron-Alith, and even the blot called the Gasping. Dun Rithell did not merit a single mark; indeed, only the upper thread of our river showed at the very edge of the largest and oldest chart despite the fact that once our settlement had an Elder name and my mother's ancestors had marched forth to face the Enemy in mythical times.

Yet just this morning I had sung a saga even older than that. A vast weight of history threatened to crush me.

"Just so." Taeron showed no anger, nor any discomfort; he appeared simply thoughtful, though passing grave. "To issue forth prematurely may well cast us all into the Enemy's hands. He has not moved, and even *orukhar* find the season of melt difficult."

"*Made of mud,*" Daerith murmured. "*Yet they do not swim in it well.*" It sounded like a proverb; the Elder and Northerners each smiled grimly, but I suspect I merely looked blank.

"Solveig." Arneior spoke softly, and her woad glared in the tent's soft light. "I am reminded."

"Of what, my shieldmaid?" Another shiver went through me; I knew what those words meant, especially in that quiet, pitiless tone.

For it was her duty to remember what I said when prophecy was upon me.

"Just before we reached Redhill. You were delirious with the cold, and you spoke." My small one paused, as if unwilling, but a shieldmaid does not shy from duty. "It rang true."

"What did I say?" My mouth had turned dry as summerdust on the ancient paved road outside Dun Rithell's gates.

"*He knows I am here*," she quoted. "You said it more than once. And, *North, amid the ash*."

Daerith breathed something highly impolite in the Old Tongue, turning away; Aeredh's eyes burned. "So she did," the Crownless agreed, in a near-whisper. "I remember it too."

"*My brother.*" Eol sounded stunned. "*Perhaps he somehow...*" And if Arneior was pale, the heir of Naras now looked deathly ill, two feverish spots standing high on his cheeks and a ghost of stubble roughening his jaw.

"Do not let it trouble you so deeply, son of Tharos." The words held only kindness; Taeron Goldspear was indeed a lord worth following, for at that moment he sought to comfort a two-skin Secondborn. "The Enemy sees much with many spies, even among the birds and beasts."

"*Beasts.*" Eol half-swallowed the word, staring at the lowered tent-flap. His shoulders were rigid, and swelled under black cloth. "*Thus the Enemy cursed us, and it became truth.*"

"*Peace, my friend.*" Aeredh laid a hand upon the wolf-captain's arm, his fingers digging in—not harshly, meant to steady instead of wound. "Your house did not serve him then; you do not serve him now."

Charged silence descended, and perhaps the High-helm thought no more would be accomplished that afternoon. For Taeron rose gracefully from his seat.

"It is the first day of spring." The silvery fillet at his brow gave a single sharp flash as he moved. "Much has been said, and much must be thought upon at length. Yet this should not keep us from celebration, for many completed the course today and my daughter's joy must be shared with all."

With other fair words he dismissed the last council of Laeliquaende, and when he left the tent it was with his daughter and Tjorin, all smiling broadly to meet the gazes of their people. Floringaeld and

Daerith accompanied them; Aeredh ushered a silent, grim-faced Eol out.

Arn and I were left to our own devices, perhaps because I had been too bold. Still, I did not mind.

When we stepped forth into a bright warm afternoon, I was temporarily blinded. A hint of smoke reached me upon a soft cool breeze, though the Elder in that valley did not use open flame for heat. Still, a mortal blaze is cheersome, and I thought it likely some might gather around bonfires amid the groves and vineyards as the sun descended.

I was wrong, but I did not know it then.

Cups of springwine were pressed into our hands by passersby. Arn drank with a will, no doubt glad to be free of endless talk. I was troubled indeed, but there was nothing to be done.

No matter how much of their delicious vintage I poured down, a deep unphysical weariness remained. And I wondered much, as we were hailed by groups of Elder and invited to share some amusement or another, upon the words Arn had remembered. I could not say I had spoken them, being half-dead with cold before we reached Redhill, but I knew better than to doubt my shieldmaid.

I wondered as well upon the exact nature of Eol's curse, the illness of a faraway Elder high king, of gems even the Allmother's first child could covet. But there was nothing to be done at the present moment, and many were the voices calling.

I would chew these thoughts at leisure when we retreated to our quarters, I decided, and did my best to appear cheerful.

Hand in Hand

To be Wise is to serve, for power used selfishly sooner or later slips in the hand like a bad sword. A warrior may lose blood from such accident, but a volva *will lose far more.*
—Idra the Farsighted of Dun Rithell

The sun had dropped far into the west when we happened across Soren and Gelad, the former wearing his victory wreath at a rakish angle and the latter surrounded by half-a-dozen chattering Elder children, a small blonde girl perched upon his shoulders and calling in a babble of Old Tongue as her steed moved with an easy stride saying he had been put to such use before.

I had to laugh, and even Arn smiled. The littles immediately clustered her, and their questions came in swift succession, like wheeling starlings—how had she gained her spear, why did she paint her face, did other Secondborn women do as she did, what did her name mean? I translated as well as I could, suppressing no few chuckles, and she bore this interrogation with good grace. For once I was considered less interesting than my shieldmaid; had they been steading children I would have been pestered endlessly for small *seidhr*-tricks.

Finally Gelad lifted his rider earthward, and Soren sent the small ones on their way with a mannerly proverb in the Old Tongue about ducks returning to water. I took note, and also watched how they linked hands, filing away while singing in high sweet voices, the taller ones leading and following, the smallest protectively fenced.

"A mighty war-band." Gelad rubbed ruefully at his lower back. "I would almost rather face a *trul*."

"*Avert*," Soren replied, laughing, and made a gesture with his left hand to ward off ill-luck. "For once I am glad you are taller; I am a poor mount by comparison."

Arn watched the children disappear between a line of gaily colored tents, shading her eyes with one hand. Rarely was her grin so broad. "They are very well-behaved. But enthusiastic."

"And have never seen a shieldmaid." More laughter bubbled in my throat; I sought to keep it contained.

" 'Tis an impressive sight; we have none in the North." Soren attempted to straighten his wreath again; the wolf sigil at his shoulder wore its own lolling smile and the plain metal swordhilt over his shoulder winked through the crossings of leather cushion-wrapping. "A few more of your kind, my lady Minnow, and we might well need no armies at all."

She accepted the compliment with an amused salute, her armor glittering. "We are not so rare. There were two downriver from us at Dun Odynnslek, and we often heard tales of others to the south and east."

"*Seidhr* and shieldmaid oft go hand in hand." I lilted the words to the drinking song and my small one made a battle-face, sticking her tongue out and crossing her eyes as she used to before we both achieved our first blooding.

"Ai, what I would not give for some mead." She rolled her shoulders and smiled afresh; children make the rest of us feel young, as the saying goes. "These Elder draughts are well enough, but I long for something real."

"They are real enough, and healthful." Gelad tugged at his tunic's hem, settling the cloth. The slight disarray suited him, and his gaze held no shadow of fatigue. "If you are weary, simply drink more."

I did not think it would work, and in any case had no appetite. I looked to the far peaks, sparkling under sunlight no longer winter-thin but full of burgeoning richness. An invisible balance had tipped, and the breeze held softness it had not before dawn.

"I am surprised our Minnow is not watching the sword-dancing." Soren's heavy eyebrows raised. "There are archery contests as well; Efain has been called to judge a few."

"Sword-dancing?" Arn immediately turned to me. "That sounds promising."

The thought of another crowd, even Elder-fair and agelessly polite, threatened to throttle me. "I see no reason why you may not view such a wonder, small one. I will be well enough returning to our quarters."

"There is no danger." Soren even bowed in my direction, very like an Elder guard though he risked losing his circlet entirely. "We are in Laeliquaende, and should you need escort—"

"I thank you for your pains," I hurried to answer, "but 'tis not necessary. I can find the city, and am passing certain I can also find the palace within it. One need only look up to catch sight of the spires, after all." A few short hours with my own thoughts seemed a wondrous gift, for all I was unused to truly solitary pursuits. Always, at Dun Rithell, there was Arn.

And I had not been alone during our journey save upon one of the first fogbound nights. The memory of that evening spent in freezing vapor was still terrible.

"Solveig…" Arn hesitated, weighing duty to her charge against the prospect of witnessing a new form of combat-play.

"Go." I laid my hand upon her arm—after all, she had not even attended Dun Rithell's last riverside fair, overseeing the stacking of the solstice bonfire with my mother's steward instead. I wondered how Hopfoot was faring, and the thought caused another momentary pang. " 'Tis a festival day, after all; there is no danger. No riverside fair to tempt me either, and I hardly think I shall be accosted by more Elder children, for I am very dull to them indeed. I shall return to our quarters, or to the riverbank. Some part of me lingers upon the water, I think, and I must call it back."

"I can still feel the oars as well." Gelad spread his hands to show as much, though little trace of blister remained upon him either. "This is a safe place, my lady Minnow. Our *alkuine* will suffer neither insult nor injury among Taeron's folk."

"I doubt I shall meet very many, in any case." I gave Arn a gentle push. "Go. You performed a wonder this morn; take some well-deserved amusement."

Arneior decided it was permissible, and her brow smoothed. "No less than you, my weirdling. Take care."

"I shall," I promised. "And I expect a full report upon your return."

So it was that I left behind the sound of rejoicing. I did intend to return to the city, but my feet were drawn in another direction. I found the beach where the race had ended deserted save for the boats pulled high upon agate-strewn sand. The sound of water slid past, soothing the ragged edges of my subtle selves.

Our craft was where we had left her, in no danger of entering—or even touching—the river. I climbed into her; she was full of westering sunshine and I was able to stretch out upon her damp floor, feet flat and knees up. I arranged my hands upon my breast and exhaled, tension falling away.

The day swirled inside my head, from the massive *seidhr*-effort of the morn to the council in Taeron's tent. Arn did not seem to think my outburst unreasonable, and so long as my behavior met her approval I did not worry overmuch for anyone else's estimation. Clearly these matters would be discussed again, the next time the High-helm summoned us to a meeting.

It seemed a lingering way to do business, but then again, the Elder had all the time in the world.

There were other, darker thoughts to be weighed as well. It was fantastical, absurd—the Enemy, the Allmother's firstborn, the great brooding thing even mighty Elder feared, knowing of *me*?

Even if I could not fully believe, I could still feel wariness at the prospect. And perhaps a tinge of outright fear.

I thought I would continue chewing over the discussion, but the river's voice was so soothing. The sun dropped and the sky was fathomless above me, its color deepening from winter paleness to a softer tint. I could have been on Dun Rithell's green at the end of a late-spring day, listening to the small voices of growing grass, small animals, and the distant mutter of a sheep-herd. Sounds of celebration reached me, but not in overwhelming waves.

My subtle selves nested more securely in my physical being. For the first time I felt wholly at peace in Laeliquaende, and I drifted into sleep.

Orange Stars at Twilight

> *To dream is not to wake*
> *Though to the Wise there is little difference.*
> —*Saga of the Third Riddle*

*T*he room was small and round; its stone walls had, by their look, known Elder shaping. A window-casement was clothed in dark wood; my glance was drawn to it, unwilling and yet compelled.

"No," the man standing near the hearth said. The fire in that cavern burned violent, vile yellow, and its heat lay wet upon every surface. "I would not risk a single feather of your plumage, little bird."

Gold was his hair and rich his raiment, though black as Northern cloth the latter was sewn along Elder lines, comfort and grace evident in every line as he turned from the flames. His hands seemed dipped in living metal—rings were stacked upon every finger, whether of plain ore burnished to a fine luster or bearing jewels both dull and glistering. Some of the gems stared at me, avid eyes drinking in every detail, and those gazes were foul as they crawled upon my skin. Over his knuckles other spider-thin strands were woven, the bands reaching his wrists, vanishing under black cuffs.

My heart beat clot-thick in my throat, the fine hairs standing high and hard all over me. Tiny sounds pattered upon the floor at my feet— broken beads, red coral singing faint high noises of stress before splitting, their cries semi-musical as they landed.

Knowledge trembled behind the thunder in my chest, a whirlpool of horror. For his face was a blankness, a softening mass like clay in warm running water, and I knew this creature was neither Elder nor Secondborn.

"Be not afraid," he continued softly, and the greater terror was how sweet and reasonable his voice was. "For my Eye hath been upon thee for a long while, and I have anticipated—"

I woke with a start, my mouth full of the taste of rotten ash, like the dregs of burning a diseased tree. There was a deeper thread of plain smoke upon the freshening breeze; at home 'twas a constant tang, for every Secondborn steading must have a fire or two and during most of our travels a small blaze was necessity at night.

Still, I had not smelled burning of branch or log since we left the Mistwood, and perhaps that is why I opened my eyes, staring at a sky not yet entirely drained of daylight.

The dream had fled, though a measure of discomfort lingered. Had Arn been with me I might have tried to name the nightmare, to describe some fragment, but she was not. I felt at my braids with trembling fingertips, for some reason, and was deeply comforted by familiar round or columnar red coral beads.

Why?

In the distance, Elder yet sang. The instruments still hummed, drum and pipe and string resounding, but the rhythm was a little slower. It sounded very much like the lull in a greathall while sleepy littles are taken to bed and older children make their formal fare-wells, practicing adult etiquette with somber care. Even the hounds would be surfeited upon scraps and finding places to catch a measure of slumber; the pigs would have been long since abed, awaiting morning slops.

I did not know how those of Laeliquaende spun their cloth, for I had seen neither goats nor sheep at grazing while roaming the valley with Naciel. Nor were there other kine, nor pigs or granary cats, and the only hounds I had seen among the Elder had been Caelgor the

Hunter's, in lost Nithraen. There were no pets in this valley, unless one counted the birds Elder sang to in the hedges and groves.

They do not cage the feathered—what need, when wild creatures will approach merely for their asking? The Children of the Star are friends to all free beings, though I thought they often disdained Secondborn too easily. The way of the flint knife, the pit, or the osier cage is not theirs, though we mortals received it from the gods themselves.

I blinked and stretched, the dream utterly vanished. Finally I felt wholly Solveig again, instead of half-dislodged from my own flesh.

The days had indeed grown longer. No stars glimmered overhead, though it could not be long before they appeared; the Moon waned, I knew, and would not show herself until deepnight.

Smoke-scent vanished as I sat up, reaching for the gunwales. Yes, it was evening; Waterstone shimmered in shades of pearl and cloud, snow and bleached linen. Seen from here the city was a floating dream, and when I looked elsewhere the river reflected the sky, her broad back smoothly rippling as distant rapids added embroidery to the music's long unwinding.

It was beautiful. I rose from the boat, stretching again. At that moment I could forgive anything—being pried from my home, the terrors of our travels, even being held against our will no matter how safely. I was so rarely alone, and though Arn was a familiar comfort I was glad to be a solitary witness to this aching wonder.

The sand gave easily under my slippers. I reached the embankment, and found an easy flight of stone stairs to the small terrace Taeron had stood upon to watch our victory. Perhaps it was ill-mannered to use the vantage, but the thought of seeing the river, its opposite bank, fields and the long shadows of groves starred with Elder lanterns, and the far peaks still holding the last scraps of the day... well, it called to me, and I deliberately did not raise my head as I achieved the balcony. I walked to the iron balustrade, laid fingertips upon its cold support, and only then let my gaze lift.

It did not disappoint. Elder families lingered outside their dwellings amid the blue glitters of their lanterns, and the wind was full of faraway voices. A piercing settled in my chest, sweet and longing at once. The snow-gilded peaks floated silver instead of white, and as I watched they turned shadowed, for the Sun had left upon his nightly journey through the underworld and the star they called *Maedroth*—the Watchful, like Taeron's sister-son—began to glimmer over the mountain they called the Protector, *Aeredhe-il.*

In that moment I loved the valley and its shimmering heart. It happened all at once, a thrill shooting through every nerve, and had I been asked to stay until I died I would have gladly agreed. Especially if I could stand here every year after others won the race, alone and whole, watching the day fold softly, seamlessly into night.

Twilight deepened. My eyes welled, blurring, and the sky was a deep aching blue—not woad and not indigo, but perhaps either dyed fast into good cloth and after a few years' worth of washing, a hue soft and endless. It looked almost like a summer sky, and I thought it might after all be almost pleasant if Arneior and I were here to see another solstice, a brief bright night full of hay-scent and easy warmth.

Another hint of smoke touched my nose. Suddenly uneasy, I blinked several times. Hot water slid down my cheeks; I wiped it away and rubbed my eyes like a child staving off weariness in order to hear a few more tales at the feast.

Upon the dark mountainslopes, stars appeared.

At first I thought it a new manner of Elder celebration. Then I wondered, for the orange gleams arranged themselves into lines, and were definitely, swiftly moving. Rivers of sparks poured down, and the burning scent upon the breeze intensified.

Fires? Maybe, but...torches? They have the lanterns, why do they use open flame?

I watched, puzzled. I had dreamed of this, yes, and awakened screaming; Arn had dreamt of orange stars too. Perhaps it was merely some strange custom, and yet...

A deep tolling cut across the music, floating uneasily with the smoke upon the back of swirling wind. More orange stars appeared, but larger—smears, instead of pinpricks. They clustered at the foot of the glittering streams, and I realized the rhythmic notes were bells in the city's towers, sounding in unison. Singing faltered into confusion, and I gripped the metal before me, hands aching.

I began to hear cries among the tents. *To arms, to arms!* Running feet, shouts, and the clanging of metal. Over it all the bell-strikes mounted in furious cascade, the city sending peals of warning in every direction.

The yellow-orange gleams were flaming brands in the hands of *orukhar* and other foul things, for the dreams had been a warning neither I nor my shieldmaid deciphered in time.

The Enemy had found Laeliquaende.

PART THREE

CITY BETRAYED

Small Trinkets

For many long years the Enemy searched, and could not find. What dark joy must have been his when news of the traitor was brought; what foul glee must have filled the ironbound heart! He refrained from movement for some short while, for little gives evil greater pleasure than brooding upon the ruin of its victims.

—Gaeran the Vine-singer, *Lament*

I do not know how long I stood, numbly gripping a cold metal balustrade. Orange pinpricks raced along, flame passed from hand to hand—while darkness fell and the Elder celebrated, attackers had infiltrated, veining the valley's margin with unlit torches. Outlying halls, cottages, wineries, and other structures fell swiftly and were set alight.

Even the ravens upon the peaks, bringing Taeron word of the outside world, had not seen the Black Land's forces. Tucked so close to that dread place was a certain safety, yes—the Spur, as Laeliquaende's mountains were called, came from the Marukhennor both high and broad, fading into a long chain of hills running between Nithraen and Dorael—but only so long as the Enemy did not know precisely where to strike.

The deep blue of twilight gave way to a shadow stretching from the north, blotting out weak, wavering stars. It was not merely physical, that darkness; an ill *seidhr* wove through as it unfurled. It followed the torchlit companies as they ran, the vanguard full of hardy *orukhar* chosen for size and speed, their pale hides now safe from the assault of sunshine and their heavy swords with triangular flags at the tips whistling. *Kwiseirh* the Elder called that sound, deeper and far more terrible than a grappling-arrow's song.

Moving swiftly between marching columns as they fanned across the valley floor came smaller ashen-skinned fighters smeared with crimson paint, straddling noisome mounts bred in vast kennels under Agramar. The scale-covered things were vaguely doglike in shape, ferociously clawed and fanged, selected for viciousness and speed, trained for war, and encouraged to consume the flesh of fallen foes.

The bells were a welter of confusion, sounds of flight and havoc mounting. Yet I was in a small space of silent stunned calm, a floodborne branch temporarily wedged between rocks. I could not move, watching the approaching disaster and unable to guess at its true dimensions.

More cries, now drawing closer. The music was gone, shivered into fragments, and the sound of the river could not surmount this chaos. I might have stayed there mired in horror longer yet, if not for movement at the edge of my vision, a shadow suddenly looming.

My heart leapt into my throat, and perhaps I made some sound as I was spun, hands clasping my upper arms bruising-hard. A stray reflection showed a face, blue eyes near incandescent and stark fear leaping in my chest like a spark to dry tinder.

Aeredh held me pinioned for a moment, his gaze searching, and his lips moved slightly. I did not know what he said, but his expression was terrible even as it turned to relief scarcely less intense than previous fury. The breath left me in a rush, and the Crownless did a strange thing.

His grip changed; he pulled me forward, off-balance. A brief, clamp-grip hug, the sudden warmth of his body underscoring how the wind from the water had turned cold by degrees—I had not noticed, for gradual changes creep upon one slowly as a hunting granary cat.

Aeredh let go, but only to seize my hand. "Come." He had to

shout over fresh tumult; those a little farther from the city were now attempting to reach its safety. "Come with me."

I could not have gainsaid him, and indeed never thought of it. He near lifted me off my feet and drew me between two tents, their fabric sides trembling as the breeze rose.

We plunged into a stream of hurrying Elder. In such a crush one may be thrown down and turned to paste, people turned to senseless beasts by terror. But the Elder held fast to one another, the taller bearing up the slighter and shorter, so we were carried along much as the boat had ridden riverspray that morn.

The road's shining pavers were lost under a crowd. A young dark-haired child sobbed, standing at the wayside, until a passing guard scooped her into armored arms and vanished with more-than-mortal speed, his boots flickering. Aeredh aimed us between groups of running Elder, seeming to know when and how they would separate. Small glittering ornaments fell from hair or wrist, neck or finger, many breaking against the stone; a tent collapsed, its lines snapping with high sweet sounds.

I was breathless, shaken, and surprised the slippers were not torn from my feet. But they hardly touched the ground; such was the son of Aerith's effort that the high narrow northwestron gate of Laeli-quaende swallowed us well before the vast vineyards of Tahn Emael were set ablaze.

The bells echoed through every stone-paved valley between buildings. Elder were hurrying to the armories, rushing to the walls. Some attempted to impose a measure of order upon the throngs streaming through the gates, and were nearly drowned out or buffeted from their feet. But Aeredh carried me along, and a dizzying succession of houses, workshops, repositories, arcades, and other structures blurred by upon either side until finally the palace loomed above us. Such was its size that when we raced through a postern—a guard with a set expression under his tight-buckled helm recognizing us both, a naked blade in his grasp full of faint blue steelglow—the clamor was muted somewhat.

I finally gained some breath and a measure of wit. "Arn," I said, and sought to arrest our wild career. "*Arneior!*" I might as well have attempted to halt a landslide with a single piece of firewood.

Aeredh glanced down at me, a single flash of blue. "Naciel," he said, and it was one of the few times I ever heard him breathless. "Or Eol. They will care for her."

No, I am her charge, and she will be looking for me. I attempted again to stop, but he took little notice, like a mother with a resisting youngling. "Stop! Aeredh—"

"Soft, gift-of-the-Blessed. I will let no harm come to thee." Our speed diminished, a garden's cool dimness enfolded us. The bells still pealed, and the city trembled, but as we finally slowed a fountain could be heard and a green hill, silvered by twilight, rose underfoot.

At its crown, bone-white, a doorless tower reared.

⬤⬤⬤⬤⬤

My skirts swung heavily as he set me down, and I staggered. Aeredh moved to steady me, but I struck his hand away, an instinctive recoiling. His arm fell to his side, and in the shadow I could barely see his face. Just those eyes, like blue gems.

"Solveig." How did he sound so gentle, even as his ribs heaved? He recovered far more swiftly than a mortal would. "The Enemy has found this place, by what means I know not. It is no longer safe."

Orange stars. I shuddered. *Seidhr* had indeed warned me of this— but not with enough clarity. "Yet you dragged me here."

"Carried, I would say." He glanced over my shoulder, a flicker of motion. His hair was a dark mass. "It will take time for them to breach the city, and even more to break into the palace. But we should hurry."

"Should we not flee?" I backed away—a single step—and froze when his hand twitched as if he would restrain me, the small movement visible even in the gloaming. "I must find Arn; Eol will be looking for you. Why are we here?" I wanted to add, *of all places,* or something even less mannerly.

Was he planning on ridding the world of an *alkuine* to keep her from his Enemy's forces? The thought would not leave me, and I took another cautious rearward step.

"I know you do not trust me. But listen, please." He did not move;

the swordhilt rising over his shoulder was familiar from our journey, though he sometimes had not carried it in the palace.

Had he suspected this might happen? I could not remember if he had worn it to the council in the great tent, and that bothered me.

It is not like a *volva* to forget such a detail.

I sought to order my thoughts, control my ragged breathing. "The tower has no windows, no doors. Only the king knows the secret of its opening." My voice shook. "I can do nothing here; we must flee. And quickly."

"Taeron is not the only one who knows the secret, now." Aeredh still did not move, but I sensed readiness quivering in him, a serpent-spring coiled tight, waiting for release. "You and your shieldmaid aided Tjorin son of Hrasimir, and he asked a boon of the High-helm. You were not present during the event."

Waterstone's bells rang frantically, no longer in complete unison. The clamor, though distant, still pressed against ear and throat, constricting my lungs. "He wanted to marry Naciel," I whispered.

"I thought he would ask for that too." An easy shrug, as if Aeredh did not after all care about a union between one of his kind and my own. "But the princess informed her father she was already wed, whether he willed it or not, and Tjorin asked for summat else."

"No. I wanted to help him, not you." The truth bolted from my mouth like a panicked horse, and the Crownless outright flinched.

The ageless, immortal Elder who had driven away a lich upon the road to Nithraen, who had carried me through the killing cold, stiffened and shrank slightly. As if I had struck him.

When he spoke his tone was measured, though urgency burned behind each word. "I did not ask Hrasimir's son for this manner of aid, though I suspect you will not believe me. I assumed Naciel would tell you after the celebration was over, we did not think— please, Solveig, I beg of you, we have no time. I know how to gain entrance to Taeron's tower, and inside it you will find one of Faevril's masterworks. I ask that you bring it forth, so we may take it—and you—to a place of greater safety."

"Oh, is that your plan? To move me from one Elder prison to the next, along with this weapon you wish me to wield? I cannot,

Aeredh. I will not." I turned, though there was little hope of fleeing him—and if I did, where would I go? I had to find Arneior.

We might yet be able to run, swift as Naciel had taught us, for the Hidden Passage and the Ice Door beyond. The guards there might not gainsay us under these conditions. Perhaps they would even be glad to see our backs.

"Solveig." Aeredh lunged, and his hand closed around my right arm. He did not squeeze, but the strength in Elder fingers is such that he could easily snap a bone if I attempted to break free. "'Tis not for myself I ask. The Enemy cannot wield what he has taken, for even when he had all the Jewels—harken to me, I know not what the things are capable of, for Faevril never said and before they were stolen…" His grip was iron, though it did not bruise, and I sought frantically to pull away. "Stop, Solveig. Listen. The Enemy does not merely wish to reclaim Lithielle's prize. He will want you as well, and if you think me cruel it is nothing to what he will do if his servitors acquire you."

I leaned away from him, uselessly, with no more chance of escape than a rabbit deep in a wolf's jaws. *Acquire* me?" Like a thrall, a sheep traded between halls—

"He does not send the Seven to fetch small trinkets, my lady, and we were hunted by more than one of those riders all through Mistwood and the Glass." Aeredh set me gently upon my feet again, and the only thing more frightening than the strength in his grasp was the care he must have taken not to mark my mortal flesh. "The Enemy knew of you well before we reached Redhill, probably before we reached the Eastronmost. I suspect that was why he attacked Nithraen after many hundred years of waiting, and why he has not yet moved against Dorael or Faeron's lands." He looked up again, scanning our environs; the garden was deadly quiet. Once more I was in a bubble of hush while the world outside disintegrated into chaos. "It is not for myself I ask, Solveig of Dun Rithell. It is to save your people as well, for if we are defeated the Enemy will reach out his hand to the South and beyond. Would you like me to beg? I will, upon my knees or even my face. Please, *alkuine*." He had never sounded thus before—pleading, desperate—in all our journeying. "Help me. Help us, and your own mortal kind."

"You could have simply asked me to travel hence," I whispered. "To take up this thing. You could have explained." Still, would I have believed him in Dun Rithell? Or even at Redhill? At Nithraen?

"Could I?" The inquiry was sharp, almost as a shieldmaid prodding her charge to proper behavior. "Our errand to the south was urgent and secret enough, for we knew the Enemy was stirring. Once we found you…I do not know if whispers of your existence had already reached him by then, for his spies are everywhere. And once we arrived here I thought it best to give you what peace could be found, for your grief and weariness were plain." His shoulders softened, and so did his tone. "I thought we had more time."

The bellsong changed once more—no less strident, but a pattern asserted itself. "What is that?" My lips were numb. The rest of me, limbs and central pillar, could not decide whether it was warm or cold, trembling or still.

"Closing the city gates, I think." At least *he* had some certainty, some idea of what was transpiring. It was an unexpected comfort. "We must be swift. Please, Solveig. Will you enter the tower?"

Once more upon that terrible day an Elder and I resonated like twin strings, and such was the Crownless's desperation that he was laid open to my *seidhr*.

His despair was real enough, a creeping dark flame eating at bone and vitals alike. He was not like Taeron, winterwine refined to clear stinging strength. The cold blue glow of Elder suffused the son of Aerith, subtle selves burning with inhuman vitality, and though he ever kept his counsel close at that moment he was almost transparent to me.

I do not know what it cost him, for baring yourself to that degree is never comfortable. But I found that he believed what he said to be true, and furthermore, that he regretted what he had done to me. That remorse lay cheek-by-jowl with another feeling, one so strange and alien-powerful I retreated from it with all the speed my own *seidhr* granted, lunging away.

It was a purely internal movement, for my physical self could not stir a single step.

His hand fell to his side. "Please," he repeated, and behind the word in my tongue lay the older form in his, vibrating low and broken. "*I beg of thee, my lady. The Enemy's forces approach. You are the only hope.*"

I would have looked to Arneior to see what I should do, but she was elsewhere—and now I had only one hope as well, that she was not outside the city searching for me amid a tide of fell creatures. The sheer number of orange flame-pricks and streaks flowing downhill into the valley defied belief.

I had seen what just a few *orukhar* could do. What if there were *trul* as well? Liches, whether of the Seven or the lesser kind? What else would the Enemy send?

"If I take this thing, we will find Arn? And flee?" I sounded very small, even to myself.

"Naras will care for your shieldmaid; they do not leave their own behind." He said it with such certainty the strange sense of comfort returned, though it vied with sharp ale-bubbling fear. "Naciel is no doubt with her now. Take heart, my lady."

My gaze was drawn to the glowing, secretive tower. I had to turn in order to regard it, and Aeredh must have taken the movement for agreement, for he passed me, and climbed the gentle hill.

I had little choice but to follow.

<hr />

Of the word the Crownless spoke to open Taeron's tower all the sagas are silent, and I must be as well for 'tis not mine to say. When it was uttered the hush became thick for a moment, almost cloying, but the silvery cries of Laeliquaende's bells pierced through in many places until, threadbare, the dread quiet drained away. All that remained was an open archway at the tower's base, black as the sides and spire glowed milky.

Aeredh moved aside, and I stared at the entrance. The darkness seemed almost a living thing, and it occurred to me that perhaps he could seal me inside and leave, escape the city; if the building could not be reopened, the Enemy would find both Elder trinket and mortal *alkuine* beyond his grasp.

As if he heard my thoughts, Aeredh drew. His sword's blade, dappled Elder steel, gave the same faint blue radiance the palace guard's had; I had seen it before, albeit much brighter, when the Crownless did battle with a lich.

I froze, staring at him.

"*It might be treachery*," he said, softly, and the Old Tongue made the blade scintillate. "If so, my lady, whoever betrayed Laeliquaende might think to come here—and if not, one or more of the Enemy's servants may yet appear. I will guard the door for you." He paused. "But I would ask you to be swift as you may."

Still, I hesitated. The bells rang, and rang.

He said nothing else. Perhaps he sensed my struggle; there was no shieldmaid to look to, nothing but the confusion in my own heart.

I mistrusted him, yes, even despite the *seidhr*-granted glimpse of his regret. The far greater difficulty was myself.

After all, I had been inwardly, secretly pleased at the chance of adventure, though I never truly wished to leave the comfort of home. And I had chosen his hidden destination instead of Dorael, telling myself it was for my hard-won allyship to Naras instead of my buried desire to see what few other mortals had. Not only that, though. Who but myself had gained Tjorin's victory upon the river, for Arn would not have stirred a single step to grant aid if not for my decision?

And Eol of Naras might not have lent his back—and the backs of his men—had I not pressured them.

Now a tower none but an Elder king had entered was opened, and even if Faevril's *taivvanpallo* had threatened to consume me, what was inside this place could only be used by an *alkuine* and they told me there was no other.

Oh, the son of Aerith had hidden his purpose, and Eol had aided him with surpassing loyalty. But my own striving for glory had done far more than either man, and blinded me to much greater degree. I could not blame them for what I was about to do. All my show of unwillingness was simply that, a pretense to salve my own wounded pride.

I did not fear the thing in the tower, nor did I quail at the thought of being the only *alkuine* in the world. I longed to test myself against the Elder thing even as I dreaded the event, for my fear lay elsewhere.

It was not the gem that frightened me, but the specter of yet another failure.

You wish to be great, my teacher Idra had oft chided, and I heard her again upon that hill, before that darkened door. *Ambition is good, for those with the weirding must ever strive. Yet it is also poison—a little may be healthful, too much and you will rot as your* seidhr *twists within you.*

My hands were fists. The bells kept ringing, and though they were muffled they filled my skull to brimming. I could not think clearly, and fear clawed at my throat.

Aeredh gazed past me, his blade glowing in the dark, and—terribly, with faultless Elder politeness—he left me to make the only possible choice I could.

A Cloak and a Casket

Then did Lithielle give both treasures to the king, for even the bliss of the West palled against her grief. "Do not thank me," said she. "These things are a burden, shifted to your back. For that I am sorry."

Thus did Taeron reply, "I and my house shall bear it uncomplaining, daughter of Melair. Rest, for you have performed great deeds."

Like gems were the tears of Aenarian's child. "There is no rest for me. For my love is gone to mortal death, and I cannot follow…"

—Saga of the Great Quest

What did I expect? Stairs, certainly, winding around the tower's interior, and at the summit something unspeakable.

Instead, the darkness in the archway parted like a curtain, and I stepped onto flat black stone. The interior was curiously spacious, but breathlessly still. The curved inner wall was black too, and highly polished. What light there was came from tiny blue pinpricks like stars caught in the glossy depths of stone both underfoot and sheathing the tower's inside; for a single vertiginous moment it seemed I had been cast into a void sprinkled with weak candleflames. I swayed, my Elder-woven skirts whispering, and almost went to my knees.

It was utterly quiet, the silence thick as cold butter. No bell-clamor, no running feet, no cries.

The void over my head bore dim dry star-glimmers as well, but I could not tell if they were upon a roof or if the interior walls simply met at some point high overhead. I wondered how any air could enter this place.

A shadow in the round room's exact center was a gloss-glassy pedestal, thankfully not full of wavering light-dots. Atop it rested an indeterminate shape. To the side was a clothing-stand of the type I had seen in our palace quarters, and upon its spread wooden arms rested a living darkness, distinct in shade and composition from the rest.

The thing upon the stand was a hooded cloak of Elder design, I decided, and approached with caution. If I focused on the shapes lacking starry glitters, I could move without nausea. I even dared to touch the garment, and it felt just like ordinary Elder cloth—if anything that folk made could ever be called *ordinary*.

This close, I could also see what the pedestal held. A coffer, two of its sides slightly too long for the whole to be called a square. It appeared to be constructed of dark iron, with intricate designs deep-carven upon each side. The top was sealed, but there were intimations it could slide free; so much I saw, bending close enough my breath touched metal and stone.

'Twas not very large—at its longest, it measured roughly from the tip of my longest finger to the meat of my forearm, avoiding the hollow of my elbow. Was this what the Enemy sought, what the Elder prized enough to hide so thoroughly? My *seidhr*-senses swept the tower's interior as Idra had taught me, but whatever was in the iron box was silent and the cloak merely whispered, its hem ruffling.

What if Taeron hid the thing elsewhere? A grand jest that would be. I tried not to think upon what was happening outside. My hands shook like pale leaves as I brushed the cloak with reverent fingertips. Aeredh had asked me to bring out what was here, but...

Perhaps this was a test of some kind? I looked to the doorway, a blank black slice in the starry night just as opaque from this side as without. The silence was stifling. Had he closed the door?

We had escaped the wrack of Nithraen through tunnels much

darker than this, but the men of Naras had an Elder lantern to keep the underground night at bay. My breath came short; I had never been afflicted like Albeig with the fear of close spaces before the wrack of that city.

Now all I could think of was the door sealing. Of being left alone in here, starving in the dark. Or I might die of suffocation before then, saving both Enemy and Elder all the trouble a lone mortal *alkuine* represented.

There could be more elementalists, I told myself. But I did not believe it, and my own arrogance was the deadliest trap of all.

I gathered the cloak in my arms. My hair was still damp from the bath, caught in coral-starred braids that suddenly felt far too tight. My hand closed upon the coffer; I paused, expecting something to happen.

Nothing. The quiet, star-ridden night inside Taeron's white tower did not change.

The iron casket was cool but not cold, and whatever was inside it slept. Yet a faint tremor passed through my bones, like a small animal nestling *seidhr*-struck upon a *volva*'s cupped palm, and I sucked in a harsh breath.

Outside a valley was under attack, a city waiting for siege, an Elder man standing guard. My shieldmaid was somewhere without me, and so were any friends I had in this place. All those things were terrifying.

But that slight feathery quiver was far worse, simply because I *recognized* it, though I had never felt its like before. It was as natural as the weirding in me, as intimate as my own pulse.

The casket did not weigh much. I picked it up, again expecting some noise or disturbance as it left polished stone. How many mortal years had it sat here? Did the thing inside it wait, or was it insensate?

There was no dust in this place, I realized, and that fact unnerved me more than any Elder weirding.

I turned, trying not to look at the starry walls, and hurried for the deep black void that meant escape.

I was afraid I would simply run into blank stone, that Aeredh had sealed the tower and left me behind. Instead, I plunged into a cool spring evening, and the scent of smoke was now much stronger—or I was now noticing it afresh after being granted brief respite. The reek of burning fair slapped me as I gasped, my arms full of soft dark cloth, and whatever was inside the coffer vibrated uneasily.

"Solveig?" Aeredh steadied me with one hand, holding his blade well down and away. *"Thank the Blessed, I was half afraid…"*

"There were no stairs." After the tower's dimness the garden seemed almost bright as noon, and the sound of distant bells nigh unbearable. For all I disliked what the Crownless had done, I was also deeply, cringingly grateful he had not closed the door. The two feelings fought for me, and I heartily wished they would find other prey. "Only this—a cloak of some kind, and a casket. Take it."

I pushed the iron box in his direction; Aeredh sheathed his sword with a sudden graceful movement, denying the gift. *"Lithielle's Shroud,"* he said, softly. *"Woven of shadow itself."* He cleared his throat, and shifted to southron. "Here. Let me."

In a trice he subtracted the fall of material from my trembling arms, shook it—no dust flew from its folds, either, but a ghostly sweet scent billowed free, cleansing the burgeoning burn-stench—and cast it about my shoulders. I found the sleeves; it was cut very much to complement an Elder gown underneath its flow.

A mantle then, not a cloak.

"There," he continued. *"No gaze may pierce this veil, said she, and the night itself agreed."* The phrase held an odd rhythm, as of saga or song, and he fastened the mantle's laces swiftly while he intoned it.

"I do not—" Again I tried to push the iron box into his hands, but he avoided its bestowal once more, stepping gracefully away like a granary feline disdaining a bit of tripe. "Aeredh, take this thing. I do not like how it feels."

"Lithielle's Jewel, and the first thing you can think of is to give it away?" Wry humor tinted his southron, and he let out a sharp breath. I had oft heard my brother make the same noise, bracing himself for a task requiring both strength and attention. "Come, *alkuine*. Now we must escape."

"Arneior." The shadowy mantle dragged upon the ground, having been made for one much taller—of course, I had not even Astrid's height—and I still held the iron box awkwardly at arm's length, as if afraid it would spring to life and bite like Lokji's serpent-dagger. "I cannot leave without her."

"I would not expect you to." He might have said more, but his chin lifted and he whirled. His sword reappeared, whispering free of its home; the blade's soft glow was eerie, for it cast no shadow as even faint starlight will.

"Solveig?" a different voice whisper-called, fierce for all its restraint, and a great flood of scalding relief filled me from toes to braids. "Sol, are you here?"

'Twas my shieldmaid, and to this day I owe Naciel Silverfoot much indeed, for she had found my Arn amid confusion and shepherded a mortal shieldmaid through the crush at the city gates just before they closed.

The first *orukhar* riders had reached Laeliquaende's walls.

Haugr and Lich

Open battle does not thrill them, for the servants take after their master. What they relish is falling upon the unwary, overwhelming the unknowing. There is no shame in subterfuge, for war is war—but the lord of the Black Land does not fight for aught but domination, and his thralls only out of fear and the lust for pillage and rapine.

—Aenarian Greycloak, *Aphorisms*

W*e must make for the southron quarter,"* the princess said, urgently. *"Come, this way."*

The palace of Taeron Goldspear was curiously deserted, holding only soft light from unheeded lamps, the wavelike song of distant cries, and the throbbing of bells. The guards were called to the walls and other points to provide direction, for though the king thought his secrecy secure he still required his folk to practice for emergency, and his warriors had not forgotten readiness.

"Riding a giant wolf." Arn was not breathless but flushed, and a faint sheen clung to her forehead. "Or it looked doglike, but it had scales and smelled surpassing foul. Efain leapt upon it; Gelad shouted that I was to find you, so I ran."

"Tjorin? And your father?" Aeredh was upon my other side, and between him and my shieldmaid all I had to worry about was

clasping the iron box to my chest, sharp corners digging through cloak and layers of Elder dress.

"My father charged me with finding the alkuine, *and rendering any aid I might."* For once Naciel was not barefoot, her slippers moving over carpet, stone floor, or inlaid wood with hardly enough force to draw a whisper. Her skirts rustled, running with silvery gleams, and her hair shone. *"My husband has his own work; this was not entirely unforeseen. Yet I wonder..."*

"They were closing the gates." Arn glanced aside, but there was no motion in the hall we ran past; we plunged down a short staircase and out of golden palace-glow into yet another shadowed garden. "I think most Elder are inside, but there was a child screaming and..." She shuddered as she ran; my own heart sank in response.

The shadowmantle swirled, and the cloth was strange. It seemed to drink light, not even giving back the faint sheen of well-woven stuff. In garden gloom it turned wholly indistinct, as if I had no body. If I gazed at my feet only the tips of my slippers peeking from under the too-long hem were visible, popping in and out of sight.

Such weirding roiled even my stomach. So I did not look down.

"We are betrayed." Aeredh sounded grimly certain, and his sword scintillated, the blade alight and hilt clasped in his left hand, for his right was occupied with bracing me. *"Is there a secret way from the city?"*

"Naturally." Naciel turned aside, and we followed her as a pack of hounds at a rider's side. My bee-torc bumped my collarbones, and 'twas a good thing I had slept in the boat's embrace, for I felt oddly rested.

But very, very frightened. "Eol." Why was I not saving my breath for running? "The wolves. And the other Elder—Daerith, Kirilit—"

For though they were disdainful, the Elder from Nithraen had also suffered through Mistwood and the Glass with us, and had taken every care with their Secondborn companions. I misliked the thought that they might be left without aid in this fresh catastrophe.

"I do not know." Arn's jaw set, her hazel eyes alight and leather-wrapped hornbraids slapping armored shoulderblades. "The wolves may find us, but if not..."

"Here." Naciel turned again; the palace revolved around us, dizzying vistas in every direction. I had not seen a quarter of its glory,

but then, I had only been here some few moonturns. The thought—
How truly old is this place, I never asked—spun through my head
and away. "We will be in the streets soon, and you twain must stay
close. In the southron quarter, the Street of Ten Alleys—if we are
separated, Aeredh, look for the sign of the *kaelaia* bird."

Aeredh's grasp tightened upon my arm; I could not even wonder
if he would wield his blade left-handed. A wall reared before us, and
Naciel hardly paused before throwing wide an iron door, its outside
disguised with a thin veneer of white stone. We were suddenly in an
alley, other garden-walls funneling down a slim rock-walled throat.

Naciel slowed. The bells were ringing differently now, one set
jangling discordantly against the frantic music of the others. "*The
eastron gate has been breached*," she said, and the princess was pale
as a mortal, though her dark eyes burned. "Stay close, my young
friends. We may yet..."

The alley spat us onto a sloping, gently curved street lined with
yet more gardens and graceful pale houses. Their beautifully carven gates—wood or metal—were almost all askew, and the emptiness
was eerie. A tangle of bright color turned out to be a cloak wad-
ded against a blue-flowering shrub; a tiny, painted child's cart-toy,
already shattered, crunched under Arn's boot.

A patchwork of streets, and other living creatures appeared—at
first just single or paired Elder hurrying intently in one direction
or another, hardly seeming to see us or Naciel. Then small groups,
and finally crowd-streams as the streets widened into avenues, each
rivulet with a gleaming-armored guard at its head as well as a few
studded along its length to provide aid and guidance.

It was the first time I saw actual fear upon ageless faces. The few
children were somber, even older ones carried by an adult and the
very small clinging to their caregivers; despite that, none of them
wept save quietly, and their damp cheeks glistened in the soft glow
reflected from whitish stone. The similarities all Elder share—high
ear-points, prominent cheekbones, the shape of their eyes, the grace of
their movements—gives an unsteady feeling to any mortal observer.
Or perhaps only to me, for I was afraid as well, though I do not think
I was even so brave as the youngest of their little ones.

The press thickened; we cut across a broad pillared concourse. My head swiveled, I searched for any familiar face and found none. My feet tangled; I almost fell headlong, but Arn and Aeredh hauled me along like a piece of wet laundry.

Two things happened at once. The bellsong changed; one of its constituent voices was stilled. And Naciel halted between one step and the next, her golden head held high as a wary doe's.

Aeredh stopped too, and I was yanked savagely aside by Arn's continued motion before she came to rest, her spearblade dipping, giving a single venomous flash.

A ruddiness bloomed along the street to our left. Flames twisted, flattening as they streamed against stone, consuming even that resistant fuel in grasping finger-ropes. A cry went up from two cavalcades of fleeing Elder, for before them a hulking thing stamped, cracks radiating from its hooves. The *seidhr* it carried ribboned in corkscrews; it was taller than the moss-skinned thing we had seen near Nithraen.

And it *burned.*

One misshapen fist rose, and its whip was not a length of rope tarred with some excrescence but a heavy iron chain running with noisome yellowish flame. The weapon cracked, shearing through a mass of fleeing shapes, and the screams, by the gods, the *screams…*

This was the *haugr,* also sometimes called *belroch*—a taller, much stronger cousin to the *trul,* both horrors of the North. It howled, mouth widening, and inside its throat was sickly yellow-white flame, the heat smoking from its splitting, reeking hide enough to scorch-crack granite. It wielded a length of terrible chain in either fist, and its horns dripped with fire.

Yet that was not the only terror. Drifting past the monstrosity was a sable smear with a high-spiked iron helm, disdaining the heat with ease for it carried its own freezing. Its cloak spread, orange fire-glow stabbing through tatters, and where its mailed foot landed the paving split, caught between its cold and the *haugr*'s blaze.

The lich's helm rose, and two dim gleams in the void covering its face fastened unerringly upon me. It lifted a tarry-bladed sword, and struck down one of Laeliquaende's bright-armored guards with a sound unheard through fresh cacophony.

"*Go!*" Aeredh cried, letting go of my arm. He shifted his blade to right-hand as he ran with the swiftness of a young stag, somehow avoiding fleeing, maddened Elder. Screams rang in my ears.

I could not look away from those terrible, knowing gleams under that spiked, frozen iron helmet. It was not of the *nathlàs* or the greater liches we had met upon the Glass, but even the smaller variety of those undead horrors is terrifying enough. *Seidhr* snake-struck from it, but the Crownless was there, bright blade flashing blue as he turned aside the invisible attack, and he fell upon the thing like one of Odynn's own battle-mad warriors.

"Solveig!" Arn shrieked, and dragged me after Naciel. Clutching the casket to my chest, I sought not to be a burden.

We ran, hearts pounding and throats sour, for Laeliquaende was not merely sieged but breached.

⬕⬔⬕⬔⬕

Another bell-tower fell silent, but Naciel did not remark upon it, nor did she pause. Lightly the princess danced, through fleeing groups or empty, disarranged streets. We were not so swift, but she held her pace to one we could manage, though black flowers bloomed at the edges of my vision and even Arn was winded by the time we turned parallel to the high, thick outer wall of Waterstone's southron end.

Great columns of black smoke rose from various points in the city. Screams lifted alongside, and with the eastron gate shattered—and the northwestron treacherously left open, though we did not learn of that until some time afterward—many of the Enemy's fouler creatures swarmed through. *Haugr,* liches of both lesser types, other malformed monstrosities, all accompanied by countless *orukhar,* for their dread lord wished not just to siege but to wreak vengeance.

He hated the Elder, did the lord of the Black Land. He hated Faevril and his sons, hated the lords of Dorael and their kin of Nithraen. But Taeron Goldspear the High-helm he both despised and feared, for there was great prophecy of that line. Not only that, but once before the spike-helmed lord of a hidden fastness had arrived unlooked-for, dealing a stinging defeat at just the moment the Enemy thought triumph achieved.

The shimmering city was valiant; its warriors stood and died so others could flee. But the entire valley was ringed, and any hope of escape slim indeed.

Neither I nor my shieldmaid questioned our guide, in word or thought. We were wholly in her hands, and she led us at the edge of steadily expanding chaos. Bestial roars and forlorn wailing mixed with bellsong and the rush of flame as smaller streets branched from our course with the regularity of pine needles from a twig. She slowed, and I thought perhaps our goal was near…

…but there were ash-pale shapes before us, rearing out of the burning gloom.

This time Arn halted first, and I nearly ran into her. Naciel slowed, her skirts swaying, and it occurred to me she must be worried for Tjorin. Where was Eol? And Aeredh, facing that terrible burning thing and its undead-cold companion.

Before us were *orukhar*—a good half-dozen, ashen hides spattered with filth and gold-tinged Elder blood, their heavy iron armor pitted and scarred, spiked and deadly. The largest wore no helm; his hair was stiffened with chalk-ash, shaped into a high crest like some warlords of the far south past the Barrowhills were said to do with clay. That hulking captain grinned, showing strong polished teeth in a terrible mockery of merriment, and amid the hulking of the Enemy's most numerous servants was a much more graceful shape.

Maedroth the Watchful had laid aside his black cloth and armor. He was in silver and green, the velvet and silken garb of Laeliquaende's most noble citizens, and his gaze fastened hungrily upon Taeron's daughter.

One of the *orukhar* rumbled something in their strange, unlovely language; it bore little relation to the Old Tongue or southron. Yet I thought I discerned a shadow of meaning, for the phrase lifted interrogatively near the end.

"As you wish," Maedroth said in southron, enunciating clearly. "The smallest one is what your master wants. Leave the Elder; she is mine."

"*Cousin.*" Naciel's chin rose. The Old Tongue's word for their particular degree of close kinship was cold, and she spat it like a challenge. "*And who are these friends of yours?*"

Arneior's head cocked. "Solveig," she breathed. Her left arm lifted, and she pushed me back. I did not stagger, though my legs were caught between wishing to flee in any direction and realizing just how far we had already run. "Stay there, do you hear me? *Right* there."

She had never said the words so solemnly before. It was the caution of a shieldmaid who must know, absolutely, that her charge will not move during a battle—so she may defend what she has sworn to.

"I hear," I whispered, numbly.

"*Naciel.*" Maedroth's lips shaped her name almost tenderly, accenting it in the way of Laeliquaende's dialect. The *orukhar* moved, spreading out, and one or two made heavy snapping noises, champing their sharp, eggshell-colored teeth.

"*How could you?*" the princess whispered. "*My father trusted… You are his kin. Just this afternoon he defended—*"

"*I do not care.*" The Watchful's lip curled; he did not even glance at Arn or I, consigning us to whatever the Enemy's servants had in store. The iron coffer bit my arms and chest, and though the too-long mantle did not weigh upon me like my heavy green woolen one it was still a burden I would gladly shed if it would give us some chance of escape. "*I will take you to the forest where my father met my mother. Soon you will not even remember that mortal's name.*"

"*I would rather die,*" Naciel informed him, and drew herself up, a frail hedge indeed. One of the *orukhar* feinted in her direction, with a deep rumbling chuckle. She did not move, did not even glance at the foul thing. Perhaps her will clashed with Maedroth's in the way of Elder, their subtle selves engaging in combat more than merely physical.

I do not know. The screams in the distance mounted another fraction. Smoke now tainted every breath.

"Sol." Arn, again, grimly determined. "Sing."

What? I could barely breathe.

She tapped her spear-butt against the paving, and all of burning Laeliquaende echoed that single blow. The sound caromed off the buildings on either side, sadly watching this small drama amid larger ruin.

Then my shieldmaid gave a cry like those of the Black-Wingéd tasked with dragging malefactors to the underworld, and hurled herself into battle.

Shieldmaid's Rage

Do not name your weapon
Until the mighty deed is done.
—*The First Saga*, attributed to the hanging Odynn

She killed one while I stared, my mouth a dry cavern and pressure mounting behind my burning eyes—a lateral strike, spearblade a bright blur as it opened the throat of an *orukhar*, unerringly finding the weakness in its armor. She stamped at the moment of impact, driving through, and then she was among them, leather-wrapped hornbraids flying, a low deadly whistle as steel cut air.

Sing, she said. Fear clawed at my vitals. They were many and she was one, straight and slim and so vulnerable, avoiding a swordstrike by leaning aside so far she looked almost boneless, one booted foot flashing out to crash into an *orukhar*'s mailed knee. It gave with a crack like well-seasoned wood, and the creature howled.

I sucked in a smoke-freighted lungful. The thing in my arms quivered; had I been the same girl who left home as weregild several moonturns before, I might have frozen in terror, useless again.

After all, every other battle I had witnessed so far produced that reaction in me.

Yet I was no longer that Solveig. And just that morn I had infused laboring rowers with strength, as is a *volva*'s duty. Mortals with *seidhr* may not touch physical weapons, aye—but we are not helpless.

We merely do battle in a different way.

Another song burst from me in a gliding wave, weirding the color of bright-spilt blood. I tasted copper as it burst past my lips, and was dreamily surprised at the words and also at the voice, for it was not mine although it used me, nor was it the deep sonorous bell-thrum of divinity.

It came from some other realm, I know not where. Neither did I care.

Of shieldmaids I sang, a recitation of names from sagas and drinking-songs. First named was Astranna, wounded grievously after she took up her husband's spear to protect hall and children from the rampaging monster that had killed him, carried away by the Black-Wingéd when her battle was done. Of Greselint the Cruel, who killed thirteen treacherous warlords at her charge's own table after they broke the sacred law of hospitality and afterward dared any man to judge her; then came the traditional mention of Erlitha One-Eye, the first outright taken by the *valkyra* at birth, marked by miracles and battle all her days.

My voice flashed across paving, scattered a widening pool of oddly dark, exhausted blood spreading from Arn's first kill who had hardly touched earth, and jolted into my shieldmaid's back. *Seidhr* leapt between us, a flash like lightning amid clouds on a hot summer evening.

Arn whirled, avoiding another strike, her lips drawn back in a feral grin of effort. Her teeth gleamed fanglike, and the sound from her throat was not a battle-cry but a blood-trill, high sawing laughter as her spear flicked lizardtongue-quick to open an *orukhar*'s belly. A grey slither of intestines spilled forth, and such was the force of her strike that the creature's helmet was knocked free as well, ringing an oddly musical note upon the stones some distance away.

The silver flicker of a flung knife, but she twisted from its path with hipshot grace. I swayed too, her motion echoed in my own flesh, and *felt* the slice along her arm as a flag-tipped blade reached through the defense of her speed, glancing off mail and kissing just below the elbow.

Of Haskenior I sang, the defender of Aen Jaeran's lady Gwenhargra; they were not merely shieldmaid and charge but lovers, and when the latter died of old age the former climbed upon her pyre, making not a sound as the flames took them both to Odynn's halls. Brynhild the Fairest, Oestrelia Quickhand, Mecia the Bearded, Lette Darkling who could strike from shadow and vanish—their names and deeds rolled from my tongue as Arn's spear cleaved another *orukhar* from life.

She retreated a few steps, spear held loose as a lover's tender hand, its tip making tiny precise circles. The leader and two of his warband were left, spreading out to flank her, but my small one was not deceived.

The smaller pair of *orukhar*—both broad-shouldered, taller than even Aeredh—attacked from either side. Arn leapt, one boot smashing a filthy ash-pale face while her spear's blunt end cracked against the other's helm so hard blackened blood sprayed from the creature's mashed nose and contorted mouth. The skullsplit one was dead before his knees met stone, and Arn landed catfoot, spearblade singing as it batted aside the leader's heavy, ugly, *kwiseirh*-whistling sword.

Aino the Lonely, I sang, *who visited steadings in deepwinter to grant justice; Tiril Shipwright, who pretended dishonor for seventeen years to lull her charge's murderer before tearing his lungs out and murdering all his blood-brothers in a single night*. Of Sithir and Yalna I chanted, the words dropping from my lips like rain; I sang of shieldmaids both famous and obscure, and those of whom only the ghost of a celebrated name remains.

A shadow darted alongside the battle, but I had no time, breath, or attention to spare. Arn pressed forward, the crested *orukhar* seeking to bring his greater weight to bear. His only remaining helper sought to attack from the side, but her spear's blunt end struck the sword from that creature's hand almost contemptuously. She stamped as she lunged, but the crested one staggered back, saving himself just in time, and his companion darted in with a knife.

My shieldmaid leapt sideways like a fish dragged from the river, landing light as a leaf. My voice throbbed; I sucked in another starving breath, my eyes falling half-closed.

Her spear whirled in a semicircle, the blade flicking forward to bury itself in the smaller one's eye. The crested one saw his chance and lunged, but I shrieked of Rekhilde the Cold who fought with her bare breasts woad-painted and of Caes the Maiden, taken by the Wingéd though she had been born shaped as a son, charged with protecting Gwenhaelm the Small who spoke to the dead during the Years of Grieving.

Arneior tore her spear free. Her face was blank-shining with trust and effort both, her woad-stripe a lick of blue flame along the underside of a dry log. Her spear's blunt end struck the ground, she crouched, and such was her swiftness that she was braced when the final *orukhar* spitted himself on the blade. Then she drove forward once more, defiance in her high silverthroat laugh; her spear pierced iron armor, dug deep, and found his heart.

I gasped, swaying again. A rancid draft reached me; there were only three paces between my toes and my shieldmaid's back heel. The crested creature's breath wheezed forth, a hot noisome draft, and that was what I smelled, along with the metallic, ordure-thick reek of battledeath.

Arn surged upward. Sideways her final opponent toppled, his sword hitting before he did. He landed upon his own blade, breaking the metal with a terrible sound, and she ripped her weapon free of flesh and armor both. The strange blackened, brackish fluid serving the creatures for blood splattered from shining steel, and her spear's haft bore but a few pale scratches. *Seidhr* died away inside me, a bubbling spring vanishing into sand. My ribs heaved; so did hers, like the small summerbirds whose wings blur with the speed of their hovering flight.

I could not speak, I could not think. I could only stand, and marvel that we were not dead.

But Arn was moving again. Her boots thudded as she bolted, and I realized my song was no longer hiding a high desperate sound.

It was Naciel's shrieking as Maedroth dragged her. He had struck his cousin, dazed her, and now hauled her along the road by her bright golden hair.

My shieldmaid ran, her weapon held high by one bent arm. A twisting, massive effort, silent as the dead bodies twitching in her wake, and she loosed almost before my stunned eyes could focus enough to understand what they beheld.

Her aim was true.

Naciel screamed afresh as the blade sank deep into Maedroth's back. Speared like a wolf was he; shieldmaids often hunt those creatures when they prey overmuch upon a steading's flocks. Tainted with *orukhar* ichor, the steel forged in Dun Rithell made a heavy sound as it sheared ribs and punched through the Watchful's chest, protruded dripping from his front.

And Arneior was close behind, the fury of the Wingéd Ones hard upon her. No man may treat a woman so while a shieldmaid is nearby.

Her hands closed about the haft; Arn dug her heels in and ripped the weapon aside with a coughing cat-growl of effort. Bone cracked, gold-tinged scarlet spray-splattered, and Maedroth the son of Alaessia made a nightmarish sound somewhere between a scream and a gurgle. Naciel scrambled aside, a confusion of silvergreen cloth, strands of hair torn from her head still caught between his clawing fingers. The silver ring upon his hand flashed, a dart of sickening light wrung free and splashing unheeded against Laeliquaende's stone.

Arneior had her balance now, the rage upon her sure and deadly as that upon my father who they named, in awe, *the Battle-Mad*. She kicked at the back of his left knee; Maedroth staggered, still vital despite the horrific wound. Her spear-butt dropped, jabbed forward, and hit his lower back—a horrible sound, accompanied by more bone creak-snapping, and he was flung like a doll, landing upon his face.

Tiny flakes of ash began to descend, black snow. Much of Laeliquaende was burning, and those small weightless feathers had once been beautiful things, whether cloth, wood, stone... or flesh. I reeled past fallen *orukhar*, bile whipping the back of my throat—she had told me to stay, but the battle was over—and had to hold up the shadow-cloak's hem with one sweating hand. I reached Naciel's side and dropped to my knees with a jolt that clicked my teeth painfully together as Arn stood over the fallen Watchful.

She lifted her spear and struck, but not with the blade this time.

No, she meted out a punishment due to violators, whether of hospitality or innocence, and bludgeoned the rest of the Elder's immortal life from him with her spear's blunt end. The pounding did not stop until his skull was cracked like a flung egg, and now I know the look of Elder brain when it is dashed from that strong, attractive casing.

The ruins of his head she hacked free with a flick of her spearblade, and lifted it by black, blood-matted hair. The golden tinge to his crimson ichor made strange patterns along dry stone, and she dropped the ruined thing upon his buttocks, so that when he met Hel in the afterworld that goddess would know by his condition what he had done.

Of course the Elder go somewhere different after their physical bodies are irretrievably broken, but we were mortal, my shieldmaid and I, and she meted out the vengeance due by our laws.

Naciel did not protest. And much later, when we learned just how the shining city of Taeron had been betrayed, the punishment was held to be fitting—not that it was ever mentioned in Arneior's presence.

Or in mine.

The ash-fall was thickening, a tide of whirling grey and black speckles. I helped Naciel upright as best I could, and she leaned upon me. Clutching each other, the iron coffer tucked in the crook of my left arm like a swaddled babe, we approached my shieldmaid.

Arneior stood for a few moments, looking at what she had done, and when she turned to us the blood upon her, both *orukhar* and Elder, glowed no less than the woad.

"We must move," she said hoarsely.

Goldspear, Broken

Once was Taeron warned by Ulimo himself, the lord of the seas standing giant amid waves. Twice was he warned by a gaunt Secondborn, who found the door to his realm by chance. Thrice was he warned by the Doom of the Elder, in a voice not her own. Yet he stayed, and as he strove with the greatest of the nathlàs *the burning tower fell upon them both, for though the High-helm had slain two* haugr *their flame does not cease until it has eaten its fill.*

—Saedrin the Winemaker, *The Burning of Coraquaende*

We were upon the Street of Ten Alleys, Naciel said between deep shuddering gasps as she sought some measure of calm. Clashing and cries resounded from the wall far above. Archers upon the battlements were attempting to fend off attackers both outside and in, and no few fleeing Elder were saved, however temporarily, by a shaft from the smoke-lensed sky.

The sagas say few of those upon the walls survived the battle; since that night, I have met none.

"There." The princess had regained her breath, but she was pale, and her hair was disarranged. Her arm across my shoulders was no longer a weight as we staggered together; instead it was a support, for my legs were distinctly watery.

Arneior blinked, following the line of Naciel's pointing; ash starred her ruddy hair. She did not speak, nor did she look at me, restlessly scanning our surroundings as if she feared more *orukhar* would appear.

They did not. Instead, small groups of Elder corpses lay scattered about, hacked and grievously misshapen. I could not tell if Maedroth's companions were responsible for that work, and I did not want to think upon it.

A small house tucked against Waterstone's massive outer wall had no garden, but above its dark, half-open door a carven bird looked askance at us, its lines so sharp and detailed I half expected it to shift, long tailfeathers rustling along one side-jamb, and burst into wild flight with a feathery cough.

Naciel drew me through the doorway; Arn pressed hard upon our heels. A bare stone cube greeted us, but the livid firelit gloom outside filtered in to show a tangle of other carvings upon every wall. The princess hurried for the back, deeper into the shadows, and as she did a slight sound, as of a flat rock dragged across a spinning millstone, threaded under the bell-cries and clamor.

A slice of the back wall opened, blue glow outlining the opening door. Arn's spear dipped; she shouldered past me, but the glow was an Elder lantern, and its fine thin filigree chain hung from a familiar hand.

"*Thank the Blessed,*" Floringaeld said, deep feeling filling the Old Tongue's lilt. He wore armor but no helm; his golden hair was just as messy as Naciel's, and clouded with ash and dust besides. Two hilts rose over his shoulders—a short sword and a longer one—and a half-familiar armoring clasped his left hand, dull silvery metal with a single cloudy green gem on its back, above the knuckles. He had been wearing the gauntlet when we met him, too. "*Come, and quickly.*"

"*Has everyone else—*" The pressure of Naciel's arm against my shoulders did not abate, urging me onward.

I twisted, looking to Arn, who cast a glance behind us and visibly decided not to quibble.

"*You are the last.*" The captain beckoned with his free hand; the lantern trembled. "*All else who knew of this route have gone ahead; I swore to your father I would wait for you.*"

"*My father?*" Hope brightened the princess's tone. Past the doorway were wide, easy stairs, the prints of other feet in a drift of fine, floury dust. That in itself was shocking; we went down half a dozen steps and halted—or she did, I was willing enough to let her set our pace.

"Ah." Floringaeld cleared his throat; as soon as Arn was safely past he made a gesture, and the stone slab moved along the floor, sealing itself. Soon the lantern's glow was our only illumination, and as the aperture closed the sounds of wrack and bell-screams cut off cleanly, as if sliced by a sharp blade. "There are not many steps, yet we must hurry. I do not think the city is fully invested yet, but 'tis only a matter of time."

He brushed past us, lantern swinging and shadows dancing over smooth white stone walls, but Naciel caught at his armored shoulder. "Floringaeld."

I could only see his expression in profile, yet that was enough. Grief may age an Elder where mere time does not, and it was like seeing a building crumble once its beams collapse. Swiftly, thoroughly, the captain of Laeliquaende's royal guard staggered without moving, and thick silence held us all spellbound for a moment.

"*How?*" Naciel breathed.

"*Haugr, and worse,*" he answered, shortly, and set off again. "*Come. I promised my lord I would see you to safety, princess, and I will not be forsworn.*"

For the second time, Arneior and I hurried through a tunnel while an Elder city was destroyed. Great blocks of grey stone held up an earthen roof; we stayed in the circle of blue lamplight, drawn in Floringaeld's wake like small boats lashed to a raft. He stopped at intervals, cocking his head, wearing a grave, expectant look which almost managed to erase the grieving.

Naciel smoothed her long tresses as we walked. I held up the hem of the shadowmantle, and though neither had remarked upon it I did not think them unaware of my wearing an Elder treasure—or of the iron casket borne awkwardly in the crook of my left arm. After some while, though, I noticed the mantle seemed to have shrunk, for it no longer brushed the ground. Perhaps some *seidhr* was at work within the strands; it was one I would have been much exercised to find the source of had the situation been otherwise.

Imagine, being able to shorten a mantle or dress so. I thought of the sewing Astrid had carefully packed in my mother's second-largest trunk, so I would have something of home to work upon during my year-and-a-day as weregild.

Oh, gods. The lump in my throat was unwelcome. I swallowed several times. My vision blurred, and I had to blink rapidly. A hot finger traced down my cheek.

Just this morning I had brought my grey travel-dress from the trunk, rummaging for my needles as well, for I thought it likely the day would bring some damage to the gown. Where was it now, I wondered? Still in the tent where Arn and I bathed after the race?

"Sol?" Arn husked my name.

"I am well enough." The thickness of my tone gave the lie away. "Your arm. When we halt next…" It was my duty to heal that wound; doubly so, for she had gained it in my defense.

"Hush," Floringaeld interrupted, though not unkindly. The edge of the lantern's glow touched a set of wooden stairs, gleaming with dark varnish. "I ask for silence, Secondborn. We must go swift and quiet if we are to escape the valley."

"Yes," Arn whispered for both of us, and when he doused the lamp a faint gleam lingered still upon the stairs' lacquer, enough to aid us as we climbed.

A low stone arch sat in the middle of a tangled grove, dark-leaved evergreens pressing close and friendly. The bells still rang frantic, clamoring over each other like competing saga-singers, but they were behind us now and the noise of battle had also retreated somewhat.

We passed through the archway and into the night. Branches were silent as the Elder slipped through, Floringaeld before us and Naciel behind, a small clear space somehow around us at every moment. I moved carefully, aware of roots, but the ground was level as the tunnel floor had been.

We were not to be so fortunate for long, however. Floringaeld halted, indistinct except for the gleam of his hair and a glimmer from his gauntleted hand, raised in warning.

Arn and I froze. I tried to not even *breathe* loudly, for I heard it too.

We were almost at the edge of the grove. Beyond the trees' shelter was rolling green which should have been silvered by starlight.

Instead, it was greyish velvet full of twisted shadows, for the sky was choked with gloom and Waterstone's vastness burning freely. The bellsong changed, becoming less complex—another tower had gone silent.

Closer, though, were voices. Harsh and unmusical, speaking in a tongue we had just heard from a half-dozen *orukhar* now dead at a shieldmaid's hand. A heavy tramp of boots running in unison, thudding no less than my fevered, leaping heart.

They faded into the distance, but Taeron's guard-captain did not move. And he was right not to, for there was stealthy motion nearby as well, a faint jingle and the creak of leather under shifting iron plates and rings.

Oh, gods. I wondered if it would pass us by, wondered if I should sing, what form the *seidhr* would take—or if I could reasonably be expected to add my paltry strength to an Elder warrior's. The thought of seeing more bloodshed sickened me, the cries from the wracked, riven city scraped my skin, and the sudden rushing in my ears perhaps meant I was going to lose consciousness like a sparrow weirding-whispered from a thornbrake, finding itself trapped in a human hand.

The creaks slid nearer, along with a strange whuffling noise. It sounded like a hound with a malformed nose, and Arn's spear dipped—slowly, so slowly, avoiding any contact with leaf or twig. I felt the tension in her, and perhaps Floringaeld did too, for his hand twitched, a peremptory motion no less intense for its silence.

The snuffles crested. The Elder's gauntlet flashed as he sprang, the dark-green gem giving a dull gleam as of rain at night. There was a *crunch*, almost lost in the bellsong, and when he straightened there was black ichor upon the metal shielding his left hand.

"*Come*," he whispered in the Old Tongue.

I could not see the shape at the trees' feet clearly, save that it was on all fours though its legs were far too long and oddly splayed besides. Naciel crowded close behind me, herding like a shepherd's hound with a recalcitrant member of its flock, and I fixed my gaze—adapted to the dark now, at least so much as mortal eyes could—upon the deeper shadow of Arneior before me.

Stealthily we crept from one shelter to the next, avoiding bands of roving *orukhar* and more of those strange, snuffling beasts. I caught a glimpse of one in the light of a burning vineyard and had to bite the inside of my cheek savagely enough to taste blood, keeping a cry bottled in my throat.

They were like their ash-skinned brothers, only they lolloped on all fours and their ruined faces bore a cavern where the nose should be, a wet void that was the source of the sniffing sound. To this day I cannot guess by what *seidhr* Floringaeld and Naciel kept them from scenting mortal or Elder flesh.

If it was indeed their doing, and not...something else.

We hid in a stand of silverbark birches, their leaves shaking with distress—the entire valley seemed to be shivering with fear and mourning. Burning homes glowed like torches, other structures shattered and aflame as well; once the frozen shadow of a lich passed in the distance, firelight peeking through its tattered, wing-spreading mantle though most of its ilk were, like the *haugr* and other fell things, more occupied within the city itself.

I did not know it then, but more than one of the Seven stalked Laeliquaende that night.

The ground became more uneven. Some Elder preferred the wilder margins, and had clearly done battle for their homes. The *orukhar* seemed to delight in punishing those, and in displaying the corpses. Arn turned away from one scene lit by leaping flames, her eyes wide and mouth contorted as if she wished to weep.

I did not blame her. I could not even look at...the bodies, what they had done, I...

Much later, we passed a tall broad outcropping of stone, left forlorn of the vast long-vanished water which had hollowed the valley from the mountains. "*Hist*," someone said close by. Floringaeld turned, right hand twitching for a hilt, and Naciel let out a soft, surprised sound.

"*This way*," the voice continued, urgently, in the Old Tongue. "*I can hear them approaching, be quick!*"

We had found other refugees.

The cave was dry and sand-floored; the entrance, like the Ice Door, was a single crack only wide enough to permit one person at a time. An Elder child—a girl with long black hair, wrapped in a deep-green mantle and cradled by a man who shared her wide dark eyes—wept soundlessly, staring into the night. Her tears glittered in dim light from some indeterminate source.

Most of the Elder bore well-wrapped bandages, for *orukhar* blades are often poisoned and require poultice. At least one had escaped a lich, for pale and silent she reclined upon the inadequate cushion of a folded cloak, clutching at her right thigh where a dark weal smoked, the edges of the wound crisped and burning with furious cold. Her sky-blue skirts, pulled high, were torn and bore pin-prick spark-burns.

"It will be dawn soon." The one who had hailed us was another guard, responsible for this group. His armor was sadly bedraggled but his gaze was clear and fell, burning blue as Aeredh's, and he did not seem wounded despite the rents in his plate-and-ring. *"We cannot move swiftly enough, and they are patrolling between us and the exits. 'Tis as if they know our evacuation routes."*

"They very well may." Softly, Naciel spoke of Maedroth's appearance with *orukhar*, though not upon the precise manner of his death. The Elder looked at my shieldmaid with no little wonder, but she did not preen under their approval.

None protested in the Watchful's defense, then or after, though he had been deep in the trust and counsel of his uncle. Even his friends—and there were many, for he was often prodigal with his help of Laeliquaende's inhabitants—could not overlook his appearance and implied leaguer with the Enemy's servants.

It is one thing no Elder will forgive, for they hate the lord of the Black Land almost as much as he despises them.

Luckily, Arn's wound was not poisoned. I drew the pain out, flesh knitting itself seamlessly, *seidhr* grinding up my own forearm in response. There was no place to flick away the injury, letting the earth bear what her children had suffered, so I simply ground my teeth and sweated under my dress and the shadow-cloak.

Then I pressed the iron casket into my shieldmaid's hands. "Rest,"

I told her, and she nodded. I did not like the haunted quality of her stare, but there were other wounded to attend.

"*I saw the king battling two* haugr," Floringaeld said. "*Large ones, and fell; they bore both whip and blade.*"

They paid little attention to a pair of Secondborn. I knelt next to the Elder woman on the cloak, and indicated her leg.

"*Let me help*," I whispered in the Old Tongue. She did not demur, shifting slightly to allow me access to her injury. Great clear drops of sweat stood out on her brow.

The wound fought me, stubbornly refusing to close as the captain told of his king amid flames and falling masonry, the giant twisted things with swords and chain-whips wounded by Taeron's flickering spear. The High-helm had slain both, but another enemy had joined the fray—a shadow burning with icy malice, left unnamed in the hurried recitation lest speaking further attract notice.

Floringaeld was not the only witness of the battle, and though 'tis embroidered some little in the sagas, what we heard that night was chilling—and impressive—enough.

"*His spear is broken*," he finished, heavily, as I finally drew the last of the lich's freezing hatred from ageless flesh. "*My lord's helm is cast down.*"

Lichburn is one of the few wounds an Elder does not heal swiftly from, especially those who are not warriors. I had read a few treatises upon their methods and manners of healing in the library, between map-studies and other interesting things; now I was glad of it.

Naciel turned to the wall of our refuge, her shoulders bowed and trembling. Arn watched, a line between her coppery eyebrows, but stayed looming at my side. The Elder woman, eyes half-closed, draped her dress decorously over her legs and sighed, a relieved sound. Her long dark hair, half-braided as was the festival fashion in Laeliquaende, was tarnished with smoke.

"*My thanks, Riversinger,*" she murmured.

It took me two tries to stand. My arms ached, and the rest of me was none too happy. So much *seidhr* takes a toll upon the body—as does fleeing, and hiding, and terror itself. Arn thrust the casket back into my hands as soon as I was upright, and returned her attention to the cave entrance, gripping her spear.

"Come dawn they will find us." Gaeran, the guard who had shepherded this group, spoke low but clear. He watched the entrance to our precarious shelter as well, and gripped a jeweled swordhilt at his belt. The gems did not shine, as if they too sensed the danger. *"In darkness we may slip past, perhaps, but we will be in the open when the sun rises. They hate the day's eye, but they will do their foul work under it if they must."*

Floringaeld was silent for a few moments, and his mien was terrible. His gauntlet made a low soft sound in the darkness as the hand within it clenched. *"The princess and her friends must reach Dorael."*

Every Elder in the cave stilled, and regarded me. I clutched the casket and tried to think. *"This cloak,"* I said, trying to speak as softly as possible while enunciating the Old Tongue clearly. *"Naciel, you must take it, and the iron box. My lords Floringaeld and Gaeran should accompany you, and you may move with some swiftness; my maiden-of-steel and I will care for the wounded here. We may escape notice if I block the cave-mouth with some trickery."*

I was not, after all, brave enough to mention *seidhr* to the folk whose name for it we mortals had borrowed.

The silence was so thick an echo of bell-ring could be heard in the distance—but only one deep tolling, over and over. It halted during that hush, leaving only the faintest intimation of cries in the darkness.

"Laeliquaende is fallen." The woman on the folded cloak rose, stiff and slow but still graceful. Her torn sleeve flapped and her hands moved as if dreaming, attempting to set her garb to rights. *"And a Secondborn is teaching us how to bear the loss."*

Arn stood very close, the healthy heat of her most welcome for I was cold as I had not been since we reached this valley. There was nothing to fight, so perhaps she was taking comfort in nearness—I certainly was—yet her attention still did not leave the cave's narrow mouth. "I will give this thing to Naciel," I told her softly, in southron. "And the cloak. We will stay here—"

"And die when they find us. I can hear them, Sol." She was pale again, my small one, and though she did not quail, she also did not look fey with battle-joy either.

"Or we outwait them, and go home." My voice quivered upon the last word; I hoped I merely sounded weary, not as afraid as I felt. There was no hope of returning to Dun Rithell, but I had to fan any embers of courage in those nearby.

It is a *volva*'s duty.

"Very well." She lifted her spear slightly, thought better of tapping it to underscore her agreement. "At least my weapon has a name now."

"*Princess?*" Floringaeld approached Naciel, who put up one hand, blindly, and leaned against the cave wall. The score of Elder crowded into this space had moved aside so much as possible, attempting to give her grief some lee. Their own must have been just as sharp, yet they were polite, and even the child merely clung silently to her carrier, her arms tight about his throat.

It must have been uncomfortable, but the Elder man did not demur. His hand moved slightly upon the girl's small back, an unconscious comforting movement very like my mother's when one of her younglings was ill or frightened. I wondered what the girl had seen so far this night, and if I truly had the strength or skill to keep the cave-entrance masked all day.

I began to fumble with the cloak-laces one-handed, the casket occupying my left arm. The sense of something live and listening inside its shell did not abate; no wonder Arn did not wish to carry it.

The once-wounded woman stepped past me; she did not limp overmuch. "*I think I can draw them away,*" she said, quietly. "*Then the rest of you may flee.*"

"*Elaedie.*" The guard shook his head. "*'Tis a foolish suggestion, and you are not a fool.*"

"*My children are gone.*" Her chin set stubbornly; though she was dark-haired, she looked very much like Astrid. "*So is my wife, and my parents. I have nothing to weigh me down, and you well know my swiftness.*"

"*Ancila would never forgive me if I agreed.*" Gaeran cast an anxious look at the cave-mouth, and spoke more softly. "*You are my sister as much as she; do not be so hasty. If someone must draw them away, I will do so."*

Others pressed close, whispering fiercely; I lost track of their argument, for my head rang awfully as if one of the city's bells had taken up residence. I had dangerously overtaxed my *seidhr*; it replenishes naturally, but one may injure the subtle selves with overwork as much as the physical.

The conversation grew heated, for all it was in half-mouthed whispers, and I began to worry we would be overheard when Naciel turned sharply from the wall. She made a brusque, commanding gesture; the Elder fell silent.

"Enough," she said, soft but clear, in southron. "My father's spear is broken and his helm cast down, but there is no time to mourn. His task falls to me and I will perform it."

"*Princess—*" Floringaeld began once more, but a single glance from her sufficed to drive him back a half-step.

I had seen Naciel's beauty, and her merriment. In that moment I saw her strength, and it was very much like Taeron's. The same sense of clarity, of distillation, poured through her. A twinge of *seidhr* limned her in soft blue like the steel of their blades when battle is nigh, the glow seen not with physical eyes but the inner ones.

"You and Gaeran will shepherd our people, and you will all protect the *alkuine* and her shieldmaid." Naciel took great care with the last word, pronouncing it just the way I had taught her. "They must reach Dorael, and if the Blessed are kind some remnant of Laeliquaende will as well. That is my father's command, and mine as well."

"But—" Floringaeld fell silent again, but not under her stare.

Instead, the princess bent, and unlaced her slippers. "You are swift indeed, Elaedie." Her tone was surprisingly gentle, and as she shifted to the Old Tongue the words became even softer. "*But my mother was Laelaeithel the Unshod, and tonight I call upon Uellar Orolim, who rode under starlight before we knew of the West.*" She stepped out of her shoes. Her feet glimmered, pale and perfect; as she straightened she reached into a skirt-pocket and drew out a small velvet bag.

From it she freed a glimmering thing. It was a necklace, a colorless gem hanging from scrollwork of dark metal, and Floringaeld drew in a sharp breath.

"*The Watchful made that for you,*" he said.

"He did." Naciel fastened the clasp at her nape; her hair fell in unbound waves as the gem settled just below the notch between her collarbones. "Tonight I will use it to undo whatever I may of his treachery. I charge you with their protection, my lord Heavy-hand; do not disappoint me."

"Princess..." Gaeran's southron was heavily accented. "I can hear them; the filth are close. Please, do nothing rash."

Naciel looked to me then, and I sucked in a sharp breath. The edge of her loveliness was like a knife that night, an Elder blade keen enough to cleave a whisper, sharp enough its touch would not even hurt at first. She smiled, and if Tjorin had witnessed her in that moment he might well have expired of the sight.

I thought she would speak, but instead she whirled, the hem of her dress fluttering. Floringaeld's gauntlet twitched as if he thought to restrain her, but she was past him in a trice, and her shadow in the cave-mouth was but a flicker.

As she burst free of confinement the necklace gave a vivid flash, not of lightning but as Fryja's veils, yet coruscating white and blue instead of green, red, and other nameless hues. She cried aloud in the Old Tongue, calling upon the Blessed, and the sound was a silver clarion, sweet as fallen Laeliquaende's bells.

"*Uellar!*" she called, and it echoed far upon the night wind, overpowering the sounds of wrack and death from the burning city. "*Ai, ai, Orolim the Hunter! One calls upon thee, mighty rider! Ai, ai, ai!*"

"Fishguts," Arn breathed, wonderingly. "She is mad."

Floringaeld hurried to the cave-mouth; for a moment I thought he meant to plunge after her. But he halted, and his gauntleted fingers sank deep into the stone on one side as he fought the urge.

We heard her cry out once more, her voice trailing into the distance.

Thus began Naciel's Run.

Naciel's Run

'Twas the huntsman of the Blessed who found us in the shadowed dells before we knew the West. The Star-Kindler we love best but to Orolim we are grateful; to swift-hunting Uellar, the One Who Rides, we owe great honor. He would not rest until he had gathered what he could of our wandering folk, patient even as we fled him. We were afraid of horn and hoofbeats, for in those twilit days the Enemy hunted us as well, to kill or to enslave...

            —The Song of Waking

The sagas tell of what Taeron's daughter did that night. Some say she was half-insane with grief, others that a vision of the Blessed had laid a divine geas upon her. Still others contend she heard her husband's voice upon the wind, and meant to seek him out.

All agree, however, that she called upon Orolim the Hunter; all agree there was a light upon her, sparking in the necklace at her throat. A glow rose from its colorless gem, perhaps reflecting the conflagration of Laeliquaende—for the city was utterly wracked with flame now, even the stone of its buildings consumed by unwholesome *haugr*-fire. Like and unlike the balls of illumination gathering in a swamp was the luminescence from her jewelry, and it bobbed over her head as she ran before bands of *orukhar*.

The light seemed to entrance them, or maybe they thought her a prize worthy of being taken to the Black Land. For the troops of the Enemy gave chase, legs pumping, their armor creaking with hollow noises as they jogged.

Most of the lich, *haugr*, and other fell things were still inside the burning city, completing its ruin. Those of the Enemy's forces net-spread through the valley were stealthier and weaker than their commanders, meant to catch fleeing refugees terrified by sudden betrayal.

A dancing glow was before the Enemy's thralls, and a sweet voice calling. They forgot their tasks, giving chase, and though it seems near impossible every survivor of Laeliquaende will swear they glimpsed her that night.

Naciel was upon the hills of Kaen-em-Anlas, flitting before a dish-faced, sniffing monstrosity and the detachment of *orukhar* it guided between hiding-places. *Orolim, Orolim*, she called, and those hiding nearby took heart, for no thing of the Enemy's would name the hunter of the Blessed, him they feared almost more than daylight. She drew away the filth, and those fleeing found strength to carry on a little farther.

She was seen in the vast burning vineyards of Tahn Emael, her hair a banner and her feet flashing as mounted ash-pale *orukhar* sought to trap her. Yet she knew the hills, glades, smaller valleys, and streamlets better than any spy, and stayed just out of reach, mocking them in clear ringing tones.

Along the river Egeril also named Naricie where her lover had won just that morn she was seen, and those who had the presence of mind to slip away in boats felt new strength fill them. They made haste to land where their princess called to them, avoiding the rapids, and found the beaches empty of enemies, the way of escape clear.

The shadowed vale of Tarithin, the rocky moor-expanse of Gil-brannaeth to Laeliquaende's east, the westron hall of Coraquaende where Taeron oft retreated when the hazy red star of Oroduel rose to mark short midsummer nights—the building now burning, but its light strengthening the glow over her head as she called to defenders and fleeing Elder alike—and yes, even unto the precipice of the Leap she was seen, crying her father's name over the sound of the whirl-pool, dodging aside at the last minute as a group of pursuers mounted upon scaled, vaguely canine horrors could not turn in time and fell from that high place to their doom in the maelstrom-deep below.

Those hiding in the evergreens of Selaan, survivors of the fierce battle to the north of the city where the hardy folk of Anricil the Winemaker stood fast at Tahn Jaelin and refused to retreat even as their sheds and presses burned, numberless Elder fleeing along the white-paved roads, hiding in bushes and mourning burning copses full of trees they had planted, the people of Maedenna in the extreme westron end of the valley—archers of renown, and few indeed survived for even their children took up bows that night—all glimpsed the daughter of Taeron as she mazed their attackers, flickering before stunned *orukhar* and leading them astray.

The night was long, and lurid with fire. Thrice the princess of the burning city circled its ruin, and ever she called the names of the great huntsman, the god we Secondborn call Uellar. In the dead watches after midnight when the shadow from the north was thickest her voice did not falter; it seemed to the wounded, despairing survivors that hoofbeats answered her call and the gold of her hair gleamed like Vardhra the Star-Kindler's.

I speak truth when I say the sagas are right, and whoever escaped the fall of Waterstone owes it to Naciel Silverfoot. The *orukhar* chased her, the sniffing excrescences confused by her appearance or struck with a following madness, refusing to turn aside even as she led them to ruinous plummeting from promontories or miring in riverside mud. Their mounts were unable to run her down, behaving like maddened horses, straying with their helpless riders or galloping until they collapsed, heart-burst.

There was time to use secret ways from the valley, not merely the Hidden Passage but threadlike passes between knife-sharp peaks, well-hidden waterways that Taeron's foresight—or his daughter's—had stocked with boats and provisions, stairs cut into rock or tunnels bored into stone. Deep in the counsel of the High-helm was the Watchful, but even he did not know everything, and the Silverfoot ensured a remnant could flee.

Of course many of those given the hope of escape stumbled, or fell to mischance. And there were no few dark things stationed at likely points to forestall their flight—but such was not her concern. The princess did her duty that night, and more.

As the grey of dawn rose she faltered, having circled the entire valley nearly thrice. Amid the rolling hills she slowed, just south of the bleeding, burning city turned to a ruddy glare in silver mist. The name of the Blessed's horsemaster was husky upon her lips, and a ragged group of mounted *orukhar* brought her to bay.

The sagas sing of Naciel turning, ready to face her death, tearing the gem from her throat and cursing her pursuers so foully in the Old Tongue the stones of the great road from the Hidden Passage to the gates of the city cracked and blackened. I do not know about that, but I do know what happened next.

Black shadows burst from the rising fog, shaggy forms with mad-glittering, feverish eyes. They closed upon her, and Naciel flung the necklace—the first gift Maedroth the Traitor ever made for his fair cousin, presented upon a day of celebration—past them, its gem giving a final agonized glitter.

But the *orukhar* were not to have her, for the shadows were neither lich nor *haugr*, nor any other of the Enemy's creatures. The wolves of Naras had been busy that night as well, leaping from darkness upon stray ash-pale attackers, foxing the sniffing things with false trails, leading small groups of Elder to safety. They were swift and deadly, for desperation was upon them and their captain perhaps mistook the gleam in the distance for some other woman singing pursuers into thornbrakes and mire.

They took the princess up and bore her away, vanishing into thickening fog as the valley wept for the loss of its inhabitants. Dawn arrived, and the fall was complete.

Laeliquaende was no more.

Another Doom

Doom arrived,
Carried to our door in strong arms.
Yet worse
Was the rot within, the danger
I did not see.

—*The Heavy-hand's Saga*, attributed
to Valis Swift-harp

H*old*," Floringaeld mouthed, and his gauntlet glimmered as he raised it again. We had been going uphill for a long while, the dark before us thick as cold batter. A *volva's* eyes are sharp and so are a shieldmaid's, but we were both near-blind once far enough from the glow of a burning city. Elaedie held my arm, limping as I swayed with exhaustion, but between us we managed well enough; Arn's helper was a slim Elder girl, her dark hair sheared raggedly at her shoulders and her clothes full of smoke. She held my shieldmaid's left elbow; one woman led, the other followed, and I could not say who was more thankful for being given a task to concentrate upon.

Elder men stayed at the edges of the group, bearing staves, daggers, or whatever else might serve as a weapon; the captain of Laeliquaende led us and Gaeran took the rearguard, grim-silent, his eyes glittering blue.

I had no idea where we were, or what we aimed for. We walked, and walked. The gloom seemed endless, and though not truly cold—soft spring night, the breeze faint and the grass dew-heavy—I shivered often. Ash kept falling, sparse flakes whirling like hesitant snow in autumn, the kind which melts the next day but still warns of frozen, impending hunger.

We halted. Elaedie's fingers tensed upon my arm, pale against the shadowy cloth. Before us, the child in her father's arms did not cry, but her breath came quick and light. I tried to think of something fit for soothing a little one, but a lullaby would make too much noise and I was drained of *seidhr*. A few stars struggled through the blackness that was not cloud; the Moon was up, but waning and rotten-cheese yellow, a worm-eaten scytheblade leached of all beauty.

Every time we halted that night, I sought not to think about what might happen. We had not encountered any more *orukhar*, but that did not make the frequent halts and waiting less terrible. Battle is awful but anticipation... well, it is not entirely *worse*, since avoiding further chaos and bloodshed is preferable to almost anything else I can imagine, even now.

And yet.

The sounds of carnage and flame, bellsong and metal meeting metal, were also extinct. Only the ruffling of the breeze and the faint, numb echoes of distant cries broke the night's silence. The world held its breath, and even the faint sigh of the tired Elder child as she wavered upon the edge of sleep seemed loud.

"*Lirielle, Lirielle,*" someone whispered nearby. "*Whither dost thou wander?*"

It had to be from a song, for the accents were most pleasingly arranged, if somewhat archaic. Elaedie let out a soft, ragged gasp, but it was Floringaeld who replied.

"*Do not look for the star, she has left us.*" The captain half-turned, the sword in his right hand giving a dull gleam. "*Who goes there?*"

"*No* orukhar *would speak so, my friend.*" A shadow melded from the darkness, another in its wake. They were Elder, of course, and I thought I recognized the voice.

No. It cannot be. "Aeredh?" The iron casket's corners pressed even harder through the shadow-cloak; I swallowed the rest of my disbelief.

"Solveig?" A different voice, not Elder, but I found I could recognize it as well. "Is Naciel with you?"

It was indeed the Crownless, Tjorin beside him as well as a group of other Elder, mostly warriors in battered armor, their blades bare. They surrounded our group with alacrity, having shepherded a few others to points of escape; I gathered, from the murmured conference, that we were the last.

Tjorin moved closer, eager for news of the princess. I could not think of what to say, but I had to produce some manner of news. "She…she drew them away." I sounded numb and breathless. "The *orukhar*. So we could…so we could escape."

"Ah." Tjorin's face was shadowed, and he paused. "We heard a voice upon the wind, and saw a light. Some trick of the Enemy's, Daerith thought, but Aeredh said nothing of *his* would use the name of the Hunter. So." He shook his head, and hurriedly resheathed his sword with a soft sound. "Who needs aid? I have some *sitheviel*, and managed to gather some healwell too."

I wished for my own embroidered *seidhr*-bag, but it was in the palace along with everything we had brought from Dun Rithell. Only a bee-end torc remained, resting comforting and warm against my collarbones—that, and the red coral in my hair.

Arneior had her spear, too. But everything we wore was of Elder make, and a sudden sharp pain speared me. I had to swallow, hard. "Elaedie—she was wounded in the leg. And there is a child; she may be sleeping now, but…"

"Say no more." Tjorin produced a small silver flask gemmed with bright blue slivers, and there were grateful murmurs as the most grievously wounded or exhausted were granted a sip of *sitheviel* or a bit of poultice-pungent herb pressed against their wounds. We set off again amid his ministrations; the son of Hrasimir spoke soft encouragement to all and even pressed a mouthful of cordial upon Arneior.

Elaedie's limping eased. I wondered what it cost Tjorin to sound so cheerful while his beloved risked herself, and was once again ashamed of my own weakness.

"*There you are.*" Aeredh had dropped back; Floringaeld consulted with another of the new arrivals in an undertone, and our pace improved. I still could see almost nothing but the gleams of the Crownless's gaze were familiar, and he touched my shoulder. An almost weightless brush of fingertips, yet a bolt went through me, not *seidhr* but almost as intense as the sharing of vital energy at the edge of the Glass while I sought to remove a killing shard from Eol's shoulder. "I feared the worst," he continued, the words mere shadows to match their bearer. "Are you injured?"

I could not have said. I felt nothing save savage exhaustion, and fear. And the thing in the iron coffer, thrumming like birdwings. "I do not think so. Here." I thrust the box at him, but again he would not take it.

Instead, his hand found the back of mine, a gentle palm-touch, and he pushed my cargo to my chest once more. "'Tis yours to bear, my lady *alkuine*." So softly even the Elder around us might not hear, he spoke. And he moved closer, as if we were in the Wild again, though he did not put his arm over my shoulders. "I am relieved to find you safe."

"*Hush*," someone whispered. "*We are not in safety yet.*"

Indeed we were not. But the darkness did not seem so deep, and I could hear Arneior breathing just past Elaedie, who no longer leaned so much upon me. My own steps seemed more certain, though the ground was rocky and I felt every dip and rise through thin slippers.

I could not hear Aeredh, but the warmth beside me was familiar and I was even grateful for his presence, as a fisherman tossed from his boat could be glad of any flotsam nearby. We were now steadily climbing, if the ache in my calves was any indication.

Some while later—I could not say how long, for I might have slept while walking, my subtle selves burrowing inward to escape fear and fatigue—I blinked, and realized a faint thin greyish line was rising to our left. It described a high sharp tooth, and another more indistinct stone fang rose upon our right.

I realized the line was incipient dawn, and the teeth were the folds of a mountain.

We had escaped the valley.

Almost.

The Elder woman next to me was no longer a mere shadow but the soft suggestion of a tall form, dark hair falling down her back, her face a pale oval. Beyond her was a brighter glimmer—Arn's spear-blade, rising and falling as she walked, the young girl between them bearing some faint resemblance to Astrid as she walked with my mother and shieldmaid, perhaps eager to visit a riverside fair.

I turned my chin slightly; to my left was a shape that could only be Aeredh. A blue glimmer was his glance, and his hand curled around my elbow as if I had stumbled, warm even through shadow-cloak and dress-sleeve.

The light strengthened. Soon I realized I could see the Elder before us as well. We were in loose file, threading between two high walls of rock. The wind was chill, and ruffled ragged fabric; the greens and silvers of their cloth melded with the grey almost as nat-ural vegetation. Even the warriors' armor seemed less gleaming, as if it understood the need for camouflage.

My own mantle moved uneasily on the stiffening breeze. I could not decide if the cloth was still solid shadow or merely a deeper grey, and looking down at it—even at my own sleeve—made my stomach uneasy. Perhaps I had torn the hem after all, for it did not drag and 'twas silly of me to think *seidhr* could be used for mere alteration of a garment, even an Elder one.

As soon as it was light enough the girl at Arn's side took Elaedie's arm instead; they moved before us, and my shieldmaid fell into step beside me as if she had never left. It was a relief, but Aeredh still held my left elbow. Perhaps he wanted to make certain I did not drop the iron box.

The Crownless's cloth was singed and chunks of his dark hair crisped to nothing; the swordhilt at his shoulder bobbed as he walked and his cheek bore a dark, slowly-healing weal that did not look like lichburn. My throat was dry, and though I longed for some suste-nance more mortal than Elder draughts I would not have turned one away at that moment.

"Eol," I finally whispered. "Did you see him? Soren, and the others?"

Aeredh glanced at me, a blue flicker before his gaze returned to the ground before his scarred boots. He steered me around a clump of stone, and I realized he and Elaedie had been herding me all night. I had not stepped upon a single twig, much less a toe-bruising stone among many littering the defile.

They were careful shepherds, the Elder guiding night-blind Secondborn.

"I did not see him, but keep heart." His fingers tightened briefly upon my elbow. " 'Tis not easy to trap a wolf of Naras, my lady."

Arn slowed, her chin tipping up as she studied the line of Elder before us. "Hidden pass." Her voice was a mere husk of itself. "I think we go just over the mountain's shoulder, see there? Well-nigh invisible from below, but we shall feel the cold soon."

"And outside the valley?" Suddenly I could think again, though each consideration struggled through a thick blanket of resistance. "Still winter, I wager. The melt cannot be fully underway just yet— Floringaeld said so, at the council."

"Ice, or mud." She glanced past me. "Well? What say you, Elder?"

"We shall make for Dorael." Aeredh sounded just the same as he ever had, though quiet enough his voice would not carry to our other companions. "Once there…"

"Another Elder city to destroy." I hunched over the casket in my arms, wishing I could drop it. A group of my kind fleeing catastrophe might well leave a trail of broken or too-heavy implements, but the Elder did not—from discipline, I thought, or perhaps they had nothing else to lose. "Taeron said I was doom."

He made no answer, nor did Arn. What could they say?

My shieldmaid was correct; we were very near the snowline. There was little foliage, merely scrub between great knife-edged boulders and greyish lichen upon black rock. The faint colorless light in the east turned golden and rosy by degrees, then orange.

I looked back once, craning over my shoulder as Aeredh's grip tightened upon my left arm.

I could see a few Elder behind us, though I knew the line stretched farther. Their garb blended with the mountainside; every one bore some mark of battle or escape, and ash starred their flowing, silken hair. The valley lay below, full of boiling mist randomly scarred with the very crowns of the tallest evergreens in certain groves. A venomously orange smear in the distance showed Laeliquaende yet burned, and a column of dark greasy smoke lifted from it. For a moment the rising vapor was full of contorted faces, mouths open in silent agony.

"Careful." The Crownless set me right as I faltered. "Do not look, Solveig. It is not of your making; you did not come here willingly."

I did. There was no use in explaining. I turned away from the wrack of yet another beautiful Elder city, and it was just as well my throat and the rest of me were so dry, for it meant I could not weep. Still, my eyes stung. Arn walked beside me haggard and ash-starred as the Elder, the woad upon her face flaking. The look upon my shieldmaid was that of a woman in a nightmare, determined to endure the worst.

Certain Signs

The weirding protects from many dangers, yet attracts others. The Wise need fear neither malediction nor riddle, neither storm nor adder's bite. But the voice in the dark, the eater of flesh, the thing unseen? To be Wise is to know true dread.

—Naethron One-hand of the Barrowhills

There were several hidden routes from the valley; each household under Taeron's rule knew at least one—only to be used in extreme calamity, of course, and perhaps that is the difference between Elder and Secondborn. For I could not see any of our own inquisitive folk obeying the dictate of secrecy so well as the people of Waterstone. Every mother knows the best way to induce a mortal child into attempting a feat is to make it forbidden, and every father knows how far afield his sons will stray in search of honor or gain.

Then again, even the children of Taeron's realm knew of the Enemy and his works. Perhaps a mortal clan might achieve something similar in the face of such a dire foe, but I doubt it.

My breath came in silver puffs. So did Arn's. When Tjorin appeared, moving easily along the line of Elder, his hair bore both ashflake and small melting bits of ice. "Snow," he said, softly—we were apparently permitted to speak in low tones instead of whispers now. "Yet others have come this way before us. Floringaeld says there are certain signs, and we are now beyond easy pursuit. How fares the lady *alkuine*?"

"Well enough." I tried a smile, though my face felt masklike again. "But is there something for Arn? She is pale."

"I endure," she said immediately, but Tjorin once more produced his flask gemmed with blue slivers, the stopper a marvel of fluted gilding.

"Endurance is all very well." He settled into an easy stride beside her, avoiding loose rocks and other detritus with expedience, if not grace. "We have some supplies, and the Elder know how to travel after such things. All will be well."

I wondered if he sought to reassure us, or convince himself.

Arneior took a scant mouthful, and handed the flask to me with a look suggesting I had best not quibble. It was indeed *sitheviel*, a comforting heat like mead and the taste of summer flowers in bright meadows unreeling upon the tongue. It cut the sour remains of burning, relieved my thirst, and the world looked a little brighter after a single swallow. I wanted more, but there was little enough in the container and it was awkward to restopper one-handed.

"Aeredh?" I offered him the flask, for after all he had faced a burning horror much larger than a *trul*, and a lich besides.

The Crownless shook his dark head, though a pained smile curved his lips. "No need, my lady. We are almost at the crest."

"Just there." Arneior pointed, and whisked the small blue glittering thing away, handing it back to Tjorin. "Do you think the filthy things may track us?"

"If they do, we shall know soon enough." The Secondborn man glanced back, and I wondered how he had arrived in Laeliquaende. He did not speak of it, and neither did the princess. "But Taeron and Naciel planned well." His calm faltered for a bare moment, a grimace rising swiftly and vanishing with the same speed.

Aeredh slowed, which meant I had to. A ripple was passing down the line. Tjorin stiffened, nodded courteously in the Crownless's direction, and hurried forward. Elaedie and her companion halted at the hillcrown, their arms linked, staring at something ahead.

The defile broadened as it reached the top of the mountain's shoulder, tendrils of old snow drifting onto the path. The freeze thickened upslope, turning whiter and whiter, vanishing into a membranous haze hanging about the peak. We arrived at a knot of refugees standing solemnly, gazing at a broad space populated by snow-shrouded boulders with wet-dark, gleaming sides. In the middle of the expanse three huge, rectangular grey rocks, of a different type than the surrounding stone, leaned together conspiratorially.

There were other shapes, too, and a confusion of tracks across the thinly snowed field. It took a few moments before I realized what I saw, and my heart gave a sickened thump.

"*Oh, no,*" Elaedie breathed, the Old Tongue full of mournful despair. She and the girl now clutched each other, staring at the bodies.

For that is what they were—Elder, scattered about the field like so many broken earthenware vessels, some half-covered with flung snow. The wind rose, tugging at my sleeves; Arneior muttered a term I had only heard the warriors of my father's hall use before, and never kindly.

The thin snow was not dirty, for it had fallen after the murder. Before that, though, the bodies had been savaged, scarlet fluid spattered widely, gold tinges fading at puddle-edges. Deep gouges scarred the field—I looked to Aeredh, an impulse left over from our earlier journey.

We had learned to trust the Crownless's certainty, even when death drew nigh.

His dark eyebrows had drawn together. Aeredh stepped forward; his right arm extended before me, sweeping gently back. Did he wish to block such a sight from my view? Arn did not move, but her eyes had narrowed and her spear dipped.

"Bare feet?" Her coppery head cocked, and she looked puzzled. "But large, and so many."

I peered around Aeredh. The stones in the middle looked almost like the massive bluish dolmens at the eastron end of Dun Rithell, always holding a chill even on midsummer afternoons; Frestis the wiseman knew their secrets, and propitiated them with the flint knife every solstice and equinox. Yet while dangerous and watchful, the stones of my home did not seem...malicious.

Not like these.

Whispers raced among the gathered Elder. Tjorin unsheathed his blade, and it glittered in the rising dawn. Floringaeld drew too; they conferred, blond head and dark bent together, and my heart was in my throat.

"No," I heard myself say. Cold earth thrummed under my soles, a quivering communicated through thin Elder slippers—they had held up well so far, but no doubt I would soon be binding rags about my feet.

"Solveig?" Arn's head turned, but very slowly; the word drew itself out too, long and low.

"They are not..." *Seidhr* reawakened inside my bones. The thing in the iron casket hummed, a high drilling whine akin to the song of bloodsucking marsh-insects on wet, warm autumn nights. "Arn, they are *not stones*."

Tjorin pitched forward, perhaps meaning to do battle. But Floringaeld was quicker. The captain's gauntleted left hand shot out, closing upon the back of Tjorin's tunic. He dragged the son of Hrasimir back as the three grey columns shifted, *seidhr* blurring and rippling, curltwisted like wood shavings from a master's chisel.

No. Not precisely like that, but 'tis the closest I can describe what I saw with eye and weirding both. The twisting continued as one rocky shape stretched, rising, its cloak rippling. Fierce cold radiated across the corpse-littered field, biting as a lich's hatred. The rock melted into a bipedal shape, much larger than even the tallest Elder. Its companions did likewise, stretching and swelling, and noisome, obscene *seidhr* clotted thick about them.

The first thing turned with a scraping, ear-piercing screech. What could be mistaken for stone was naked, greyish skin marred with frostburn—not the sort called *Lokji's kisses* or the playful touches of black-ice sprites. It was the lividity of a frozen carcass, and its huge, discolored face was a corpse's as well. It wore the expression of a man starving to death in a snowstorm, glimpsing something horrifying between curtains of falling white.

"*Draugr!*" Tjorin yelled, and my knees turned loose.

Who does not know of such creatures? Stories of their depredations were told far more often than those of Elder or the Black Land, usually in deepwinter when the wind howls about the greathall's roof and the snow lies thick in every direction. They were never my favorite sagas, Astrid disliked them too, Bjorn and even Arneior grew somber when such things were mentioned. A traveler infected into a restless undead thing, rending its garments to nothing, growing as it feeds upon travelers caught amid the drifts—who would not shiver at the thought?

Worse than the swollen, blackened faces and the high drilling *seidhr*-whine was the way they moved. The first one jerked into motion, its right hand clamped upon the hilt of a massive, rust-notched sword; it darted across the snow much faster than anything that size should.

Its gaze, yellowed orbs protruding like boiled hen-eggs from filmed, rheumy eyesockets, settled unerringly upon me. They are things of ill weirding, and there is nothing *draugr* like better than draining the *seidhr* from one who has more than a whisper of talent. Luck, heat, and life—those are the things they feast upon, as well as the flesh of their prey.

Floringaeld met the thing with a crash of metal. "*Go!*" he cried in the Old Tongue, and two Elder—one was Daerith of Nithraen, I saw now, and was amazed he had once more survived ruin—grasped Tjorin's arms, bearing him away. More Elder hurried in their wake. Elaedie let out a single sobbing noise before grasping the girl beside her about the shoulders and pitching forward, forcing both of them into motion.

Laeliquaende's finest captain leapt, hanging in the air for a breathless moment, and the force of his landing drove the thing back a few steps. Yet there were two more, and the foul *seidhr* upon them was terrible. The air cringed as they ran upon naked, flayed, gangrenous feet, their jaws champing, slablike yellow teeth making a horrible clacking that echoed upon the mountainside.

Arn's spear leveled, but Aeredh half-turned. His fingers sank into my arm, and suddenly we were running, the Crownless somehow

between me and the *draugr*. How he withstood the invisible weight
of their stare I do not know; my feet skimmed thin snow and once
more I could not even fall, so swift was his passage.

Arn bolted after us, and Floringaeld streaked sideways. The sword
in his right hand glittered like ice under hard bright sunshine, the
shorter blade in his left reversed, the gem on the back of his gauntlet
no longer dull but giving a sharp viridian flash. One of the *draugr*
fell, its head hanging from its neck by a thin thread of frost-bit tis-
sue; its scream sent heavy awl-needles through my ears. It did not
bleed, for their humors are frozen, but it dropped to all fours with a
sound like thundercrack and began crawl-lolloping on all fours. Even
then it was unholy swift, and it still clasped the hilt of its rust-rotted
blade, which scraped a great dark furrow in ice-hard earth.

※※※※※

The whole night of fire and rapine, death and terror is lamented by
the survivors and also their kin of Dorael, Galath, Faeron-Alith, the
Harbors—the whole North, and not just by Elder but by the Secondborn who heard of it. Of them all, though, 'tis only the sagas of that
last lonely battle I cannot listen to.

Floringaeld must have been weary, and he grieved the loss of
his lord. Yet he drove the three *draugr* back, spinning among them
like a whirlwind, singing as he fought. The warriors shepherding
exhausted refugees sought to offer some aid, but so swift and deadly
was the combat none could approach. Against the slope he pushed
his opponents, the crawling one with its head hanging by a thread
seeking to tangle the Elder's legs.

His gauntlet flashing, the Heavy-hand gave true death to a pair of
the foul things as the mist froze around them and the snow thickened
underfoot. The third and largest he forced up, into the fog, and 'tis
said that any traveler in that lonely place will still hear smithy-echoes
when clouds touch the peak.

Once the tail-end of the ragged ash-daubed line of refugees
was prodded to safety a handful of warriors turned back to render
both chase and aid, but a thunderous warning interfered. Those few

witnesses barely avoided a wall of snow and rock hurtling downward, freed from the mountainside by the noise of battle. When the
rushing rumble faded the clearing lay beneath a fresh covering of
white several bodylengths deep, the hidden pass was blocked, and
Floringaeld of Laeliquaende was never seen again in those lands or
any other, save perhaps the blessed, uttermost West.

PART FOUR

TO DORAEL

Regret My Hope

Only later was it learned that the traitor had been captured during one of his secret expeditions outside the valley, for he increasingly broke his uncle's law and wandered far seeking rare materials. Brought before the Enemy's most dangerous lieutenant was Alaessia's son, and no torture was employed, for such was not that dread lord's way.

No, indeed. Instead, the Eye offered him a gift.

—Gaemirwen of Dorael

The treeline rushed up a boulder-studded slope to swallow us, and Aeredh did not slow even when we were deep among snow-hooded evergreens. When he finally halted my teeth clicked together and the world revolved sickeningly before I stopped, too, my ear to his chest and his hand cupping my coral-braided head.

The iron casket trapped between us dug into my flesh, but I could not move. His other arm was about my waist, and the Crownless pressed me to him as if to muffle a child's screaming.

There was nothing, I had not the breath. The forest was quiet save for the stealthy unsound of dawn, the creak of an occasional bough, and the thunder of an ageless heart under my cheek. I heard his pulse, slow and strong; I shut my eyes, wishing all this would go away and I would somehow find myself in our closet at Dun Rithell, Arn beside me, hearing the creak-clamor of a greathall waking to another day of irritations, annoyances, boredom, and all the duties I had chafed under.

His grasp gentled, but he did not turn me loose. The warm hand upon my hair stroked once, twice. My slippers were cold, for we were outside the valley now and winter still held the world in her bony fingertips. We rested upon snow as the Elder could, not sinking below its crust; the sensation was familiar, and the heartbeat in my right ear repeated *I am, I am, I am.*

It sounded like my mother's when as a youngling I would rest against her, or Arn's when I woke late at night from ordinary dreaming. Or my teacher Idra's as I leaned listening-close to her chest during her final illness, though the slowness of her mortal pulse was that of illness and age, and an Elder's is…otherwise.

"*Peace,*" he finally murmured in the Old Tongue. "*Fear nothing, sun-girl. I am with you.*"

Perhaps he thought me a horse, or some other brute creature in need of calming. In truth I felt like one, shaking with exhaustion and terror. The sound the *draugr*'s teeth made, clacking together—I knew, with miserable certainty, I would have nightmares from it. They would have to jostle aside those from the screaming, the ravaged corpses, the dark inside Taeron's tower, the column of smoke bearing horrified faces…there was no shortage, I was replete with horror.

"I do not want it," I said numbly. I could not even dream of my kin or my home, only of war and carnage. "I do not want it, take it away, why did you do this to me?"

"If I could…" The words died, and Aeredh took a deep breath. His arms tightened almost unbearably, and his fingers tensed upon my hair. "I cannot regret my hope, or our meeting. I live in fear of some harm coming to you; yet you are mortal and I will grieve unto my own passing when…" A shudder, his or mine, passed through us both.

"Let go." I could not move, could barely breathe. "Aeredh. Please."

"*Should I?*" His hand fell from my braids, though I still could not move. "*Not even if they hang me from the walls of Agramar.* Tell me—" His tone changed, became practical and businesslike, a man with a task to perform and a wary animal to shepherd. "No, never mind. Are you hurt?"

My head throbbed, the *draugr*'s cry still reverberating, and I could not think with an Elder holding me so.

Or, perhaps, only this particular Elder. "I cannot tell." I was abruptly conscious of being alone with a man amid snow-choked trees. There is no such thing as propriety during battle and precious little of it during disaster, yet a hot wash of shame—married to some other inarticulate but terribly powerful feeling—suffused me. "Arneior. I have to...where is..."

"Probably upon our trail." His heartbeat continued against my ear, and he was warm. If not for the sharp edges of the iron coffer squeezed between us, the closeness might even have been comforting. "I would not put it past her to hunt an Elder, even one taking great care."

It was a compliment indeed, but I was not cheered. "She will find me." The hope of that event was a slap of cold water, dousing every other feeling. "You can take this accursed thing and the cloak, and go where you will."

"And leave you alone in the Wild? You think so little of me, my lady." Aeredh did not move; the words vibrated in his chest along with his heartbeat, humming under my cheek. "The Enemy knows of an *alkuine*. Should you return to your riverside it will only be a matter of time before his servants descend upon the place. Dorael is better; even he cannot pierce Melair's barrier, else he would have long before now."

"You thought Waterstone was safe." My voice shook. "Yet now this. If Arn and I return we can warn them, we can hide—"

Even I did not believe as much. But what else could I do, or say? Like a trapped bird battering itself against cage-walls, I knew only the desire to leave, to run. To go *home*, no matter if I foundered in the attempt.

Knowing I would not, could not, did not alter the urge.

"If you are held by the Elder, he has little reason to seek out your folk." Quiet and logical, the Crownless continued. "He has ever considered Secondborn less, though amenable to many of his plans."

"Just as the Elder do." I stiffened, sought to pull away. My feet sank slightly in the snow-crust, though the thin, heavily embroidered shoes were not sodden yet. "Tarit is right. You care nothing for mortals."

"Were I mortal we would both be dead several times over, Eol and your shieldmaid as well. But perhaps you are right, my lady." Finally, he let me loose—though not by much. Now he had my shoulders, and examined my face. I wished my braids were fallen or I had the mantle's broad, comforting hood to hide in. "I will bear your hatred; I deserve it."

There was no place to seek shelter. Aeredh studied me; I could not help but return the favor. He held me above the snow, and there was no wall or lock behind his blue eyes. I did not know how to name what was in his gaze, only that it struck something akin inside me and I could still feel his heartbeat upon my cheek, resounding in my own wrists and throat. Perhaps it was merely some manner of *seidhr*-sympathy between us, for he had kept me alive during the freeze before we reached the Ice Door, and I had used his aid to draw a lichblade's splinter from living flesh.

I had called, doubting even my own weirding, yet he answered. He asked me to go into the darkness of the tower, and I had. There was no way to blame him that was not also holding myself to account.

"*I do not hate you.*" Unsure and unwilling, the words left my mouth of their own accord, and in the Old Tongue as well. "*I do not think I could.*"

"*Then I am content.*" His grasp was oddly gentle, and his right thumb stroked my shoulder, a tiny movement. "We will rejoin your shieldmaid, and the others. Fear not."

I had every reason for terror, but the sound—*I am, I am*—still echoed in my own pulse. I nodded, clutching the iron box, and either its trembling had eased or mine was so marked I could not feel otherwise.

Aeredh took me under his arm again. We set off, his steps shortened to match mine, leaving only faint impressions upon the time-packed snow.

Laggards from the Fire

Hope is sharper than fear.

—Elder proverb

Arneior was indeed upon our heels; a short while later she burst from thick shade between two white-swathed trees and fair skidded to a halt. Naciel's lessons served her in good stead, for 'tis no small thing to match an Elder's speed. Still, a spray of old snow lifted as she stopped, her mouth crumpled, and I sprinted from Aeredh's side. My feet sank, the slippers soaking in melt after three steps, but I cared little, and flung my free arm about her.

She did the same, her spear held well away, its end sinking into frozen white. My shieldmaid cursed long and low, breathing a warm spot amid my braids, and I could say nothing through the sobs caught in my throat, aching for release.

"—run off," she finished, her arm so tight it rivaled Aeredh's, near crushing the breath out of me. "Do not do that ever again, Solveig. Do not *ever*."

There was no use in saying I had little choice in the matter. A shieldmaid who has lost her charge is forsworn; that is an unpleasant state indeed and after the night we had just passed neither of us were in best temper. The wonder was that she did not scold me more harshly, and perhaps give a clout to my ear as my father would to Bjorn.

Finally, her grasp loosened, and she pushed me slightly away, eyeing me critically. "Are you hurt?"

"No." I could not suppress a shudder; it is well known those with the weirding are *draugr*'s preferred food, and they can easily infect us with their rot. "It had not time to strike me. Did you...Floringaeld?"

"I do not know." There were dark circles under her eyes despite the *sitheviel*, and the edges of her woad had flaked free, leaving a faint yellowish tint on cheek and forehead. Still, she essayed a grim smile. "I am beginning to dislike the North most mightily, my weirdling."

Oh, indeed. At least she could still jest, however bleakly. "We are still alive." However long that dubious mercy would linger I could not tell; nor did I dare think that perhaps its cessation might be preferable to more terror and bloodshed. "Are you injured? Tell me."

"Nothing but my wits half-gone from worrying about my Solveig." She magnanimously turned her glare upon Aeredh next. "Well, Elder? What now?"

"Now we strike for Dorael, as swiftly as possible." Aeredh studied the trees, wearing a listening look. The dark weal upon his cheek, clearly visible in brightening mornlight, was now smaller; marks from a *haugr*'s whip, like lichburn, tax even an Elder's ability to heal. "There will be survivors moving in the same direction; we shall not be alone for long."

"Another Elder city?" Arneior, like her charge, plainly thought little of this plan. "Because the last two have fared so very well."

He acknowledged both the sarcasm and the truth it contained with a wry expression and a graceful shrug, the hilt at his shoulder bobbing slightly. "A different power holds that land, my lady shield-maid, and in any case we have no choice. The Enemy's forces will be at their work in the valley for some while, and the routes from thence are narrow and laborious. Taeron's plans will have taken that into account, giving survivors the best chance of flight, and some will no doubt close the way behind them. Yet soon enough his creatures will be watching the ways into Dorael." The Elder still scanned the forest, alert to any further pursuit; I wondered if he spoke to Eol in this fashion. "What worries me most, though, is the ice-dead upon the Pass. They should not be there."

"Those things should not be anywhere." Arn's knuckles were white upon her spear. "I thought them foul stories only."

The iron casket quivered against my left arm; a new day crept between the trees. My eyes were dry and grainy, the rest of me aching though a steady glow of *sitheviel* burned inside my ribs. Yesterday morning was a lifetime ago; by this time we had already been upon the water.

Pressure mounted in my throat. I could not tell whether I wished to scream or weep. The shadow-cloak, though thin, was warm as my great green mantle with its lining of wolf-fur—was it burning in Taeron's palace? Had an *orukhar* taken it as spoil?

"I wish they were," Aeredh said gravely. "Come. I shall help you both by turns; let us step lightly as we may."

My shieldmaid embraced me again, a hard, fierce one-armed hug, and we set off through the woods.

◄░░░░░░░►

We spoke little, though we were presumably much safer; in any case, the cold, while nothing like new-winter freeze, was still enough to trouble a mortal wearing only armor. Arn's ribs moved steadily with the warming breath, stoking the body's fires, and so did mine. The trees were thick, the undergrowth winter-dead, and the snow packed tightly as often happens just before the thaw turns many a drift into rotted traps for the unwary. Boughs creaked under wet white, though thankfully there was little wind and the sky, iron-grey, threatened precipitation that never fell.

Aeredh's listening look increased as the day wore on, and as the day's eye fell from noon-height we turned due south instead of south-and-west. I saw no sign of passage, but both Arn and Aeredh halted at intervals, glancing at each other, and as dusk hung purple veils between the trees we emerged into a deep-shadowed dell busy with soft activity.

An iced-over stream was beginning to shake off its torpor, a thin silver rill in its very center refreezing nightly, judging by the delicate scallops at its margin. Well-shielded blue *aelflame* provided warmth and illumination, and a buzz of welcome greeted Aeredh.

Our approach had been remarked, of course; the survivors of Laeliquaende were both weary and wary. There were small tents hidden among the trees, not brightly colored as the festival cloth-houses but of natural dye, taking on the forest-hues around them almost like the shadow-cloak.

"Thank the Blessed!" A mortal voice rang among the murmurs of Old Tongue, southron strong and clear. Tjorin had arrived just before us and hurried from the largest tent; I bit back a gasp of relief. For pushing aside the flap was a slim, familiar shape, a long fall of bright hair—Naciel winced slightly as she padded from that shelter, where those most weary or wounded among the survivors were receiving aid. "You look half-frozen; fear not, you have reached safety. Many will wish to see you, my friends."

That was not the only shock. Other hurrying footsteps, quick but not quite so light as Elder, sounded in the gloom, and from the shadows figures in black Northern cloth appeared.

"Minnowsharp!" Efain, his eyes bright though his hair was singed and his tunic near-shredded, shouldered Tjorin aside. He thrust out his left hand; Arn, bemused, moved to take it by the wrist as warriors do in the North. He yanked upon her arm and clapped her upon the right shoulder, almost embracing her, and—even stranger—she allowed it, though a shieldmaid does not often let a man treat her so. "I knew it. I *told* Soren you would arrive before dark; I won the wager."

More shadows resolved into Gelad and Karas, who crowded close. There was much good-natured buffeting, as reunited warriors often express relief in such terms, and even low laughter.

"Ah, he bet against me?" The pale, pinched look Arn had been wearing eased, and she allowed Gelad to clasp her left wrist as well, accepting his buffet upon her opposite shoulder with a clap of her own, though with caution for her right hand was full of spear-haft. "I shall have to send him into the mud twice the next time."

I held the casket awkwardly, watching this, and Naciel arrived, as near to breathless as an Elder could be. She was no longer barefoot; inside her slippers were linen bandages, wrapped tight and clean.

"*Thank the Blessed.*" The princess repeated her husband's greeting, but in the Old Tongue. For the third time that day I was embraced, and she hugged me hard enough to send hot water trickling down my cheek; I was grateful for the twilight to cover such evidence. *"Oh, my friend. I worried for naught; is Floringaeld with you?"*

"Against you?" Soren appeared too, his heavy eyebrows peaked and his grin visible even in the dimness. "My lady Minnow, I wagered you would arrive here before us, and ask what kept laggards from the campfire."

"We have not seen him since…" I could barely produce the words, between the vise-grip of Naciel's arms and the leap of my heart into my throat. *"What of the others? Is…"*

I could not say what I truly wished to know. The question simply refused to rise from my throat, for if I asked and the answer was *no*, what would I do?

"Solveig!" A familiar voice, and the knot of Northerners separated. Another shadow thrust between them. Naciel's arms loosened; she drew away, smiling, and reached for Tjorin's hand. *"Solveig!"*

It was Eol, his blackened armor ragged and smoke-tarnished, his swordhilt heavily wrapped once more so the gleam of the gem did not give it away. He pushed past Arneior almost rudely, descending upon me. My shoulders were grasped, the world wobbling before catching like a skirt upon a fence-nail.

Everything was ash and bloodshed, yet now something had been set aright.

"You are alive." His teeth gleamed as the dell slid deeper into darkness, the blue glitters of *aelflame* shuttering themselves as if even the fires knew we were hunted. *"I feared the worst."*

It was not so much the words as the tone—he sounded like my brother scolding Astrid, or our father when Bjorn had committed yet another blundering bit of mischief. His fingers sank into both shadow-cloak and flesh beneath; he held me at rigid arm's length.

"Eol." His name caught in my throat, and the relief was like a live forge in my chest. I could not find the Old Tongue, though I had spoken it near-daily for months now. "Where were you? How did you escape?"

"It matters not." He paused; a hush had enfolded the small camp.

Most of the Elder were looking away, Tjorin wore a curious smile, and Arneior studied the air over Eol's head, graciously not taking exception to a man handling her charge in this fashion. *"I swear, I will never let you out of…"* The heir of Naras stopped short; his grasp softened. "Ah. You must be weary, and cold."

"R-relieved." More hot water trickled down my cheeks, but I could hope it was not visible. "Nobody had s-seen you, or your men, and I…"

"No need for worry." As quickly as he had seized me he let go, but otherwise did not move. "We are all accounted for, even those from Nithraen; Daerith was wounded after his arrows were spent and Kirilit requires some rest before he may move with any speed. But all in all…we are well enough. There will be much joy at your survival—and our lady Minnowsharp's," he added hastily. "We have travel-fare, and fire. It shall not be so difficult a journey as before. You must take some food and sleep, both of you." Belatedly, he glanced over my shoulder and caught sight of his friend. *"Aeredh, by the Blessed, I should have known. What kept you?"*

"Oh, nothing large." The Elder's smile was instant, and he clasped the captain's wrist. They yanked each other close, shoulders meeting with bruising force, and embraced as brothers do in the North. *"A thing with two whips, a lich, a few pale excrescences, and a trio of corpses. Tell me there is some wine, my friend, and I shall bless you."*

We were the last to arrive, though I did not care at that moment. It was enough that there were fires to keep the cold at bay, leftover Elder vintage carried in haste from the valley, and shelter from lingering winter. The tent for the wounded and children was not overly crowded; Arn and I were shown to a hastily constructed bed of downed fir boughs and torn cloaks. The instant I dropped into its shelter consciousness fled me, and at least for that night I did not dream.

But I clutched the iron casket close, waking with its imprint pressed into the skin of my upper arms, over and among the marks of a man's fingers.

A Lamp of Belief

*What houses have remained Faithful, disdaining the
Enemy, adding our small strength to the Elder war? Too
few by far. The list grows ever shorter, and yet we endure.
The price of our alliance is steep.*

—Tharos son of Ildar

Dawn was made of freezing fog and stealthy sounds, tree
branches groaning under fleecy coats growing heavier as melt
tiptoed closer. I lunged into full wakefulness when Arneior moved
upon our couch and had to rub at my eyes. Naciel leaned over us,
her finger to her lips; the princess beckoned. We followed her out of
the tent, stepping quietly between the huddled forms of Elder taking
what rest they could.

It is not often those folk seek such surcease; sometimes they
dream with their eyes open and 'tis good as mortal slumber. Only
when driven to extremity—or when they wish it—do they do as tired
mortals will.

Naciel did not quite limp but stepped very delicately indeed, and
her bandaged feet bore loose slippers which did not match her torn
skirts. Yet her beauty was unabated, every tear and tatter merely
accenting its depth.

The camp was silent; shadows moved in the fog as the midnight
watch returned for fire and a mouthful. The High-helm's folk had

lived in Laeliquaende for a long time but the Elder do not forget what they have suffered, and before any city of theirs was founded they well knew how to move swiftly over hill and through forest, how to guard their younglings while doing so, and how to confuse pursuit.

Tjorin was before a much smaller tent, perched upon a boulder with his knees drawn up, watching a campfire. *Aelflame* burned, the fire's fingertips blue; I knew the *seidhr* of kindling it now, thanks to Aeredh.

Yesterday seemed dreamlike; I could not imagine another Elder city simply, entirely gone. I still felt a strong, slow heartbeat upon my cheek. And my upper arms remembered the feel of Eol's fingers, too. It meant little; both Elder and captain were merely afraid of losing their captive *alkuine*.

And yet.

Naciel touched her husband's shoulder as she passed, a brief tenderness I had to look away from. Arneior was busy attempting to keep watch in every direction, her leather-wrapped braids disarranged but the dark rings under her eyes erased. For all that, she moved a trifle stiffly, and I creaked like an old woman.

Idra's pained expression on damp-chill mornings made much sense now, and I was probably wearing a variety of it.

The tent—stocks of them had been hidden along escape-routes, I later learned—was lit by a filigreed Elder lamp upon a small folding table, both cunningly and beautifully designed. A jug and two cups sat beside, and she poured us each a healthy measure. "How do you feel?" Her southron was marvelous clear now.

"Like I am made of wood, and the axe-mites have been at me," Arn muttered, taking a cup with alacrity.

It was springwine clear and fierce, in some ways better than sleep. I had to lower my own goblet and gasp for air; I saw the princess's gaze settle upon the iron casket.

Which I still carried. It did not seem right to lay it aside, and I had little enough left. The idea of losing aught else gave me an unsteady feeling no Elder draught could allay, but if she would take the cursed thing I would not gainsay her.

I might even express my thanks in song, could I but find the breath.

I finished my drink in more leisurely fashion; Naciel poured Arn another cupful. My shieldmaid saluted her, and set about sipping instead of quaffing.

"We must speak," Taeron's daughter said, finally.

"About this?" I set my cup—wooden, and smoothly elegant—down, and the iron box beside it, glad to be free of its bulk. " 'Twas in your father's tower, princess. I shall leave it in your care."

"No." Her mien grew passing grave though no less lovely. She had drawn her hair back; the golden flood rippled past her waist. "You do not even know what it holds, do you?"

"A jewel." I sounded very calm, all things considered. "Made by Faevril, and wrested from the Enemy by an Elder princess and her Secondborn lover. It seems right such a thing should go to you—"

"And have Faevril's sons seek to slay me for it?" She shook her head and glanced inquiringly at Arn, indicating the jug—but my shieldmaid did not wish for more. "No, my friend. I may call you that, may I not? You are my friend, Solveig daughter of Gwendelint?"

Why do you ask? "I met Faevril's sons in Nithraen—Curiaen, and Caelgor. The latter offered his aid, though he had not time to render any." I was not at all certain any help Caelgor the Fair offered would be to my liking, either. "And yes, Naciel daughter of Taeron, I am your friend; I do not know why you would ask as if you doubt my regard."

"Indeed I do not. I could not, after what you have done." Naciel's mouth drew down at either corner and her expression grew even more grave, if that were possible.

I thought I knew why and crossed my arms, palms cupping my elbows. "Your city." I could not speak very loudly; the weight was in my throat again, and perhaps my voice had not fully recovered from smoke or battlesong. "Your home—your father, too. The Enemy's servants were chasing us, perhaps we led them to—"

"Oh, no. Do you think that traitor cousin of mine did his work so swiftly, only beginning it upon your arrival?" The Silverfoot's dark gaze kindled, and a glimpse of that knifelike edge turned her beauty sharp again, though no less weary. "No, I had my suspicions of his wanderings in the far hills of our valley for more than a few mortal years. He was careful, and clever, and after all none believed my father's own kin would traffic with the Enemy. You may rest assured we were betrayed by our own, not by any doing of yours."

I could not decide if it was mere politeness or an honest estimation of Maedroth's treachery, for I knew Taeron's daughter possessed a kind heart. "Are you so certain?"

"Oh, aye." Her mouth pulled down bitterly once more, but even that grimace did not alter her loveliness. "I warned my father, but he would not listen, thinking his sister's son merely prey to an... an unwholesome affection, and struggling against it. So I made ever more secret preparations, without his knowledge or my *cousin's—*" It was almost a silent snarl; she clearly could not bring herself to say Maedroth's name. "And I ensured supplies over and above those already laid by; I held my peace, thinking my sire would see reason before 'twas too late. Even the Blessed warned him. *Do not over-cherish the things of your own making*, Ulimo said, not once but thrice. Our fall was also of our own making." She gazed at the lamp upon the table, her hands tense amid ragged skirts. "As always."

If she meant comfort, it was of a bleak variety indeed. "Nevertheless, I am sorry." And uneasy, for Tjorin had mentioned Ulimo as well—the great blue-robed lord of the deeps we Secondborn also name Njord, whose daughters sometimes sun themselves upon rocks, singing so sweetly mortal sea-travelers are drawn to wreck by the sound.

"And I." Naciel moved restlessly, wincing as she shifted her weight. Her feet pained her still that morning—I still did not know what she had done, hearing the tale shortly afterward, but I suspected the dimensions of her bravery well enough. "Yet I am about to ask even more of you, weary and troubled as you are. You should have found shelter and care among us, not this."

"We have." There was no denying it. "You have been kind to us, Naciel. You and Tjorin both."

"Have we?" She took a deep breath, looking past me at the drawn tent-flap. I had the sudden, uncomfortable idea that Tjorin was standing guard instead of merely warming himself as all mortals like to upon a chill morn. "There is summat I would ask of you, Solveig of Dun Rithell. I have no right; you have done more for me than any other. I owe you—*both* of you—my very life, not to mention my husband's, and more. It is not meet that I should beg for aught else, yet I do."

Arneior's gaze rose over her goblet-rim, met with mine. The same look had often passed between Aeredh and Eol during our travels, or Tjorin and Naciel in Waterstone; I was ever glad of my shieldmaid, though at that moment the joy was sharp as a blade.

"Enough." Arn set her wooden goblet down. "Let us hear what you would have us do, princess. We are allies to the House of Naras, and have proved our faith to you and your husband besides. Say it, and be done."

"Even if it is something..." Naciel's bright eyes half-closed, her head slightly averted as her chin dipped and a bright sheaf of her beautiful hair fell over her shoulder.

She looked, of all things, ashamed.

"My Solveig would never turn away from a friend in need," Arn said, and the certainty shining in her features shamed me, because I also suspected what Taeron's daughter meant to ask.

I could be wrong. Please, let me be. "Say what you will, Naciel. Faithless is the one who turns away from a troubled ally." The proverb did not quite sting my tongue...but it did threaten to catch upon a rock in my throat.

"Very well." She faced me again, her shoulders pushed back; straight and slim the princess of Laeliquaende was, though footsore and heart-aching from many losses. "Only my father could open the tower. But the Freed Jewel rests within that casket, and I am the one who knows the secret of its opening. I would unlock it, and have you take up what Lithielle won at such cost."

Oh, sheepshit. Once or twice Idra had remarked that there was no greater curse for a *volva* than being right, and that was the moment I understood what my teacher had meant. The knowledge, like all gained in such circumstances, was bitter as spring herbs. "You know I cannot use the thing—even one of Faevril's minor toys threatened to boil me from the inside. I am Secondborn, Naciel, and—"

"I do not think it has a *use*, my friend. Please, listen." Her hands were before her now, and it was the first time I saw an Elder's fingers twist together so hard they turned bloodless, like Astrid when she feared a particular task but must perform it anyway.

Had I not done the same more than once upon the winter solstice, dreading failure? I subsided, yet I felt that anxiety once more—distinct from the terror of a shattered city and *draugr*, a far more familiar and entirely unlikable companion.

And I felt the iron box's quivering in my arms as well, though it rested innocent and demure upon the table.

"Indeed Faevril never used the Jewels, only wore them." Now the princess spoke almost eagerly, with the speed of one who must impart much before they are interrupted. "But an *alkuine* made them, and only he knew their secrets. You are the only other of that kind I have ever heard of, Solveig—the only other Aeredh has, or my father, and Odynn's ravens brought him news of the wide world for hundreds of mortal years. To have you appear now, while the Enemy is resurgent and taking our kingdoms after a long watchful peace...Aeredh believes it means something. He believes the Blessed have sent you for this very purpose, and he is not one to trust lightly, nor to say such a thing without gravest proof." The light in her eyes intensified; Naciel of Laeliquaende's own belief shone like the filigreed lamp.

I did not need weirding to see it. "What if I attempt the thing inside that casket and it kills me, princess? What then?"

"It will not." And she sounded so sure, but Taeron's daughter had no *seidhr* save the share granted to every Elder as a matter of course.

For all their beauty and their power, we sometimes do what they cannot.

She pressed onward. "And if another *alkuine* holds Lithielle's Jewel, Faevril's sons may somehow be brought to reason, or at least alliance. We have little chance against the Black Land, but what there is lies in our leaguer, not our division. So Aeredh says, and I agree." Naciel took a deep breath, and her knotted hands now pressed into her middle. "Please, Solveig. Bjornwulf was a Secondborn like you; Tjorin is one as well. Take up what the first won, and help me save the second."

Arneior made a restless movement, but I was still, and my *seidhr* sharpened. "Ah," I heard myself say, in the peculiar tone of a *volva* speaking truth that is not quite prophecy but close enough. "You do not wish your child born fatherless."

Arneior cocked her head, examining the Elder woman afresh. One bearing new life is sacred to all, and shieldmaids will protect them hardly less assiduously than an oathbound charge. Naciel was not showing yet, but I knew my guess correct when the princess's gaze met mine, holding for a long moment.

Knowing herself holding such a fragile treasure, she had still drawn the Enemy's forces from our hiding-place. Her bravery shamed me all the more deeply, for I did not share it.

"I have so little time left with Tjorin, after all. He is mortal." Naciel's mouth crumpled; for a lone moment an ageless Elder looked younger than my sister. "And afterward the Enemy will pursue both dam and foal until he achieves our extinction, for he hated my father—and my husband's too, no less than he feared them. You are our only hope."

My mouth opened and I drew breath, but the words died unsaid. I was, for once, struck utterly speechless.

Her brittle self-possession returned, Naciel turned to the table. Her strong, slim fingers flickered upon the lid of the casket. She made no attempt to hide the trick of its opening, and fool that I was, I could not look away. A *volva* watches such things in order to learn, it is as natural as breathing and as inevitable as sunset.

There was a click, a soft sound like a sleeping child's sigh, and a smaller rectangle upon the deep-carven iron lid lifted. It did not open completely, but the tent's fabric walls rippled uneasily.

"I cannot force you," she continued. "I can only ask, and I have no right to. Yet I do, my young friend. I have no choice."

With that, the daughter of Taeron nodded at my shieldmaid, and passed by us half-limping with a sweet brush of torn, silken skirts. The door-flap moved, the sound of a winter dawn and soft Elder voices slipping through, and we were left to our own devices.

Lithielle's Jewel

Thus was Lithielle granted a mortal death, singing as she clasped her lover's body. Some say a great light flashed, others aver a deeper music answered, still others that a vast silence descended from the sky. All agree upon the vanishment, all agree that ever after ildora *grew not only in Dorael but in other places. And a raven brought the news to the Greycloak's throne...*

—The Vanishing of Lithielle, *attributed to Daerith the Elder*

Arneior stared at the table as if she expected something venomous to appear and lunge for us. A thin, sweet unsound of *seidhr* blur-buzzed not just in the space near my ear but also behind my heart, the pulse thumping in my chest nowhere near as strong and sure as Aeredh's. I waited, but nothing happened.

Finally, my shieldmaid turned her head slightly, to catch me in the edge of her sharp vision. "Well?" she said, softly.

Oh, please, Arn. Not you too. "Well, what?" I eyed the jug of springwine; perhaps another draught would settle me, or make the trembling in my limbs recede. " 'Tis an exceeding small box, to be pursued by such great folk."

A pathetic attempt at jesting, playing upon a secondary word for a woman's most private parts, but it drew a pained laugh from us both nonetheless. My small one gave her spear a thoughtful quarter-turn, its blunt end digging into cold earth scraped bare of snow. These tents had no carpets, but they were far better than sleeping in the open.

I exhaled, breath shaken into small pieces by a shiver. Another awful silence rose like cold water, filling the tent to the brim—such quiet should have been comforting, because she was with me. Yet 'twas not, because I sensed what *she* was about to say, too.

It is a good thing to have a shieldmaid, but measuring one's own actions against their uncompromising is not comfortable at all.

"Well?" she repeated.

"Arn..." My arms hurt, as if the bones inside them had not finished growing and were forced to do so quickly. My knees were sopsoft, and my back was unhappy in the extreme. Last night's pure, untinctured terror still quivered all through me, like the casket's steady feathery motion. How much more of this could I endure before I went utterly, gratefully mad?

There are stories of what happens when fear—or agony past mortal bearing—eats one possessing the *seidhr*. It is an unpretty end indeed.

"You wear the bands." Oh, she was pitiless, my small one, for all she meant to render aid. "That thing is weirding, not something I can set my spear against. What are we to do with it?"

"Did you not hear what I said?" Frustration nipped at my throat, along with the dryness no Elder wine could erase. "It could kill me, Arneior." *Or worse.* I could not tell what frightened me more, and that is dangerous.

I had wished for adventure, for great deeds. How many times had I chafed at my own limitations, even as Idra said, *Large does not mean effective, the small has its place, try again*?

"But you are *volva*." Clearly Arneior did not credit such a fate for her charge. The tent's walls rippled slightly as faint dawnbreeze mouthed them. "And why would the gods bring us here if you were not meant to wield it? That makes no sense."

"We cannot go home." The words were ash upon my tongue, like the flakes of burning still clinging to us both. If Naciel was ragged and Arn smeared with smoke-shavings, I was grateful I could not see what a sorry sight I myself presented at the moment. "The next time an Elder city falls some dread thing may well murder us both. If not, we shall be caught between Aeredh and Faevril's sons, grain between millstones. Or that thing in the coffer, whatever it is, might not kill me but burn me to witlessness, leave me insensate as a beast. Can you imagine that, Arneior?" I did not think she could—none who lack weirding can compass the particular horror of that fate. "What say the Wingéd? Will they offer aid the next time we face a lich, or *orukhar*, or—"

"I have been afraid." She half-turned, disregarding the table to face me, shoulders square and chin set as if we were about to spar upon a training-yard's beaten-earth floor, a far more serious affair than the play of dodge-dancing we often engaged upon at home. "Since we left Dun Rithell, I can barely think for the fear. I was afraid when you were lost upon the Elder Roads, I was afraid during Nithraen's fall, I was afraid when we faced the *trul*. I was deathly afraid when I could not find you last night, for you were not in our rooms and those foul things were already upon the riverbank. Then I was afraid again when the *draugr* screamed." Her freckles stood out, and the ghost of her woad-stripe was bright against chalky paleness. "I am *terrified*, Solveig. But every time I look to you there is some comfort, for my wierdling is a *volva*. You know what to do; you will not fail here."

Oh, gods. I depended on her certainty far more than my own clearly inadequate abilities, but how could I say so now? "You turned three of Naras's wolves and a clodfoot drylander into a rowing team fit to win an Elder competition, Arn, and in less than a nineday. You faced a *trul*, you've killed half-a-dozen *orukhar* at once, and you rescued Naciel from...from *him*." I found I could not say Maedroth's name aloud either. My tongue simply refused. "If the Wingéd are not pleased it is no fault of yours, and I say so freely in their hearing."

"So you trust me, but not my trust in you? For shame, my weirdling." She did not smile, her generous mouth pulled tight. "I shattered an Elder's brain-casing and cut off his head, and the thought does not sicken me as it should. I hardly know who I am, now." Her spearblade scintillated in lanternlight, the merest hint of motion though she held herself stiffly upright. "You were meant for great things; I have always said so. At least look upon this bauble they wish you to wield."

"I hardly know who I am, either." It hurt to say, but there was also sharp relief like lancing an infection, drawing out the foulness so healing may begin. She had admitted her own fear, yet I still hesitated to bare the depths of mine. "I could not even turn Aeredh and Eol aside when they took us from Dun Rithell with a lie."

"Perhaps you were not meant to," she pointed out, reasonably enough. "And in any case it does not matter now, Sol." A deep breath, Elder armor glittering with the movement. "I do not think we will ever see Tarnarya again. I have not since that first night in the fog."

Oh, Arn. I took two steps, noiseless in my borrowed slippers, and found I could unclench at least my right hand. I touched her arm below the armor-sleeve, covered only with quilted fabric; flesh I had sealed, but the jagged slice from an *orukhar*'s blade could not be mended until I had some time with needle and thread.

Those were lost in Waterstone's ruin, too.

The shadowmantle hid my own arm, even in the lantern's glow. But the sleeve was pushed back and the lowest band upon my wrist showed, blueblack ink forced under the skin. My shieldmaid looked down at me.

There was no defense against the faith in her gaze, any more than against the sound of Aeredh's heartbeat or Naciel's entreaty.

For who had chosen to go to Laeliquaende, after all? Who had said, *We are the allies of Naras, we will go where we are led*? Who had entered the tower despite repeating her refusal, because the lure of something so powerful could not be denied to one such as I?

High time for truth, even if I would only admit it to myself. I was not really frightened of the thing in the iron box, and the lack of fear was disturbing in and of itself. What truly terrified Solveig of Dun Rithell was her own ambition, the yearning to be more—to have a saga, perhaps, to be thought wise and honorable…and then miscarrying the feat, becoming merely a jape, a cautionary tale, or worse, forgotten entirely.

The knowledge was bitter indeed. I swallowed it, for there was little other choice, and nodded. "We will not," I agreed. "But at least we are together, and that is something."

"Oh, aye." Her spear moved again as she shifted, leaning into my touch. "Will it be enough, do you think?"

I do not know. "It has to be." Despite the springwine, I was cold. There was no way to avoid what came next; all my struggle and striving had availed naught. "This is weirding, and you know what that means."

"I shall make certain none touch you during the event." Arneior nodded briskly, and the sudden easing of her expression was painful, for I could not share it. She patted my hand upon her arm, warm callused fingers. Then I had to let her go; she brushed past me to the tent-flap, standing guard no less than Tjorin outside. Perhaps Naciel had joined him, waiting for whatever would happen.

Yet she turned from the flap, and spoke again. "Sol?"

I looked to my shieldmaid, half hoping she had changed her mind. "Hm?"

"You sang, last night. In battle." Arneior wore a small but definite smile, encouraging as my mother's while teaching Astrid to walk. "You've never done that before." *And you have never done this*, she meant, *but look, there is hope.*

I tried to smile in return, but my face was frozen. Instead, I turned to the table again, and pushed my sleeves—both dress and Elder shadowcloth—higher. My bands were plainly visible now, and I walked to my doom with them displayed.

⬚⬚⬚⬚⬚

A few moments' worth of study, and I saw how the lid could slide wholly free. My hands were so cold; not even midsummer's sun could have warmed me as I stood before that small table. Deep in the woods, in a tiny camp full of stunned, wounded Elder and exhausted warriors, in a small tent still smelling of the sweet herbs packed with its cloth…it was not a setting worthy of tale or saga.

In fact, 'twas rather threadbare, and the great epics never speak of the discomfort in one's stomach from sheer terror, nor the clumsiness of mortal fingers. They do not speak of the clamor of battle or the fear which holds one frozen amid the blood and bowel-cut, nor of the silent weeping of children as they cling to any safety amid fire and rapine. I have sung many a saga before and since; they linger in the breath of all who have heard them, and music burrows into brains both mortal and Elder.

Even *orukhar* sing, after their own fashion, and thus, it is said, perhaps some distant day they will be free of their service to the Enemy and his dread lieutenants.

But no song tells of those things, and I wish at least one did. Yet who would listen to such laments? They do not grant courage, nor ambition, nor strength in the hour of need. All they might give is some compassion, and the world's stores of that treasure oft seem slender indeed.

I rested my fingertips upon cold iron. Ash and travel-dirt clung to my nails, though the shadowmantle was pristine. Underneath it, sour sweat no doubt dyed the dress I had been gifted. Elder cloth will turn aside dirt and sometimes rain, but Secondborn flesh does not, and I was wholly mortal.

Arn faced the tent-flap, her spear easy in her grasp. She did not look back, even when the lid sprang aside almost of its own will, as if the thing underneath it yearned for freedom.

The songs say Faevril's work was beautiful, but the word is pale beside what he achieved. Light poured from a bed of black Elder velvet, richer than silver and brighter than gold. Like sunshine it was, and moonglow, and yet unlike either, and also different from the fire of torches or the dry pure burning of stars. It could be said that it was not light at all, though the faceted jewel reflected every flicker of illumination that came its way, magnifying and hallowing even the smallest gleam.

No, not light. Perhaps *clarity* is a better word, or *force*. To name is to explain, but the term has not yet been found in any song save that of the very first Making itself.

To see a Jewel was to understand why the Allmother's firstborn coveted such beauty, for the glow was tender and forgiving, radiating in every direction. To understand why the one who had wrought such things had guarded them jealously and sworn bitter vengeance when they were taken, yet also to understand why Bjornwulf had cast this shard of brilliance at the feet of Aenarian Greycloak, saying, *Take your bride-price, king, for I value my wife more.*

Of Aenarian's scorn much is said elsewhere, and of Lithielle bending to pick up the ornament, casting one look at her father, and turning away even more is sung. She left the land of her birth directly afterward, to their long lamenting.

Of surpassing loveliness was Lithielle's Jewel, and her gifting it to the king of a hidden valley where she and her lover finally found refuge was a great and powerful deed. So was Taeron's binding it in a box only his daughter could open, for he had access to the tower— the temptation to return and view the treasure, over and over, would have been too much for even one of his will and wisdom.

It was warm, and its facets slick. It shone in the darkened tent, stinging my eyes to weep-blurring with hot heavy tears, and all the *seidhr* in me recognized the language it spoke. Before that moment, none could hear its voice save he who made it, and I glimpsed Faevril again as I had in Nithraen—a tall bright-eyed Elder, a streak of paleness amid his dark hair, his face alight as he finished a crowning masterwork.

For the Jewels were of no material mined or found even in the uttermost West, but *made*. The secret of his craft vibrated in them, plainly visible yet unable to be read by Elder, Secondborn, or even the gods themselves, for they are not *alkuine*.

To see how great one is compared to one's fellows is a fine thing; men will do anything and women hardly less to feel that grace. Yet the one who could hear the Freed Jewel as she held it also saw how small, how insignificant she was next to that light, and though I cupped the radiance in my palms I would fain rather have done as Bjornwulf and cast it away. Anywhere, into the whirlpool under Waterstone's Leap or the sea I had not yet seen with my physical eyes, into a mountain crevasse or the grinding ice of the Glass.

It was small, yes. But so heavy, and when it touched the hollow between my breasts, melting through cloth and finding my skin like a lover's hand, I cried out from the agony.

I fell to my knees, and in my chest was a live coal. The burning pain, hovering just past the edge of pleasure like a sharp blade's kiss, did not end.

It never will.

Seeing, Understanding

Three things make an alkuine: *fire from air, water from stone... and light from darkness.*
—Faeron One-hand, *My Father's Words*

Sol?" A small quiet voice, from very far away. It passed through a vast muffling silence, and I blinked, wondering why the sky was so strange—though not lightless, for a soft glow lined dark creases and drapes. "Solveig?"

Tent. I'm in a tent. The realization swam heavily to the surface of the soup serving as my thoughts; I blinked again, realizing I did indeed have eyelids. Which meant I had eyes.

Did I?

The rest of me came slowly back, subtle selves jostle-crowding into the container I was born with. Fingers slack and useless. Toes in soft Elder slippers, askew. Wrists where thin lines of fire danced, their needle-burn receding as I became aware of it. My legs were insensate clay, my arms numb wood. My chest ached fiercely, and a cramp sank into my ribs as lungs sought to draw in air I still, after all, needed.

Vision warped; my eyes were full. Hot tears trickled down my temples, for I was on my back, flat upon cold earth. *Felled in one blow like a sapling,* I thought, and it struck me as funny.

Or at least, it might have if I could breathe. My mouth worked like a landed fish's, and I might have drowned in clear air had Arneior not, in a move born of desperation, struck me across the face with no little force.

Normally one who is working *seidhr* must not be touched, but she had seen Idra wallop me upon the back a few times when my subtle selves refused to seat themselves properly and I choked upon nothing. The shock rammed me home and I coughed, turning onto my side, curling like certain armored insects found when one lifts a damp woodland rock. Arn hovered uncertainly, but at least I was breathing, each inhale a tortured gasp and its twinned exhale a scraping almost-retch.

More voices filtered through my ringing ears, the Old Tongue sharp and worried. Bit by bit the fit eased, and finally I lay limp, blessed cool air pouring down my throat and passing back out with little difficulty. My cheek throbbed, and the iron-hard dirt under me was at least wonderfully supportive, if not comfortable. I saw the legs of a small Elder table and a blue glow from one of their cold-burning lanterns.

Memory returned—fire, battle, terror in the snow. Everything in me cringed away from the last few minutes, or had it been hours? From touching the loosened top of an iron casket to the impact of Arn's callus-hardened palm across my face was a confused jumble of impressions, receding like a particular tree upon the bank while the river carries a boat swiftly past, and I was glad to have it so.

I did not wish to think upon what had just happened ever again. It had to do with the burning in my chest, buried between my lungs. It was *within* me, nestling like a mockbird's get among sparrow's young, and though it did not seem likely to kill me just yet I still heartily disliked the intrusion.

It pressed against my heart, and it *burned*.

"Stay back," my shieldmaid said, sharply. "I struck you once, Elder; I will do so again. She is not to be touched by your kind."

A tense, stinging silence. Running footsteps, a tearing of cloth. *"What happened?"* The Old Tongue, though in a mortal mouth—Eol.

I did not like the idea of him—or anyone else—seeing me thus, even my Arn. My fingers flexed, I shuddered, and I managed a weak embarrassing sound, like a baby's mewling.

"*What did you do?*" Eol barked. "*By the Blessed, what did you do to her now?*"

"*Peace, my friend.*" Naciel, soft and soothing. "*What happened was of her own will. Such things cannot be forced.*"

"I can help her." Aeredh was much closer. "As I did before, shield-maid. But should you strike me for it, I may move less swiftly tomorrow when the Enemy's thralls are upon our trail."

I found my voice. "Stop," I husked. "Talking."

They did. Arneior knelt at my side—I saw her mailed knees through the blurring of tears. I found I could move my arm, so I did—weak and uncoordinated, a foal's first staggering steps.

But as always, she was there. Her hand closed around mine, and the shock of another breathing, thinking life poured through me. It was a second blow, one I welcomed even as my head snapped aside for it returned me fully, though each idea passing through my skull was far slower than it should have been.

With her help I curled half-upright, and though she was upon her knees she still gripped her spear, its blunt end sliding to one side of the table. By then, I suspect, no one in the small fabric-walled space thought her unready even in that position, her cradled charge shuddering with the aftereffects of a massive, wrecking *seidhr*.

Her legs dug into my side, but that ached less than the burden in my chest. I rested against her and found I could yet breathe, which was a relief. "Hurts," I whispered, and disliked the tentative child's whine in the word.

"Tell me what to do." She did not look at me, though, gazing upward as if in challenge, and the light in her hazel eyes was that of a shieldmaid ready to kill.

"Drink." I could speak further, I found, though reedy-piping as a chick. "Is there? Something?"

It was Eol who approached the table, poured a healthy measure of the remaining springwine, and dropped to one knee before us, disregarding her spear. "Here." His skin rippled, the wolf inside turning restlessly; he was pale as milk under a mess of dark hair, traces of ash still clinging to the strands. His swordhilt bobbed at his shoulder. Arn braced me, he held the wooden goblet, and the liquid filled my mouth.

I choked, managed a swallow. Then another. My hand rose, closed over his fingers—fever-hot, another swamping sense of hot mortal life exploding through both physical and subtle selves—and I finally drank in long, endless swallows. Not only the draught but the vitality burning in him helped; I did not let go when the cup was empty.

My head fell back, against Arn's armored chest. I stared at Eol, and found I could clearly see the beast sharing his flesh. Long and lean was he, broad in the coal-furred shoulder, and deep in his gaze was a stillness—a moonsilvered glade full of bleached bonelight, silent as a barrow on a long winter's night.

Oh. Why did I not notice it before? Very odd. But, as Idra said, everything is there for those who know. 'Tis not the seeing that is the difficulty, but understanding what is already and ever before one's senses.

Had she known she was training me for this?

Eol's motionlessness was that of an animal. He barely breathed, and I could not name his expression, then or now. "More?" His eyebrows raised slightly, his lips shaped the word, but the rest of him did not move so much as a muscle.

I shook my head. My fingers loosened, slid to his wrist, grabbed as tightly as I could manage. The weight in my chest was awful, but I could gain enough air if I were careful. "Up," I said, and they both understood.

He glanced at Arn, a flicker of coordination, and they surged upright as one, bearing me along and setting me upon numb feet. I staggered but was steadied, and earth under my slipper-soles provided its own aid.

"*Blessèd,*" Naciel breathed. A soft blue glow about her shaded into clear shining at the fringes; deep in the bowl of her belly a tiny flame flickered. "*It … she is bearing it. Inside.*"

"*I see it, yes.*" Aeredh stood beside her, the burning of an Elder limning him as well. "*I hoped … I did not think …*"

Behind them, Tjorin lifted the tent's flap and gazed outside, his head cocked, listening intently. At least he looked blessedly mortal, the heat-haze of a living thing clear and rippling as the distant shimmer over summer fields—though I could see the shadow of some great ill-will upon him, held in abeyance for now.

That's seidhr. *And powerful; someone hates him enough to leave a mark…ah. The Enemy.* Another violent cramp seized my chest. I doubled over, cough-choked, and the thing inhabiting my ribs turned as well, settling like a tired hound. The clear waterburn of springwine fought with coppery blood at the back of my throat; I coughed again, rackingly, and the worst of the hurt eased all at once. It felt like the woozy relief after a great bout of vomiting, when the body is wrung dry and knows there will be more pain, but not yet, not yet.

"*By the Blessed,*" Eol said raggedly. "It is killing her. What did you do?"

But I could straighten, so I did. Both Aeredh and Naciel shifted slightly, their eyelids lowering as if they gazed into bright sunlight.

"*I am not dead yet.*" It was easier to speak the Old Tongue; the thing nesting inside me had, after all, been born amid its cadence. "*And you are not cursed, heir of Naras.*"

"Naciel?" Tjorin looked over his shoulder. "The sun is above the horizon. They await you; we should strike camp soon."

"*I…*" For once, the princess sounded neither amused nor at ease. "*Aeredh, are you certain?*"

"*A small group, light and swift—we escaped the Enemy's creatures thus before. And if we do not, we shall draw some of the pursuers after us and lessen your danger as well. It is a good plan. Even Daerith agrees.*"

Eol's gaze dropped. He freed the goblet—and his own hand—from mine, with exquisite care. Then he stepped away, busying himself at the table.

Arneior moved to my side, and I found I could stand. I thought I could even walk, though the heaviness did not abate. Nor did the discomfort; it had merely become bearable. My body was a tired horse, and I the rider forcing it a few more leagues.

"Solveig?" Naciel approached, her hands folded before her as if she asked the gods for some favor, and her eyes shone. "It is true. The Blessed sent you to us."

I doubt that, princess. I was too occupied with balancing my suddenly tricksome flesh; would I have to learn to walk anew, child-staggering through the wilderness toward some new Elder city-trap? *"I am not traveling with you?"* I sounded weary, and any benefit gained from a night's sleep was gone. *"That is what you are saying."*

"Slower, and harder to hide." She reached out as if to touch me, but I shied away, leaning into Arn. Naciel's hand fell to her side. *"Forgive me. We shall hopefully draw them after us; Aeredh and his companions will go with you as they did before. May the Blessed guard you, my friend."*

Of course there would be no rest, of course I would not be allowed a moment to digest this turn of events. Perhaps I should have said something comforting, but I could not. I simply nodded, and the princess of Laeliquaende followed Tjorin from the tent.

A Patient Beast

How few, how few remain
The dead outnumber us, and yet
Perhaps they are fortunate.
For they rest in the Shadowed Halls
And that is in the West.
                    —*Lament of the Uncrowned*

Some few horses had been brought from the wrack and burning, slender-legged cream-colored Elder beasts with wise dark eyes. The steady discomfort of the thing resting in my chest swallowed any other pang I might have felt at their appearance.

I gathered that our small group had the best mounts, and the few others were left for carrying children and those Elder too wounded or grieved to move swiftly as necessary.

So few had survived the burning—threescore and a little more in this camp along with the children. There were other collecting-points for those who had managed flight, but they had to make shift for themselves.

All the rest of Laeliquaende's folk, the festival throngs and city crowds, the builders of vineyards and high-prowed boats, beautiful stone houses, the gardens, the fountains...all gone. The crystal-roofed library was no doubt turned to ash and shards, for *orukhar* were not likely to see its utility and were, in any case, under orders to erase everything Elder they could reach or affect.

Nothing else satisfied their lord. Those wonders proving more durable or valuable could be judged by their commanders and carted back to the Black Land by liches, for though the Allmother's first son hates the Children of the Star, he also yearns to own what he cannot make.

He can no longer create, only twist what he has not wrought. Or so the sagas say.

I had to lean upon Arn, my legs weak as a newborn's, and I was surprised my feet did not sink into the ground, though it was still hard-frozen. The heaviness made it difficult to move, and I wondered if my wits were also slowed. I hoped not; they were all I had—*seidhr* is many things, but chief among them is cunning, knowledge, the tongue to move through both and song as well.

The Elder paused as my shieldmaid escorted me past. A few shaded their eyes with a hand, though the sky was a grey infinity promising snow. I could taste the weather as any child of Dun Rithell learned to, especially in winter, and decided nothing would fall today but the night would be cold indeed.

It was a barbed comfort to be out of the valley's temperance. For all its discomforts, I knew mortal weather much better, and that morn I welcomed it as an enemy so old and familiar his appearance is almost greeted with a smile by opposing warlords.

A murmur passed through them. I tried not to hear the whispers in the Old Tongue, but a *volva*'s ears are sharp as a shieldmaid's.

…the Crownless…from the South…with our princess…River-singer…the Enemy…

Did they hate me for bringing ruin to their home? Each Elder was surrounded by that strange glow, subtle selves burning as mortals' do not; my eyes were sharpened beyond anything I had ever dreamed, but the *seidhr*-sight was distracting. I would have gladly given it up if the thing in my chest would cease its pressure, the aching relentless smolder.

My mount was to be a tall mare with a placid gaze and beautifully tooled Elder saddle; I hoped I would not bring her grief. She eyed me sidelong, her tail moving gently, and I could not approach. Arn thought me perhaps stricken with some new weirding-ill, for she watched my face anxiously, and her arm tensed.

" 'Tis heavy," I whispered. The language I thought of as my own was unexpectedly difficult, twisting in my mouth. "The poor beast cannot bear it."

"We'll ride double." Arn bumped me, a chivvying movement; she had been given a salvaged mantle of greygreen cloth, for though a shieldmaid loves the cold she was also Secondborn. " 'Tis an *Elder* horse, Sol; it could carry four of us. Or so the sagas say."

A jagged laugh slipped between my lips, but it also eased the discomfort inside my ribcage. To hear my practical shieldmaid speak of the old stories we had been so certain were merely tales to frighten or delight the littles, like Lokji's long-backed eight-legged horse and the price for riding her…Bjorn and I had teased Astrid, not unmercifully but certainly more than our mother liked, with grim tales of the Black Land too.

I could almost see Dun Rithell under a coat of heavy snow, the river glittering as ice-floes bobbed past—our water-mother under Tarnarya's black bulk had not frozen completely since the time of Gwenlara my own mother's distant progenitrix. The gilding upon the greathall roof, the thin cheerful pillars of smoke rising from nearby steadings—

"Sol." Arn jostled me again, and we were at the horse's side. "Up you go. Better than walking, and they say we must travel far today."

Who says? But it was my Arneior asking, so I reached for the saddle-horn and gathered myself. She stepped back slightly, cupped her hands, and I found I could lift a foot. Into the saddle she flung me, and indeed almost tossed me over the horse itself. I swayed, righted myself, and found to my amazement that the patient beast merely flicked her tail again, not staggering splayleg under the weight in my chest.

"See?" Arn watched me for a few moments. "Can you ride? I will climb up after, if needed."

I did not cherish the thought of how I would feel at the end of the day, but it would be cruel to make the horse carry this hideous weight and more—though Arn would be slight indeed compared to the thing burning in me. "I can ride." To prove it I gathered the reins, and fixed my gaze upon the horse's ears. They looked like Farsight's; that mare had ever a mischievous air.

She had done her duty well, endured more than any mute beast should, and I wondered again if she had escaped Nithraen's fall. *I hope you had better luck than your rider, my fourfoot friend.*

The sounds of the Northerners mounting were familiar, from Gelad's slight chirruping noise as he settled a-saddle to Soren's habitual *Blessed make us swift* muttered like a prayer. Eol wasted no time and bid no farewell, touching his heels to his horse's sides and striking for the edge of camp, Efain in his wake.

Arn vaulted atop a charger whose ears flattened, but she patted his mane and the Elder horse visibly decided a Secondborn with a spear was less upsetting than the previous night had been. The saddle even had a sling for her weapon, and she looked glad to be riding once more.

Aeredh shrugged into another mantle, though of rough black Northern cloth, while speaking softly to Naciel and Tjorin. The motion behind them—Elder breaking camp, the tents struck and furled with swift efficiency, even the children helping with any task their size and quickness could accomplish—was strangely stilted, for they often stopped to look in our direction, squinting or shading their eyes. I could not tell why; if anything, the clouds were darker than even winter had a right to be.

Perhaps I was merely exhausted.

Aeredh clasped Naciel's hands, murmuring something—a last farewell, perhaps, a congratulation, or simply a few words of comfort. She nodded, and her chin rose. He smiled at Tjorin, gave them both a nod as good as a deep bow for the respect it carried, and turned to his own mount. In a trice he was a-saddle, and the Northerners closed about me. The mare knew her business was to stay with her fellows, and I sensed her eager to be gone. She set off, and the rhythm of a steady walk lengthened into a jog. At the edge of camp the snow rose, a smooth ramp, but Elder mounts are well used to such footing and stepped lightly, barely sinking into old, packed drifts. There was little sign of Eol and Efain; Karas and Gelad dropped back to take the rearguard, Elak and Aeredh bracketed Arn and me. It was just as it had been upon leaving Dun Rithell, right down to the sound of hooves, the slight jingle of tack, and the occasional chuffing as a horse scented something upon the wind.

We had not gone far before two more white horses appeared between shrouded evergreens—Daerith, tall and proud, his hair lifting upon the breeze, and Yedras the spearman, blue eyes vivid and his weapon slung like Arn's. The harpist carried his great bow and there were two quivers upon his saddle, both loaded to match the one upon his back; his expression betrayed nothing though Yedras's eyes half-closed and he studied me intently. They took their places with not a word, and I thought the rest of Nithraen's folk wished to stay with their kind—or were perhaps more wounded than Eol had given me to understand.

I clung to the reins, trying not to sway too badly atop my patient mount, and it was little comfort that I would be too miserable from the Jewel's weight to notice much of the soreness being a-horseback again would grant before nooning, let alone the day's end.

Thus the Flight to Dorael began.

Made for This

We fled the Gasping that terrible day, and what remnant reached the Taurain found the Greycloak's folk riding to save who they could. Shelter we sought in the great forest past the plain, and not for the last time. Yet below those boughs is dusk perpetual, and no mortal may bear the dimming for long. When we judged the danger less we went forth to rebuild, little by little, aided by our Elder neighbors. For we are Faithful, and well they know it—and the curse did not fall upon them.

— Hravald the Second, Lord of Tavaan

Southward we struck, and though I knew Arn and I would never see home again it still cheered me to be wending that direction. The woods were thick, the snow packed and frozen enough for solid footing. Though shadows lingered between the trees, daylight was a blessing—and besides, 'twas downhill. These hills fell from high peaks of the Spur which had cradled Laeliquaende, meeting the immense wall of the Marukhennor to the north, east, and west yet distinct from those terrible crags.

Taeron and his folk had hidden next to their Enemy's land like a dagger to his thigh.

I barely saw the trees. The mare's gait was easy indeed, though at every step I feared the weight might prove too much and she would

founder. Yet her hooves did not sink into the snow more than any of
her coevals', and come the nooning I near-fell from the saddle into
Arn's waiting arms.

She caught me as if I weighed little, and set me upon my feet. My
legs buckled with the jolt, the thing in my chest twitching, but after
a few moments the weakness faded somewhat and I found, carefully
placing my slippers, that I could balance upon the snow-crust.

I held my breath, dreading to break through and be sent sprawling. Arn's boots were light, but she and the Northerners left definite
tracks. My prints were barely visible.

Like Aeredh's.

I thought I would be called upon to offer *seidhr*-aid to the horses
as I had before, but Yedras and Daerith went to each in turn, stroking their legs and speaking quietly in their ears. I was left standing
useless, for Arn and the black-clad men of Naras were occupied with
checking each other's armor and equipage now that we had ridden
some initial distance, buckles and weapons inspected so they would
not fail at sudden later need.

Aeredh halted beside me, blinking against snowy grey daylight
and producing a flask carved from soft white stone. "*Sitheviel*," he
said, quietly. "How...forgive me for asking, but how does it..."

*How does it feel? As if I have swallowed a live coal, and it sits
between my lungs.* "Uncomfortable." I had to search for the word in
southron; the Old Tongue wanted to bolt free of my throat. "Heavy."
Concentration was necessary to lift the container; the summery
sweetness of Elder restorative filled my mouth, slid down my throat.
It assuaged the burning for a moment, but only that.

"Can we...is there aught that would aid you?" He had never
sounded so anxious before, and I did not like the change. If he became
tentative, how would the rest of us fare?

How would *I*?

I shook my head, and my fingers were clumsy upon the stopper.
I looked past him, at the trees surrounding this tiny clearing. Both
evergreens and the winter-naked others bore white shells, yet the
wind was not so sharp as it would have been a moonturn ago. Under
the metallic edge of freeze another scent lingered, the earth not quite

waking but stirring in its bed, not quite yawning but hearing the clatter of another season's work approach.

A gleam of *seidhr* limned every trunk, trembled upon each bough like the glow upon a living mortal or over distant summer fields. Small stealthy sounds tiptoed around us, a patter of tiny feet and the snapflut-ter of small wings. It was like being atop Redhill again, though the music of living things there had ridden the early edge of new-winter freeze.

I could hear almost everything, including the strong slow pulses of Elder heartbeats, the near-soundless steps of the Northerners, and Arn's breathing soft and quick, the clink of metal as she tightened a buckle for Efain. I heard hares scratching amid the snow, foxes leap-ing from drift to drift, birds dodging heavy spatters shaken from branches where their larger cousins lighted or flightless tree-dwelling creatures ran upon roads far above the forest floor.

The earth was waking, atremble on the cusp of melt. My subtle selves quivered alike, and but for the *sitheviel*'s warmth I could have stepped free of my flesh and flown as well.

"Solveig?" A hand on my arm, strength humming through fin-gers careful not to squeeze too tightly. The shadowmantle's cloth slipped slightly under his grasp; startled, I found myself returned to a snowbound glade, the activity of a nooning-halt nearing its end. Across the clearing Daerith stroked a horse's face, murmuring in a tilted ear; a tail like a waterfall twitched as he whispered.

I could almost hear the words.

It was fishgutting *distracting*. I lifted my right hand, gazed at the fingers. Thin threads of weirding branched through bone and ten-don, blood-channel and muscle. At least the shadowy cloth made my arm look natural and reasonable again.

"*I am seeing things,*" I murmured. "*Hearing, too.*" It took fresh effort to remember southron speech. "The weirding is very strong."

"Lithielle wore it upon a necklace." Aeredh's tone was very gen-tle, all things considered. Some attempt had been made to trim the evidence of charring from his hair, and the disorder made him look the youth we had thought him in Dun Rithell. "But you are *alkuine*. I did not think...do you doubt now?"

"Did you know it would do this?" I forced my attention away

from the song of small lives and restless-sleeping trees around us, my hand dropping forgotten to my side.

"I do not know precisely what it has done."

Well, at least he did not pretend. Since he was disposed to answer a question or two, I settled on the most important. "How am I to use this thing?"

"I do not think it can be *used*." He let the flask dangle from one hand, watching me closely. "Even Faevril only wore his greatest works, and the Enemy as well. If there is some power in the Jewels other than the hallowing and their beauty, I cannot say."

I did not like the thought that their Enemy had worn something now burrowed into my very body. In fact, the thought filled me with queasy revulsion, and the weight in my chest grew sharp as if it longed to burst free, eating its way out with small sharp granary-mice nibbles.

"Sol?" Arneior was at my other side now, her spearblade bright in grey noonlight. She glared at the Elder. "Come. Time to mount again."

Oh, gods. Another eternity atop a horse. Hot water gathered in my eyes, but there was no help for it.

Why would Aeredh do what he had done, bringing me through such danger to Taeron's city, risking so much, when he did not even know what the curst thing was meant to accomplish in the hands of an *alkuine*?

Of course, it was not properly in my hands, but that was beside the point.

The urge to sink onto the snow, weep-screaming, and kick like a youngling in tantrum was only held back by the knowledge that the thing nesting in my ribs would hurt even more if I acted thus. Even as a child I had not behaved so; no daughter of Gwendelint's would dare, especially under Albeig our housekeeper's eye. And by four summers high I was already training with Idra.

"*My lady*," Aeredh said. "*The Blessed made you for this. Of that I have no doubt.*"

Little comfort that was. Arn's lip curled, and her glare deepened. "Have you not done enough?" she said, quietly but with great force. "Leave my charge be, Elder."

He stood upon the snow, the small glowing-white flask in his hand, and watched as she shepherded me away.

Downhill the Elder horses moved, as the sun fell upon its own course. We rode past sunset, until the last scrap of light was pressed from the sky, and from the grim looks the men exchanged I could guess why. Arneior was silent and watchful, keeping her mount close to mine. The two were in step more often than not, sounding more like one beast instead of a pair.

When we halted I thought I would be called upon to light the fire, for that had been my duty during our earlier travels. Instead, Arn and I were left standing while the others attended to making camp; Aeredh kindled *aelflame* with flint-and-steel. Winter-lean coneys had been hunted by the men of Naras. The smell of roasting meat should have been comforting, yet it turned my stomach; instead, Daerith brought a wineskin and a small wooden goblet carved with fluid Elder designs.

"Here." He took care to speak in southron, and his leaf-stamped boots of Laeliquaende make rested easily upon swept-clean, frozen earth. "Springwine, my lady *alkuine*. There is enough and to spare; take what you need."

"Do you not wish for—" Arneior looked alarmed, but I shook my head and accepted the Elder draught instead. The Northerners appeared, took a few bites, and disappeared into the darkness by pairs, melding into latewinter night. By the time I had finished my second measure of springwine fir boughs had been taken, shaken free of snow, and piled to provide a blanket-draped bed for us, and such was her exhaustion my shieldmaid fell asleep near-immediately, still in her boots, her spear easily to hand.

I had managed to find a reclining position that did not overly disturb the thing I carried, and stared at the small circle of tree-choked sky I could see. The clouds were pale and thick, yet I could distinguish tiny struggling points among them, like candleflames in distant windows upon a summer evening.

Except the flames were silver, not the warm gold of beeswax or tallow. Watching them helped, as did Arn's steady warmth.

But not enough.

Careful Use

Three from Nithraen, mighty lords and fell,
Six from Naras, the wolves proud and strong,
A pair rode together, maiden-of-steel and mighty spear,
And in their midst...
    —Anonymous fragment, *The Flight to Dorael*

The fire burned for a long while on very little fuel, as *aelflame* will. In the dead reaches of the night a wolf's voice rose in the distance, answered by another in the opposite direction. Low, lonely songs, and I almost understood their modulations like sagas in another accent—mountainfolks' speech, instead of our riverside softening of vowels and elision of certain consonants.

I moved from the bough-bed so quietly Arn was not disturbed, and in any case I did not go far. Just to the fireside, where a downed trunk had been dried by its heat, providing a handy seat.

There was no sign of the Elder, but I did not think them far away. Yet 'twas not Aeredh who appeared from deep shadow between ghostly snow-covered firs, nor his friends from Nithraen.

Eol approached, silent as the shaggy shape of his other self. He eyed me sidelong for a moment, then reached as if to free his ragged black mantle. A plain silver pin held it gathered on his shoulder.

I shook my head. "I'm not cold." The Old Tongue poked and prodded behind the words.

"Ah." He settled on the trunk beside me, stretching his legs out and thrusting his boots almost into the fire; their soles steamed. After a few moments he drew them back with a soft hiss, and I could not help but smile. "Go ahead, laugh. It still feels good."

It was something Bjorn might have said; a chuckle caught in my throat. The Jewel settled, no longer a spiked misery. For the first time since the morning's *seidhr* I could take a deep breath, and I did so with gratitude.

And much caution, ready for the pain to return.

He still watched me, but not directly. His gaze settled upon my hands in my shadow-clad lap, cupped as if I still held the glittering thing one Elder princess had worn and another sealed in iron. "You should rest," he said, finally.

"I cannot sleep." *It won't let me.* And indeed, the weariness was neither better nor worse than it had been that morning. Perhaps slumber would be denied me while I carried this—but to what end?

He nodded as if he understood, a slight silent motion. The light reflected blue highlights in his tousled, hack-chopped hair; he had clearly trimmed the burnt parts with a knife, because of course he would. The swordhilt at his shoulder did not glitter through its wrapping, but the gem still sang its own half-heard melody.

Another howl lifted in the distance. "Soren." Eol's tone was thoughtful, nothing more. "We watch through the night, though not…as men. Daerith and Yedras are ahead, scouting tomorrow's route. Aeredh is with Efain upon our backtrail; if pursuit draws close they will harry, and warn." He paused. "You have never been unguarded, my lady. Not even in Laeliquaende, by day or by night."

"Save that first night upon the hillside." I almost shuddered, thinking upon the fog and the *grelmalk*, the sweating, terrified horse, and the cold. Suppressed the movement just in time, for I suspected it would make my chest hurt. "And the last, at the riverside. But that is not your fault."

"We would have searched until we found you. Both times."

"I know." And strangely enough, I did. The knowledge settled in me as a sending from far away might, another of the Wise reaching across long distances to warn or comfort a fellow bearer of the weirding. I could not tell precisely when it had arrived; once such things are noticed, it seems they have always been with one.

The fire mouthed its fuel. Fallen wood was stacked to one side, but there was no need of it just yet.

"The heartseeker." Eol continued watching my hands, as if he thought they might do something untoward. "I never truly thanked you."

There had not been time, and in Laeliquaende we had spoken of other things.

"There is no need. And I could not have done it without Aeredh's help." That was strict truth; I could not accept any talk of debt unless it were for his help upon the Egeril, risking both himself and his men. "A *volva* aids her allies thus. After the battle your work is done, mine just beginning." Thankfully, it did not hurt to turn my head and study his own callused fingers, resting against armored, black-clad thighs. "On the river, the rope struck you." Had it only been yesterday? Or were we past the night's center now? So much had happened, and I could not keep my balance atop galloping events.

He nodded, a single brief motion. "That it did."

"Does it hurt?" Could I offer any *seidhr* to ease the wound, with the thing burning inside my ribs? 'Twas uncomfortable not to know.

"We heal quickly. Of most things, at least." His mouth turned down at the corners. "'Tis one blessing in the curse, I suppose."

"I see." Now that was odd. Did he consider being two-skinned a malediction requiring *seidhr* to lift? "There were other marks."

He did not shift with embarrassment, though something told me he perhaps wanted to. The fire sang an entire saga-stanza before he spoke again. "My father oft tried to beat the curse out of me. Since I am eldest, and my brother...Arvil did not carry it."

His brother, slain by mine. "We know of the two-skinned in the south." I chose my words carefully indeed. "Our sagas say such strength is prized, for with it a warrior may hold back bandits. Or accidents."

" 'Tis a gambit of the Enemy's, making men into beasts." His tone was flat and distant, though courteous enough.

If the gift sprang from that source, why did southron sagas speak so highly of it? Certainly one must hold a two-skinned's strength in caution, even as one pays proper deference to those with *seidhr*. "Or a gift from the gods, deserving careful use."

Power, physical or otherwise, demands prudent handling. It was why my father gave Bjorn many a clout about the ear, why those with *seidhr* are trained from childhood—and why every young warrior practices with blunted weapons first.

A steel edge is power of a different sort.

"It did not show until the Day of Ash, when Naras fell. Tavaan and Uld too, and Jormgaard—those settlements in what is now the Gasping, you see. They once kept watch upon the Cold Gate. Those near Faeron-Alith were struck as well, and their warriors slew their own kin in the confusion of the first change." Eol's right hand twitched, fingers curling slowly into a fist. "I should not mention such things in darkness. Forgive me." He moved as if to rise.

"Don't." I could not say it very loudly, but the word arrested him. "The thing—the Elder gem. It hurts."

His broad shoulders hunched, as if the rope-end had struck again. Yet he stayed, motionless as a wolf eyeing a sheep-fold, waiting for a single moment of shepherd's inattention—or still as the shepherd's dog, alert to danger from its wilder cousins.

Eol did not move when I shifted, cautiously. The burning abated, and I laid my head against his armored, mantle-clad shoulder. It took some doing, for the coral in my hair was just as uncomfortable as mail or ring. I do not think he even breathed, or if he did it was imperceptible.

The heaviness did not vanish entirely, and neither did the Jewel's ceaseless, aching flame. Yet it eased, and I could draw full breaths around the discomfort. I could even let my eyes half-close, and though I could not sleep some rest was found.

Aelflame whispered softly. Another howl lifted, a lonely sound amid dark forest, and the clouds were at last soft with moonlight.

So passed the first night I bore the burden. It seemed to last forever, and not long enough. Before dawn we were a-saddle again, for dark things had boiled forth from fallen Laeliquaende, not to mention other places in the Marukhennor's wall.

The Enemy's thralls were on the hunt.

Not Far Enough

That great battle is named Skalda-en-kar, and the flooding afterward swallowed the bodies of the fallen. Deep they sank, the marsh drawing foul nourishment from its meal, and when winter came the first lights hovered above deep-riven ice. It remains an unwholesome place.
—Barald of Jormgaard, *Song of Northern Battles*

We had crossed the Glass during the deepfreeze; now, we had to brave it before the melt arrived to turn the entire bowl into quagmire. Leaden skies in this season are often a warm blessing, but now we hoped for clear icy nights to keep the snow a little firmer underfoot.

Gone was the constant howling wind, though strange colors still played nightly over great crevasses and in daylight massive tangles of thornwrack, sedge, and other scrub bore hoary hanging daggers of refrozen moisture. For the first two days our travel was almost pleasant, at least in comparison to our former journey across the great ice-swamp. I did not even have to light the fire, and so long as their frozen carapaces were shaken free the thorn-branches were reasonably good fuel.

The ground was slippery, but Elder horses are surefooted. Still, the cream-colored beasts grew weary and spent many of our halts with heads hanging, tails barely twitching while Daerith and Yedras sought to infuse them with strength. We traveled as soon and as long as there was any light at all, and the nights were uneasy.

On the third day, a soft slithering pervaded the Glass. Imperceptible at first, it strengthened bit by bit, akin to the sound of a scaled belly dragged over dry dusty grass. Near nooning it intensified, and I realized my breath, while still a silver plume, was not nearly so dense as it had been.

Arn lowered me to the ground. "Melt," she said, softly, and there were shadows under her eyes. Sometimes I suspected she slept in the saddle, her chin nearly upon her chest and leather-wrapped hornbraids dangling over her shoulders, swaying gently with the horse's steps.

She was right. I could taste the shifting weather, dry cold softening as sap under the world's skin began to thaw. The gathering whisper made me think of the Enemy's giant serpent at the roots of the world, blindly chewing. It was only the music of water-trickle echoing through giant rifts in the ice…and yet.

I half-turned, my gaze drawn unerringly northward. The mountains had receded; the Marukhennor itself was a smear of darkness like distant thunder. I thought I could discern tiny flickers of crimson upon that horizon as well, but any torch or bonfire would be well beyond the reach of mortal eyes.

The Jewel gave a twinge as I stared. Did it yearn for its siblings, trapped league upon league away?

"Solveig?" Arn touched my shoulder. The shadowmantle seemed to keep me from shivering, and oft I wondered upon the secret of its weaving as I rode, testing the fabric between my fingertips. It was a relief to think upon a *seidhr* I had some faint hope of unraveling. "What is it?"

Of course, it could have been the live coal amid my ribs staving off any chill. "Look. Do you see the darkness, far to the north?"

The mare stamped restlessly, her warm bulk shimmering with *seidhr*-haze. Even the ice-freighted scrub was beginning to kindle; I had never seen spring's return so clearly.

Arn gazed at the northern horizon, hazel eyes narrowed. Thin threads of gold and green gleamed in her irises. "I do not know," she said, finally. "But I am uneasy. Soon this place will be a morass."

At least there are no liches yet. A bleak jest indeed, and one I kept prisoned behind my teeth. It was comforting to stand so near my shieldmaid, her living heat a balm and the soft brushing of the Wingéd humming upon her shoulders like Hel's feathered mantle. Her spearblade glittered almost angrily.

She drew breath, but whatever she would have said was lost as a thin, piercing sound rose far away. It did not quite strike the ear, nor the place where *seidhr* hums between palate and hearing. Instead, it vibrated in the teeth and sent a pang through my bones, sawing at marrow like an old rusted blade.

My arm touched hers. She did not move; the contact may have brought some comfort to us both. Her woad-stripe needed repainting, and her cheekbones stood out starkly.

"*Hunting horns.*" Daerith had approached; he stroked my mare's neck with long, light fingers and shifted to southron. "The Enemy's servants have found some manner of trail. We can hope it is not ours."

"Naciel," Arn said, quietly. "And the rest. They had children with them, and wounded. I wonder…"

"She is quick, and Tjorin canny. Besides, they have warriors who survived the ruin." Though I was quick to offer reassurance it felt hollow, for I only half believed. "You need something substantial to eat, small one."

"Salted pork," she muttered. "Albeig's new-winter bread. The last, darkest honey, upon buttered oatcakes."

"Even hot ale sounds appetizing." I generally had to hold my nose to imbibe such a thick, yeasty drink. "Pickled fish. Stuffed puddle."

The game might well make our longing for real food sharper, but it also distracted us from the piercing, distant howl. Daerith murmured to the horse, and Efain approached with a measure of spring-wine for us both.

The Northerner's scars were pale, and he urged Arn to drink deep. "We may press on through the night if the horses can bear it. I like not how the wind smells, and Gelad agrees."

Arn glanced at me, her throat working as she swallowed fiery-clear Elder vintage. I read her concern plainly; no doubt she also saw mine. We both sought to keep the other from worrying.

"Perhaps…" I took a deep, testing breath. The Jewel did not thorn-jab, but once I was a-horseback, it might shift as I attempted *seidhr*. The thing had a mind of its own, and any moment I was granted a measure of relief I could not tell what might make discomfort return.

I was even more useless than during our first journey, and little did I like the feeling.

Arn lowered the goblet, and though her color was much improved those dark circles under her eyes taunted me. "Thinking of weirding? That Elder bauble might be of some use, instead of merely keeping you from sleeping."

Of course she had noticed my restlessness as well. I did not wince, even internally, for the slightest motion might provoke some reaction from the Elder thing. "It seems to do little but weigh me down. Like a festival goose, fattened so its liver swells."

At least I did not feel like coughing. The idea that blood might rise from such an effort was unsettling, to say the least. Was this what lungrot felt like? The last outbreak of that dread illness at Dun Rithell had been in my paternal grandmother's time; her bee-end torc rested easily against my collarbones.

I still possessed that one small piece of home.

"Hm." Arn wiped her mouth with quilted undersleeve, the goblet brushing her cheek. I had not yet had time to repair the gash in the material, and indeed had no needle to make the attempt. If I could find a thin enough sliver of hardwood, perhaps I could unravel a bit of thread from elsewhere and attend to it. "We shall have to carry you into the hall upon a great carven platter soon."

"Ai." I suppressed a chuckle, relieved it did not hurt. In fact, it lightened the burden for a few moments, so I could take a healthy measure of springwine as well. "Garnish me with spring herbs, but only after my feathers have been plucked."

Efain's eyebrows shot up. He looked mystified; Arn's laughter was a bright banner on the cold breeze.

"We can hunt as we run," the Northerner said. "Everything we find is winter-lean, but—"

"I am well enough." My shieldmaid sobered. "I do not think we will have time to roast a few coneys tonight, either. The melt will only quicken, unless an ice-wind strikes." Her gaze settled upon me as I drank.

Your weather-sense is as good as mine. I wanted to shrug while quaffing, but could not. At least the burning was also ameliorated somewhat while I swallowed Elder distillations, though it never vanished entirely.

"We may reach the edge of the Glass before the snow rots. We are aiming to the west of the Mistwood, so soon enough will come to the Taurain and Barael-am-Narain." Efain almost smiled, as if the thought was a pleasant one. "There are steadings upon the plains, though perhaps our people have taken refuge in Dorael already."

I might have made some reply, but as I lowered the cup another shrill, distant hunting-cry floated skyward. The mare snorted, tossing her head, and Daerith leaned into her side. *"Far away,"* he murmured. *"But not far enough."*

"How do they make such a sound?" Arn tugged at the hem of her tunic with her free hand, settling cloth and mail more comfortably. Her grip tightened upon the spear. "Like a needle to the ear."

"Their horns are of bone, with blackened metal chasing." The scar along Efain's jaw flushed as he gazed to the north, and I wondered if he saw the sparks amid the faraway pall. "They will be riding, taking shelter only when the sun is highest."

"Those scaled things." Arn stretched, her spearblade dipping slightly.

"No, too cold." A muscle flicked in Efain's cheek under a scruff of dark stubble. "Now they will be upon *vargen*, for those are furred."

"Wonderful." My shieldmaid showed her strong white teeth. "Come, Sol. Walk for a moment, you're probably stiff as old leather."

She took my arm as Efain hurried away to perform other duties. Daerith turned back to the mare, whispering in her ear. At least the beast looked pleased at that event, and her tail twitched.

Some few steps we managed—not nearly enough for privacy, but her whisper was soft indeed. "You do not sleep." Her brow furrowed, her jaw tightening. "And I *know* that look. Speak, quickly."

What could I say? The words crowded my throat, jammed against a weight akin to that of the Jewel a little lower down.

This thing burns, but does not consume—or does it? I can see fires in the North, and I do not sink in the snow-crust as a mortal should. I feel the chase upon our back, and I know I do not sleep, my shield-maid. I am as weary as when this started, never worse and never better. "Weirding." The word was hoarse, and dry despite the wine. "This is not like the *taivvanpallo*."

"Is that not good?" Her eyebrows rose anxiously. "You were afraid it would burn you."

It does; if you only knew how much it hurts. But I could not explain, and there was none other with *seidhr* in our group. No wise-man, no bard—though Daerith was a songmaster he was Elder, not mortal, and their invisible wisdom is not like ours. No *volva*, no cloudshaper or stone-whisperer. Idra was dead, the others in Dun Rithell unable to offer any aid even if I could gather the concentration for a sending, and I could not even dream of my mother, let alone the rest of my family.

My shieldmaid was at my elbow, her fingers upon my sleeve, and yet I was utterly alone in a way I had never been, not even upon a fog-drenched hillside or the sandy agate-glittering bank of Naricie Egeril.

"Solveig." Sharply, as Arn hardly ever spoke to me. Her hand tightened upon the shadowmantle's sleeve.

I realized with a start that I was gazing north again, over the crazyquilt-cracked surface of the Glass, ice starred with clumps of frozen sedge and thornbush, silvery mist rising from the crevasses. The shadow lingering upon the horizon was unchanged, tiny red spatter-flickers too far away to be definite yet terribly sharp, too clear, and entirely awful.

The tiny motion of surprise caused a shifting in my chest, and I had to quell a flinch that probably would have driven it deeper. Transitory relief faded; the stealthy slithering of melt filled my ears as the Jewel began to burn afresh.

"To horse!" The voice was Aeredh, in the southron tongue for our benefit. The men were mounting. Daerith held my mare's reins, and his gaze was upon me, eyes narrowed as if with suspicion.

"Come." My tongue felt too large, and clumsy against my teeth. "I think pursuit is closer than even they guess, and so is warmer weather."

A Single Bone

Turn your gaze to the North and sharpen your blades,
For the Enemy's vargen *are coming.*

—Northern counting-rhyme

By the time the sun fell below the westron horizon a great silvery fog was breathing from every crack, fissure, and ravine in the Glass. The men drew close with Karas in the lead, for he was counted the best pathfinder among them and even the Elder deferred to his skill.

Daylight died, but the dark was not complete. Even during the worst of freeze strange lights, in colors both earthly and indescribable, rose from the claw-marks in the Glass; now, with the melt whispering below the surface those heatless flickers returned, reflected through chilldamp vapor.

Arn was a shadow at my side, the Northerners deeper blots amid shifting freeze-veils. The forms of the Elder were limned with a faint bluish cast different than the unwholesome flares elsewhere; the vision reminded me of our flight to Nithraen. The mist lacked some essential quality of the deep fog upon the Elder Roads, but even a *volva* would be hard put to describe exactly how.

The horses plodded on, and I could not have said which direction we wandered. Often I thought we doubled along the edges of deep ice-chasms, retracing our footsteps; a few times Karas pulled rein and we halted while he dismounted, vanishing into the night to return a few breaths later, and we would go on.

Our halts grew shorter, the jog-trots longer. When sunlight found us again even Arn's great charger hung his head, though the mist flushed rose and gold for a short while before grey crept in to muffle every breath, every footfall. Karas stayed before us, and as the day mounted we slowed again.

The melt was still a mere trickle, but our mounts' hoofsound changed—snow was hollowing out underneath us, and each drift would soon be a false friend at best. Sedge-banks and other frozen vegetation loomed at irregular intervals, and their blurred edges were reminiscent of a lich's mantle, tattered stains spreading in defiance of wind or calm.

Nothing looks familiar when the clouds come to earth. But at least we did not hear the hunting horns again—until after sunset.

Another night spent a-saddle. Arn swayed wearily, and I am certain she slept as she rode though her hand did not loosen upon her bucketed spear. Half the Northerners' saddles were empty in the darkness, and though there was no wolfsong I often caught a gleam of eyes to one side or the other as they ranged about our small herd— not as predators but as sheepdogs, protecting and guiding.

Had the weather grown much warmer we may well have vanished into the morass, but on the third day the mist turned freezing and the snow firmed. It was a mercy of short duration, we well knew, and every face was grim or worried. The Elder spoke often to the horses, whispering courage into their ears, running their hands down slim pale legs, sharing vital heat and strength. Fodder was produced, I know not from where—perhaps by the same *seidhr* that had carried my lost trunk from Dun Rithell.

I longed to help. Neither Aeredh nor Daerith would allow me to, turning aside my attempts with graceful though mostly silent courtesy. And I held myself so stiffly in the saddle, seeking to avoid sharp jabs or greater burning from the thing tangled inside my ribs, that I could not concentrate enough to whisper a thread of strength into my poor mare, whose eyes stayed half-closed even at noon. She moved as if dreaming, and I did not blame her.

Then, in the deep cold darkness before another dawn, I realized we were struggling uphill. Back and forth up the incline, gentle zigzags like hurried stitching to reinforce a seam or protect a raw woven edge from unraveling. Our route managed to avoid sagging drifts, and miraculously none of the horses faltered upon the slope. Only the Elder, Arn, and I remained mounted, yet the beasts continued trudging together, held to their task by wills much greater than their own.

We had much in common, the pale, slim-legged, dark-eyed creatures and one tired *volva*.

A short rest, a swallow of *sitheviel*, and I could barely struggle back a-horse even with Arn's aid. We had no sooner started off, the riderless horses plodding steadily and Arn's charger blowing out a dissatisfied sigh, when a terrible brazen cry lifted, far nearer than the hunting horns had been before.

The fog cringed in thick ropes. The horses did not halt, but white showed about their eyes and every set of ears was pricked, including mine. I looked to my right at the shadow that was Arn, and the faint gleam from her spearblade watched me in return.

Yet when dawn came, stinging red like spilled mortal blood in the east, the mist had thinned to a smoke-thin veil and the undulating ground bore no fissures or masses of winterdead scrub. A wandering breeze hummed over well-packed, wind-sculpted snow, and the thick coppery tang of incipient thaw rode heavily upon its back.

Aeredh rode at my left, Daerith at the head of the ragged column, Yedras on his own weary mare last of all.

"Taurain," the Crownless said, barely audible over the sound of moving air. "Between the Mistwood and the Gasping, with Dorael at the southron end. There are no few Secondborn settlements here."

I nodded, though I could not concentrate enough to see again features of the maps studied in Laeliquaende's treasure-trove. The snow was not quite hard as stone, but not nearly so soft as the Glass's slog either; where the winter blanket was scraped away by wind the prickles of long winter-yellowed grass showed through.

The Taurain only looked flat, gently rolling in every direction. At first the sudden space, the sweep of iron-clouded sky and rippling white, was almost shocking, and I was glad the light rose by slow degrees as the mist wore off. Old tracks crisscrossed the hillocks and dips—fox, hare, musk-mouse, long-glutton, lemming, the tiny scratches of bird feet, the prints of horned deer and wolves too. Shadows melded out of the grey distance, and the Northerners in their black cloth loped to join us one at a time, swinging into the saddle between steps, maneuvers so perfectly timed the horses did not even flick an ear. Last of all was Eol, shaking blown snow from his hair, glancing up and down the line, and nodding to Aeredh.

Like a gift the sky opened, shyly, slowly. I cannot say when I first noticed blue overhead, but streaks turned to stripes, the color widened, and finally bright sunshine turned the haze in the distance white. Though old, the snow was blinding, yet full of flittering shadows as the animals of the Taurain went about their daily business with little concern for our presence.

I felt as if I could truly breathe again, and the sensation was welcome even if the thing in my chest poke-prodded incessantly.

The horses picked up their pace, glad of the light as well. Arneior straightened, her mussed braids molten copper and the remains of her woad-stripe gleaming down the left side of her face, darker than the sky but just as blue save for the yellow fringes where the dye had worn loose. She glanced at me, and her smile was like that of a child whose long fever has broken. Even the breeze did not disconcert her, bringing a flush to her cheeks, her freckles glowing.

I did not think of how vulnerable we were upon this bright expanse, for it seemed one could see forever in any direction. I was simply, marvelously grateful; even the sudden appearance of steep-sided gullies after our short nooning halt, sneaking out of the snow-glare like the Glass's endless crevasses, did not sully the feeling.

Well past dark we took shelter in one of those cracks, called *bailkah* in the Old Tongue. After spring or autumn cloudbursts they are prone to floods so swift and foaming even an Elder may well be carried away upon the torrent, but in that season they provided shelter and the horses could find a manner of grazing along dry riverbeds, the snow easily brushed free with gentle hoof-scrapes. Not enough, certainly, but there was apparently still some fodder left.

When married to Elder *seidhr* even a mouthful might suffice as a full meal.

There was little brush to use as fuel; what could be found fed *aelflame* that night. The ground was cold, but every saddle-blanket and mantle was piled atop a huge clump of dead grass for Arn. I sat next to her couch and did not shiver; with the shadow-cloak drawn close, I could have been a stone for all the chill I felt.

I even managed to hum an old lullaby, one my mother had sung to all her children. No doubt my small one remembered it as well, for as soon as she closed her eyes she was gone into sleep's arms. There is a limit to even a shieldmaid's endurance.

So strange, to guard her slumber as she had so often mine. I watched the slight movement of her breathing safely inside her fabric nest, and the song found an answering thrum deep in my chest.

Minor and inconsequential, it was still the first *seidhr* I had attempted since the Jewel burned its way into me, and my eyes prickled with tears. I had not lost the weirding; I was still *volva*.

The difficulty lay in delicacy, for only a thin trickle of vital force was necessary. Yet a weight lay behind it, a vast dammed-up cauldron that could have been my own impatience, my longing to *do* something rather than be carried from one place to the next like baggage. A pair of Elder cities were burned and broken now, we had been chased to and fro through the Wild, and though we had won a river-race and survived our travels so far both victories seemed paltry indeed.

If Aeredh was correct and I had been chosen, what in sheepshit did the gods expect? I needed direction, yet dreams were taken from me and the concentration necessary to perform other divination robbed by the Elder thing burrowed into my flesh.

A wolf's cry lifted in the distance. *Karas*, I thought, and rested my chin upon my knees, gazing at the fire. Another answered—most certainly Elak, though he was the most silent among them. Aeredh and Yedras had vanished as well. Only Daerith remained, the harpist moving about our small camp attending to what was needful before approaching, his step soundless and his dark hair bearing missing chunks, scorched bits trimmed away with more care than Eol or the Crownless had shown.

"My lady?" Tentatively, in the Old Tongue. He had rarely spoken to me, and even less so formally. *"Is there aught you require? Something to drink, perhaps, or...?"* His southron had improved immensely, though it still bore the accent of Nithraen.

I shook my head.

He folded down to sit on iron-hard earth brushed free of snow, glancing once at the lump of Arn's couch. "The way will be easier now. There are Secondborn settlements between here and Dorael, and we will warn all we pass that the Enemy's servants are riding. Though I would be surprised if they did not already know; they are not unwary here."

Did he mean to comfort me? There was no solace to be found in my own thoughts, yet I wished he would leave me to them instead of altering his haughty Elder ways at this precise moment. Still, he had lent his great bow to Efain, and perhaps he was uncertain as well.

Or mayhap he was curious about the thing I carried. "It sounds almost as if you admire them." My tone was polite, but only that. His disdain for mortals was not so marked as Yedras's... and yet.

"You are the Allmother's most favored children." The shadows were kind to his face, leaching some of the essential alienness of Elder beauty. He could have been a man from south-over-sea, where they have strange ways but are still wholly mortal. "Even the Blessed say so, and they do not lie."

"One of them does." I did not turn my head, and in any case I could not look northward from the bottom of this ravine.

Yet I felt it. The darkness was like a sore tooth, tempting the tongue to circle, to pry. Distance did not seem to ameliorate the pull—no, in a strange fashion, it threatened to strengthen. Perhaps the Jewel did long for its siblings, trapped and suffocating in the Enemy's iron crown.

The thought induced deep nausea, though there was naught but Elder liquid in my stomach.

"Yes," Daerith agreed. "And we have fought him since before the first sunrise, Lady Solveig. We have lost, and lost again, and won at dreadful cost that is a loss in itself. Yet what can we do? The way home is barred; we are fading exiles. The Enemy will not cease until we are eradicated; your kind he wishes to rule, ours to erase."

If the Elder could not fight him, what on earth could mortals do? "I thought at first that Aeredh wished me to use this thing in battle. Yet I cannot tell how." I hugged my knees gingerly, listening to the cold, sibilant breeze over the *bailkah*'s top. There was nothing to halt the world's breath on the Taurain; it wandered where it willed, a constant song like the breathing of a river.

Or the sea itself.

"My lord believes the Blessed themselves sent you." Daerith's ageless face was somber, and he seemed...uncomfortable, or as near to discomfort a graceful Elder could display. "And for my part I must believe so as well, for there is no other explanation. Yet we can only guess at the purpose. Certainly Faevril never unlocked any power in his greatest work, save their beauty and their sacredness. What you bear is holy; you must feel it."

I feel nothing but discomfort, my lord Elder. "Yet if the Enemy acquires a Secondborn *alkuine*, he may find a way. That is what you Elder fear, is it not? I might be used against you, so you took me from my home and seek to keep me hidden like a brooch buried in a trunk. And after all I am only mortal; it will not be so long, as you Elder see it, before I am dead. The only wonder is that none of you have sought to hurry the event along." My mouth stung, both with bitterness and with truth.

For I had thought long and hard about the Elder, even Naciel, while riding. And in my weariness I grew ill-tempered, the pain sawing at my innards near-unceasing and married to the fear breathing upon my back.

A cold wind from the North, indeed.

"Yes," he said, quietly. "But I would not lower myself to strike at children."

We regarded each other for a few moments. Daerith's eyes were half-lidded, and finally he turned his gaze aside as if he could not bear to look upon me. Perhaps it was the fact of a mere Secondborn holding something so sacred to his people; I could not tell.

Finally, he spoke again. "What do you know of Lithielle, my lady *alkuine*?"

"A princess," I hazarded. My time among Laeliquaende's books and scrolls had not been spent delving for such lore, though what I had absorbed served me well enough during the river-race and in treating some small lichburn. "Aenarian Greycloak's daughter, who fell in love with a Secondborn. They went to the Black Land and took a Jewel from the Enemy." I hesitated. "We sing of a Bjornwulf in the south, but he was a king who fought monsters and died much-wounded upon a mountainside when all but his cupbearer deserted him. I do not think it the same man."

"Indeed he was not. Lithielle's love was a Northerner, son of a great but fallen House. Aenarian Greycloak refused to give his blessing to the match, and an Elder who loved the princess betrayed Bjornwulf to the Enemy—who did not kill him, instead keeping him chained as an amusement." The harpist grimaced slightly, making a restless motion. "I do not think you have the patience to hear the tale sung; I am reducing the feast to but a single bone. Suffice to say Lithielle set out from Dorael wearing the very robe you do now. She braved the iron gates and the halls of the Enemy himself, and when her lover saw her in danger, he broke his chains. They took the Jewel you now carry from the great iron crown, and fled. Eventually they found refuge in Taeron's lands, but by then her Secondborn husband was wounded and ailing. When he died she cast off both robe and Jewel, gifting them to Taeron, and herself chose mortal death."

A princess with a glance like a knife. I had heard bits and pieces, of course, and a *volva* does not forget even partial sagas. I studied the harpist's profile in uncertain blue-tinted firelight. "Some little of this I knew. Not all."

"There is much more—Hjorin the Faithful, the Return to Dorael, the Vanishing. The greatest and most complete saga is in three parts and hardly ever sung even among us, for it was made by the one who betrayed Bjornwulf. He was my kinsman. My uncle, in fact; I bear his name, though they call me *the Younger*." Daerith hunched, shoulders rising, almost as if he wished to make himself smaller. "He died of shame after singing his masterwork."

"Ah." I did not have an uncle—my father's brother had gone to Hel's country before I was born—but I could perhaps imagine the loss. What Daerith spoke of must have occurred long ago, and to bear the pain for so long... "I am sorry. You must grieve still."

"Yes. We are not like you." His right hand tightened, not quite curled into a fist. The motion was akin to Eol's, but I would not have said so to this proud Elder. "A Secondborn may love again; your heart may eventually turn to another if the first does not accept you. We cannot. Once given, our... affections remain constant, even when we go into the Halls. Sometimes they consume us. Perhaps being able to do otherwise is another gift from the Allmother, since she loves your kind so well."

"Do you really believe that?" I longed to know more of *into the Halls*, but it seemed rude to inquire too deeply upon. "We sicken, we die. Do not the Elder disdain us for it?"

"Some may. I think it more a blessing, for there is great weariness in a long life." A short, flickering sideways glance. "Lithielle is the only Child of the Star granted a Secondborn death, for she would not be parted from Bjornwulf even then. The Blessed answered her, mayhap because she was the only being to *give* one of Faevril's Jewels away."

I took his words as a warning, and tried not to grimace. "Have no fear, my lord harpist. The instant I may do the same, I will with great haste."

"Would you?" He stilled as the wind shifted direction, his head cocked.

"If you knew what it felt like, you would not ask." If I held very still, the thing in my chest did not chew or burn too badly. "I do not want this. I long to be free of it."

"And yet it shines in you, so brightly we almost cannot bear to look." Daerith unfolded gracefully, catlike. "Were it not for Lithielle's Shroud we might be blinded, and our pursuers drawn as to a lodestone."

"What a lovely thought." Perhaps the Jewel was simply hiding like a worm burrowed into a sheep's guts, or the whip-infection in sickly fish. I could not even shudder, for it might poke at my innards—just how aware was the thing?

It seemed alive, in some quiet, questing way. But was it conscious?

The harpist now regarded me with a rueful smile, perhaps surprised or even amused at mortal sarcasm. He sobered quickly, though. "We may move with more swiftness now, and so may pursuit. Your shieldmaid is wise to rest while she may."

Another thing I would do if I could. There was no point in saying as much, so I simply watched as he bent near a pile of gear to retrieve his bow. Then, armed and solemn, Daerith faded into the shadows on the other side of the fire. The horses slept standing, pressed together for warmth; Arneior's breathing continued, soft as the sound of *aelflame* and the brushing of the wind.

Even wolves in the night were less lonely than one small *volva* huddled at the bottom of a ravine. And in the quiet, the pull against my subtle selves—and all the rest of me—sharpened.

It longed to draw me northward.

I did not have to climb the *bailkah*'s sides to look, for the view thrust itself upon my inner vision. Looming darkness upon the horizon, and the reddish glitters—fire in smoke, sparks refusing to fade.

It would be selfish to wake my small one because I was afraid; if I called into the darkness, perhaps one of the men would answer...but perhaps something else would, instead.

I could only sit, endure the burning in my chest, and wait for morning.

An Empty Steading

*The Enemy has many captains, and they vie with each
other to work his will. No doubt he prefers it so, for if they
are busy with each other they do not seek to unseat him. It
is ever thus with the greedy, be they small or large, weak
or powerful.*

—Caelgor the Fair

Windbreath never fades upon the Taurain's expanse, no
matter the season. We were lucky to be upon the cusp of
spring, for the snow was packed and a thin scattering of fine granules
rode the back of moving air. The ground was still frozen, not yet
deep sucking mud, and there was welcome additional forage for our
mounts under the white shell. Added to the Elder *seidhr* of care, it
was enough for survival.

The first settlement was a collection of shadows upon the southron horizon long before we reached it. Arneior straightened in the
saddle, her mount sensing the change and all but prancing despite
weariness; my heart lifted with a strangling leap almost as uncomfortable as the Jewel's sharp burning weight.

Two black blots—Elak and Karas—preceded us, drawing toward
what I realized had to be buildings before vanishing into the middle-
distant haze. For a long time the settlement stayed where it was no
matter how the Elder horses jogtrotted, then suddenly the wooden

bulks separated from a billow of driven ice-flakes, looming larger with every approaching step.

Greathall, outlying halls, stables, pens, smaller houses—all in the customary pattern, though their backs were turned to the North and they used a great deal of turf instead of timber. Still, wood had been brought from the outskirts of Dorael's great forest and the Mistwood itself, and the building's shapes were blessedly mortal. If not for some minor differences in construction it might have been one of Dun Rithell's neighbors, and a mingled edge of pain and wonder pierced deep when we passed through an unguarded opening in the palisade. The twinge was only matched by another when we trotted between drifts fetched up against other structures and saw the greathall with its stone steps rising out of wind-thrown snow.

Yet I could not feel much joy, even though 'twas a relief to be out of the incessant onslaught of tiny icy pellets. For the place was deserted.

Doors were largely unlocked, yet all shut tight. The houses were empty and had suffered some small damage from winter's gnawing. The snow was not cleared, there were no pigs in the sheds, no hounds milling about and belling in excitement over visitors. No flocks huddled in the barns, nor in the well-fenced paddocks. No children gawped, no women peered from the doors or from under mantle-hoods, and no warriors held the palisade. I suspected even the granaries were empty. It was eerie, and the only sound was a banging from a pair of shutters upon a smaller westron hall loosened by some recent storm.

Still, it was shelter, and the light was failing. The greathall's stables were empty, clean, and still held fodder, albeit frozen. As soon as my slippers touched ground and I inhaled the faint fading scent of mortal steeds trapped in the building, my knees nearly gave.

"*Ekfar's people must have gone to Dorael,*" Eol said, handing his reins to Efain. "*I would have thought him too stubborn.*"

"*If Lady Gelveig left, he would follow. Stubborn he is, but not foolish.*" Efain actually smiled; the Northerners seemed greatly relieved. "*And he prizes his wife, as he should.*"

"I do not like this," Arn murmured, steadying me. "Not even a granary feline left, it feels like."

"At least we will not have to camp in a ravine." I looked up—the hayloft was precisely where it should be, and after so long spent in the Wild or Elder houses, it was a joy to see mortal carpentry again. "Maybe we can sleep there, and pretend to be hiding from Albeig."

The thought of our housekeeper cheered me immensely; had this been our home she would be busy with the work of arranging guest-greeting, fretting over the proper mulling of the welcome cup, and sending servants in every direction for this or that. One who can organize a greathall is held in high honor, for woe betide you if winter arrives and she is unhappy. My mother relied upon Albeig's wit and work almost as much as her own hands.

I could picture travelers being greeted at home, but not what might happen were Arneior and I to reappear. I could not even imagine my mother's embrace, nor Astrid's likely bursting into relieved, joyous tears. What would Bjorn do, if we ever saw each other again? Or my father—Eril was ever gruff and forbearing, keeping any joy under a screen of fierce rectitude, and I could not compass how he would react to his eldest daughter's return.

The greathall, though well-constructed, reeked of damp and neglect. Even a single inhabitant may save a place from complete ruin, but buildings wholly abandoned begin to fray in short order. Upon the dais was a high table—made of stone, and hauled to this place by what feat I could not tell—and upon *that*, a thin board with carven falling-runes lay, gathering dust and whispering its tale into the dark.

Read by the cold blue glow of an Elder lantern, the mystery was revealed. Some short while ago a very large raven had appeared at bruise-dark twilight, winging hard from the north and settling upon the roof of Lord Ekfar's hall. And, as befit such a creature, it had spoken.

Taeron Goldspear hath fallen, it croaked in the Old Tongue. *The Enemy is moving. Flee, or prepare for war.*

Thrice it repeated this message, then it took wing again with a sound like the whirling winds which sometimes race across the Taurain in spring or late summer, shaped like spinning children's toys but full of horrendous power. Wherever those swift-racing storms touch the earth with a fingertip all is harrowed, and even their fringes cause great harm.

When I heard of that, I wondered what *seidhr* Northerners work to turn aside such things, and to this day I do not know.

The letter stated the raven flew south afterward, perhaps for Dorael. If it gave the same message at settlements along the way, Ekfar's people could not guess. But Lady Gelveig who had written the warning added that their House, being Faithful, had caused their entire folk, old and young, ill and hale, to set forth along with whatever supplies, kine, swine, horse, and hound could be moved.

I did not blame them. Had such a thing occurred at Dun Rithell, the elders and all with *seidhr* would have been called to hasty conference. Frestis and I would have been asked to divine, but such clear sign from the gods themselves—for those giant birds are sacred to Odynn, and even their smaller kin oft carry his vision or intent among mortals—could be ignored only by fools.

The hue and cry must have been considerable. It spoke well of the lady, and of her lord, that they had organized their flight so thoroughly. There was very little left behind; the greathall was tidy, but horribly empty. The tables were bare, benches and chairs placed just so, the floors swept clean even of sand or sweet rushes, the hearths cold.

Some slender stores were left—dried manure-pats and scrub enough for a fire, at least, and a single barrel of ale. We made camp in the greathall, the hearth looking very glad indeed to hold a blaze again, and the Northerners spoke of other settlements between here and the great forest's edge. Who was likely to leave, who would stay, who might send merely their children and elderly with a few warriors' guard…they named many I had never heard of, and normally my ears would have worked until they tingled, storing away such details as a lord's daughter must to aid in future negotiation.

Instead, I settled near the fire, watching my shieldmaid as she drank warm ale with every evidence of enjoyment. Winter-skinny coneys were put to roasting, some hard cheese left in a cellar was found, and a few jars of preserved stuffs added to what was a virtual feast.

The Elder were merry as well, though they left the mortal provender to their Secondborn friends. And I could not stomach it; strangely, even the good healthful aroma of roast meat made me lightheaded. A double measure of springwine did not induce the deep rolling nausea, at least, and I tried not to watch longingly as the marrowbones were cracked and Arn sighed with pleasure.

The Northerners even sang a few songs while the Taurain's breath mouthed the corners of the hall. Apparently Gelad was polishing a few verses about rowing in my shieldmaid's honor, which caused great—and very respectful—mirth. *Minnowsharp in the prow was she*, the refrain went, *and kept calling tai-yo! Tai-yo! She kept calling tai-yo!*

Of the fall of Laeliquaende they did not sing.

Daerith was called upon for at least half a saga. He chose a song I had not heard before, of the creation of rabbits, and Lokji—who the Elder call by a different name—spear-marrying one of their princesses. It tread close to the ribald, but I could not help smiling and even Arn laughed at the last few lines.

Normally 'tis a *volva*'s delight to partake in such things, but I could not have crafted even a couplet, let alone a song. The burning in my chest, only slightly quenched by springwine, turned and sawed.

My shieldmaid and I bedded down in a servants' closet near to the hall, with an Elder lantern to keep us company. It was slightly damp but a great and welcome change from outside, and I thought perhaps I could finally find some rest.

I managed a half-doze for a long while, listening to the sounds of a wooden building on a cold night and Arn's soft breathing in my ear. Sleep would not come, despite the comfort of her arm over my waist.

I did not mean to attempt *seidhr*. But 'tis natural as breathing for one with the weirding, and besides…I am not quite certain it was entirely of my own will.

⬙⬙⬙⬙⬙

A white bird glimmered in the dark, winging northward. The pull was strong; once I ceased to resist I barely felt the burning. In fact, the heat amid my ribs was proof against deep chill. Snow undulated below, the Taurain's expanse swanfeather-soft. Seen from above the pattern of cracks from storm runoff became clear, as well as the hidden groves of silverbark birch and shiverwood, their naked limbs hung with ice partly melted every noon, refreezing at night—though not for much longer.

The land dropped away into a vast misty cauldron, and from above I saw the lights over the Glass's ice-chasms.

What are you doing? *A soft, secret voice whispered in my invisible ear.* You fled with such haste and effort, why return?

I did not know. By all rights I should have been flying hard south and east, hoping to at least glimpse my home before I was called back into my aching, feverish physical shell. But the urging drew me on, and its source was not the horrified fascination of smoke and fire to the north but a wordless impulse from the gleam cupped amid a hollowboned chestcage, granting strength to stretching, long-pinion'd wings.

Fear brushed me, soft as feathers drawn along bare skin. I veered westward, balanced between the northern call and the draw of my left-behind body. Between the two I veered upon a thread-thin edge, and below me shadows gathered. Freezing mist receded in long fingers, and the land was now snowbound but flat as the grass-plain could never be. No hillock, no valley, no ravine, nothing but soft featurelessness. The first blot upon the landscape looked like a skeletal, begging hand, and I realized I had dropped—no longer moving at hawk-height, but skimming-treetop like a hunting crow.

The thin bony shape wheeling below was a blasted tree. Others recurred sometimes, reaching from soft grey like a shadow. I realized the wind was full of tiny flakes as well, but they were not snow. Nor were they ice.

Ash, *the inner voice whispered.* But it is so cold here; what is burning?

I was afraid I would see Laeliquaende afire still, but what spun under my bird-belly next were ruins of riven stone and blackened timber, deep grey drifts clinging in every hollow. A terrible cataclysm had come over this place; the shape of the buildings was not quite Elder nor that of my people, but somewhere between.

The darkness upon my right was very close, and along with it a low hateful sound. Agonized groaning or cries of pain, rage or terrible cutting mirth? I could not tell. Lurid bright flickers were fires cracking through the ash, burning though denied any fuel, not the tiny starlike points I had seen from the Glass but much closer. They hissed continuously, and I dropped lower still. Fatigue beat alongside a steadily mounting pain in my chest.

Where am I going? For there was some purpose here. The call was too loud to be otherwise. A tower reared in the distance, its wholeness a shock amid such desolation. It was a graceful spire, and at its top a yellowish glitter blinked lazily. There was a pattern to its stutter, but one I could not decipher for I was moving too swiftly now.

Too late I realized the trap, and my wings beat soft-frantic as a pigeon in an osier cage, strapped to a wicker tower and waiting for the fire. The tower loomed closer, and others reared below it—more Elder than mortal construction, but still familiar enough.

Behold, *another voice whispered, and I knew I had heard it before in a forgotten dream.* **This was Naras, lost in a single night of flame and lamentation. Now it is home only to darkness, and to beasts.**

I strained to break away, an egg of fire cracking in my chest. The flame raced through me, wingtip to claw, beak to tail, every vein suddenly full of burning. My gaze was torn from the yellow light at the tower's top, and I tumbled through darkness and keening wind, my mouth full of hot copper...

...before thumping into my own heavy, painful body, every muscle rigid, staring at the shadowed ceiling of an abandoned closet. The Elder lantern set upon the floor brightened, and Arn muttered in her sleep, her arm tightening. My mouth was open, but I could not scream—I could barely breathe, drawing in shallow sips of air that tasted of desertion and fire's cold leavings in a dirty hearth.

I lay choking and paralyzed for a near-eternity before the thing in my chest shifted. It did not hurt me less, but at least I could fill my lungs. Hot tears trickled down to my temples, sinking into my hair. My braids were deeply awry, and sharp edges dug into my scalp.

Two of the larger red coral beads had split, and their broken bits were what I felt.

Not only that, but my hair was heavily frosted with ash.

Uncanny Before

Our houses turn their backs to the North, but that does not make us less vigilant. Even the Elder rely upon our watchfulness, for though they are mighty their increase is slow. We are far more frail, yet who else do they have to turn to?
— Gelveig Steelheart of Aen Taurieth

"**W**hy did you not wake me?" Arneior peered out the door, into the hall. It had to be near dawn; she had risen naturally through slumber-veils to find me sitting upon the floor, my lap full of red coral, attempting to shake firecorpse from my hair and rebraid the dark mass with only my fingers to help.

I did not even have a comb. Just an Elder dress, the shadowmantle, my torc, and the thing trapped in my chest. And the beads, but two of those were riven.

What more would I lose upon this journey?

"You need your rest." I sighed, braced myself, and lifted my arms. The Jewel did not poke too badly, but all the same, even twisting my hair was a torment now.

A soft, almost unheard vibration of wind added to wooden creak-groaning made any silence more a matter of degree than quiet. Yet the entire hall felt somewhat wrong, for there were no distant foot-steps, no intimation of a kitchen beginning daily clamor, no hounds clicking their nails upon the floor, and not even the dozing sense of other mortals breathing amid the rooms, halls, closets, cellars, or stairs.

My fingers encountered a knot they were ill-equipped to separate with blunt ends. "Sheepshit." It felt good to curse, especially in my own language, while I tugged at the obstruction. A sharp yank against my scalp was merely temporary pain, but it was of a kind I knew and understood instead of the thing in my chest and its contradictory, unfulfilled scorch.

Arn turned, regarding me curiously. "You don't even have your *seidhr*-bag." As if she had just realized it.

"I left it in our rooms. Maybe the *orukhar* now wear my gowns." I tried to make it into a jest, but my voice wobbled slightly.

Arn stalked across the small room, pushing past me as if to climb back into the bed. Then she dropped to her knees, wedging herself between me and the wooden frame. I had to move—but carefully, with a lapful of none-too-fresh ribbons and clicking red coral. Her spear she propped easily to hand, and poked at my shoulder. "Sit still."

"Arn…" The lump in my throat would not go away.

"I cannot give you hornbraids. Those are for shieldmaids and wives won by bowshot." She pushed my arms down. "And I do not think I can use as many beads. But you have a pocket or two."

I will not cry. I will not *cry.* The Jewel subsided as my hands dropped into my lap, and Arn began separating and braiding.

"Now." She was not gentle, but neither did she pull with sharp almost-random intensity like Astrid. Instead, my shieldmaid was ruthlessly efficient, and swore under her breath at a few knots until they yielded to her far superior force, no doubt ashamed of themselves. "Tell me what you remember."

In short order I had four tolerable beaded fishscale braids upon my head, which Arn plaited into a thick cable once they fell free of the scalp. We almost ran out of ribbons, but two short ones were left, ready for the remaining red coral to be threaded like pierced chits upon a rivertrader's counting-string. And through it all ran my halting recitation of what I had witnessed—or what I could remember of the vision, since such things slip swiftly from the waking mind's busy fingers.

"A tower." She tugged slightly at the bottom of my hair, tying the ribbon with a knot more suited to securing armor than anything else. "And this stuff in your hair. Doesn't smell like burning, but..."

"I think it was Naras, in the Gasping." I chewed at my lower lip, gently. The slight discomfort did not distract from the Jewel, which was now as quiescent as it ever became, as if it listened to our tiny Althing. "Which would make sense, perhaps, because their men are here? Yet I like not that the thing couched there seemed to know me."

"What thing? One of the Enemy's..." She exhaled sharply, grabbing her spear as she rose. Her knee brushed my shoulder, a casual touch threatening to stagger my precarious equilibrium. "I cannot believe I am saying such things. Mentioning the Black Land like an elder sister scaring fractious littles."

"And Elder, and two-skins, and *trul* and *orukhar*." Wonders we had been agog at while listening to sagas, but now all too real. I missed the warmth of her against my back the moment it left.

"Well, we have two-skins in the South, and never heard tell of one breaking pax." She pushed past me again, clearly done with an unappetizing duty. "I like them better than the Elder, certainly. Sol, does it strike you that..."

It was true we knew of two-skins, but they were held to be distinct from such things as *varulv* and other ill *seidhr* treading upon the edge of malignant bestiality. Rather, those who shared a wolf's skin, or a bear's or great feline's, were held to take some nobility from their other form.

Every saga said so, and I had been thinking upon such things as we rode as well, turning the problem of Eol's malediction over and over inside my aching skull.

I waited, stringing beads on the pair of leftover ribbons. "Does what strike me?"

" 'Tis passing strange." She peered out the hall door again, though there was not a sound or even the feeling that we might be listened to at the moment. "You do not sink in the snow. Light as thistledown you seem, and your eyes... I cannot say."

I could not tell what was wrong with my eyes, save that they smarted with snow-wrung tears all too frequently of late. "What are you saying?"

"You look, well, you don't look…" She shook her head, turning her spear's blunt end a grinding quarter upon the floor. "Ai, listen to me. I sound like a wanderwit herder."

"What don't I look like?" The shadowcloth over my lap was neither grey nor black, nor even precious, expensive indigo. It lingered in an uneasy amalgamation of darker tints, blending into the patch of unlight under the bedstead. "I know my braids are bad, but you cannot blame me for that."

She didn't laugh. Her knuckles whitened upon the spear. "You look a little like *them*."

"Like a two-skin? I only have the one, and 'tis sore enough at the moment." I found a pocket to hold the bead-strings just where I would expect such a convenience in a mantle, and tried not to think that the fabric itself had responded to my need as it had somehow shortened during our flight from Laeliquaende. Thus I was left with the broken coral-pieces, lying in my palms like bright bloodclots.

"Like Aeredh, and Naciel, only not entirely." Arneior made a restless movement. "You were uncanny before, but now you even sound like them when you speak their damnable Old Tongue."

"An Elder wouldn't have knots in her hair." I could have taken it as praise, I suppose, for the Children of the Star are beautiful.

But I did not feel complimented in the least.

"It is that thing you carry. You do not sleep, you ate nothing solid last night, and when you think I'm not looking you frown as if pained." Arn still faced the door as if she stood guard, only turning her head so I could see her profile, thoughtful and pale. "What is it doing to you?"

Nothing you need worry for. A tart reply, and uncharitable even if she had been so thoughtlessly quick to assure Naciel of our aid. "As soon as we find a safe place to rest it, I can return to being Solveig."

"That is it, exactly." Her woad-stripe was worse for wear, though still bright. When the snow melted I would have to find more for her, and bless the water for the dye. "Sometimes you do not even look like yourself."

Well, who am I then? Asking such a thing aloud while carrying what I did was unwise, so I swallowed it. The morning seemed destined to go badly, for what I said was almost worse. "Do you not know me?"

"You are my charge." Thankfully, she sounded certain. "But you do not even *smell* like yourself, either. That is what is so odd."

"I feel ripe enough." My nose wrinkled. "We've been riding for days. Maybe 'tis the Elder cloth, keeping us from sourness."

"Perhaps." She shook her head slightly, and ground her spear-butt again. "They are stirring like mice, and building up the fire. Let us not be laggard; I want breakfast if any is to be had."

I almost told her to go without me, since there could be little danger in an empty hall. But she finally turned from the door to give me a fierce warning glance, striking the thought before it could be uttered, and I refrained.

The last time I had thought there was no danger, we had learned otherwise at dusk. "The orange stars," I said, instead. "They were the torches in the hills. *Orukhar*, and other things."

"Yes." She had paled, her freckles standing out. "I did not recognize it beforehand."

"Nor did I," I admitted. "And I am supposed to be a *volva*."

"There was no way you could have, even with weirding." She tapped the floor, marking the statement—but softly. "You cannot see what the gods themselves hide, Sol."

Yet that is exactly what a wisewoman is supposed to do. "Hm." Clutching broken beads, I managed to rise—slowly, and cautious lest the Jewel decide to take offense. Arn hurried to help, but I gained my feet without her aid, my smile stiff as a mask. She did not need to hear more of my fruitless uncertainty. "Well, then, breakfast. Perhaps we should have looked for a sauna last night."

She laughed, but there was a new light in my shieldmaid's hazel eyes. And as we navigated through halls that could have been our home—save they would never be so bleak, so cold, or so dark—her free hand cupped my elbow as if she feared I would falter between one step and the next.

While she had frequently done so at home as well, the anxiety in her solicitousness was new.

I did not like it.

Imaginary Offense

Long vigil held we, and towers we built
The cold iron gates we watched.
Some said the danger was over,
But then came the Day of Ash.
—Bjornvald of Aen Sevras, *The Fall of Jormgaard*

Even if the walls are thin and roof turned into lace, a night's rest inside does anyone a world of good. The wolves of Naras were cheerful, even ruddy-haired Elak whistling a snatch of some song or another as he and Soren set about saddling the horses. The sky hung low and infinite, the wind flirting-unsteady and tasting of chill mineral freeze.

Spring snow. It began midmorn, as the horses picked up their hooves and flicked their tails with anticipation. Heavy wet white feathers made wind-curling curtains, erasing any slight depression left by Elder mounts. I listened to the breeze, to the massive silence of snowfall, and my unease grew sharp as the sun descended, precipitation becoming fitful but the silence remaining.

After so long in dry, deep cold the advent of air warm enough to grant flakes nearly brings one to sweat. There was no soft rushing trickle of melt, but even the drop in temperature after sunset was not so bad as it could be.

I could tip my head back, staring at a sky that should have been featureless and dark, and discern tiny struggling lights. They were no longer strangers since our time in Laeliquaende, but the stars should not have been visible to any glance not freighted with piercing *seidhr.*

Yet I saw them, without any trouble or effort. And that was not all. Thin silvery notes hit the space behind my ear where weirding oft makes itself known. There is no music softer, nor any more aching, yet no creature living under the night's small fires can hold more than a snatch of the melody. The sharp brazen-throated hunting horns were silent, but I was not comforted.

If anything, I grew more nervous. The Elder did not speak upon the cessation of those terrible cries, but Yedras and Daerith often exchanged meaningful glances and Aeredh stayed with whoever had the duty of end-guard, always the last to approach our daily shelter. The wolves of Naras spread out, those running in their other forms leaving their horses to crowd Arn's and mine, and we traveled well past dusk each day. Snow passed over us in waves until night fell, halting only until the next sunrise wrung more free; winter had not yet finished her last dance upon the windswept plain and her presence kept the drifts reasonably firm.

Perhaps it was the daily fall of fresh white that mazed our pursuers.

The journey wore on, every possible speed wrung from Elder, Secondborn, and horse alike. Small settlements and steadings rose out of whirling white curtains, approached us, and faded away; we sheltered in them if we could, but more often in a *bailkah.* Not a soul remained in any mortal structure, and the closed but unlocked houses were disturbing. So was the constant wind-moan and the idea that our pursuers had not withdrawn but were simply...waiting. There was no more singing, saga or otherwise, even if we stayed in a dark, abandoned hall, and we roused long before dawn to be on our way.

We reached the tower of Barael-am-Narain twelve largely silent, nerve-fraying nights later. That day the drifts underneath us softened at noon and refroze at dark, the sky clearing as the sun sank.

And finally, we met a single Northerner.

Just as it has ravines, so too does the Taurain have hills. Even a slight prominence can afford a view for leagues in that country; the settlement stood in thick dusk atop a huddled group of rises arranged for defense and strengthened with palisade and abatis as well as a graceful stone spike at its highest crown. The tower was a rarity, its top sheared by some unimaginable storm. Even broken and at a distance the spire gave much evidence of Elder aid in planning and construction; the bloom of ruddy flame at its base near drove the breath from me.

Snow parted, flakes thinning swiftly. A flicker, a moment of mistrusting my eyes, then my heart attempted a leap into my throat as I realized what I was seeing—that gleam had to be evidence of some habitation. The Jewel pinch-prodded, its quiet burn receding somewhat, and when I glanced at Arn I knew from her expression that she had seen it as well.

"Torch." Soren's eyebrows held a few pieces of ice, but his smile was wide and genuine for the first time since before Laeliquaende's fall. "Don't worry. 'Tis the Old Wolf's tower, and he will not have gone to Dorael. Not yet."

"Old wolf?" If there was a riddle in the term, I could not find it.

"Aye. Probably already scented us." The stocky Northerner paused, swaying with his mount's gait. He did not often ride upon that journey, spending most of it in his other skin. "I crave your pardon, my lady."

What on earth for? "I might grant it just for the asking, did I but know why." It felt good to weigh the words, both his and mine; I had been struck near speechless by my burden, and that is never comfortable for a *volva*.

There are several forms of *seidhr* in silence, but I wished no more of them at that particular moment.

"Ah. Well." His horse eased closer. "I had no time, you see. To gather your trunk from the palace."

I glanced at Arn again. She peered around me in the winter gloaming, bright-eyed and interested, her spear's blade glistening. The torch in the distance bobbed gently closer with each hoof-fall.

"The city was overrun and you..." I wanted to laugh, but further jostling in the saddle might hurt. And he had waited how long to offer this apology? Either he dreaded my reaction or this was some manner of jest—or, perhaps he meant to lighten my mood, I could not tell. "My lord, I cannot pardon an entirely imaginary offense."

" 'Twas my task, and I am pained by not performing it—I have been seeking a spare moment to speak of the matter." He regarded me steadily, not quite scowling but certainly downcast. "We promised you would travel as one of our own, and with every care."

He seemed serious; I was glad I had not made light of his apology after all. "I count it a great victory to be still breathing; the wolves of Naras have indeed shown every care in that regard." Curiosity invaded me, a welcome tonic after days of being too dazed to think properly. "Of course, were you to tell me how you managed to carry it all the while, I would listen most intently."

"A small trick, performed by members of my family. Sometimes the…when we receive the curse, we are granted something else as well." His head lifted slightly; at the head of our column, Karas and Daerith drew away, their mounts quickening. In the distance, the orange torch-spark bobbed again like a small boat on a placid river. "Lord Tharos discourages use of such talents."

But Eol does not, for all he considers his wolfskin a curse. The mystery of the captain's grimness was somewhat solved, yet it was nothing I could affect, for there is no way to remove the second skin from one who has the gift. At least, so our sagas say.

So, Soren had an additional talent, but it clearly was not *seidhr* since he bore a blade. Ordinarily I would be thrilled at finding some new thing approximating weirding in the world.

The lord of Naras disliked both the second skin and these additional talents, but his son welcomed those afflicted. No wonder Eol's men followed him so faithfully. He cared for his own, and that is a quality which keeps a warlord's underlings loyal—if the man who would rule knows what he is about.

Was my task here simply to argue the wolves of Naras into considering their gifts afresh? If not for the Elder thing burning in me, I might have found the solution to this particular riddle entirely risible, in the manner only one of Lokji's pranks could be. "Yet they are useful," I said. "Such a cunning talent would be worth much in the South."

"I am better here." Soren's smile returned, diffident but pleasant to see. "But I must also speak of summat else, my lady Question. You may well be surprised tonight. Lord Tharos keeps to old ways, and is much concerned with tradition. All his folk know better than to act otherwise."

It was luxurious to have a problem or two I could solve looming before me, whether it was explaining *seidhr* to warriors or using my tongue wisely before a lord in his own hall. "You wish me to be mindful of my words. Have no fear on that account."

"Indeed I fear not, for you are a quiet one. 'Tis more likely our Minnowsharp there will be offended, though the Old Wolf is ever courteous to a lady. It is more that…" He fell silent, and when I turned my head I saw a shadow in the snowy night.

A tall rider, urging his horse past. But I would know him anywhere—Eol, and probably listening to every syllable.

Wolves, like Elder and shieldmaids, have sharp ears.

"Worry not, Soren." The Old Tongue rang under my words, turning their consonants sharp. "My brother killed Lord Tharos's son. I shall do all duty demands, as both ally and weregild."

The horses sensed respite was near, and our pace quickened despite the danger. Finally we rode into Barael-am-Narain, *Hill of Broken Spears* in the Old Tongue.

But among themselves, those of Naras called it *the Old Wolf's place*.

And, more quietly, *Home, for now*.

Upon the Threshold

Welcome strangers, but do not trust them. Be courteous and wary; many are the Enemy's snares, and any gift accepted from that quarter bears steep cost. Even a friend's face may be seeming; was not even Arnan the great songsmith taken in by Olvrang the Cruel?
　　—Nethael the Drunk, advisor to Uldfang the Third

There were no other lights, and the turf-and-timber buildings shared the same air of hasty abandonment as previous steadings and settlements—all except the tower, where a perfectly mortal brand glowed despite the wind, shielded by a trick of Elder construction and illuminating a point-arched ironbound door.

I did not like looking upon the tall stone spire, for its shape seemed familiar in the way of dream-seen things. At least there was no yellow gleam at its shattered top, and while the night was still thick with cold and metallic snow-scent no flakes fell from the sky, ashen or otherwise.

A single black-clad figure stood upon stone steps as hoofbeats echoed on packed earth swept clean of all ice. Karas was already opening the stables; dismounting was undertaken with alacrity by every man save Eol.

My Elder slippers had proven amazingly durable, and touched the ground with gratitude. Arneior steadied me. The Jewel did not burn so much, nestling softly inside my ribs, but I sensed its sharp edges could turn in a moment. My mount shook her snow-clotted mane, impatient for shelter, and I peered around her familiar warm bulk.

In Northern cloth, spare and angular, our host bore a great iron-colored mane as well. A greying smallbeard was suffered to remain upon his chin and upper lip, but no beads would find a congenial home there, for it was far too short. A golden torc, its ends plain instead of fancifully cast or carved, lay over his high collar. He wore no sword. Instead, a single dagger with a glowing pearl at its pommel rested at his belt, and his narrow hands were crossed before him as he examined what the wind had borne to his door.

Eol finally dismounted, handing his reins to Efain. The heir of Naras approached the steps, and the Taurain's snow-choked wind did not keen at the tower's corners but muffled its tone, whispering conspiratorial.

"Father." Eol halted, and bowed—but not as to me or Arn, and not as he would to an Elder. Instead, the movement seemed perfunctory, but I did not know Northern customs. "We have passed many an empty steading. I thought to find you gone to Dorael."

"*I said I would stay here until my son's return.*" For such a lean fellow, Tharos had a deep resonant voice with an edge of growl, especially in the Old Tongue. Though the cloth was Northern the pattern of his robe was very close to Elder, and a golden ring with a great dark stone glittered upon his left hand. "*Thus, here I stand.*"

All in all he was very lordly indeed, though my father might have muttered, *A cold one, that man.* The shadowmantle's hem fluttered uneasily, and I would have shivered if I felt the wind's chill.

I had not for some while now, and I did not think it entirely due to Elder garb.

Soren led my horse away. Arn's head turned as she studied the space before the tower, the shuttered buildings looming close by, the pattern of paving spreading for a short distance from the stairs. It faded into hard-stamped, frozen earth, melding by degrees as Elder stonework so often does.

I had not immediately seen the wolves of Naras—or the bears of

Tavaan, or Uldfang's men—for what they were. But in Tharos the lord of lost Naras I saw an aging beast with a shaggy iron-colored coat, his lip quivering though not quite raised yet and a warning gleam lost deep in dark, narrowed eyes.

Prickling apprehension spilled down my back. I was no longer truly Eol's weregild, but my brother had killed this man's son. A powerful debt, all else aside, and an uncomfortable one.

Had I not been *alkuine*, would they have taken Bjorn or Dun Rithell's roof-gilding instead? Or would I have been brought directly to this place upon the plains, spending a year and day under this man's stony shadow?

"Naras is faithful," Eol said, the Old Tongue mellifluous as if he quoted a proverb. *"So we have ever been, and so we remain."*

"Oh, aye. Even unto those who wrong us." Tharos glided down a step, another. A ripple passed through his skin—a warning, the wolf shifting inside its bearer. My breath caught, though the movement was subtle and he paid no more attention to me than to the sharpening breeze. *"Or those who betray their own kin."*

Had we not been traveling together so long I might not have sensed Eol's tension. He was taut as Daerith's bowstring. *"I would give you the news privately."*

"And what news would that be?" Another step. Now Tharos loomed over his eldest son.

Aeredh arrived at my left side, and though I had not heard his step I must have somehow sensed him, for I did not flinch. The edge of his warmth touched me, different than the unfelt snow-chill, and his mouth was a thin line. He regarded the two Secondborn narrowly, father and son framed against a closed door, torchlight limning them both.

"Very well." Eol gazed upward, a statue with shaggy ice-dotted hair. *"Arvil has gone West, my father. I lit his pyre myself, the day after winter solstice."*

It is never pleasant to see an old man stagger under ill news. 'Tis even worse when he does so without moving, physical stillness unable to contain or turn aside a sudden shock.

"And you, still breathing," Tharos murmured.

"*I am.*" Eol sounded, of all things, bitterly amused. "*Despite all efforts to the contrary, including my own.*"

A pang jolted me. Maybe it was the Jewel turning afresh, dissatisfied with its new home—or perhaps the thing was interested in this saga-stanza, for it was a scene worthy of one. Eol gazed up at his father, who twitched into movement, descending the last few stairs with stiff grace.

He was not as thoughtlessly, efficiently lithe as the others, but perhaps age—or grief—robbed him of that fluidity.

Tharos's ringed hand flashed. The blow snapped his son's head aside, and well it is that those with two skins are more durable than other mortals. For even in his senescence the lord of Naras was strong, and he did not restrain his fist as my father would while disciplining Bjorn.

"*You should have tried harder,*" the Old Wolf said. He turned with a flicker of black robe and climbed once more; when he reached the ironbound doors he pushed the left half open. More ruddy torchlight spilled from that aperture, and I did not realize I was moving until Arn stepped onto paving at my shoulder.

Eol stayed as Tharos had left him, head turned and chin down, staring at the ground. A muscle flickered in his stubbled cheek, and his black mantle bore small rips and thin spots that could not be seen at a distance. Had I a needle, I could have attended to that as well as Arn's sleeve.

He did not give me a chance to speak. "Enter, and be welcome." The southron tongue, crisp and clear with all due politeness, rolled from Eol's mouth—but he still did not move. "Nothing more need be said, my lady. 'Tis a matter between my father and myself, and you are a guest here."

Not weregild? The words trembled on my tongue. Others slipped past them instead. "I will explain." Was the tingling in my hand some *seidhr*, or did I simply wish to touch his shoulder, his elbow, imparting whatever comfort I could?

But I did not, for I was after all too far away and his tension had not abated.

"Oh, no." Eol laughed, a single sarcastic bark. "Do not, my lady. If you care for me at all, do not."

With that, he turned upon his heel and stalked for the stables. Efain was returning, his expression grave and dark eyes burning. The rest of the Northerners were looking elsewhere, either with studied indifference or tactfully busy at other tasks; Daerith was busy examining my mare's foreleg as if suspecting incipient lameness and Yedras had halted in the middle of the open space, gazing at the blank, snow-pregnant sky.

Did he see the stars past the clouds as well?

"Come." Aeredh was beside me again, offering his arm. His expression was set, yet I thought a flicker of distaste lurked in his gaze, shadowed the straight line of his mouth. "In the North the guests enter first; the sooner we do, the sooner Eol may."

But he did not; the elder son of Tharos made for the stables, and there he stayed that night. And I stepped over the tower's threshold with deep misgiving.

I knew the ways of the North were different and guessed the folk of Naras had taken all they could carry to safety, leaving a bare minimum for their lord's use. Still, it was an exceeding cold welcome.

Oh, the fare was better than it had been for a long while, certainly. Not only was there a haunch upon a small spit but also ale, cheese that had not been forgotten, and even hard winterbread softened in the ale until it was almost as melting as Elder waybread wrapped in leaves. There was also a cask of winterwine; no house of the Faithful in the North would be without a vintage or two, brought by Elder friends and saved for any later visitor of their kind.

No, the chill radiated entirely from our host, who presided over the feast from a high-backed chair upon a dais, his board a massive black wooden slab with ferocious carving upon its legs. Teeth and eyes glared from the chisel-marks, along with the roughness of wolf-pelt. Aeredh was seated to his right, Daerith and Yedras to his left; I was given the place near Aeredh, with Arn upon my other side.

Eol did not appear. I tried not to stare at the great doorway from the entry-hall, expecting him at any moment.

The rest of our companions made do with a lower table, and they were not merry at all. Their hush was extreme, broken only by sounds of consumption and a fire half as big as it should be in the massive stone hearth. Efain arranged the repast at the high table while the others were made do without bond, thrall, or servant to fetch and carry. There was no singing, no jests provoking laughter, no telling of old tales; when Tharos did speak it was only to Aeredh, and in the Old Tongue as well.

"*One of the Blessed's own ravens, upon the stable-roof. I should think its croak would not reach our ears were it to perch upon the tower.*" Tharos gazed into his great wooden cup; there was meat upon his dish, but he ate slow and sparing. The ring upon his hand gleamed, its stone bearing a single bright spot. Some trick of its carving made that pupil dilate or shrink with every small motion. "*When it left, it was to the south. No doubt the Cloak-Weaver will hear all tidings. Her husband is kin to Taeron, after all.*"

"*We came light and fast, but not wingéd.*" Aeredh drank steadily, and his gaze lingered upon the shadowed doorway at the hall's far end as well. I might as well have been invisible for all the attention paid me, and was well content to have it so. "*You should ride with us in the morn, my friend. What follows the survivors of Taeron's folk is unpleasant at best.*"

"*Let them come. I swore to bide here, and I will.*" The lord of Naras did not speak of his younger son, and I was acutely aware of my own embarrassment, nearly sharp as the Jewel's claws.

The fishgutting Elder thing had returned to burning as well; winterwine did not help, nor did it taste as it had before. There was no mouth-filling, no cascade of memories from the liquid, merely a slight amelioration of the heat and a dozy trickle of strength returning to my limbs. I studied the ceiling-beams, the construction of the hearth, guessed at other rooms in the tower's bulk—for though it looked slim, the inside was surprisingly roomy. The hints of Elder knowledge and craft in stone and timberwork were plain, yet I could not say if I liked the melding.

Beautiful, durable, and of a certain comfort was Tharos's lodging, yes, but a damp, nasty tinge lingered within. Later I learned only warriors were allowed in the broken tower unless some attack made it the shelter of last resort, but even so, there was an entire community at its foot to supply any wants. To be left behind, alone of one's steading...the notion gives even a *volva* who likes solitary pursuits a shudder.

Tharos did not even have a bondsman or thrall to shake his bedding, yet here he stayed. Leaving a single man to shift for himself in a greathall is a punishment all its own. Nobody to keep the pantry or cellar in order, no weaving in the women's quarters, no laughter, no cooking, no song—if it sounds ugly, that is because it is. Even the loneliest shepherd ranging upon Tarnarya's slopes had a community to notice if they did not bring their flock to the green at the appointed times, and kin to visit occasionally as well, bringing news or aid against disaster.

In a saga I might have admired his determination, as iron as his hair and the streaks in his smallbeard...and yet.

"None would stay with you? I find that hard to believe." Aeredh turned, regarding our host; I was grateful I did not have to attempt conversation. *"Naras is Faithful."* The last word carried a great deal of stress upon the penultimate syllable, not merely descriptive but a title of some repute.

"For all the good it does." A glower was evident in Tharos's tone; I glanced at Arn, who was not perturbed by language she could not understand. I would repeat the conversation for her later, if there was aught of note within it.

Another small task I could take some comfort in performing, for a *volva*'s memory is well-trained. I sensed some manner of apology in Aeredh's attempts at conversation, deep reticence—and anger—in our host's.

"Do not give in to despair, Tharos. That is the Enemy's weapon." How often did Aeredh use this tone with mortals—sorrowing, and gentle? I had heard it more than once, and could not tell whether to dislike or be comforted by its advent.

All the Elder grief in the world would not bring back Tharos's other son. Yet Arvil's fellows had suspected him of treachery, which Aeredh was politely refraining to lay before his father. Perhaps he would discuss it with the lord in private, and I did not envy him the task.

I had never met this Arvil, only heard of him from Bjorn and the men of Naras. I could lay aside the matter of him insulting Astrid, for that might not be an act deserving death no matter what touchy menfolk say...and besides, he *had* died for it, whether worthy of such a fate or not.

One cannot argue with or change what has been, and sometimes not even what lies ahead.

"And what else should I think?" the lord of Naras replied, before taking a long draught. Ale or some other drink glimmered upon his lip when he lowered the cup. *"I hear a wyrm lodges where Nithraen once was."*

The Crownless did not stiffen, nor did his expression change. *"Did a raven tell you that?"*

Tharos's grin was almost triangular, strong white teeth framed by greying shortbeard. *"No. But the North is full of news, my friend, and a good nose may catch it upon the wind."*

They spoke of other things—Faeron-Alith, Galath, Isthanir, Nassan-Daele, of dispositions and relative strengths, of what had passed in these lands while Aeredh journeyed south. Neither mentioned a dead son, which was wise and polite...yet a spirit lingered in that tower's greathall, colder than new-winter's freeze.

I was glad when the meal was over.

Know, Not Tell

Those with the curse are vital well into old age and often marry late. The mark often does not show itself until near adulthood, though one with a strong beast may give sign as a child, and should be fostered with the Elder to learn control.

—Kelaas of Uld, *Concerning the Houses of the Gasping*

Not a word of any weregild, hm?" Arn scratched under her hornbraids, fingertips scrubbing hard. No doubt she longed for a sauna as much as I did, though steambreath might make the Jewel even more uncomfortable.

I could not tell, and I did not think the Elder would be able to dispel that particular mystery. Not that I would mention such a thing to any of their kind.

" 'Tis not proper feast-time conversation." I settled upon the pallet, glad to be both stationary and free of male attention. Perhaps this narrow room was a servant's closet, but it was large enough for us, a single candle in an enclosed holder resting upon a shelf by the door, a low heavy bedstead to comfortably hold both shieldmaid and *volva*, and a small, strangely designed fireplace as well as enough wood harvested from ravine-bottoms and the fringing fingers of Dorael's great forest to keep us warm for the night.

Luxuriously, wonderfully warm. I almost did not mind the prospect of the water-room down a dark, damp stone hall; morning ablutions would be a slap-shock.

"I did not think I would ever say this." Arn settled her spear against the wall and began stretching, ridding herself of stiffness from spending all day a-horseback. "But I like your father better."

"I did not think to ever hear you say such a thing, either." I grimaced, and for once my face did not feel masklike. Lingering unease had to fight with the languor of heat not provided by some Elder artifice or draught, and could not truly win the battle. I was almost pathetically grateful for the orange-and-yellow fire, no touch of blue *aelflame* in its fingers. "For my part, I like even Yedras better. And he called me a witch. Twice."

"Hm." She bent double, supple even in her armor—though it had to be uncomfortable, she clearly did not intend to sleep without its protection even in this haven. "He fights well enough."

High praise from a shieldmaid, especially for another spear-wielder. Yedras was skilled in the art of *trul*-hunting, Soren said; I had seen as much in the woods after Nithraen. Such a feat is best done in trios, two warriors with spears to hold the thing at bay, one with sword or axe to inflict a killing blow.

"They all do." We would hardly be alive otherwise, I thought. "But 'tis strange. This Northern lord welcomes his elder son with a blow, grieves the younger's absence, but also seems..."

"As flint," she supplied. "Resists until it shatters, into shards fit to cut a throat."

I gave a slight nod, for it was true, and thankfully the Jewel did not poke me. Yet it was not exactly what I meant to say. "Unsurprised," I added—not disagreeing, merely adding a refinement. "Perhaps he dreamt of his son's misfortune."

She made a noise halfway between a grunt and a murmur, neither assent nor its opposite. I watched the fireplace; soon it might be stifling in this tiny space, but no sweat prickled under my arms, or indeed in any crease. The shadowmantle should have been far too heavy for such a warm room.

Elder cloth was wondrous indeed. I could not decide if the

mantle's camouflage under any gloom, and its pale grey appearance in the snow-wastes, was a trick of weaving or of *seidhr*.

Or both.

There was no room for spear-practice and little enough for stretching, so Arn soon bedded down. I settled near the fireplace, watching the flames as if they would grant me a vision. My shield-maid's silence was almost comfortable as my own, and I could tell by her breathing that she was not asleep despite fatigue and the comfort of temporary safety.

"You are still not sleeping," she said finally.

"I wonder that you can, in your armor." My hands arranged themselves in my lap, the cupped position Idra said was best for scrying while seated. "I am weary, yes. But it never grows worse, nor better."

"And you do not eat."

"Perhaps the thing fills my stomach." I did not like the thought of my innards disarranged, and tried not to wonder if they would eventually return to their proper places once the Jewel was dislodged—whenever that happy event could occur. "I do not feel hungry; sometimes even the smell of meat sickens me. This is a heavy weirding; I will be glad to be free of it."

Arn shifted, tucking a stiff bolster more securely under her head. "And when will that be, do you think?"

I am so glad to have you, my small one. "I once thought it was intended to be used as a weapon, but it does not seem possible. I wonder if Aeredh is disappointed."

"*Pff.*" A short, dismissive sound. Her eyelids drooped heavily, but the gleams under them were fierce. "If he had left us in peace, he would not be so."

"The Enemy knew of an *alkuine* before I reached the Eastron-most, he said." All I felt was a dim, weary wonder that I could utter such words calmly, without shaking in terror. "I begin to believe him and Taeron, that perhaps there might not be another in the world."

Arn was silent for a moment, pulling her knees up and settling more comfortably. "But Idra..."

"I know. I have been wondering if she merely assumed there must be a few, and trained me accordingly." 'Twas a relief to finally give the thought some voice outside my own head. "Or if she...if she knew, but for some reason did not tell."

"Know, but not tell?" My shieldmaid snorted softly. "How entirely like a *volva*."

A soft laugh bubbled in my throat, and the Jewel did not scrape inside my ribs when it slipped free. "If I told you all my thoughts you would be bored to tears. Some things are best left locked up."

"Oh, aye, including that egg you're brooding." She sobered, her eyes closing completely. "But if not a weapon, what in Odynn's name do they expect you do to with it?"

"I do not know." My fingers tightened a fraction; it was an effort to loosen them, to take as deep a breath as the weight would permit. "What truly unsettles me is that Aeredh might not either." *Nor his Elder friends.*

"Well, he is a man." Her tone was not unkind; *it is regrettable*, she meant, *yet such creatures are only as they have been made.*

Oddly, my cheeks warmed, and the strong slow ageless thrum of his pulse echoed in my memory. *I cannot regret my hope, or our meeting.* "I had not noticed."

"Oh, no." Amusement filled the words. "Your eyes turn in a different direction, indeed."

There was no possible answer. I listened while her breathing shifted; she fell into sleep's dim country without further ado.

I envied her that boon, and watched the flames as they consumed their own feast. Was I feeling what wood does under that bright kiss? The Jewel might be a creeping fire of the type that slips underground with blackcoal, burning in the earth's very veins.

Would I eventually become ash, like that drifting over the Gasping?

There was no answer.

⬗⬖⬗⬖⬗

Moving slowly, I snuffed the candle inside its enclosure, settled a little more fuel upon the coals—the fireplace was so strange and simple it did not need much tending, long husbanding even a few sticks— and was about to sink cross-legged on the floor again. The silence was profound; in this room, we could not even hear the Taurain's constant singing.

Perhaps the subtle brush of a footstep reached my inner senses, or perhaps I had expected a visit. In any case, a soft mannerly tap upon the door was loud as a thunderclap in that hush.

Arn was awake in an instant, lunging up from the bed. Her hand shot out, closing around the spear's haft, and my shieldmaid was ready for battle.

"Soft," I mouthed, and would have moved to answer the knock.

She glared me into immobility, and glided in that direction. Bootless, her hornbraids rumpled, she was still a forbidding sight, and when she flung the door open, the golden glow of a thoroughly normal, mortal handlamp held by an iron hoop at its top cast sharp-edged shadows in every direction.

"I apologize for disturbing your slumber." Lord Tharos tilted his head slightly, and in that moment he looked much like his eldest son, when Eol searched the horizon for pursuit or some other manner of threat. His southron was highly accented, though courteous enough. "Yet there are words I must pass with your mistress, maiden-of-steel, and I would not have other ears catch them."

Speak of a Friend

What now lives in our old homes,
where once we sang and slept?
Shadows and dark things, creatures misformed.
Remember what was, but do not dream,
for the Gift-giver lurks in the corners...
　　　　—Gaelfang the Mad, once-lord of Aen Aethas

Quiet was the lord of Naras's step; he led us through the tower's passages with no more sound than an owl's muffled wing. The doorways were all arches of the Elder style, with tapering tops; the doors themselves were of heavy varnished wood, ironbound and strong though some showed signs of great age.

Finally we reached a staircase. "A long climb," our host said, "but worth it. We may go slowly."

Though it was indeed many stairs they were also well-laid, and I had little trouble even with the Jewel's weight. Still, Arneior preceded me, and was perhaps uneasy at the close confines. The lamp flickered, dancing shadows filling a stone throat. As the stairs wound upward the archways confined themselves to the left side, each solemnly barred.

Near the top, signs of wear and decay became far more marked; a low humming of wind tiptoed alongside us. The last few steps were somewhat less solid, wood instead of stone; they led to a timber roof

and trapdoor, but Lord Tharos turned aside upon the final platform
and the last door opened with no protesting squeak.

I hesitate to call what was revealed a room, for much detritus lay
scattered upon the floor and half its outer wall was gone. The Taurain's breath played across the hole, producing a mournful flute-note.
The cold was sharp after the comfort of our small room, but also
bracing. Clouds had parted; a soft glow was moonlight running over
ice and thin fingers of snow digging into the tower's hide.

For all that, the space was protected from the full force of the
weather. The hole was wide enough to permit a view of white wilderness to a far horizon turned faintly blue by the lamp of night, and
I let out a small sound of wonder.

"Gaining some height oft makes many problems appear simpler."
Tharos beckoned, setting the lamp aside on a handy protruding rock-
shelf. Its flame straightened, tall and gold. "Come, and shut the door.
We will not be heard here."

For all its weight the slab of old wood moved easily, and when
it was closed the tenor of windsong changed. The sound was still
beautiful, but I suppressed a shiver and hoped the cluttered floor was
solid.

Arn hovered at my shoulder; I faced Eol's father over a stripe of
moonlight. His hair silvered in the bleaching glow and his smallbeard holding only traces of charcoal to match his cloth, he was a
forbidding sight. He had laid aside the pearl-handled dagger and the
plain golden torc, but the ring was still upon his left hand, gleaming
wetly.

"Well?" he said, finally. "I beg of you to tell me truly, lady. How
did my son die?"

Arn tensed, though her fingers remained easy upon the spear.

I had suspected he would ask—what father could not? I had also
given some thought to my answer, and for what it was worth I gave
it steadily. "My brother struck him, my lord. Your son fell; his head
cracked upon a stone."

"Ah." He nodded, thoughtfully. "And why did your brother
strike my Arvil?"

"There were words concerning my sister, my lord." Who would

like telling a grieving parent of such matters? Sharp edges twitched inside my chest, the Jewel's prodding far easier to bear than delivering this particular tale. "It was...a mischance."

"Are you so certain?" His left hand tightened, the ring's scintillation akin to a cat's eyelid-flicker.

"I did not see the event myself," I admitted. "Yet my brother and father spoke of it, and so did Aeredh." I thought it best to be honest concerning the dead—but also as kind as possible. "Thus I was given as weregild for a year and a day. Events during our journey turned that debt to alliance instead. Yet I would ease your grief, lord of Naras, in whatever way I can. I am sorry for it." *And everything afterward.*

"Weregild." A brief nod. "I have heard of the southron custom. But that is not everything, my lady. You would not be taken to Taeron's secret fastness were it so, or now guarded so closely by three of the mightiest lords of Nithraen and the beasts of my House besides."

Beasts of his House? A mistranslation from the Old Tongue, perhaps? And he regarded Aeredh and his friends as deserving the term *of the mightiest*?

In any case, I could give a diplomatic answer. "Indeed we have traveled far."

The wind caught my words, shook them; then, dissatisfied, whisked them out through the hole. North and slightly east it looked, much larger than a window, and outside stars glimmered fitfully through snowy moonhaze as the weather cleared. I wondered what had torn away great chunks of masonry, for at the edges it looked as if a giant claw had dug through clay.

The silence lengthened, and no doubt Tharos thought nervousness might make a woman chattersome. Yet I had never been so even as a child, and traveling so long with men not of my kind or kin set the habit even deeper.

The Jewel's claws prickled afresh inside my ribcage. Mere discomfort, or a warning?

I wished yet again I were not carrying the thing, for my wits were much quicker without its dragging pressure—and I suspected I would need them both sharp and swift to deal with Tharos of Naras. He was no bandit or petty warlord; nor was he of my father's rough stripe. Cold and contained, he reminded me most of Taeron, or—more aptly—of Caelgor the Fair.

For both of them knew well how to wait, and watch. Such men are dangerous.

Tharos turned his head, watching the broken wall—or what lay beyond. "You know of our curse."

"In the South, such things can be counted a blessing, bringing great strength to protect and aid." I believed it, then and now. I had said as much to Eol, and that eve I repeated the idea to his father.

I like to think I sought to help, instead of to steer the conversation from his younger son's murder.

"In a dog, perhaps." Tharos's right shoulder lifted, dropped, a weary shrug. "But we are wolves, and to share a beast's skin is to share his hungers. Uncontrolled, we are worse than animals. And Arvil—my blessed boy—was not as I am, as that other one. He did not carry the fangs."

A father who would not even use his eldest son's name, whip-scars upon a man's back... much more about Eol of Naras's bleakness now made sense, and I could not tell if the pang going through me was the Jewel or something else. "Eol of Naras has saved my life many times, my lord."

"He does everything the Crownless asks." Tharos's lip well nigh curled under his smallbeard. I had thought he held Aeredh in high honor, being what the North called *Faithful*, but perhaps that was mere seeming—and if so, I had to be careful indeed. "He always has."

"They are friends." I sensed the drift of our host's current, and 'twas in a most unpleasant direction. My fingers tingled as if the nipping cold would turn them numb despite my newfound immunity. The Jewel shifted again, sharp edges against tender innards.

Were it dragged free of my flesh, what scar would I bear from the parting? The thought returned, and I did not like it this time either.

"Friends?" Tharos laughed, half-turning to gaze into the night—did he see what I did, the darkness well past the horizon, starred with pinpricks of flame? How keen was the Old Wolf's gaze? "The Elder call us *faithful* when we obey. But they also keep the secret from us."

I could not disagree. "They keep many secrets." Perhaps I sounded bitter as well, for Arn glanced at me; her brow was furrowed, and her grasp upon her spear changed slightly.

"There is one above all others they hoard, Lady Solveig." He pronounced my name as if in the Old Tongue, and it sounded better in his eldest son's mouth. In this man's it was near-mocking, especially underlaid by the wind's rising, jangling melody. "Have you ever wondered why we are mortal, and they are not?"

What? Did he think me simple? Of course any mortal with sense and the knowledge of Elder existence could not fail to wonder, even if the answer was in no few sagas. "The Allmother—"

"Oh, spare me Elder pandering, girl." Tharos's dark gaze sparked, and for a moment he looked very much like his eldest son indeed. "If the Allmother loves Secondborn so, if we are so much more precious and gifted, why do we sicken? Why do we die? Mayhap she prizes them above us, or does not—either way, they lie. Where is the truth of the matter to be found, then?"

Now he sounded like Idra, coaxing me to understanding. I stood very still, yet the Jewel kept turning and prodding. Bitter frustration crowded my throat, a hot ill-tasting lump; if the fishgutting thing in my chest would cease its aching I could perhaps think clearly.

Silly child. My teacher's voice echoed, just behind my ear where *seidhr* strikes. *You are* volva. *I taught you to lay aside distractions so the weirding may speak; this is no different.*

"We may ask one who knows." Tharos faced us fully again, spine straightening and shoulders pushed back. A man does not need a second skin to seem taller; he must only stand a certain way, and all will swear him nearly a giant. "And here in the North, 'tis possible to find him."

A cold fingertip touched my nape, adding to the tingling in my hands. Both sensations were all the more startling since I had not felt winter upon my skin for some while. Slow, rippling dread coursed down my back, yet even as it did I welcomed the feeling.

It was familiar, and above all, *mortal.* "You say the Elder lie, and

I know Secondborn may as well." I longed to use the Old Tongue, but the old habit of misdirecting Northern men had risen, and I did not question it. I did not know if one of our companions had let slip the fact that I knew their speech... but I did not think it likely, and there was no reason to grant this man any advantage at all, however slight. "Even gods may mislead. Is there anyone in all the world who does not?"

"There is one, my lady." Tharos's gaze locked with mine; the contact very nearly jolted me physically. "He gives gifts to those who would hear truth, and works against those who would enslave."

I did not dare break the humming between us, a fishing-line pulled taut. The contest was akin to groups of strong warriors heaving upon either side of a rope, each seeking to yank the other off-balance. I had seen many such games at Dun Rithell, and laughed when they were well-played.

There is a like challenge in *seidhr*, invisible but no less potent, a means by which one of strong will seeks to dominate another. Curiaen the Subtle and Taeron Goldspear had both sought to discern my thoughts with sharp strength; Tharos of Naras meant to overpower and lead me to some end.

Perhaps he even thought it would be easy. The wind flirted and swirled, its voice taking on a darker edge.

"The Elder fight the Enemy," I said, finally. The Jewel's prickle was an irritant, true, but it also frayed the pull of his will. He had no *seidhr* beyond that usually granted to two-skins, of that I was certain.

The power striving with my own came from somewhere else. And why was he speaking so? I had expected questioning upon the death of his younger son, not... whatever this midnight parley was. I could not even glance to Arneior, yet I did not have to.

Her warmth beside me, the steady disciplined fire of a shield-maid, never altered.

"Indeed they do, for they serve those powers seeking to enslave us all." Tharos's tone was gentle, nearly avuncular; the edges of his robe twitch-rippled as he shifted, slowly easing his weight from one foot to the other. "You and I are mortal, young lady, and not party to their quarrel. Why should we bleed for the Elder, work for them, send our children to die for them? There is another way." A feverish glare had invaded his gaze. "And what you carry is the key to it."

My attention focused upon the ring—the damp glimmer of its stone swelled, far brighter than the weak golden shimmer lampglow should produce. "What I carry." *So he knows. Be careful, Solveig. Be very, very careful now.*

"Did you think me unaware?" The Old Wolf smiled, strong white teeth gleaming with faint lamplight and the far stronger illumination of moonlight. "I knew of my son's misfortune long before your arrival, for I have a good friend, one more honest than the Elder and wise enough not to strike down our Enemy until the time is right. My own folk, blinded by Dorael's witchery, sought to entice me from Barael-am-Narain—for my safety, they said, *faugh*! But I swore not to move until my Arvil returned, and also because I knew you would come."

My heart pounded in my wrists, my throat, even behind my knees. The Jewel's burning dilated between my lungs, and I almost welcomed the pain. "You knew?" My voice was a cricket-whisper, barely audible over the wind.

"I was told." Tharos's smile widened. "By a friend you never knew you had. *He* sees you, young Solveig, and many times you have been saved by *his* efforts. I was shown your face long before this, and all has come to pass as *he* predicted."

When the Elder spoke of the Black Land's lord, they laid the same stress upon *he* and *his*. So did Eol and his men—but I did not think Tharos of Naras meant the Allmother's eldest child. Yet if he did not, who or what…

"No closer," Arn said. The warning in her tone was clear and harsh, and I realized Tharos had moved.

"There is no need for alarm." Slowly, softly, he took another padding step; he wore a warrior's boots instead of house-shoes. His robe's hem just barely brushed leaves and dust blown in by autumn-breath. "All we must do is wait."

"For what?" It was so hard to think, between the weight of my burden and a motionless inward striving to keep from being swallowed. The rope tautened, its hum deepening, and the ring on our host's left hand gave a yellow flash as unlike the lamplight as fish is to fire.

I have seen that gleam before. I strained against a dark current, sinking fast. The discomfort in my chest was oddly smothered, covered by a heavy blanket. The respite would have been wonderful and welcome...save for the fear taking its place, bright copper at the back of my palate.

"It will not be long," Tharos murmured. "He knows of your people, Solveig of Dun Rithell, and he will protect them. Mine he will cherish too, once they have been taught their error. The curse will be lifted."

The cold was all through me, now. "You speak of the Enemy."

"I speak of a *friend*, southron child." The glitter in his gaze was of no physical fever, and far back in his pupils a different spark dilated, peering as if through a long dark tunnel. "One who will heal all hurts, explain all mysteries, break the doors of mortal death and bring my Arvil back to me."

There is a *seidhr* of speaking to the dead, of course. Ancestors and kin may be drawn from Hel's many countries, or even Odynn's and Fryja's halls, to provide guidance and aid. 'Tis a dangerous act, performed only at great need...but a sudden jabbing instinct told me evocation or spirit-showing over a basin of blood and smoke was not what he meant, and my veins chilled at the blasphemy.

I shifted, a movement of my subtle selves quick as sunlight upon a leaping carp's wet scales. The rope snapped; the sound of its breaking was all internal, and I saw once more Eol at the oars, cloth upon his back parting and bright blood flying as he strained. The sting sank into my own flesh, I gasped, and the blunt end of Arn's spear leapt between me and Tharos.

Who had drawn close indeed, his ringed hand lifting as if to touch.

The strike sank into his midsection, driving the lord of Naras back. His boots scraped stone, and I saw beneath his skin as his lip lifted in a snarl.

The wolf in him was strong, grizzled muzzle and lean shoulders bespeaking hunger and survival both. Yet in its dark eyes was a yellow flame of watersick, foamjaw madness.

The Jewel blazed in my chest; for once its burning was welcome. I coughed, a dry rasping sound swallowed at its end by another.

A brazen horn-cry lifted high in freezing air, thrilling up through mortal hearing into the regions beyond. Before, the hunting yowls of the Enemy's servants had remained at some distance, but not this one.

No. It was close indeed, and loud.

My shieldmaid stepped before me, leveling her spear. Its blade gleamed, a bar of brightness bathed in silvergold from mingled lamp- and moonglow, and was pointed directly at our host.

Woad, Earned

Quick was the Minnow
And sharp was her spear
Bright was her armor
And she knew no fear...
—Gelad son of Aerenil, *The Rowing Song*

I bent stiffly, retch-gasping, and struggled to breathe. Along with the pain came bafflement—he had no *seidhr*, for we weirdlings can tell our own. Yet he had ensnared me with invisible force, and the breaking of his grip sent a shock almost to my very bones.

Not him. Something else. Which meant Arn was facing powerful, malevolent weirding, and I could barely straighten, let alone sing.

"Sol," my small one said, calmly enough. "Go to the door."

A ripple passed through Tharos, the wolf turning inside him. The others of Naras shared that small betraying skin-twitch, but his was...wrong. Instead of a fluid melding, two creatures sharing a single goal, his motion was as a jerking, string-yanked puppet.

The horns sounded again, shrilling through my skull. The sound was awful yet the pain was salutary, a sharp pinch from Idra when she tired of an apprentice's slow, clumsy work.

Try again, Gwendelint's child. Do better.

Arn was already moving. Her spear flicked, and if she felt any hesitation about attacking an unarmed man it did not show. But

Tharos was quick, leaning aside with a crackle of bones; he flung his left hand forward, a low vicious jab.

The ring gave a venomous yellow flash, and I screamed.

Inelegant, certainly. I should have been singing strength into my small one, turning aside any weirding with a chant, parrying or subverting any runnel of invisible force. Yet I could not haul nearly enough air into my lungs, for the bauble trapped in my flesh flamed like the fire-eggs certain birds lay within the cauldrons of restless, heat-breathing mountains.

Sheepshitting stupid Elder thing, behave! Frustration boiled over, porridge left too long upon the fire, and my cry hit Tharos with a crunch, driving him back. His boots scraped long furrows upon the dusty floor, and Arn's spear whispered within a fingerwidth of his throat.

I had no time to be shocked; I meant only to baffle and confuse, not fling physical force. And indeed, I should not have been able to do so.

Another yellow flash. Tharos dropped into a crouch, bones creak-popping as his knees spread. The fabric of his robe tore as his shape wavered; the close-fitting trousers underneath split along their seams as his thighs swelled. The others of Naras looked like shaggy black inkblots while they moved between one form and the other, but no merciful blurring enfolded the Old Wolf. Nor did he fully take his second shape, though hair rasp-sprouted painfully through skin and his jaw made a deep grinding noise, teeth lengthening and changing.

An unholy amalgam, caught between two-legs and four like the horrible sniffing things flushing out Waterstone's survivors, hunched its rapidly swelling shoulders and darted aside as Arn lunged again, spearblade whistle-cleaving cold moonlight. Bootleather parted, sheared by lengthening claws, and I wondered how the others kept their clothing intact during—

"*No!*" Another cry wrenched itself from my throat as the thing Tharos had become reversed with sickening speed. A chunk of masonry evaporated at the end of another scraped-clean trail, my weirding-laden voice flinging stone into the night, and stark fear filled me.

My *seidhr* was not behaving as it should.

We knew of two-skins in the south, yes. We also knew of different things—not man, not beast, nor yet a sharing between them. I had never heard of a two-skin turning into this manner of abomination; 'twas unnatural, *seidhr* of the most noisome and forbidden kind.

The *varulv*'s claws were knives, oddly translucent but sharp-honed indeed, and one paw still bore the ring upon a cramp-curled finger. Its yellow-pricked gem keened, a high sound of stress like wet rope pulled taut by heavy boat and fast current; my small one was all graceful motion, dodging Tharos's swipe. Her spear halted, spun, whistled down, but she had to give ground as he pressed. A flurry of parries, claws ringing on blade, and I struggled to draw enough air, to do something, anything other than stand witless during battle.

Arn jabbed, feinting, and faded aside as Tharos's strike blurred through the space she had occupied just a half-heartbeat before. Her face was blank and solemn, hazel eyes shining; in the training-yard at Dun Rithell or sparring in Laeliquaende she often smiled, but this was deadly serious.

Now her back was to the half-gone wall, and the wind sang a plaintive note across its mouth. She edged sideways, feet in green-grey Elder boots soft-quick as a granary feline's step, her hornbraids mussed and her woad-stripe bearing only traces of blue though the skin itself was dyed darker by its near-constant presence.

The Tharos-thing leapt for her again, its shadows from lamp and moon both distorted. My shoulders met cold, damp wood; it was the door, and I had not even known I was moving. Both combatants were silent save for their breathing, Arn's quick and deep, the *varulv*'s edged with a nasty growl. They closed, and though the one who had been the lord of a proud House was fast and fell, my Arn knows well how to hunt a wolf.

Any shieldmaid does. The final test before she may wear the woad is to go into the wilderness, naked or in a thin shift, bearing no weapon. There, she must not only survive with the aid of the Black-Wingéd Ones but also hunt to the death one of the beasts who prey upon her settlement's flocks. The sagas say the wolf offers itself to her cunning, her strength, and her trust in those who took her at birth.

But it is not a creature to give the gift lightly. A blue stripe must be *earned*.

Another shattering growl turned into a coughing trill midway, spiraling up. Pinpricks of vile jaundiced light flared in the thing's eyes, and it bolted for my small one with such speed colorless sparks struck from its amber claws.

Do something. I could not sing. My right hand snapped out, the first two fingers stiff, and *seidhr* filled me.

Empty air parted, a streak of brilliance lingering after my fingertips. I had no breath, but I did not need it to scratch a rune, did I? A single slashing line, the shape meaning a particular vowel-sound in both our language and the Old Tongue—but its edges were crisp and hard, the symbol itself named for ice in our written language, a sudden snap-freeze descending the moment winter ceases its stalking and springs upon its prey.

My left hand flicked palm-out, a brushing motion; the rune flashed as it was flung. Perhaps my shieldmaid felt the wind of its passing, yet she made no sign—most likely she simply ignored the sensation, trusting me to do my part.

I could not see its landing, for the rune vanished as it approached the abomination. Yet the *varulv* staggered before lunging at her again.

Arneior skipped aside, and I knew her spearblade was too high. It gathered moonlight, a star shining from its honed tip for a brief bare moment, and another shapeless, hopeless yell bottled itself in my aching, half-stoppered throat.

But my small one was not deceived, nor was she outplayed. Her hands flashed and she leapt as well, the maneuver perfectly timed, using all her considerable strength. Her lips skinned back in a snarl close to a wolf's itself, very much like one of the men of Naras when facing battle, and the blunt end of her spear smashed into the slavering, snarling face.

Crunch. Foam flew, the thing's howl turned into a mangled screech, but she was not done yet. No, my shieldmaid landed, knees bending deep, and uncoiled again with devastating force. Her high glassy cry of effort swallowed both her opponent's noise and another piercing horn-howl, and such was her might in that moment that the lord of Naras—or what had been him a short while ago—was driven to the very edge of the crumbling floor, arms wheeling wildly like a child attempting to regain balance atop a slippery boulder.

My right hand leapt again; this time the lines were firmer, and burned silvergold for a bare moment as I sketched in empty air. Two runes melded together, force bleeding from my fingertips—the horse-and-rider symbol, meaning a partnership, and the lightning-swift angles of a strength-rune, not the torch of day but a quick serpentine cloudflash. My left palm stung when I slapped this new weirding free, as if batting away a flung pebble.

Black veins danced at the edges of my vision. The Jewel halted its torture for a bare moment, perhaps realizing its host was upon the verge of suffocation, and I sucked in a deep, cold, endless breath.

Arn whirled, and so did her spear. A complicated flurry ended with the blade slashing across the creature's front, not biting deep but adding to its difficulty balancing. Stone groaned sharply, dust puffed, and a splash of blackened blood flew—life-fluid looks darker than usual at night, but this appeared inklike, almost as wrong as the exhausted ichor from *orukhar*.

Then her spearpoint rose, the haft sliding through her hands loose as a lover's casual touch. A thundercrack—she drove the blunt end against the floor and *leapt* with the haft's aid, her boots smashing into the beast's middle.

The blow was one too many, and the Tharos-thing—still swelling, still growling, still champing its strong white teeth amid a billow of rabid froth—was flung into the night.

I half expected her to go sailing through the hole too, but my shieldmaid dropped straight down, landing heavily as more stone crumbled.

"Arneior!" I shrieked, and staggered in her direction.

My small one almost followed the lord of Naras that night, for the floor was giving way. She pushed herself backward, gripping her spear whiteknuckle now, and collided with me. The back of my skull hit wood, and I did not mind the pain. Even now I am not certain I did not perform another lunging, impossible *seidhr*, drawing her from the brink.

Skull ringing and lungs heaving I slumped, pinned between her and the heavy, age-blackened door. "Arn," I whispered. "Arn. *Arneior.*"

She gasped, breathing deep now that the battle was done. I held her belt, fingers squeezed tight, heavy leather yielding as warm butter in my grasp.

From below rose shouts—my name, and hers. A hot, distinct tang of smoke rode the whistling breeze. But for that moment I closed my eyes, simply glad I had not lost her as well.

A Second Shadow

Orukhar *may be eluded, if one is swift and canny enough; others among the Enemy's thralls may be baffled or outraced. Even the wights, those weakest of liches, may be turned aside or granted true death. Those of Kaer Morgulis may veer aimlessly if their prey passes beyond a barrier of some might, and return empty-handed despite the punishment.*

 But those from the third tower of Agramar do not cease pursuit, save at the will of the Enemy himself.

—Farail son of Batura, *Rede of the Dead*

Arn's recovery was swift; mine was otherwise but I could be dragged. We careened down the stairs, my feet scarce touching every second step, and her arm about my waist was tight and sure. Landing with a jolt at the bottom, she set off through the passageways, and in short order we rushed past the room we had been given for sleep—a burst of warmth leaking from its now half-open door, low reddish firelight making a distorted shape upon stone flags—and from there it was a mere twinkling before the high, shadowy great hall swallowed us.

There was no evidence of the others, though we heard voices calling our names; no doubt they had found us missing shortly after the first hunting-cry shook them from rest. There was no time to wonder, and Arn took the steps at the far end of the hall in a single leap.

We burst through the tower's door and almost collided with Efain outside, the Northerner only saving himself with an astonishing sideways lunge, landing braced and ready, his blade held down and away but alive with reflected snowlight. His eyes widened, but he asked no questions. *"Here!"* he shouted in the Old Tongue, and an edge of wolf-cry rode the edge of the words. A stronger hint of burning swirled past us on cold wind. *"They are here!"*

Several paces away upon stone pavers a blackened, broken shape moved in painful, uncoordinated spasms. The stable-doors were thrown open, and movement within turned into hurriedly saddled Elder horses, their eyes white-ringed and their ears laid back, barely heeding Yedras and Daerith's coaxing.

Efain threw his head back; a ribbon of sound lifted from his throat. I flinched, for there was something close to *seidhr* in it, and Arn began to haul me for the stable with alacrity.

Yet there was a second shadow near the writhing body at the tower's foot. Eol of Naras unfolded from a crouch, the swordhilt over his shoulder giving a single icy flash though the gem was well-wrapped. Perhaps only I saw it, since the weapon seemed almost-alive in the way of named things; I had not heard its title yet, but was certain it bore one.

My brother had killed his, now my shieldmaid had slain his father. My throat was dry as road-dust in late summer; I found my right hand, fingers cramping, flattened against my chest and pressing hard as if to keep the Jewel—or my gristle-thumping heart next to it, a high hard pulse brushing sharp edges—from flying free. My lips shaped Eol's name, and perhaps the heir of Naras read what had happened upon my face.

A thin, lacy veil of smoke drifted past the tower. Something was aflame, but I did not have time to wonder. Nor did I have time to be reminded of Laeliquaende's burning.

Aeredh burst from the shadows between two smaller structures on the west side, Gelad and Elak from the east. They came together like raindrops running down a scraped-horn window, all the wolves of Naras appearing, bright-eyed despite being shaken from much-needed slumber.

"*Get to the horses*," Aeredh called. His expression changed as he sighted us and he repeated the order in southron, but Arn needed no translation. Nothing could halt her, in any case; she was bearing me along like flotsam upon a river during those damp spring seasons when melt mixes with heavy storms, ripping giant chunks from weakened banks and carrying entire trees past in a twinkling.

But I could not look away from Eol. *I am sorry*, I wanted to say. The weight in my throat would not budge, and neither would the pain.

The heir of Naras drew, his hand flickering to hilt and his blade almost burn-bright as an Elder's. The brazen hunting-horns sounded again, and this time they were so close the sound sent awl-tips through both my ears, thin invisible blades riving my skull. I cried out and saw Karas snarl, his face echoing a wolf's for a bare moment.

Even so, it bore no relation to the agonizing, congested hatred upon the *varulv*.

Yedras and Daerith were fully occupied with the horses. Aeredh reached them first, near vaulting into the saddle, and his mount wheeled, its hooves dancing with fear. He urged the snowy beast forward, and 'twas not until it loomed before us that I realized what he intended. He leaned down, shouting something almost lost in another high glassy glaring cry, and the sensation was familiar—*seidhr* thick and foul, spreading like ordure in fast-flowing water.

A lich. Or more than one, because the air grew still, knifelike cold thickening as if no spring threatened to turn the drifts of the Taurain to sucking mud.

Arn might have sensed it too, for her grip upon me changed. I was lifted, tossed like a sack of wet laundry, caught by an arm strong as an iron bar, and before I knew it Aeredh's horse had wheeled and the rattlethump of a gallop jarred my bones.

Some things that night I did not see, only hearing of them later—the corpses Soren and Elak found in a cellar, frozen stiff and with deep clawmarks showing how they had died, the fires as *orukhar* ravaged wooden buildings though they could not do much to the tower itself, a lich rising from a pool of shadow across the paving and Daerith putting an arrow freighted with cold blue Elder brilliance into the space where its face should have been, the suddenly appearing knot of mounted *orukhar* who almost pulled Gelad and Karas from their saddles before Yedras and Efain arrived, the Elder's spear flickering and the scarred Northerner's battle-cry lifting high and clear to overpower the dread horns for a brief moment.

But as the Elder horse fled, Aeredh's arms around me and Arn gaining her own charger's saddle with a leap I would sing of could I but find the words to do it justice, I caught a glimpse of a swordblade, descending so rapidly it was a solid bar of silver, as Eol of Naras put an end to the shattered thing that had been his father.

Aeredh's mount whinny-screamed and the Crownless replied with a single smoking word in the Old Tongue, clipped and harsh. The force of it thundered through all my internal halls; we shot away, shod hooves striking sparks until the ground became snow over packed earth, and there was a thunder behind us as well as beside. Arneior's charger followed, needing no encouragement, and the rest kept pace as best they could.

Barael-am-Narain was burning, a ruddy glow, and we burst from a gap in the southron palisade onto the moon-silvered plain.

Flow and Flame

A volva must know her own strength down to the last featherweight. Only then may she surpass it at need—but beware, for the price is high.
                                        —Idra the Farsighted of Dun Rithell

Jolted, shatter-shaken, the Jewel in my chest flaming like abandoned buildings or a well-prepared funeral ship, I could do nothing but huddle against Aeredh and hope I did not slip from the saddle. I was not even properly *in* it, sitting sideways, though thankfully I was not thrown over like a captive or a carcass upon a dray's back. It was uncomfortable in the extreme, yet I did not care—for the awful metallic horn-howls all but ringed us, great spatters of snow flung in every direction as pale Elder horses packed into a tight herd, racing under the swiftly clouding sky.

Perhaps the Crownless knew I was not a strong enough rider to stay atop a horse at such pace, or perhaps he and his companions were well used to such flights. In any case, he held me with bruising force, so close we were almost one being atop a wildly plunging, fear-maddened animal.

As the hills receded and the Taurain swallowed our small group, the wolves of Naras dropped from the saddle at full gallop, shaggy inkblots exploding as they changed midair, landing in their other forms. They veered away, ringing us loosely; Yedras crowded upon Aeredh's left and Daerith to Arn's right with his bow unlimbered.

Thus we fled, the wolves providing a screen and a fear-maddened horse-herd galloping in the only direction allowed.

A medley of brass-throated cries followed, along with a tide of snarls. The *orukhar* rode great slumpshouldered quadrupeds, furred and vaguely canine instead of reptilian, and that night was my first glimpse of the dire *vargen* bred by the Enemy for his cavalry. Hulking and graceless, they were nevertheless capable of great speed and endurance, and their riders were not the small among *orukhar* either. The *vargen* were not quite as misshapen as the scaled things aiding in the wreck of Laeliquaende, but they were monstrous enough and called up sickening echoes of Tharos's hunch-snarling, skittering speed.

Had there been any time or breath to spare, I might have been nauseated. But there was another danger looming; the night was cold, yes, but not cold enough.

The Taurain's drifts were giving way.

A hard, high stringsnap was Daerith's bow speaking, not upon a river's heaving back but a sea of dingy white; past the bright spot of Yedras's head was a flash of teeth and a thunderous impact as a wolf—I thought 'twas perhaps Soren, for no reason other than *seidhr* ringing inside my skull whispering his name—leapt to crash into a mounted *orukhar*, tumbling his iron-armored opponent from the saddle. The *vargen* snarled and veered away, suddenly free of spur or bridle-pressure, and bile-hot fear clawed at my dry, aching throat.

Our pursuers did not use their own bows—afterward, Arneior hazarded their reticence was not lack of willingness but orders to capture the prize as undamaged as possible. At the moment all I knew was the Jewel's burning, and the fact that I was near-worthless during yet another battle.

And I hated it. Behind the sawing edges buried in my ribcage a spark guttered, waxed. By all the gods, I was so tired of fear, of being chased, of freezing and mounting dread and men shoving me about. I was also tired of Aeredh's chin striking the back of my head as the horse nearly foundered, its hooves sinking slightly in sodden snow instead of landing light upon thin ice-crust.

Amid the terror and the ire, another emotion rose. The whole affair was *ridiculous*. Dragged from my home, pushed from place to place, hounded from the wreckage of two Elder cities, every scrap of freedom I could win or bargain turning to ashes in my palms, and the horrid, burning alien thing inside me, tormenting my flesh as it burrowed deeper—all of it, from first to last, finally reached boiling.

No. Not boiling. There was no flow in what I felt, only flame.

Be careful, my teacher Idra's voice whispered amid the great stillness descending upon me. *This is not a weirding to use lightly, daughter of Gwendelint.*

Oh, my physical body was borne along at a furious pace, caged in an Elder's arms and shivering with fearful rage. Yet all the rest of me turned inward, subtle selves slipping from their mooring with the ease of long practice. The world vanished under a silvergold glare, pitiless light flooding my inner vision, and if I burned in its killing glow, well, in that moment 'twas a price I was willing to pay.

My back arched, and Aeredh near lost his grip. Which is no insult to his strength—balancing upon the back of a maddened horse, holding it to a pace more-than-mortal while the Enemy's creatures chased, and attempting to keep a *volva* before him in the saddle? The wonder was that we had not both been thrown within a few steps, and every hoof-fall afterward a miracle.

Especially when I bent as if stretched spinecracked upon a barrelhoop, my arms rising stiffly to cloud-smeared sky. Moonlight brightened, streaming upon softening snow, yet also took on a strange aureate cast as if summer or harvest had ripened the silver fruit of night.

I whisper-screamed, fingers cramping as inked runes and bands blazed upon my wrists. The cry attempted to form words, but I had not the breath. Instead, the Old Tongue tolled in my brain like a vast bell, bursting free in every direction.

Before, I could only ask, negotiate, persuade. Now I wrenched a flood of *seidhr* from a place alien unto me, bending it to my will with sheer fury.

And the sky...*answered*.

The waning Moon above us swelled, a spreading hood-haze swallowing nearby stars. Columns of glittering light jabbed earthward, not fork-branching as lightning usually does but straight as a good heavy Northern sword driven into soft turf. Where the falling light-spears touched the snow was flung away, flash-hissing into steam, and stinking rags of *orukhar* flesh burst in strange patterns from the lips of holes scorch-carven into the Taurain's skin, punching through wintersleeping grass and stabbing deep.

Very like the pillars, Daerith said afterward, *in Nithraen's forest-gallery.*

Arneior would only say there was a great flash near to blinding her. One shard of falling light avoided Karas by a hairsbreadth, and he said it was neither warm nor cold though the shock sent him tumbling through melting drifts, his head ringing, before he gained his feet once more and kept running.

My hands fell, wounded birds. I almost slithered bonelessly from the saddle, but Aeredh cried out again in the Old Tongue; for all the immensity of that scream of effort, it went unheard after the flashes. Almost blinded, amid a storm of galloping, he still did not let me fall.

And well it was that he did not, for though the *seidhr* had struck down plenty of *orukhar* upon their furred, snarling mounts, it did not touch the liches. Fortunately the spike-helmed horrors were mired in the sudden softening of the Taurain's winter floor, and their own mounts could not match the speed of white Elder horses, galloping mad with terror toward a dark line upon the horizon.

Dorael.

We were so close, and yet upon those plains the sight of a destination is deceptive. And even long-limbed, silk-maned mounts bred by the Elder, given strength by the presence of their owners, could not run forever.

See the Curse

She was there from the beginning, the Cloak-Weaver, and she is not of our kind. Some say she was set to guard a treasure from the moment of world's making, and others whisper that she knew of her husband long before his arrival, and loved him in advance. By her will is the fence about Dorael set, long it will endure, lo! even unto the coming of doom.
—Anonymous, The Song of Nightingales

Just after dawn another ravine sheltered us for a short trembling while. Arn held a small flask of blue glass—Yedras's, and thrust upon her with haste—to my lips. The now-familiar heat of *sitheviel* filled my numb mouth, along with the incongruous taste of midsummer flowers.

"Drink," she said harshly, as if she thought I might refuse.

I was vaguely surprised to find I still had teeth, let alone fingers and feet. Idra's voice—whether hers in truth or merely my own wisdom speaking in a tone it knew I would not gainsay—was right, such a weirding was dangerous not only to those it had killed but its wielder as well. A diaphanous amazement that I was still alive after using something so far beyond my strength or skill lay over strengthening dawnlight like finespun linen, turning everything indistinct until the liquid reached my chest and heat spread in concentric rings, nailing me once more into my physical self.

"*Easy, fourfoot cousin,*" Yedras crooned to a head-hanging mare, stroking her wet lathered neck. "*All is well. All will be well, let me help you.*"

"He was not left alone." Elak's paleness made the snow seem blushing. His eyes were live coals; his hands squeezed into fists, relaxed, and repeated their clenching. Of all the wolves of Naras he was the quietest, but now his baritone held an axe's edge. "I recognized some. Haralt, and Tyony's son Aesimir, and Bjornhalt of Vestalt...he tore their guts out."

Eol gazed at the northern end of the *bailkah*. The leather over his swordhilt was scorched, the gem peering free, and his dark hair rumpled wildly in every direction. Even the Elder were snow-spattered and gaunt. Our mounts' ribs stood out—a single ride like that will melt flesh from man and horse both no matter their might.

How were we still alive? I could not tell, and still do not know.

Daerith sang softly to Aeredh's mount. The beast shuddered, great twitches passing in waves through his body.

"I saw them too." Soren swallowed convulsively. "But I could not...could not recognize..."

A second swallow of *sitheviel* followed the first, and I choked as a coppery tang pervaded it. Fortunately I did not spray the precious cordial over my shieldmaid; Aeredh held me upright and his left hand stroked the shadowmantle's shoulder, as if I were a maddened animal needing calming as well.

"Sol?" Arn lowered the flask, peering anxiously at me. Her spear's blunt end was driven deep into snow beside her; the weapon listed slightly, a few fingerwidths off true. "You...are you hurt?"

My face felt odd. I lifted a hand, staring dreamily; it seemed strange to have such an appendage. I had felt this way before, just after my first blooding when the weirding began to accelerate within me, but never so strongly.

Seidhr may well eat its bearer whole, if an act well beyond one's ken is attempted.

When I touched my upper lip, something crackled under my fingertips. I scrubbed a little harder, and realized it was dried blood.

"*He is at peace now.*" Eol's tone was harsh, too loud in snowbound stillness. The Taurain's breath soughed over the ravine's lips, a hollow fluting noise full of menace underlaid with soft stealthy trickling. He took a deep breath; when he spoke next, 'twas in southron. "And we are not safe in Dorael yet."

When I rubbed my fingers together, bloodcrust flaked free. But it was wrong—some of the fluid was still tacky-wet, and bore an odd tinge. I thought it a trick of the light at first.

"Sol?" Arn persisted. "Where are you hurt?"

I am not, I wanted to say, *only weary*. But the strange sensation was all over my face. The blood had trickled from my eyes and nose; the sides of my neck held thread-thin drying rivulets escaped from my ears. Arn used a corner of her mantle and a bit of snow to wipe, as if tending a food-eager child. Though she sought to be gentle, my skin still stung under her ministrations. Aeredh held me upright, and continued stroking my shoulder.

My shieldmaid offered the blue glass flask once more; I shook my head. Ribbon and horsetail clouds, already shrinking as the eastron horizon lightened, presaged a clear day. It was no longer so cold. In fact, a prickle touched the curve of my lower back, though no sweat rose.

"Blood," I whispered, and Arneior nodded, capping the flask with a savage twist.

"Idra would scold you." A tendril of coppery hair fell in her face. Even her freckles were pale at the moment. "But perhaps that Elder thing is useful after all."

How could I explain? "*It was not the Jewel.*" My tongue would not seat itself quite properly. The pain in my chest eased somewhat, though the burning did not fully abate; perhaps it was the *sitheviel*. Fresh strength and sense crept into my limbs, aided by a deep, soft jolt of vital force from Aeredh's grasp. I did not know how he had so much strength left, to share such a measure. "Ah." I found my mother-language again. "It was...was not the...Something is happening to me, Arn."

"Gelad, Efain." Each name held the snap of command; Eol straightened, and perhaps it was fatigue, but he looked at least ten years older than he had yestereve. There were new lines graven upon his face, spreading from the corners of his eyes and bracketing his mouth. *"Take our backtrail for a distance, see what you can smell. The rest of you, aid our Elder friends with the horses, and keep hand to hilt."* He turned upon his bootheel, and his gaze lighted upon me.

I felt it like a blow. All my inner senses were cringe-sensitive.

But when he halted next to Arn, it was Aeredh he addressed. *"How fares our lady?"* As if he had forgotten I spoke the Old Tongue, or as if he could not bear to address me directly.

"Somewhat stunned, I think." Aeredh's hand halted its steady motion as I sought to straighten, to use my own legs. *"She was not touched, the bleeding is...otherwise. Eol—"*

"I shall scout ahead." With that, the heir to Naras would have stalked away, but Arneior coughed, a harsh, ratcheting sound.

"Son of Tharos." She all but spat the words. "We must speak of summat."

"Must we?" He had already turned his back to my shieldmaid, and his profile was severe as his father's. "I am concerned with our survival at the moment, and little else."

"Eol." The word was a husk of itself, and I suppressed the harsh tickle in my throat. "Your father. He—"

"Now you see the curse." Clipped and cold, Eol pronounced each syllable very clearly indeed. "But have no fear, Solveig. Should I or any of my companions fall to it, the others will dispatch him as required."

He set off, and the shaggy inkmass of the change swallowed him before he had gone two steps. The wolf—lean and dark, its fur damp and its ears flattened—bounded up the side of the *bailkah*, vanishing over the top.

"Sheepshit," Arn muttered, and I heartily agreed.

" 'Tis merely his grief," Aeredh said, softly. "Take what rest you may. We have a few moments—most of the surviving *orukhar* now fear us, but that will not slow them forever."

As if to underscore the point, a faint chill howl rose to the north. It was not a hunting-horn of the Enemy's troops, for all it bore a hateful edge. No metallic instrument could loose such a cry; there was a tinge of agonized flesh to it, long-dead but still suffering. I tasted rancid ash and the copper of powdered blood, the *sitheviel*'s heat upon my tongue pushed aside by chill grave-dirt.

"Lich," I whispered, dryly. One of the horses sidled uneasily, too exhausted to rear, shy, or otherwise protest.

"*Nathlàs.*" Aeredh's arm tightened about my shoulders, and sudden tension turned him into one of Laeliquaende's pale stone statues. "At least one of the Seven, quite probably more. We should not linger, for even in daylight they ride swift indeed."

Only Mortal

For a long while the grief was staved off, for he loved his land and his wife. Yet bit by bit it mounted, in the way of such things; the Elder know not the Secondborn's loosening of regret. And the Greycloak had never seen the West—yet if he had, perhaps the mourning might have consumed him more swiftly. Who can say? Not even the very wise...

          —Daerith the Younger

Whatever *seidhr* kept the horses from sinking was failing, or perhaps it could not work with rottenmelt drifts. The poor beasts spent much effort to lift their feet, though a firmer layer of freeze remained a handspan or so below the surface. Blinding sunlight bounced from slump-glistening waves, and the wolves were dark shapes leap-sliding upon slick, treacherous white billows, still traveling in a loose ring about us.

I knew which one was Eol. All that day he and Karas forged ahead then dropped into our wake, checking the ground, finding a chain of more-solid footing with unerring instinct, and gauging how far behind our pursuers raced.

I gathered the liches would be weighed down somewhat by the bright golden eye of day, though not nearly so much as *orukhar*. And the dark line at the southron horizon would not draw closer no matter how we struggled, the horses slowing.

There was a skyborne pall to the north. It hung motionless until nooning, but as the sun began to fall the wind rose, pushing at our backs.

Aeredh would not suffer me to ride alone, and Arn did not quibble. I no longer had to balance sideways, though, and our mounts gained some little strength as the day wore on, even while the breeze turned knifelike and sunlight took on a yellowgreen cast. The living heat of an Elder against my back blocked the wind's edge, and his hands rested easily upon the reins before me.

I could not help turning, attempting to look behind. He shifted slightly—not to deny me the chance, I thought, but merely as a consequence of close quarters.

It was no use. I could see nothing but the approach of inimical, unnatural weather. Had anything like this borne down upon Dun Rithell every *seidhr* would have gathered upon the Stone set in our vast green, both to divine the source and to attempt mitigation.

Sky and seasons were best left to themselves, as Idra oft repeated. But part of weirding is restoring a tipped balance, too, and turning aside evil is a *volva*'s duty.

"A storm." His breath touched my temple. "Sometimes they happen upon the Taurain in spring, and yet..."

"How far?" I sounded ragged and breathless, even to myself. "To Dorael?"

"Not far." He sought to hearten me—and whoever else heard, as always. "If we can reach the trees..."

I could not hold back a small, disbelieving sound. It could have been mistaken for a laugh. "My eyes are only mortal, and yet they can tell we are nowhere near enough. Especially with the sun falling."

"Only mortal?" The Crownless sounded tightly, bitterly amused as well. His breath brushed my hair. "Take heart, my lady. We will not falter now."

I wish I were even a fraction as sure as you sound. "Aeredh..." What could I say?

"If all else fails, we shall slow them while you and your shield-maid flee." He freed one hand from the reins, and I flinched as it rose.

I could not help it.

But he merely raked stiff fingers through his own hair, shaking his head slightly. The movement echoed in my own tired, aching flesh.

"And when Dorael falls?" I stared at the dark smear of our goal in the distance. "What then, son of Aerith?"

His arm tightened, his hand dropped back to the reins. Our mount's ears flattened, but the Elder horse did not raise his head. He merely plodded, obedient to the end.

Was that my fate? Driven onward, ridden by some mad Elder purpose until I foundered? The Jewel twinged inside my chest. Its burning branched through my veins, and though I had only borne it a short while I could not remember a time without the sensation. And there was also the tinge to the dried blood on my face; Arneior had not remarked upon it, but she was not blind.

Nor were any of our companions. It was not so marked as when Elder flesh is violated, but the thin, lingering golden traceries were unmistakable. Faevril's masterwork was performing some *seidhr* upon my very body, and I was helpless to stop it.

More terrifying yet—even more horrific than the things pursuing us, or the violation of my own physical being—was the fact that the Jewel had not pulled pillars of solid, streaking moonlight from the sky to strike down the *orukhar*. It was utterly innocent of such affairs.

In fact, Aeredh was far more correct than he knew. The sodding thing could never be used as a weapon; 'twas not in its nature. *I* had brought down the Moon's own fire. Somehow, I had accessed a weirding far more powerful than I should have been able to, perhaps because the thing nestled inside my ribs was tainting me with Elder witchery.

Changing me.

A long, lonely wolf howl rose behind us. I did not need *seidhr* to hear Eol's voice in the cry, or to understand its import.

The day was failing, and the storm gaining upon us.

***

Upon the vast rolling Taurain one may watch a weather-wall approach for a long while, dreading yet entranced. At first the wind helped, pushing us along, but as it mounted tiny flickers of melt were snap-frozen and flung, collecting upon every surface like the gravel-ice of the Glass during deepcrack freeze. Our footing became ever more slickly treacherous, the plain turned to iceglass.

Had we some few pairs of sharpened bone-curves, we could have strapped them to our feet and flown like sleds over smooth ice. At home Astrid was grace itself upon such things, swooping and turning on the mirrorlike face of ponds locked in winter's embrace. I did not cherish skating, having fallen a few too many times for my pride or comfort, but both my sister and shieldmaid liked it well enough—though neither of them were so skilled as Albeig our housekeeper, who had to be fair pushed out the door by Mother before she would consent to take some manner of holiday.

Once upon the ice, though, she was a swift bright bird, finally set free.

The storm-edge was still far away as the sun's strengthless red coin touched horizon. Arneior hunched in the saddle, two of the Northerners' tattered black mantles wrapped about her—they were wearing their fur now, but probably just as miserable. Yedras and Daerith were indistinct shadows atop their mounts, save for the blur-shifting bluish gleam about them, their subtle selves burning freely. The horses moved with what speed they could, seeming to understand our only hope was reaching whatever shelter lay ahead.

I huddled in Aeredh's lee, my hands tucked into the shadowmantle's sleeves. The red coral in my sadly abused braids had long since frozen solid, and stray strings of dark hair lifted like spiderweb-strands, worked free by flight and the wind's fingers, filigreed with frost. The breath of the North reached across league upon league; amid the whirling frozen droplets I saw reddish flickers—hideous sparks, each one a gleam in some unfathomable eye.

Worse than the scream of moving air, worse than the tiny pelting granules was the choking darkness. Light faded as the storm's tattered wings settled fully over us, and its claws could not be far behind.

The wolves of Naras pressed closer. I could not see them, but the horses knew and their natural unease at the presence of predators was only outweighed by what they scented behind us.

And by exhaustion. One of the horses nearly fell, splayleg staggering, and the Jewel flashed inside my chest. The pang was terrible, my gasp lost in whirling white.

No. Please, no.

I might have tried some manner of helpful *seidhr*, but our pursuers gave me no chance. A high wavering scream pierced my skull without bothering to ride the air about me or pass through my ears. It scraped like an iron carpenter's comb shredding softwood—I had endured this manner of assault once before upon the Glass.

Curiaen the Subtle and Taeron had both tried a variety of it. One I had gainsaid, the other I had eventually allowed; Tharos of Naras's attempt had not been wholly his own. But this bore little relation to any of them; 'twas a *nathlàs*'s violation, and I forgot the cold as I cowered before Aeredh, clutching at my ears, too breathless to cry out.

Provoked past exhaustion into one final heart-wringing effort, the horses bolted. But it was no use; the liches had found us, and Dorael was still beyond our reach.

Name in Battle

Before the dark wind they galloped:
  The spearman who led the charge at Dag Aethas,
  The songcrafter of Aerith, bearing Kaesgrithil,
  The uncrown'd one, hope-winner, faithful beyond measure.
  Unveiled they rode, and so too the nathlàs
  Their wills contended. Then the battle was joined.
                    —Taeglin of Dorael, *The Saga of Six*

There are only two songs of these events, and I do not like either. They do not speak of how the first riderless Elder horse dropped, galloping heart-strain and treacherous footing finally claiming one life, then another. I felt both like bolts to my own shrinking flesh, *seidhr* flaming inside the ache-quivering mass my head had become, and the Jewel burned desperately.

Daerith dropped his reins, rising in the stirrups to nock; Arneior's spear was out of the saddle-bucket and she snapped a glance at me, the leather-wrapped ends of her braids afloat upon the storm of our wild career. On our other side Yedras's spearblade gleamed ferocious blue, and wolf-cries rose both right and left.

The liches—great and small—had almost ringed us. I felt them without needing to see, a furious chill hating all that lives, the stain of their presence spreading as the westron horizon worked to swallow a huge, terribly exhausted crimson disc.

The sun's daily death would presage our own.

Another horse screamed with fear. There was a flicker of move-ment, Gelad bursting through both his forms in quick succession, his sword giving a forlorn reddish glimmer as it cleaved a lich's head free—or tried to, colorless sparks struck from iron armor and the undead thing screeching at the blow.

The songs speak of the closing ring, and the *nathlàs* taking shape from the storm's darkness, each a whirling as of embers carried on a bonfire's breath and the scorchgleam of eyes under spike-crowned helms. They say there were three of the greatest liches present that evening, each with a complement of their undead thralls, but I do not know.

I remember only a jarring, a weightlessness as Aeredh's horse reared, its obedience finally snapping as an overstretched hawser may, and I was flung. The impact is mercifully blank in memory; so is the confusion as the mounts galloping behind us avoided my body, whether by instinct or mere chance. A jumble of images, sensations—spearblade flashing, Arneior's warcry a high bright note amid hoof-thunder and howling, wolfsnarl and the clatter of blades, Daerith's bow speaking again, Aeredh shouting in the Old Tongue—breaks over me in a wave of trembling whenever I think upon it, and I do not often do so.

It is…uncomfortable.

Somehow the Crownless was still beside me, and somehow he pulled me upright. The darkness was all around, and in that moment I saw not the storm nor the wolves of Naras, nor even my shieldmaid.

There was only the wind, full of stinging ice and heatless red sparks, and the black figures in their thornmetal armor. Their man-tles spread in defiance of howling air, darkness more than physical freighted with clot-rotted *seidhr*, and their blades were rust-pitted yet terribly long, terribly sharp. They carry mace as well as sword, and either weapon may leave a sliver in the flesh of other beings, working inward even if the prey escapes.

Before I had not seen their faces, just a blessed obscurity, but that dusk I glimpsed the ruin of things dragged from the long rest of death, given a simulacrum of life by foul acts too twisted to be called *seidhr*, and witnessing that horror might have driven me gratefully insane.

For the *nathlàs*, the Seven, are mighty indeed. They are spirits who chose to follow their master in his first rebellion against the All-mother, in a treason against existence itself, and they hate what they betrayed. They draw souls from Hel's many countries, kidnapping them to bleak servitude, and against either kind of undead nothing mortal lasts long. Contagion they bear as well as hatred, and 'tis difficult to say which burns the deepest, or coldest.

Yet I was not catapulted into madness, for between me and the terror of lichgaze was a bright blue coruscation, subtle selves burning upon their outlines as the Elder unveiled more than their physical forms. Visible and hidden are the same in them; tall and terrible was the son of Aerith in that extremity.

No less so were the harpist and spearman of fallen Nithraen, arriving to either side. I reeled, and a feverish iron bar fell over my shoulders—my shieldmaid's arm, straight and sure even if no hope remained unto us.

At least we die together, I thought, and gathered myself to strike a final blow in whatever pitiful way I could.

Arneior held fast, her spear lifted against the terrible weight of a greater lich's eyeless regard. The weapon shivered under that impact. Aeredh's sword blazed. A far sweeter refrain battled the scream of moving air, impossible *seidhr*-fueled storming, and a harsh, hate-soaked screech.

The song was Daerith's, *granr* unleashed as he had once before upon the Glass when facing both *nathlàs* and snow-hag. The music granted him was mighty, an echo of the Allmother's own making-magic, but the cacophony around us was too swallowing-vast.

Snapping, growling, a crunching impact and a whine, a terrified bugling as a horse plunged into the wall of screaming darkness—I could not worry for the wolves, nor for the Elder. All I could do was cling to my Arneior, for I knew we were going to die.

"Alcar alaëssilar!" The voice shivered around us, breaking into pieces, and a silverthread sound accompanied it. 'Twas not the howl of *orukhar* horns nor the death-fueled screeching of liches, but the

breath of a silver-chased Elder instrument, high and strong. It spoke again, and a tide of barking with it. Hoofbeats swelled, and several more cries broke in a white-foaming crash.

It is oft the Elder way to give the name of their house or its most-cherished words when charging into battle, much as those taken by the battle-madness will growl Odynn's titles or the name of a loved one, or Northerners will ken upon the deed of a much-respected ancestor at the attack.

"*Nithraen arenaënai!*" Yedras shouted, and surged to meet the foe. Daerith's bow hummed; he sang as he loosed, each bolt freighted with stinging Elder might.

They broke upon the battle like a sudden spring flood in a Taurain *bailkah*, like a towering storm-driven wave upon a pebbled beach, like a deep-frozen river suddenly shaking off its shackles and becoming a wall of water scouring the throat of its bed. More pale Elder horses, more burning-blue forms, more weapons blazing, and such was their suddenness the lesser liches broke and fled in confusion. A smaller tide clustered the white horses' legs, hounds brindle and grey, their dark gazes lambent and their teeth showing as they snarled, bell-baying at the filth.

Still the Elder horn sounded, and the battle-cries echoed. "*Alcar alaëssar! Faevril-imr alaein!*"

I did not see the *nathlàs* flee; the songs say they were driven off by the charge, for terrible is the wrath of those Elder who were born in the uttermost West, soaked in the light of the Blessed. There were many of them, overwhelming even those powerful spirits, and among their number the sons of Faevril were not counted least.

Dark Curiaen the Subtle, so named because he was regarded a craftsman nearly as great as his sire, plunged a Westron-wrought blade into the back of a lich of Kaer Morgulis that day; such was the power of his strike the thing gave a terrible grinding scream and fled, its sable mantle dispersing upon a clear cold wind. Caelgor the Fair, his blondness shining no less than the horn he wound, rode with his hunting-pack—brindle, black, and grey, sleek and quick, hounds I had complimented in Nithraen, and well they deserved it. Those beasts were rumored to have been gifts from Orolim himself, though the Fair had lost the finest of their number to an Elder princess long ago.

Their followers were of Faevril's people, much reduced since leaving the West but still loyal unto death and more than fell enough at need. Outnumbering them were a crowd of Elder warriors clad in grey, blue, and shining, their cloak-brooches shaped like silver nightingales within a thorn-circle and the mantles almost as shadowy as the one I wore.

The people of Dorael, of Aenarian Greycloak its king and Melair the Cloak-Weaver, had come to our aid.

It was Caelgor who plucked me from the ground, lifting me skyward with no more effort than a bondsmaid retrieving a dropped rag. Once more I was sideways upon an Elder saddle, and if the Fair had not Aeredh's gentleness at least he did not let me fall or simply throw me like a sack over the pommel either. His brother likewise swept up Arn, who had the presence of mind to take his hand instead of waiting to be hauled, settling behind instead of before him, and such was the Subtle's skill that neither were scratched by her spear or his sword during the maneuver.

Others bent to lift the wolves of Naras, riding double from the field; the Nithraen folk knew to expect this manner of help and were willing enough to be borne away as well. All realized, of course, that the *nathlàs* would be only temporarily dazed.

Another thunder of hooves swirled about us, this time accompanied by the excited cries of hounds as they surrounded Caelgor's great pale steed. I could not even look for my shieldmaid, my head ringing from lich-cry and terror. The Jewel quivered inside my ribs like a frightened nestling, and we overtook our few horses staggerfleeing the battle, sweeping them along—for the Elder would leave none of their friends in distress, even mute four-foots.

Like a falling star we streaked over hard sheer ice atop half-cored drifts, and either we had been closer than I thought or the speed of our passage was prodigious indeed, for it seemed only a few endless moments later we plunged between massive tree-trunks. A soft fragrant shadow enveloped us, the storm's noise cut cleanly as if by a sharp knife, and the ice faded. Hooves sank into rich loam rising through swiftly fading traces of snow, winter falling away upon either side, and over horse-sound and jinglecreak of tack there echoed a sleepy rill of birdsong.

Somewhat Late

Thus it was doom came, and the Lady of the Wood greeted its bearer.

—Gaemirwen of Dorael

Under the canopy of ancient, black-bark evergreens lay a starry night. Vines wrapped up the trunks and spread through branches, seven-petaled white flowers gleaming even upon moonless nights and providing enough soft illumination for even mortal eyes. The *eresdil*—for so the vines were named—did not harm the trees, nourishing them with subtle exchange even as they used the pillars and roof for support. And gazing from the soft ground were small blue *sudelma-lithielle*, for the plant was native to Dorael though it had spread wherever a certain Elder princess traveled.

The air was soft but crisp. My breath sobbed in great heaving gasps; a glade opened about the riders, trees drawing away as if granting space to an earnest, private conversation. My rescuer drew rein, but I was not in a fit state to recognize him. All I knew was that I had been taken from the battle and the terrors of the North into some new strangeness.

A circle of paving-stones gleamed stainless in the clearing's center. A stone fountain stood at its heart, and the sound of running water was neither terror nor warning but a sweetness, as in Laeliquaende. The hounds milled; other riders arrived, some dismounting almost before their horses came to full stop and hurrying to tend the few exhausted survivors of our own mounts—only three of the almost-dozen we had left upon remained.

Caelgor swung down in one lithe motion. I could not cling to the saddle and toppled; the hunter caught me with one Elder-strong arm, the jolt wringing a small cry from my throat.

"Sol! *Solveig!*" Arn's voice, I could not tell how far away. I was set upon my feet and the hounds pressed close, nosing me while the hunter's mount turned his head, regarding this display sidelong. No foam clung to him, and his eyes were brightly calm; he had not suffered what our horses had.

"Steady, my lady *alkuine*." The blond Elder's voice was familiar, and I peered up at his face. He kept a hand upon my arm, whether to hold me upright or keep me from ill-advised retreat I could not tell. "The foul things cannot yet pierce the Cloak. All is well."

A needle-toothed animal had me by the nape, shaking me as small dogs will the rats they are bred to kill. My knees were soft as spring-hollowed drifts, every part of me hurt, I could not draw a proper breath, icemelt dripped from my sadly abused braids, and the thing trapped in my chest throbbed like a cut artery.

My name was cried again, but it was not my shieldmaid who appeared first. The hounds parted, one or two lowering their heads and considering Eol of Naras narrowly as he loped through their press. The water-clear gem in his swordhilt blazed—every scrap of masking leather scorched away by its fury—no less than his dark gaze, and the wolf in him twitch-rippled his human skin, especially when his lip lifted, a gleam of ivory teeth in the dimness.

He grabbed my free elbow, yanking hard, and I was nearly torn from Caelgor's grasp. Then he held me stiffly at arm's length, examining me from top to toe. Bright blood painted half his face and his dripping mantle was torn almost to shreds; he glared as if I had somehow brought the liches down upon us.

I did not care. I was too grateful for our continued existence, even one tinted with absolute terror. A reek of grave-dirt and rot clung to us both, though the stench frayed in the clear air of an Elder place.

Hard upon Eol's heels was Daerith, who let out a soft wondering curse in the Old Tongue, his tone one of profound relief and his great bow hanging loosely from one hand. The Elder's hair was a wild mess, his left sleeve sodden-flopping and a stripe of lichburn visible through a rent at the shoulder, stark against pale flesh.

And finally, *finally* Arn reeled into view, her spear bobbing, and I had to look over Eol's shoulder to find her.

He let go when I leaned away. I retreated, staggering, from men and their bruising-hard hands, and though my feet made no noise in sodden Elder slippers I was amazed my step did not sound like falling boulders, for the Jewel's heaviness was upon me again.

Arn flung her left arm about my waist. I did not care how the thing in my chest poked and scraped, I hugged her as hard as I could, burying my face at the juncture of her shoulder and neck, breathing in the smell of mortal effort, snowmelt, a fading tang of blood and lich-filth. I made another low hurt sound, almost keening, and she swore into my cold, streaming hair.

Yet even in that extremity I could not weep. The tears simply would not come; only the burning as the Jewel twinged, trapped inside my flesh.

A raven brought news of Taeron's fall. The leader of the Dorael party—Estaelir—was a tall slim Elder who looked younger than Aeredh had at Dun Rithell, save for the shadow of knowledge in his bright blue gaze. He glanced my direction more than once, eyes the color of a cloudless winter sky narrowing as if against snowglare; the accent of his Old Tongue was soft and musical. *"A watch has been kept for refugees, and many Secondborn have come. The queen sent us here two days ago to wait, for the storm was building even then."*

"And we decided to lend our aid." Caelgor's smile did not alter, but he loomed very close to me indeed, and spoke in much better southron than he had at our previous meeting. Perhaps he had been practicing. "I swore the lady our protection in Nithraen, and am glad to fulfill the vow."

His dark-haired brother stood aside, his brow growing more

thunderous by the moment. Curiaen's scrutiny also rested upon me, and Arn kept watch in return. Her knuckles were white, the ghost of woad yellow upon her bruised face, and though we were rapidly drying in the clement wonder of an Elder land she did not seem soothed.

"We rode hard from Barael-am-Narain," Aeredh supplied. "Tharos of Naras has gone to the West, along with all his folk left there." Though just as draggled as the rest of us, he had the Elder trick of looking elegant despite it. Daerith hovered nearby, Yedras upon the Crownless's other side; the wolves of Naras and their leader had gathered near the fountain, being attended to by Elder. Every one of them one had suffered some injury.

But not a heartseeker. The *nathlàs* had not time to use such things, though the scar upon Eol's shoulder had split angrily during the battle, as such wounds sometimes do.

They heal, yes. But sometimes they recur, even in one blessed with a two-skin's burning vitality.

Arn refused all aid but mine, and we both had been given full measures of springwine. Dorael's brand of that vintage was less clear and far more fiery than Laeliquaende's, though perhaps the latter effect was only because we needed warming so badly.

"We must speak to the Cloak-Weaver," Aeredh continued. "There is news she must hear, and her counsel is needed."

Curiaen took a single step forward. *"Then hand over what belongs to us, Crownless, and be upon your way to her."*

"This is not your land, son of Faevril, and you do not command aught here." Estaelir did not look in the Subtle's direction, but the two Elder warriors flanking him tensed. *"The peace of Dorael will not be smirched with kinslaying; do not make us regret offering sanctuary."*

"Soft, my brother." Caelgor kept his smile, but his blue gaze grew cool. *"We are guests here, after all."*

"He is bringing to Aenarian what his father helped steal. Must we be grateful for the aid of thieves?" Curiaen was unmollified. *"And as if that is not bad enough, he put it in a Secondborn."* The word for my kind curdled with disgust, the Elder's lip outright lifting as if he smelled surpassing foulness. *"Do they think to hide the Freed Jewel from us?"*

Arn did not need to know the Old Tongue; she discerned the tone well enough and glanced down at me. I shook my head slightly. Let the men wrangle; fear still thumped within my scratched, aching heart, and the thing they all could not stop looking at still burned between my lungs.

Yet its prodding was marginally softer, drowned in springwine. There were no liches or *orukhar* chasing us, no fire or rapine or murder. I was content to stand thus, and listen.

The gods knew I could do little else.

Surprisingly, it was Daerith who spoke, and in southron too. "She did not ask to bear it, son of Faevril. What you see is a miracle of the Blessed; the Freed Jewel chose her." The words rang clear and loud amid soft birdsong; the hush of this place might have been soothing if it did not seem likely to be broken with fierce argument.

As a lord's eldest daughter I was more than used to keeping the peace between fractious warriors, but I felt no desire to at the moment. Let them do as they willed—Arneior was alive, the wolves of Naras were being tended with far more skill than one riverside *volva* could lay claim to, and my own miserable hide had been rescued as well.

All in all I had great good fortune, and was loath to speak lest it somehow vanish.

"*Chose a Secondbo—*" Curiaen's wrath boiled over. He laid hand to a jeweled hilt at his belt, and so did Estaelir.

The Subtle's blond brother made a soft *tsk-tsk* sound, almost like my mother when keeping peace among her children. "*Control yourself, little sibling.*" The term was affectionate, but the command in the words unmistakable—very much as I would quell one of Bjorn's ill-advised moments, were I nearby to do so when it struck. "We have entered this place freely once more; none of us may leave until the Weaver wills it. And in truth the Jewel is not being *kept* from us. In fact, we might even say the Crownless has returned a great treasure to our keeping, and graciously thank him for his trouble."

The Subtle fell silent, but he stared at Aeredh—who took a single step sideways, gazing past Estaelir. Which placed him between me and the dark-haired son of Faevril, as if he expected Curiaen to offer some insult or attack.

A soft clear glow showed between the trees, and every Elder in the glade fell silent.

She was tall—moreso than Aeredh, than Eol, than Taeron or my own father—and slim, and wore a great indigo mantle starred with clear white gems. A simple wreath of *eresdil* vine, heavily flowered, rested upon her dark head, with several small blue blooms of the other type worked into its circlet. Her slippers were indigo as well, and the waterfall of her shadowy hair brushed at her ankles as she walked, unhurried, over velvet sward.

Her eyes were wide and dark, and very still; her ears came to high points like the Elder's, but I realized with a start that while she might *look* like one, she was...otherwise, though I could not tell precisely what. A hint of a smile lingered upon her lips, and she was perhaps the most beautiful woman I had ever seen or even imagined. I lost my breath as the Jewel made a delicate wringing sensation inside me, each vein drawn upon for a moment as her gaze met mine.

I know you, that look whispered, freighted with bright cool *seidhr*. The shock of recognition was intense, and yet I had never seen her before, in waking or in dreaming.

Estaelir and his lieutenants moved aside at her approach, performing the mannerly Northern motions very near a shieldmaid's salute to a woman she respects—right-hand fingertips to heart, to lips, and to brow as they dropped their heads in reverence, their badges gleaming. Curiaen subsided, and even Caelgor gave a respectful half-bow.

Aeredh let out a sound very much like a relieved sigh. *"Hail, Cloak-Weaver,"* he said. *"I bring tidings, and a gift of the Blessed."*

"I know what you bring." Birdsong stilled as she spoke, though her voice melded into the call of nightingales and I suddenly knew the feathered singers stayed in this forest because *she* did. I could not even tell if her southron held an accent, and would have marveled at her handling of my mothertongue, had I the wit in that moment. "And you are somewhat late, son of Aerith, though not through any fault of your own."

Amazingly, Aeredh laughed. Relief was in the sound, and pain as well. "Better than the alternative, my lady."

He glided aside, and she bore down upon my shieldmaid and me. I could not tell if Arneior was stunned too. All I could do was stare.

Melair the Cloak-Weaver halted before us. She did not look to the sons of Faevril, nor at the Crownless, nor the wolves. She watched me, and I had not been weighed so thoroughly since my fourth year when Idra the Farsighted of Dun Rithell formally visited the great-hall as *volva*, to see if a lord's daughter were truly one who could become Wise.

"Solveig daughter of Gwendelint," she said, softly. "Riversinger, Jewel-bearer, Doom of the Elder upon these shores. And you, Arneior, taken by the Black-Wingéd, bearer of the spear-which-strikes-down-treachery. You have come at last."

Arneior's elbow touched my upper arm—not to jostle, nor to remind me of duty. She did not even mean to ask me to speak. No, she merely leaned against me, for faced with this neither of us could do otherwise.

My mouth was numb. "We have not met," I managed in a dry whisper. "Neither have I dreamt you, my lady. But I know you."

"Indeed." A single, graceful nod. "You are weary, and yet there is little time. We must speak, you and I."

Was there some new terror I would be forced to endure, or *seidhr* beyond my capabilities to attempt? I did not know, could not even begin to guess. "Yes." My mouth moved unbidden, and what answered her was not my conscious self. "I know."

"Come." One soft pale hand beckoned. She turned, and set off for the forest. No other being moved; I do not think the men even *breathed*.

Reeling upon colt-shaking legs I followed, and heard Arneior's step behind me. Into the shadowed peace of Dorael we moved, trailing the being whose immense *seidhr* kept even the Enemy at bay.

Yet that mighty fence was failing. And the storm
from the North raged on...

The story continues in...

Doom of the Elder

Book THREE of Black Land's Bane

Keep reading for a sneak peek!

Acknowledgments

Thanks are due to Lucienne Diver, tapers or no; to Nivia Evans and Angelica Chong, who worked hard up to the wire; and to Bryn A. McDonald for endless patience and wisdom. Thanks are also due to beta readers J.P., K.A., and K.W. for reassuring me that there was indeed something worthwhile in here, to Mel Sanders for the steady clarity of a best friend and writing partner, and to my children for myriad reasons space precludes listing.

Last but never least, my very dearest Readers, let me thank you as well in the way we both like best—by telling you yet another tale. Soon.

extras

orbit

meet the author

LILITH SAINTCROW was born in New Mexico, bounced around the world as an Air Force brat, and fell in love with writing when she was ten years old. She currently lives in Vancouver, Washington.

Find out more about Lilith Saintcrow and other Orbit authors by registering for the free monthly newsletter at orbitbooks.net.

if you enjoyed
THE FALL OF WATERSTONE

look out for

DOOM OF THE ELDER

BLACK LAND'S BANE:
BOOK THREE

by

Lilith Saintcrow

*Don't miss the incredible conclusion of Solveig's journey
to save her world from the greatest evil.*

The Mere of Melair

In those days the vast shadowed forest of Dorael held an intimation of the world before the First Sunrise; in deeper reaches, with starlike flowers vine-hung upon pillared trees, a mortal could swear Tyr had never shed his skin and ascended to prove his love of our kind. The twilight was a living thing, though it held no fear.

Yet my heart shrank within me as I hobbled along, Arneior and I near clinging to each other. My shieldmaid was pale, her freckles glaring and mere flakes of blue woad clinging to her skin instead of the proud stripe of those taken by the Black-Wingéd. Her spear's blunt end occasionally touched springy turf.

Normally one of her kind will not use their weapon as a walking-stave. It must have galled her, but perhaps she could blame it upon her charge. There was no shame in needing a brace after escaping the Enemy's greatest liches, even with aid. 'Tis a feat very few are able to accomplish save temporarily, with much effort or divine aid—but I did not think she would find the observation comforting.

Besides, my breath was short and the alien thing in my chest, pulsing like a second, sharp-fingered heartbeat, had decided to become heavy again. I was wearily surprised my slippers did not sink deep into soft ground, and the streaming of snowmelt and granular ice from our mantles—hers of ragged black Northern cloth, mine otherwise—sank into the forest floor with little ado. Our braids were askew, our steps as hurried as possible, yet the being before us never seemed to vary her pace.

She was taller than my father, Melair the Cloak-Weaver of Dorael; dark hair poured smoothly down her back to her ankles and her raiment was Elder-woven, soft and silken-shadowy. And just as I thought we would be forever staggering in her wake, a pair of graceless mortals led astray by some wood-spirit, she slowed, turning to glance over one slim shoulder.

Her profile was beautiful, too. The loveliness lay not in her features, though those were pleasing enough. The wide dark eyes, the mouth as generous as my Arneior's, the winged eyebrows and proud nose—all harmonious, all reasonable, but wholly beside the point. Something else shone within her; though her ears came to high points and she looked very much like an Elder, the *seidhr* in me knew she was not.

It should have frightened me, but the wrack of two Elder cities and pursuit by the Enemy's thralls through Wild, waste, and winter seemed to have robbed me of lesser fears.

Or perhaps the thing trapped in my ribcage performed that particular theft. I had the dazed, inchoate hope that she would somehow take the curst Elder jewel from me, so I could be relieved of both the weight and its poking, prodding, creeping scorch. To eat a proper meal again, or to lie down beside Arn and sleep...

"Forgive me." The queen of Dorael's southron was nearly accentless; perhaps, as certain birds do, she possessed the gift of mimicry. Only Mehem the petty-dverger of Redhill had spoken our tongue with as much facility. "You have borne more than mortals should be asked to. Both of you."

Arn slowed, so I was forced to as well—gratefully, I might add. My shieldmaid said nothing; whether she considered further speech superfluous or she was leaving converse with a being of such great and powerful *seidhr* to her *volva* was an open question.

My throat was parched despite the winterwine pressed upon us. To go from the howling of a storm, a ring of liches and *nathlàs*, the utter certainty of an excruciating death to this...

It was a wonder neither of us were raving mad. My arm was caught in Arn's, my free hand locked to her mailed elbow, and perhaps I leaned upon her so hard because I suspected I would otherwise slip my mooring and be carried into insanity with only a faint whimper of gratitude to mark the occasion.

"You are not Elder." I sounded steady enough, which was surprising. A thin fluting of birdsong nearby underscored the words, much as Laeliquaende's fountains provided accompaniment to every utterance within their city and most of the valley as well.

All gone, now—burned, broken, violated. What would the Enemy's ravening thralls do to this quiet, dim peace if the being before us withdrew her protection?

"Yet I am so shaped, live among them, have even wedded one." A faint smile tilted the corners of her sculpted lips, but she did not otherwise move. The stillness was akin to an Elder's, only different in degree.

A goat may wed a sheep, but neither is mistaken for the other. A suppressed bray of laughter whipped the back of my throat along with acidic bile, and though uncomfortable the burn was a mortal sensation, and comforting.

I had not felt it in what seemed like ages.

"And had a daughter." After the soft song of hers, my voice was harsh as a raven's. Perhaps a large one, flown from the crags of the Spur to land on a roof and croak *Beware, the Enemy's forces approach.*

Melair halted, and turned to face us fully. Even sudden sorrow could not make her less lovely, but there was nothing mortal in the expression. Arn stopped, which meant I had to as well.

A quiet, searching look, her dark eyes still as a shadowed pond. No whisper of wind ruffled that surface, but every riverdweller knows the most placid waters may well hide a riptide underneath. And even the mightiest warrior may drown in a puddle, if too sotted or wounded to move.

Of course she realized what I wore; of course she also saw what lurked inside my ribcage, its illumination veiled only by the shadowmantle her daughter had woven. *A glance like a knife,* they sang of Lithielle, and 'tis very likely she gained that look from her mother.

"Yes," Melair said, softly. "She came to great grief, did my little dancer. I would spare any mother the pain of such a thing." A slight, bitter smile, and she beckoned once more. "Come. 'Tis not far now."

What could we do but follow?

The gloom lightened as we descended a slope so gentle even exhausted mortal legs found its length free of stumbles. The trees did not quite draw apart but separated slightly like friends traveling in silence, each occupied with their own thoughts; the flowered vines were thick among their branches and falling in long swaying strings. At the bottom was a glitter of water.

At first I thought it a stream, flowing fast, and deceptively smooth as Melair's gaze. As we drew closer, though, it became a large pond with velvety banks, and rising hurriedly from the soft-silvered turf was an Elder woman clad in white. Her unbound hair was gold as my sister Astrid's or Naciel of Laeliquaende's, but with a faint moonlit sheen; she smiled as she strode to greet Dorael's queen, hem and mane both fluttering.

"Ah, it is you." The Old Tongue held a light lilting accent, somewhat archaic, and her bare arms gleamed as she made a gesture of welcome before looking past the tall dark-haired woman. *"And ...Oh. I see."*

"This is my very great friend Gaemirwen." Melair's smile returned, retrieved as a warrior does a dropped shield, settling it with habitual quickness in preparation for another bout. "She will see to the shieldmaid's comfort for some short while; Solveig of Dun Rithell and I have other work."

I looked up at Arn; my small one's jaw hardened. She did not speak, but then again, she did not need to. The Jewel turned in my chest again, and the hot acidic wad in my throat swelled.

Perhaps our careering flight from Barael-am-Narain or the great wracking *seidhr* I had performed upon the Taurain had jarred it. Or the thing had simply grown weary of being trapped inside a riverside wisewoman, longing for a more congenial home and expressing it with mute intransigence as any living beast may.

"Go." A husk of a word, dry and empty, filled my mouth. "This is weirding, and..."

I did not say *there is no danger*, for the last time I had uttered those words disaster had descended mere hours later. Nor did I say *you cannot help*, but no doubt she knew.

My shieldmaid's task was to protect us both physically. My own duties comprised all else, and I had failed time and again.

"Worry not, Secondborn friends." Gaemirwen folded her hands before her as if asking the gods for some favor; her southron was accented as Melair's was not. The Old Tongue rubbed through under each consonant, singing through the bars of a cage. "Safety is yours, and rest for your weariness."

I doubted both most mightily, but there was no choice. I let go of Arn, finding my legs would indeed hold me upright without her steadiness, and watched the white-clad Elder woman lead my shieldmaid away. Arn's spearblade winked once, a forlorn signal from a high hill, and the copper in her hair did not catch fire in the starlit gloom. She turned once to look back, and in the soft illumination the shadows under her eyes were dark indeed, as well as the gaunt hollows of her cheeks.

She looked tired unto death. I suspect I was not much better.

Melair studied me for a long moment, a look searching as my teacher Idra's. There was no weirding in it, merely close attention. A being so mighty as to deny the Enemy himself could no doubt overwhelm one tired mortal, even a *volva* granted access to every branch of *seidhr*'s great tree. Elementalist, my folk called those so gifted; *alkuine* was the Elder word, and I had thought us merely rare.

Other Elder had sought to overwhelm me with such scrutiny married to invisible force, to lay bare my intent and subtle selves or simply to dominate. Something foul had attempted the last in a broken tower as well, reaching through an old man driven mad by grief—or by another, darker purpose.

But the Cloak-Weaver of Dorael did none of those things. She simply waited, and 'tis far more effective with one of my temper.

No doubt she knew as much. Between the spirits of field, wood, or animal and the gods themselves there are many intelligences, and had I not driven almost past sanity no doubt I would have been thrilled to be in the presence of one so obviously mighty.

Instead, I was merely, simply afraid.

extras

"What must I do?" How many times had I asked Idra the same thing, knowing some feat or test was required? Since my fourth year, when she formally visited the greathall to see if Eril's uncanny daughter was one who could truly become Wise, my greatest aspiration had been to make her proud.

Or at least, not to disappoint her, and in doing so also bring shame to my mother, my father, the entire settlement. I had been so certain such ignominy would kill me; now it might not be granted the chance.

Melair's hand lifted, a graceful motion. Hushsweet birdsong turned expectant; her cupped fingers indicated the pond's smooth shining. Tiny points of light caught in its mirror reminded me of Taeron's tower, though the darkness under Dorael's roof was not nearly so complete as that within the milk-white spire holding Elder treasures.

"This is the Mere." Still the Cloak-Weaver spoke my mother-language, as if she wished there to be no doubt or mistranslation. "Since the First Song it has been here, waiting. Even the war against the Treacherous One before the waking of the Elder did not disturb its peace; it was here when I arrived, knowing whom I would meet and how I would love him. And what that affection would bring."

Some of the Elder spoke of knowing the world before the very first dawn. It was no less fascinating than it was chilling to hear this creature speak of even older things, and had not the pain in my chest mounted afresh I would have enjoyed it.

What *volva* would not? *Seidhr* encompasses ambition, 'tis the nature of the thing.

But I was so weary, the burning was all through my veins, and the sharp inimical edges of an Elder treasure prod-poked unmercifully. A small, wringing cough struck me, hot coppery slipperiness filling my mouth.

"The time grows short." Melair glided forward a step, two, and I realized she approached me as a herdsman will a skittish sheep, or a houndmaster an anxious dog not yet trained.

Did she think me likely to flee? I could barely walk. The ridiculousness of the entire affair struck me once more, though I was not a-saddle atop a wildly plunging horse chased by the Enemy's thralls.

Such great beings, such unrelenting terrors, all concerning themselves with one small, very tired Secondborn. It defied belief.

Melair touched my shoulder. A great cool wash of power spread from the contact, very like Aeredh's sharing of vital force; my knees softened but she caught me, more-than-mortal strength humming in a tall slim frame as her hands folded about my shoulders.

"Come," she said, urgently, almost kindly. "I may take you to the brink, but no farther. The final step is yours."

I know, I wanted to say, but another cough mounted in my throat and the thought of spraying effluvia over her distant, stainless beauty was too embarrassing to be borne.

I set my jaw and reeled downhill, disdaining not her aid but the indignity of my own failing body. A thin hot dribble traced down my chin; I hoped 'twas blood and not an infant's helpless drool.

Ageless, immortal, she paced beside me. The Cloak-Weaver was as good as her word; to the very edge of the water she was at my side.

The stars upon its surface shimmered. There seemed others caught in the glassy depths, fires burning in defiance of cold quenching, trembling as they sang in high silvery voices. A tearing cramp seized my chest, my slippered toes dug into the soft rim.

I folded double over the agony, and finally, *finally* the grip of a *volva*'s will upon the patient beast of flesh loosened. My subtle selves lunged for freedom, or at least cessation of the near-constant humiliations since leaving my home.

And I fell.

if you enjoyed
THE FALL OF WATERSTONE

look out for

SONG OF THE HUNTRESS

by

Lucy Holland

Britain, 60 CE. Hoping to save her lover, her land, and her people from the Romans, Herla makes a desperate pact with the King of the Otherworld. But years pass unheeded in his realm, and she escapes to find everyone she loved long dead. Cursed to wield his blade, she becomes Lord of the Hunt. And for centuries, she rides, leading her immortal warriors and reaping wanderers' souls. Until the night she meets a woman on a bloody battlefield—a Saxon queen with ice-blue eyes.

Queen Æthelburg of Wessex is a proven fighter. But when she leads her forces to disaster in battle, her husband's court turns against her. Yet King Ine needs Æthel more than ever. Something dark and dangerous is at work in the Wessex court. His own brother seeks to usurp him. And their only hope is the magic in Ine's bloodline that's lain dormant since ancient days.

*The moment she and Æthel meet, Herla knows it's no
coincidence. The dead kings are waking. The Otherworld
seeks to rise, to bring the people of Britain under its dominion.
And as Herla and Æthel grow closer, Herla must find her
humanity—and a way to break the curse—before it's too late.*

*A Note on Pronunciation: The ash character Æ/æ used in Old
English is pronounced like the a in "cat."*

1

Æthelburg

Tantone, Somersæte
Kingdom of Wessex

'Burn it,' she says.

Faces turn to her in the waning light. '*Burn it?*' Leofric repeats. 'But
Tantone is a strategically important piece in your husband's—'

'You want Ealdbert to control it, or worse, the Wealas?' Æthel
casts a dark glance at the fortification beyond the wall. Unor-
namented and squat, with greening planks of stout wood, it
would still go up – with a bit of effort on their part. 'Let us burn
him out.'

Leofric shakes his head. It's a shade greyer every time Æthel sees
him, and more than likely, she is the cause. 'I want Ealdbert dead
as much as you, but firing Tantone is a step too far.'

'We did not bring a force to garrison it,' Æthel argues, starting
to pace. 'Do you think the king will be pleased to hear we left it
behind for the taking?'

'My queen, Ine king himself ordered Tantone built. At least send word to him before making an impulsive decision.'

Æthel comes to a sudden stop. 'Ine king is my husband, and he trusts me,' she says coldly, stamping on the flicker of doubt her own words sow. 'He will support my *impulsive* decision.'

'I agree,' comes a new voice.

Edred is dressed a little too well for battle; a golden brooch pins his cloak to his shoulder, and his tunic is linen fine enough to wear at court. 'The Wealas still roam these lands,' he adds with a vague gesture westwards, and Leofric frowns. 'You know the natives – always searching for ways to undermine Saxon rule. Unless the king posts men here, Tantone is better off ruined.'

Æthel seizes the chance to say, 'And he informed me of no such plan to do so.'

'Maybe true, my lady, but equally he gave no instruction to destroy it.' Anger mottles Leofric's cheeks. 'I must insist—'

'Insist, Leofric?' Edred raises an eyebrow. 'To the Queen of Wessex?'

Æthel straightens her mail shirt while the man splutters, although she would rather not win this battle by rank. *It's a sensible decision. Any good commander would make it.* Edred's agreement is a surprise, however. He is her husband's brother's man and not one she knows well. Æthel regards him through narrowed eyes. Perhaps he seeks to win a favour from the king and hopes for her support. Whatever the reason, she'll make use of it.

'All I meant,' Leofric says through gritted teeth, 'is that—'

'The queen has decided. Your protests now are improper, if not downright defiant.'

Æthel presses her lips together before a smile can ruin her poise, but she has probably made an enemy this day. *Well, it can't be helped.* 'Burn it,' she orders her men.

After a moment, Leofric nods infinitesimally, and that small motion kills any humour Æthel had in her. How dare he give his permission – and the men look to him for it? It gnaws at her heart: the knowledge that Ine's gesiths think nothing of her prowess in the field. No matter how many successful campaigns she fights, how swift her thinking or strong her arm, to them she is still only a woman. 'Burn it all.' Her tone is harsh and Leofric walks away. Ostensibly to supervise, but his displeasure is a chill that even the rising conflagration cannot banish.

When the buildings beyond the palisade are fully ablaze, she picks up her spear, unshoulders her shield and ensures her sword and seax are loose in their sheaths. 'To me.' A yell from the assembled men, and Æthel bares her teeth as she leads them up and over the earthen ramp, covered by arrow fire. Her blood thrills. Wild-eyed men are tumbling from the fortress as the flames spread, and she cuts them down, her anger at Leofric turning her blows savage. It is only after a dozen have fallen that she remembers they ought to take prisoners. And where is Ealdbert, the traitor she came here to fight?

They have brought a hellish dusk. The night is orange, the air choking and thick as old stew. A man – *boy*, she amends on seeing his thistledown beard – lunges at her out of the stables, carrying with him the frightened squeals of horses. She parries the blow, but the boy's eyes lock with hers beneath her helm and widen.

'The queen,' he shouts, 'it's the queen!' In moments, another five of Ealdbert's men surround her. *Shit.*

'Lady Æthelburg,' the eldest says with a mocking bow. 'How considerate of you to provide my lord with such a fine ransom. How much will your husband pay to have you back unharmed?'

Æthel flinches at the thought of Ine's face if she were to arrive trussed like game at the gates of Wiltun. She can picture his pained look perfectly. *He* would not blame her – he never did, even if he should – but the men of the Witan are a different story. Ine would be forced to make her excuses. Æthel's fist clenches on the hilt of her sword. 'I doubt he'd pay a silver penning,' she tells her assailants, already hearing the apologetic speech he would give the Witan. 'I am far more trouble than I am worth.'

The man chuckles: her only warning before she is forced to parry a backhanded blow meant to knock her unconscious. The others are grinning too – at least for the first minute. One by one, their smiles fade as each attack fails to land. Æthel can feel her face set in a frozen grimace. Batting aside the sword of the man who mocked her, she sees an opening and takes it, thrusting her spear into his ribs. His leather slows the strike, but does not stop the spearhead sinking deep.

'*Bitch*,' the boy snarls as his companion staggers. Æthel tries to pull her spear free but it's stuck fast. She draws her sword just in time to block the boy's rage-fuelled swing.

A second man lunges for her. She catches the blow on her shield and spins to deflect a third that slices into her arm. *Damned if I'll let them take me.* Yelling wordlessly, Æthel launches a flurry of blows hard and fast enough to send the boy to his knees – if it wasn't for the fact she is facing four other men too. All of whom are starting to wonder whether she needs to be taken alive. Dodging a blow aimed unambiguously at her kidneys, she thinks, *How dare they?* Fighting for her life against the Wealas – Britons – is a given, and against the men of Mierce and the east to be expected. But these are her own people, Wessex born. How dare they raise arms against her?

The roof of the stables is afire now; Æthel can see her men hustling the valuable horses out of danger. Most of Ealdbert's small force seems to be fleeing into the night, but where is *he*? A horrible thought hits her, along with another glancing blow. Was he ever even here? He had fled west; she'd spent a month driving him from place to place until she had cornered him here at Tantone. At least, she had thought him cornered.

Her sword is knocked aside. Throat sore from gasping smoke, Æthel watches it thump to earth cracked by summer sun and pulls the shorter seax from its sheath. Another man goes down with the weapon planted in his neck, and she snatches his sword as he falls. It is a poor substitute for her own pattern-welded blade, but they are forcing her onto lower ground where she cannot reach it. She coughs; the smoke is thickening, making her eyes stream. Æthel drags an arm angrily across them.

Blinking, she thinks she sees Edred's face, but grey rolls across and a streak of silver swings at her in the dark. Everything slows. Æthel watches the blade part the smoke and knows she cannot raise her shield in time to block it. *How ridiculous*, a stray thought says. How incredible.

The iron stops an inch from her flesh. Still braced for the blow, Æthel blinks again, but the sight before her becomes no clearer. The boy warrior's mouth is open, his eyes bulging. With the sureness of a woman born to the battlefield, she knows that he is dead.

Screams pierce the dark. Not the cries of the wounded, or the desperate fury of those fighting for their lives, but lost bitter wails. Æthel shudders. The next instant, sheer instinct throws her flat just as a blade scythes the spot where she was standing. Her helm slips; she pulls it off before it can blind her, to see riders among them like ragged ghosts, steering their mounts through the spear-din. Men are falling beneath sword and hoof; the slaughterhouse stench of spilled guts is thick in her nose. Æthel frowns, trying to gauge numbers, but the chaos is absolute. That is, except for one still point. She raises herself, sticky with mud and blood, and looks.

Like the eye of a storm, unreally calm, a woman looks back. Mounted atop a horse larger than any Æthel has seen, armoured in leather and fur, one of her gauntleted hands is curled around a blade as dark, surely, as the roots of the world. Many small braids tumble out beneath a horned helm pushed back from her face.

Something inside Æthel stutters, stops . . . and the figure is gone, become the chaos. She licks dry lips, tastes blood. Perhaps she has taken a blow to the head. 'Leofric!' she yells, staggering to her feet. She does not expect a response, but the gesith answers from somewhere east of her and Æthel follows his voice to the edge of the earthen ramp that guards the fortress. 'What's happening?'

He is grim-faced. 'That traitorous bastard must have had horsemen. They swept through and cut down two dozen of us before we even knew they were here.'

She curses. 'If they're Ealdbert's, where are they now?'

Leofric shakes his head and Æthel wonders whether he saw what she did: that person – wild and beautiful and dangerous beyond all measure. She grimaces. A trick of the smoke and the pain of her wounds. More likely the riders belong to Ealdbert and she is a royal fool for failing to find them before the attack.

'You're bleeding,' the gesith says, and she is surprised to hear a note of concern in his voice. Probably concern for his own hide – it will not look good if she dies on his watch.

Æthel shrugs. 'It's nothing.' And it mostly is, but the wound on her arm will need stitching up. 'What of Ealdbert himself?'

'No sign.'

Although Leofric's tone remains neutral, condemnation is writ large in his lowered brows. Tantone, he thinks, has burned for nothing. Men have died for nothing. Æthel looks away. 'It's one less place for him to hide.' Their losses are heavier than she had planned for. 'Did we take any prisoners?'

'Two.'

Edred emerges out of the night, wiping his sword – the only dirty part of him – on his cloak, and Æthel recalls her brief conviction of seeing him among the men who cornered her. 'Where have you been?'

'Ensuring we have these to question.' He gestures over his shoulder. His men are dragging a pair of smoke-stained prisoners, their wrists bound.

'Soften them up.' Æthel makes sure they can hear. 'I will question them later. If they do not talk, kill them. I won't feed traitors.'

Leofric nods approvingly and Edred bows. 'Your will, my queen.' The men are led off, staring wide-eyed at the fortress that sheltered them. Clearly it had never occurred to Ealdbert that she would choose to burn the place. Æthel adds the absent ætheling to the list of men who have underestimated her . . . or think her merely unhinged. It is a long list.

Tantone is a beacon in the night. Those riders . . . She cannot convince herself they were Ealdbert's. *Else they'd have stayed to rout us.* But if the fire had alerted them, it would alert others. Æthel turns her head west. 'Gather the dead and bury them quickly. Geraint may have eyes in the area.'

'The King of Dumnonia is not brave enough to face us,' Leofric says. But he too turns to look westwards, where the land rises and falls in the first of the valleys that give the people of Dumnonia their name. Night blankets those forbidding dales; Æthel shivers at the thought of them. She was raised in open country, on a plain disturbed only by the ancient tombs of people gone before. Gentle, grassy mounds – unlike the tangled hills that hide the Britons. Space for a horse to run without pause while she clung to the reins and the wind and the sound of sun drying the grasses. She used to plait them while she waited for her horse to catch his breath. *Keep your hands busy*, her mother had said, *and they won't suspect your mind is at work too.*

Æthel smiles at the memory; the sad smile that comes with knowing her mother cannot give her more advice. 'I could do with it,' she murmurs under her breath and goes to oversee the collection of the dead. Despite her attempt to banish them, a pair of eyes burning brighter than the fire goes with her.

'Holy God, Edred. I said *soften* them, not beat them to within an inch of their lives.' Æthel crouches in front of one of the rebels. In the dawn light, his cheek is split and blood crusts his swollen mouth. 'They do need to be able to speak.'

'Crazy she-wolf,' the man slurs.

Before Edred can raise a hand to strike him, Æthel catches it. 'Peace. I don't care what he calls me.'

'By insulting you, he insults the king,' Leofric remarks, and she keeps her expression blank with an effort. She would bet that *crazy she-wolf* is exactly what he thinks of her after tonight.

Æthel forces down exhaustion, leans forward and grabs the rebel's chin. If he wanted a she-wolf, he could have one. 'Where is Ealdbert?'

His lip curls. 'If the king seeks him, why didn't he come himself?'

'We are not talking about the king. Where is Ealdbert?'

'Gone.' He spits. Æthel ducks aside and it lands on Leofric's shoe. The gesith makes a sound of disgust. 'Ine won't find him.'

'Few places would extend him welcome.' She flicks her eyes at Leofric. 'Sussex?'

'Nothhelm would not dare. After the beating Cædwalla meted out, the realm's sworn to your husband now.'

'You don't know where he is, do you?' she says to the rebel. 'Might as well admit it and save me the trouble of torture.'

The man glues his lips together, but she knows she is right. Both are likely no more than ceorls pressed into the ætheling's service with promises of wealth. She tips her head on one side, considering what to do. Ine would probably exile them . . . and they'd swiftly join up with Ealdbert again. The hard decisions always fall to her. 'Kill them,' she says and forces herself to watch while it is done.

The events of last night are blurring in the late-summer dawn. Searing heat, metal on metal, the scream of tired muscles – all seem a fancy. Except *her*. Æthel could not forget those eyes if she tried. They are there even now when she shuts her own, along with a face haunted by pride and grief. She shakes herself. Foolishness.

'The riders,' she begins and stops. A blackbird pipes gaily; the breeze is gentle. From where they are camped, Tantone is a slur on the green, its watchtower a smoking ruin. But something is moving. Æthel squints at a ripple in the grass, and her blood chills. 'Leofric!'

'What is it?'

Æthel nods at the frisks of distant movement. 'Look.'

Leofric follows her gaze, raising a hand against the glowing sky. 'Deer, surely.'

'No,' Æthel says. 'Wealas.'

'What?' Edred joins them. 'Dumnonii – here?'

'I *knew* Geraint would investigate. He'd be on us already if we hadn't moved our camp.'

'I cannot see any men.'

'And you won't until it's too late.' Æthel wheels round to bark out orders. 'Move! Strike camp. Be quick about it.' No man looks to Leofric this time. They can hear the alarm in her voice.

'Why not face them?' Edred catches her injured arm and Æthel winces. 'If Geraint is foolish enough to bring the fight to us—'

'Foolish?' She almost laughs. 'Our forces spent the night fighting, burying bodies, and then marching out here to put some distance between us and Tantone. They are in no shape to take up the sword again so soon. Geraint is not foolish. It's the perfect opportunity.'

'What do you mean we won't see him until it is too late?' Leofric asks slowly.

Æthel hesitates. Plenty among the court do not believe what she has witnessed with her own eyes. And the bishops come down hard on such talk. 'Geraint employs . . . unusual methods,' she says meaningfully, and prays he takes the hint. 'You know the Wealas and their superstitions.'

'Superstitions can't make up for strength of arms,' Edred says.

Æthel grinds her teeth, determined not to spell it out. Her credibility has taken enough of a knock. 'Look at the men,' she says in a low hard voice. 'They have been up all night while Geraint's forces are fresh. Only a fool would stay and face him.'

'What forces? Some scouts, perhaps, but nothing more.'

I have seen them appear as from air, she tells him silently. As if Geraint and his men could blend seamlessly into the world around them. No battlefield prowess can explain that. And if those flashes of movement are anything to go by, he – or whatever power he prays to – is doing the same now. The Dumnonii will be on them while they stand here and argue.

'Enough.' She lowers her voice, so only Edred and Leofric can hear. 'You know I value your opinions in the field.' Æthel draws a breath. 'But, as you pointed out last night, Edred, I am queen. If I say to retreat, you will retreat, and I am not beholden to state my reasons.'

They glower. She has had this conversation more than once, and every time she wonders whether *this* will be it – the time they openly defy her. She wonders what she would say, how she would react. They are important men, trusted in court, and have proven themselves good counsel. It would cost Ine to exile them, but he would do it if she asked. He has never denied her anything. Except *that*. And as the years pass, she – not he – bears the consequences of his decision. In her darker moments, Æthel wonders whether it is guilt that urges him to support her, to defend her, rather than belief in her ability.

Between blinks, the blood drains from Edred's face. There they are: lining the brow of a hill. She does a clumsy count – at least five score warriors – and shock courses through her, leaving no room for the pleasure of vindication. Only an overwhelming force would have the confidence to declare themselves so openly.

'We'll pull back to Gifle,' Leofric says tightly into the silence. 'Once we have walls around us, we dispatch scouts to keep an eye on Geraint.'

'And send a message to the king,' Æthel adds, eyeing the Wealas – more and more appearing by the second. 'I have never seen the Dumnonii show themselves or their forces so blatantly.'

Leofric grunts agreement and Æthel mounts her horse, her thoughts in turmoil. First Ealdbert, then the nameless riders, and now Geraint. Foreboding cramps her chest like a winter ague. As she turns her horse south-east, she imagines she can feel Geraint's eyes across the intervening distance, the mass of Dumnonia brooding at his back. *What does he want?* And more to the point, why did he show himself? His decision to drop his disguise, to threaten them openly: bluster or something else?

Æthel bites her lip. After years of uneasy truce, it's as if the King of Dumnonia wants war.

orbit

Follow us:

f /orbitbooksUS

X /orbitbooks

▶ /orbitbooks

Join our mailing list
to receive alerts on our
latest releases and deals.

orbitbooks.net

Enter our monthly
giveaway for the chance
to win some epic prizes.

orbitloot.com